THE SECRETS BETWEEN US

High in the mountains in the south of France, eighteen-year-old Ceci Corvin is trying hard to carry on as normal. But in 1943, there is no such thing as normal — especially not for a young woman in love with the wrong person. Scandal, it would seem, can be more dangerous than war . . . Fifty years later, Annie is looking for her long-lost grandmother. Armed with nothing more than a sheaf of papers, she travels from England to Paris in pursuit of the truth. But as she traces her grandmother's story, Annie uncovers something she wasn't expecting: something that changes everything she knew about her family — and everything she thought she knew about herself . . .

Books by Laura Madeleine
Published by Ulverscroft:

THE CONFECTIONER'S TALE

LAURA MADELEINE

◆

THE SECRETS BETWEEN US

Complete and Unabridged

CHARNWOOD
Leicester

First published in Great Britain in 2018 by
Black Swan
an imprint of Transworld Publishers
London

First Charnwood Edition
published 2019
by arrangement with
Transworld Publishers
Penguin Random House
London

A catalogue record for this book is available from the British Library.

ISBN 978–1–4448–4185–5

Published by
F. A. Thorpe (Publishing)
Anstey, Leicestershire

Set by Words & Graphics Ltd.
Anstey, Leicestershire
Printed and bound in Great Britain by
T. J. International Ltd., Padstow, Cornwall

وملـح خـبز بينن____ا

There is bread and salt between us

An Arabic saying expressing an alliance,
a bond, an oath not to be broken

They say Lot's wife was turned into a pillar of salt for looking back.

I have tried to write of the future, but I cannot find the words. I have tried to write of freedom, but I can't remember its taste. And so, look back I must, to the beginning of what might prove to be my final summer on this earth. If my punishment for that is salt, so be it.

It has been a summer stolen. A summer of sky. A summer of riches. Of clear water tasting of far-off winter. Of meat and blood, the flesh of the mountain, carved from bone. Of wild fruit, ripe as honey, sundering at a touch. A summer of wheat, ground by stone and transformed by an ancient recipe, of bitter herbs and oil as old as a distant land across the sea.

Mountain and flesh, sweat and skin, bread and salt: life. Love. This summer has drained me, drenched me, wrung me dry, but still I reach for more.

I reach for you.

How far must I go back? The root of this summer is buried in the bleak, hard earth of February 1943, when you were cold on the mountain and I was cold by the shore, and neither of us knew the other one existed.

I will unearth it for you, my love. I will try to remember how I came to be sitting here. I will

1

look back, so that you can live it again, through my eyes.

Then, whatever comes next, whatever happens to us, these words will remain.

Saint-Antoine, Alpes-Maritimes

February 1943

They say that April is the cruellest month, but for me, it was always February.

The last gasp of the season, the short, fretful days before spring. Not like midwinter, beautiful and treacherous as glass. February was a month that wheezed between sickness and health, when the sheets of ice on the mountain groaned before they fell.

On the February day when everything changed, I had a headache from the sky. It was leaden, made me want to crawl into bed beneath the blacked-out window and not wake up again until spring.

Instead, I forced the barrow down the street. The wooden wheel jarred and rattled over the cobbles, the unease working its way into my bones. An afternoon mist was rolling down the mountainside. Soon, it would tumble into the narrow streets and settle there, closing us in for the rest of the day. In February, Saint-Antoine felt like the fortress it once had been. Ancient houses, squashed together, like animals huddled for warmth on a bare outcrop, so close you could hear every word of every argument, see the stains on other people's washing, strung from windows and balconies.

3

I stopped to catch my breath on the main street, where icy water trickled down the *gargouille*. It had confused me as a child, to learn that the ugly stone monsters that spouted water from the church roof were called the same thing. Our *gargouille* was different. It wasn't a monster at all, but a waterway; a stone channel as old as the town, running from a fall in the mountains, all the way along our steep, main street and down into the river. Generations of people had channelled the flow so that it seemed to spout on almost every corner. Its water washed our clothes and bathed our children, filled our cooking pots and drenched our thirsty plants in the summer. It was the throat of the mountain, and we drank from it.

I shivered and pushed the barrow towards the town square, the cold wrapping around my wrists, exposed by my too-small jacket. In the doorway of a closed-up café, a couple of Italian soldiers were hunched, waiting for the bus.

'*Madre mia!*' one of them called out at me. I ignored him, until the other stepped into the path of the barrow.

'*Zitto, l'ho vista prima io,*' he said, grinning down at me. His face was wind-tanned, a shadow of dark stubble staining his chin and cheeks. Beneath his jacket, his shirt-collar was undone.

I stared straight past him, annoyed at the heat that crept on to my face.

'*Principessa, vuoi che ti accompagno a casa?*' the first one said, leaning closer.

'You!' A shout echoed across the square. 'Stop that!'

4

Old Madame Gougeard had come puffing around the corner, a basket in her hand. When he saw her, the Italian removed his boot from my path.

'*Ciao, nonna,*' he catcalled. '*Non vuoi divertirti?*'

Madame Gougeard jerked her chin at me. 'Come, Ceci,' she said, throwing them a filthy look.

Together, we turned our backs on the Italians and went to wait on the other side of the square.

'*Sales Piémontais,*' Madame Gougeard muttered as we walked. 'You should not encourage them, *poupée.*'

I forced down a wave of frustration. Eighteen and still I was a girl to most of the town, a doll to be protected. As we walked, I snuck a look into Madame Gougeard's basket, which clinked as it moved. There was a bottle of brandy in there. No surprise. The Gougeards ran the hotel, and everybody knew they were masters of *le Systéme D* — 'making do' in a way that often bordered on illegal. They were always able to get hold of things the rest of us could not.

'Are you meeting Olivier from the bus, Madame?' I asked innocently, though I already knew the answer. Madame Gougeard was as hungry for gossip from Nice as the rest of us were for butter and sugar.

'I am. He has been there on an errand.' She slid a look at me, letting me know that *she* knew something important. Behind us, one of the soldiers let out a bark of laughter.

'Louts,' she muttered, not caring to keep her

voice low. 'Look at them, they do not even dress like soldiers any more. Have they no respect?'

It was true, the Italians had begun to look ragged as the winter wore on, ever less like occupiers. One of the soldiers behind us had mislaid his belt, and the other wore woollen mittens that I was certain were not part of his uniform.

'No, Madame,' I said.

'They should go home and eat Mussolini's bread.'

I pressed my lips together. I did not like the Italians, but even I knew it was more complicated than that. The Germans may have taken the rest of the south back in November, but here it was the Italians who had marched in, clinging to German coat-tails.

Madame Gougeard was sneering at the soldiers. '*Un coup de poignard dans le dos.* They are cowards, aren't they, Ceci?'

I nodded, and fought to keep silent, though I wanted to remind her that half of her own relatives were from across the border, that my own grandfather had been Italian. The Gougeards were our main customers. Mama would murder me if she found out I had been rude.

Madame Gougeard sniffed. 'At least that brother of yours has the spirit to stand up to them. Your father should be proud. We need more young men like him.'

My smile was growing tight at the edges, and I began to wish she had left me to fend off the Italians on my own. Perhaps she sensed this, for her voice grew softer.

'You have had no news of him, then?'

6

I shook my head, staring into the damp mist, wishing the bus would arrive. 'Papa went to Menton early this morning,' I told her, 'to try to petition for his release.'

I said nothing of the envelope Papa had carried in his jacket, the collection of francs inside that had taken us the best part of two weeks to scrounge together, but Madame Gougeard nodded, as if I had.

'God willing, the *capitano* there is blessed with greater intelligence than his inferiors.'

'God willing,' I murmured, and for once, I meant it.

As usual, we heard the bus before we smelled it, smelled it before we saw it come wheezing through the mist and into the square. The *gazogène* engine on the back made a terrible racket for something so useless. It was no match for the steep mountain roads. Sometimes, passengers even had to get out and push. Still, it had come all the way from Nice, where there were cinemas and department stores with goods that no one could afford, and restaurants that could still serve you meat, if you had money and knew the right way to ask.

I hurried towards the slowing bus, looking for my father through the fogged windows, looking for the familiar face he might bring back with him. I was so busy looking, I almost collided with a trio of soldiers who were disembarking, duffel bags on their backs.

'*Scusi, mademoiselle.*' They smiled, showing their teeth and touching their buttoned-down caps. I looked away, heard them barging other passengers aside to greet the soldiers who had been waiting in the cold, all shoulder slaps and hair ruffling; raucous young men, perhaps the same age as my brother. One of them caught me looking, and winked.

I turned my head. Papa was shuffling down the bus's steps, head lowered beneath his cloth cap.

'Leon?' I asked uselessly as he stepped down to the square.

He shook his head, and I knew I would get no more out of him, not here, in the open, where ears were always listening.

'Did you bring the barrow?' he said wearily.

By the time I returned with it, he was already hoisting himself up on to the wheel arch of the bus, loosening a tarpaulin tied to the roof to reveal the slumped shapes of sacks beneath.

'What did you get?' I asked, trying to shove down the disappointment, the fluttering anxiety that filled my chest.

'Two wheat,' came his muffled answer. 'Two bran. And chickpeas.'

Before I could groan I had to brace myself to take the weight of one of the sacks. The familiar, dusty scent of cloth and flour filled my nose and I took a step back, only to slip on one of the cobbles.

Hands caught my shoulders, steadied me. I looked up, face hot, as Paul took the sack from my arms and dropped it into the barrow.

'Merci, Paul,' Papa called, already stretching for the next one.

'De rien.' Paul brushed the white wings of

8

flour from his dark gendarmerie jacket. 'I'll help you with the others as well. They're too heavy for Ceci.'

I threw him a withering glance.

'Ceci,' Papa said, catching the look, as Paul dropped the second sack into the barrow, 'go and tell your mother I am home. Both of you wait for me in the kitchen.'

I left him with Paul, made my way slowly back to the bakery. My brother's name echoed with every step as I walked. *Le-on, Le-on*: strong arms lifting me far easier than a sack of flour, a boisterous laugh, the beginnings of a dark beard. *Le-on*, cried by my mother when he was once again in trouble. *Le-on*, muttered by my father, summoning him into the kitchen for another 'talk', now that he was a man and too old for the strap. But that anger, that exasperation, always faded into fondness, a chuckle, a shaken head at my brother's devious expression. *Le-on*, people tutted, dragging out the sound as they smiled, *Le-on*.

Ce-ci sounded small in comparison, and however hard I tried, I could not outstep it.

I stopped in the street outside the bakery, not wanting to see my mother's hopeful face, the shape of my brother's name on her lips. From here, the place looked sombre. Melting ice had slid down the window, leaving trails in the winter dirt. Inside, the shelves already stood empty.

Five years ago, they would have been stacked high with herb-flecked *fougasses* and flour-dusted *bottles*, leaf-like *epis* and sticky *fougassettes*, fragrant with orange blossom and honey. I would

9

have been able to sneak a fresh *brioche* from the tray, the dough slicked bright, or pilfer one of the first, rich croissants of each morning's batch, made with only the best butter from neighbouring farms, where cows grazed on sweet grass and herbs in the high pastures. Such things had once been my reward for a night of sleepless work, for piling the baskets and shelves high with loaves of all shapes and sizes, ready to feed the town, to delight the tourists.

At fourteen, Leon would take the loaves we made and fly like a demon through the streets on his bicycle, delivering them to the villas of wealthy families who came to take the air. At seventeen, he would smile at their daughters when they came in to buy their picnics, the baker's smock rolled up to show his tanned arms. At eighteen, he began to take his pay down to Nice in the evenings, sneaking away when he should have been working, leaving me to take his place in the kitchen. At twenty-one, being a baker was the only thing that had saved him from being called up but still, he didn't care for the life, still he was wayward, and still Papa turned a blind eye. Perhaps, if he had been more stern with Leon's excesses, if he had said something sooner . . .

I pushed open the door.

So much had changed since those years of brightness and plenty, but not the smell of the bakery. The deep nuttiness of a crust forming, the sweetness of wheat, the tang of proving dough that caught sharply in my nostrils. My stomach, always taut with hunger, constricted a little further. I shut the door behind me, closing out the grey day, the Italians in the square, Madame Gougeard's gossip.

Mother was sitting at the end of the wooden counter, behind the box we used for money. The accounts book was open before her. Too few inked lines on one side. Too many on the other. She looked up, a frown creasing the skin between her brows.

Leon? she asked silently.

I shook my head, and turned away to rearrange the two remaining loaves of heavy *pain bis* in their basket.

'Papa said to wait for him here,' I told her, and glanced towards the empty window. 'Mama, what if — '

'Ceci,' she stopped me. She did not want to hear my wonderings, not about Leon. 'Why don't you go and make the coffee?'

I turned and did as I was told.

Cheshire

April 1993

'Want some coffee, pet?'

I look up in shock. A waitress is standing over me, pot of filter coffee poised. How long has she been there? I've been miles away. Decades.

'No,' I hear myself say automatically, before I realize it sounds rude. 'I mean, yes, thank you.'

She makes a face as if to say *suit yourself*, and pours. The coffee looks watery, slightly yellow. I don't really want it, but too late now.

'Early start for you, then?' she asks. I risk a glance up. She looks bored, tired beneath the thick make-up. We are the only people in the hotel breakfast room.

'Yep,' I tell her, looking at the coffee.

She stands there, waiting for me to say more. Music is playing in the background. 'Up here for work, is it?' she tries again, after a moment.

I nod.

'Come from far?'

'London.'

'London,' she repeats, making the syllables bounce. 'That's nice. You like it there?'

Yes, I want to tell her, *I live in a tiny flat in Bloomsbury, above a grocer's shop. The windows rattle when buses go past and it's hot in summer and freezing in winter, and the hallway*

12

always smells of overripe bananas. But it's close to my work and the library and just about big enough to put up my mother when she comes to stay . . .

I don't. The words would tangle themselves in my mouth. Instead, I nod.

The waitress doesn't quite manage to keep down a sigh.

'Well, enjoy your day,' she says, giving up.

'Thanks,' I murmur, but she's already gone.

My cheeks are burning as I reach for the sugar bowl. *Pathetic, Annie.* The sugar is in cubes, the hard, brilliant white kind. Carefully, I break one in half.

Someone else walks into the dining room. I glance up, hoping it isn't one of my colleagues. I'm in luck. It's a businessman, smiling broadly at the waitress. She'll have more success with him.

I stir the sugar into the coffee, take a sip. It's awful. I put it down again, and turn back to the file that's open on the table beside me, with its lists of catalogue numbers. So much to do. And the sooner we are done with it, the sooner we can go back to London.

Back to what, exactly? I push the thought down and pick up my highlighter pen.

The dining room has started to fill up, voices bouncing back from the drab, peach-coloured walls. My stomach complains, finding the coffee and nothing else. I don't want the full English breakfasts that have started to emerge, greasy and piled high, from the hotel kitchen. We never had them when I was a kid. *Because we're not*

English, Mum would always tease. *Fried bread? Your grand-mère would never forgive me.*

I could have toast, but that would mean walking past the waitress to get to the buffet . . . With a sigh at myself, I close the binder, grab my bag and leave the coffee unfinished on the table.

Quarter to eight. Too early to go to work, even by my standards. Ducking my head as I pass the receptionist, I make for the alcove with the payphones and take out twenty pence to dial my answerphone in London.

'You have no new messages.'

I press '1', listen to the last saved message.

'Hi! Annie!'

My mum's voice fills my ear. I know exactly what the message says. She left it a week ago, to say that she had landed safely in Australia, to tell me about her colleagues and the project, about the onwards flight they will have to take to the islands. Listening to her, my heart gives a squeeze. She sounds bright, but tired. I hope she's taking care of herself. I wish I was there to make sure that she rests, that she takes her medications on time.

'Anyway, I have to go,' I hear her say as an airport announcement booms in the background. 'There's . . . another thing I want to talk to you about, but it can wait until next time we speak. *Bisou, chérie. Ciao!*'

Outside the hotel, the morning is cool and clean as freshly washed skin, not yet dirtied by day. I take a breath of it, trying to smooth away the worries. *Another thing I want to talk to you*

14

about. She would have told me if it was health-related, surely? What then? I grip the handle of my bag tight. There's no use speculating. Nevertheless, as I walk briskly towards the bus stop, I can't quite stop the thoughts, or dreaded words like *legacy* and *executor*, from creeping through my mind.

The office isn't far; a short bus ride out of the town and into the Cheshire countryside, where spring has peppered the winter hedgerows with brilliant green buds. I'm the only person to get off at a nondescript-looking compound, a sign that reads CHESHIRE NORTH SALT MINE above the gate.

No one else is here yet, apart from the security guard. He always nods and says hello to me. Once, he smiled a little longer than usual and asked me where I was from. I pretended I hadn't heard and hurried away. It's a question without an easy answer, too complicated to explain to a stranger.

I can feel myself flushing at that memory as I step into the silent reception. 'I — ' I dig through my bag for my ID badge. 'I'm — '

'It's OK, I know who you are,' he says easily, dark eyes creasing. 'Early start, eh?'

I nod. Part of me wants to stop there in the corridor, wants to chat with him about the morning, about anything. I want to, but when it comes to it, I can't find the words. Anything I say always seems to come out wrong. Easier to stay silent. I look away, and escape through the door.

I dump my bag on my chair and am heading for the kettle when I see it: a delivery note, lying conspicuously on Iain's desk, marked CONFI-DENTIAL. My fingers twitch. I shouldn't look at it. I'm only supposed to be working on administration, data entry, getting the new catalogue system up and running. I shouldn't even be *touching* the archives, even though I'm as qualified as the rest of the team.

It's not a demotion, Annie, my boss had insisted, it's just that during your time off Iain has really stepped up. He's a more natural fit to manage this project. And we need someone like you to do the admin, someone who's conscientious, good with computers, someone who'll knuckle down.

Turning my head away, I walk past and go to make tea. But even as I stand there, with the kettle rumbling and steam rising, I can feel them, those red-stamped letters just behind me, waiting for me to take a closer look. I glance into the corridor.

The envelope is a thin, brown one, only lightly sealed. I wouldn't even have to tear it, just ease it open. My fingers seem to be a step ahead of my thoughts, because they're already working at the flap, freeing it, pulling out the piece of paper inside.

I recognize the crest at the top of the letter immediately. Foreign Office. That means the delivery is a whole new series of government files, declassified for the first time ever, waiting to be checked, inventoried, safely archived. *This* is the work I should be doing, not sitting behind a computer, punching in endless numbers. Above, the clock reads half past eight. The others

16

won't be in for half an hour. Who would know if I went and had a quick look?

Across the compound, I step into the lift that will take me down into the old mine, descending through layer after layer of rock. The moment the doors open on the holding bay I see them: new archive boxes, stacked one atop the other. I creep forwards, the soles of my shoes raising clouds of salt dust. It never settles here, not really. When I return to the surface it will be with the taste of salt in the back of my throat, on my lips.

I stop, listening. The miners haven't yet started the machines for the day, haven't yet begun to claw rock salt from the walls. It's eerily quiet, makes me feel tiny, insignificant. Gently, I brush the top of one of the archive boxes. My fingers come away rimed with pinkish dust. If I were to go back thousands of years, I could be underwater, at the bottom of a vast inland sea that stretched for hundreds of miles across Europe, its salt tinged pink by the sand blown in on desert winds. Now, that salt is dug from the rock to coat roads in winter, to flavour cooking pots, leaving caverns behind to be filled with history of a different kind.

Dry and cool and sparkling, these caves have been chosen to hold the past. Precious documents, hundreds of years old, scrolls, medical records, government archives, army lists, court cases and tax papers, all safer down here than in any building above ground. My head spins when I think of it all. No wonder Iain is so precious about security clearance. With time and the right

17

know-how, a person could find anything . . .

My hand rests on the stack of boxes. I certainly *don't* have clearance. Iain saw to that. We've been in competition for the same jobs ever since we were interns. Now that he is finally above me, he won't let me forget it.

Abruptly, I haul the top box down and gingerly lift the lid. The sugar-sweet smell of degrading paper rises around me. The files are from the 1940s, I can tell that just by looking at their covers. They're a dull government green, stamped and stapled and scrawled on by many hands, perhaps shoved into a filing cabinet in Whitehall fifty years ago and never thought of again, until now. Until me.

Curiosity killed the cat. But I can't help myself. I look through them, peering at the names and dates, until one in particular catches my eye, its cover torn. I ease it open and come across what looks like an official communiqué, a handwritten note that probably should have been shredded. A historian's dream. I turn the pages, one after another. They teem with clues. One letter bears a coffee stain on the top right corner, another is smudged, as if by rain. I lower my nose to the surface of a paper and close my eyes. Yes, the smell of old ink and must, but something else too, dusky and cloying, cigarette smoke and . . . a woman's perfume?

'Annie?'

I straighten in an instant, blood rushing to my face. Iain is standing behind me. I hadn't even heard him approach. My cheeks burn, so hot they almost hurt.

'What're you doing?' he asks, eyes narrowing.

'I — ' My throat is dry with salt dust. 'These Foreign Office files. I was just checking them.'

'Checking them,' he repeats flatly. 'You don't need to check them. That's Marta's job. You shouldn't even be down here.'

Someone else would make a joke right now or snap back and tell Iain to mind his own business, but I can't. I mumble something like an apology; place the file back in the archive box.

'Annie,' he says, sounding pained, 'you're not drifting around some library in Bloomsbury now. These are *government* archives. The PRO takes security very seriously. You're a junior staff member without clearance. What if you damaged something, or lost it? How would I explain that to head office?'

'I wouldn't,' I murmur. 'I . . . I'm sorry.'

Iain gives a frustrated sigh as he walks over to the boxes and pointedly rests his hand upon the stack. I have no choice but to duck my head and make for the lifts, my face burning with embarrassment.

'Annie,' Iain's voice reaches me, the moment before the doors close, 'don't let me catch you down here again.'

Saint-Antoine

February 1943

The bitter smell of roasted acorns filled the bakery kitchen. I couldn't remember the last time we'd had real coffee. The acorns were similar enough, I supposed, in that they were hot. I wrapped a cloth around the pot handle and brought it to the counter, poured the dark liquid into four cups. Mama, Papa and Paul watched the steam as it rose.

'Here.' Papa stood up from his stool, brought something over from the ovens. 'This one burned a little too much to sell.'

Gently, he set down a loaf of *pain aux noix*. It was blackened at one end, but only slightly, just enough to excuse keeping it back from the customers. Paul and I exchanged a glance, trying not to smile. We both knew that Papa would never allow a loaf to burn by accident. I took a slice when he cut it, dipped it into my acorn coffee and let the taste of fresh bread and tiny shards of walnuts fill my mouth.

'Did you speak to the *capitano?*' Mama asked, a strange expression on her face: anxiety and hope plaited together.

Papa put down his piece of bread, cleared his throat. 'I went to the gendarmerie first, to see if they could intervene. I mentioned your father's name, Paul, but they said that since it was the Italians who arrested Leon, they can't do anything about it.'

'Surely in the city they have some power to — '

'They don't.' My father sounded curt. 'They have to answer to the Italians like the rest of us. They had their guns confiscated too.'

I could tell he was trying not to look at Paul, at the empty holster that sat on his belt.

'And the *carabinieri?*'

Father held up his hand, trying to keep my mother's questions at bay while he gathered his words. 'The Italian *army* arrested Leon, and the Italian army locked him up. I — I went to the barracks where they are keeping prisoners, tried to speak to the captain, but he wasn't there.' He looked at us. 'Neither was Leon.'

'What?' I think we all asked that, but my mother's voice was loudest, edged with panic. 'Has he already been released? Or transferred?' That bland, official word came chained to dread now, to knowledge of the internment camps scattered across the south, or the work camps in Germany that had swallowed so many of our young men.

'He was released,' Papa said, but there was something in his voice that stopped us from breathing out. Awkwardly, he took the envelope full of francs and laid it on the table. 'Someone got there before me.'

'Who?' I burst. I could not stop myself, not when my mother's face was so white. 'Leon doesn't know anyone with that kind of

21

influence.' I looked at Paul. 'Does he?'

Paul shook his head, his eyes wide.

'Then if he's out, where is he?' My voice rose. 'Why doesn't he come home?'

'You don't think he's joined the *maquis*?' my mother whispered. 'Jean-Claude's eldest did, to avoid the draft.'

We sat in silence, that word and many more hanging over us. Paul and I met each other's eyes, and I could tell we were both thinking of the many times Leon had done something rash, something foolish. He had always been able to bluff his way out of it in the past. But this was different. None of us could predict what might happen, not any more.

'There is no use in speculating.' Papa's voice was heavy. 'Wherever he is, we just have to hope that he's safe, that he'll be able to send word, sooner or later.'

No one spoke for a while. The coffee pot made a clicking sound as it cooled. My stomach grumbled, wanting more than bread.

'Nice was crowded,' Papa said, to break the silence. 'Never seen so many people at the market. Nothing there, of course. No vegetables but old cabbages. Saw one man cutting up a cauliflower to make it go around. And more are arriving every day, they say, some with little more than the clothes they stand in.'

'Jews?' Mama sounded distracted still. 'Where are they all coming from?'

Papa shrugged. 'I have to say, many of them did not look well.'

'And the Italians are letting them in?' Paul

asked, hand on his belt. 'Don't they have orders to stop them, turn them back? From the Germans, or — '

'If they do have orders, they're ignoring them.' Papa drank the dregs of his coffee, grimaced. I could tell he had more to say, and was thinking of how to say it.

'I saw Olivier on the bus,' he told us eventually. 'He seems to think that the Italians will send some of them here.'

'Send who?' Mama frowned. 'Not the foreigners? The Jews?'

'Yes. He said that the Italians don't want them in Nice, so near the coast, that they will be sending some of them to the villages.' Papa breathed through his nose, not enough to be a laugh. 'The Gougeards are obviously expecting business. I saw Olivier buying back all those sheets he pawned before Christmas.'

Abruptly, I remembered Madame Gougeard waiting impatiently for her son to step from the bus, with his news from the city.

'But why *here*?' Paul asked, frowning.

'It is not as if Saint-Antoine is short of space,' Papa said, 'all those holiday villas, standing empty — '

'There is not enough food to go around,' Mama said quietly. 'Not with the Italians already taking so much.'

Nobody answered.

Paul pushed back his cup. 'I should be getting along,' he said. 'My father will want to hear about this.' He smiled at me — a small, pressed-lip smile — and all at once I was filled

23

with gratitude towards him, for being here, when Leon was not. 'Thank you for the bread, Madame Corvin,' he said.

'Here,' Mama turned to find a napkin, 'take some for your mother.'

I walked Paul to the bakery door. On the other side of the thin wall that separated the kitchen from the shop, my parents had started up talking again.

'You shouldn't blame yourself about Leon,' I murmured, opening the front door. 'It isn't your fault he got arrested.'

Paul shook his head. 'I shouldn't have let him go to that bar. I knew he was spoiling for a fight with the Italians, but I never thought he would be so stupid as to . . . ' He trailed off. The distant sound of the river crept up the street, filling up the space where his words had been. 'I'm here for you, though,' he said softly. 'Whenever you need. You know that, don't you, Ceci?'

All at once he was too close. I felt myself flush despite the chill from the open door, felt acutely aware of my parents, only a few paces behind us.

'I know,' I said. 'Thank you, Paul.'

He smiled, looking into my face. For a moment, I thought he would say more, but then he was raising his hand in a mock salute and striding away down the street.

Cheshire

April 1993

I grip the office door handle, not wanting to go inside. Iain's words are lingering in my mind, making my eyes burn. Alone with the archives, I feel so sure of everything. There's a number for every file, a stack for every box. But out in the world everything's a jumble, too big or too small, all tangled up and confused, and however hard I try, I can't seem to make anything fit.

Inside, Marta and Kai are working away, Marta poring over a stack of documents, Kai clacking at his computer terminal. I focus on walking. The cheap carpet snatches at the soles of my shoes, threatens to make me trip and embarrass myself in front of them, but I make it to my desk, sink into the prickly office chair with relief.

'Morning,' I force myself to say into the stuffy air.

'Hi,' mumbles Kai. He's the youngest one in the team, always hidden behind his hair, his headphones. We've hardly spoken, but he seems all right. He's another number puncher, like me. Before I can look away, he meets my eyes. 'Message for you,' he says.

For a second, I wonder if I've misheard. No one leaves me messages. 'Sorry?'

Marta hears. 'Message,' she says slowly, as if to a child. 'On the machine. From your mum. What's she doing, checking you got to school on time?'

My cheeks flame as I dial into our work messages. The message is a short one: Mum calling to leave the number for a satellite phone where I can reach her. The line is fuzzy and faint. Hurriedly, I scrawl down the details. She called at seven thirty this morning, probably forgetting the exact time difference between us. Perhaps if I'm quick, she will still be in range. I punch the digits into the phone, hold my breath as the international dialling tone rings, once, twice. A crackle, a moment of silence and then . . .

'Hello?'

The voice is muffled by distance, but it's hers, distinctly hers.

'Mum!' I can't keep the relief out of my voice. 'Mum, *c'est moi*. I'm sorry I missed you — '

'Annie! It's so good to hear your voice.'

I press the phone hard to my ear, not wanting to miss a word. 'Where *are* you?'

'In the middle of the ocean, somewhere east of Cairns, if you can believe that!'

I close my eyes while she tells me about the trip, imagining myself there with her, surrounded by waves, the growing heaviness of a tropical storm in the air.

'Don't let me get carried away,' she breaks off after a while. '*Et toi, ma chérie?* How is everything there?'

'All right, I guess,' I answer cautiously, glancing at the others. I switch to French. 'The work isn't exactly challenging. I miss London.

Here I'm stuck with — '

'People?' Mum asks shrewdly.

I don't need to answer for her to know she's right.

Her snort of laughter is quick, warm. 'What did I do to make you so antisocial, Annie?'

'I'm not antisocial,' I protest. 'I just — ' I stop, short of saying, *I just don't know how to talk to people*. 'I just didn't inherit your charm.'

'You have plenty of charm, *chérie*, but I'm afraid you got your grand-mère's stubbornness, too.'

A silence stretches between us, over continents, vast distances. Talking about my grandmother always makes her sad.

'Mum,' I change the subject with mock-sternness, 'are you looking after yourself? You sounded tired on your last message.'

'I was tired, but that was just the flight. I'm fine.'

'You promise?' I wish I was there to see her face. 'You can't overdo it. You're still not completely over the operation.'

'Annie!' she laughs. 'I'm supposed to worry about you, not the other way around.' When I don't answer, she sighs. '*Chérie*, I'm all right. I'm doing everything the doctors said. I'm even resting. There was no way I was going to miss this trip, you know that.'

'Just because they gave you the all-clear, it doesn't mean — '

'Enough,' she says gently. 'There's something more important I want to talk to you about. Something I thought about a lot during all that treatment. Do you have a minute?'

Iain has come back in and is staring at me, but I don't care, not now. 'Of course,' I tell her, my stomach knotting. 'What is it?'

I hear her take a breath. 'I don't know if it's everything that's happened,' she gives a dry sort of laugh, 'being ill or turning fifty this year, but I've been thinking a lot about Grand-mère.'

Back to my grandmother. I lean on the desk, glad she can't see my frown. Whenever I've tried to question Mum about Grand-mère in the past, she has always clammed up. *Too painful*, she once said. 'What about her?' I ask.

There's a long pause. 'I want to try to find her,' she says quickly, as if she's worried the words will disappear before she speaks them. 'I want to see her, tell her that what happened between us doesn't matter now. I want to apologize, tell her I never should have said the things I did — '

She breaks off. I hear her gulp and I hold the phone tighter, wanting to step out of it and hug her.

'I shouldn't have stopped you from looking for her before,' she carries on, slowing down. 'I just didn't want you to get hurt. But it's different now. We were a family once, the three of us. I'd like that again. You deserve a family, Annie.'

Even from far away, over the vast distances her voice is travelling, I hear the words she is not saying: *You deserve more family than just me, in case* . . . Tears wash into my eyes.

'Mum — '

'What do you think?' she says briskly. 'Will you

28

help me look for her? I can't think of anyone more qualified for the job.'

I manage a weak laugh at that. 'Of course. If it's what you want.'

'It is. We can make a start when I get back.' I can hear my mum's smile, even down the phone.

'Well,' I say, trying to sound more cheerful, 'when will that be?'

'In just under a month, now. It's a bank holiday weekend there, isn't it? Do you have plans?'

'A few things,' I lie. 'I'm really busy, with all this data.'

'Annie,' my mother says warningly, 'promise me you won't sit at home worrying, that you'll go outside, at least once. You're young, you should be enjoying yourself.'

'*Bien, je sais*, Mum,' I reel off, 'I will, I will.'

'All right then. I had better let you go. *Á tout á l'heure, chérie*, love you.'

'Love you too,' I murmur.

There's a rustle, a click, and then the phone goes silent. It's only when the dialling tone starts to whine that I remember to put it down. Noises filter back in to my hearing.

' . . . not listening to you,' someone says.

Marta and Iain are both staring at me. 'Annie,' Iain says, beckoning me over to his desk. 'A word?'

I push the desk chair away and walk over, my mind still reeling from the conversation.

'Was that a long-distance call?' Iain asks when I get to his desk. 'A personal one?'

I stare at him, at the disapproving slant to his eyebrows. 'What?'

29

'You know you shouldn't be making those on company time.'

'It was just once,' I stumble. 'It was important. My mother — '

'Annie.' He sighs, a short, impatient sound. 'We're behind schedule as it is. I can't have you wasting time when there is real work to be done. If you're still struggling to concentrate even after all that time you took off, then — '

All at once I can't stand it any more. I turn and hurry out of the office without a word. In the toilets, I run cold water over my shaking hands, splash my face, the awful worry of the past few months welling up in me again. Iain doesn't know that the weeks I took off work were spent with Mum. He doesn't know they were filled with appointments and scans, with holding her hair while she was sick, caring for her in the wake of operations. I can't blame him for not knowing.

The smell of disinfectant in the toilets is overwhelming, too much like the hospitals, but I'm not ready to return to the fishbowl of the office, not yet. I shunt open the narrow window above me, lean against the wall, breathing in the mild spring air.

After a while, a squeal breaks through my thoughts, a scraping sound. I hear the murmur of voices, the sound of a lighter, and fresh cigarette smoke begins to drift in through the window. The fire exit; the others are always going out there to smoke. And Iain goes on about *me* wasting time.

'What do you think all that was about?'

30

It's Marta.

'God knows,' Iain answers, around a lungful of smoke.

'I thought she was about to cry.' There's the sound of an indrawn breath. 'You probably shouldn't have said that to her, about the phone call.'

'Why not? It's true, none of us go around calling the bloody ends of the earth just to speak to Mummy.'

Marta shushes him. 'Annie's mother's quite famous, you know,' she says idly, 'in academic circles. She's an anthropologist. I read an interview once, about some tribe she studied in New Caledonia.'

Iain snorts. 'And she ends up with a library nerd for a daughter. Gutted.' There's a thump, as if Marta has hit him on the arm, but they're both laughing. 'What?' Iain protests with mock-indignation. 'You know I'm right. She's weird.' He lowers his voice, but it doesn't matter, I can still hear. 'You know, when I went down to the mine earlier, I caught her *smelling* one of the files.'

Marta snorts and coughs, dissolving into laughter. 'You did not . . . '

I shut my eyes tight, clench my jaw until I can hear the blood rushing through my ears, blocking them out. Eventually, there's a scrape, a slam and they're gone.

Saint-Antoine

February 1943

Over the next few days, rumours about the Jews from Nice spread through Saint-Antoine like a fever. No one seemed to know what it meant, how long they would stay, how many would arrive. All I heard, over and over, was that 'they' would come soon. No one could say what 'Jews' even meant exactly, whether they would be old or young, rich or poor, French or Russian or Polish.

We were used to tourists in Saint-Antoine, or at least we had been before the war, but this was different. Across the alleyway, I heard our neighbours whispering about criminals and communists. It wasn't fair, some said, that Saint-Antoine should be expected to accommodate them, not when we already had the young men of the Italian Fourth Army eating us bare.

It was true, the soldiers stretched the town's supplies, especially at this time of year, when the harvests were long gone and summer was so far off. There had been reports of thefts, of soldiers seen stealing vegetables from gardens, chickens from coops. We fared better than most. The *capitano* had come to see Papa, and had made an arrangement. Now, we delivered bread to the soldiers once a day, and if we received a little extra money, or occasionally a bottle of precious olive oil for our trouble, we did not speak of it.

Still, we were always short of something. Our meals were scraped together: meat boiled with bones, cabbage leaves, a few potatoes. And so, like many other women in the town, Mama decided that we would rent our tiny apartment above the bakery to the foreigners, if and when they came.

News began to creep up the mountain from the lower villages of buses arriving, bringing dozens of people, and all of them in need of a place to stay. There was no point in preparing the apartment until 'they' arrived, I had argued, but Mama insisted. She said we needed to be ready.

On a gloomy Sunday evening, I began to pack up my room. I did not have much: my Sunday skirt, a few chemises and blouses, some much-darned woollen stockings. But it wasn't only my possessions that needed to be taken care of. Slowly, I drew back the curtain that divided the little room into two halves. Papa had hung it a few years ago, to give Leon and me a little privacy, now that we were grown. Sometimes we'd leave it open at one end, so we could see the gleam of each other's eyes as we talked at night. Other times, Leon yanked it closed, right up against the wall, and I knew I wasn't allowed to disturb him. The room felt strange with that length of old brown fabric pulled aside. Suddenly bare and cold.

Leon's half was as he'd left it the evening he went to Nice: bed hastily made, washbowl on the table, mirror and comb and razor scattered around. A picture of a red-haired woman in a bathing suit and sunglasses tacked to the wall next to the bed.

It felt wrong to touch his belongings. I knew he'd be angry when he found out, but I didn't have a choice. Mama had asked me to pack them up, like mine. I balanced on the end of the bed to drag the old, leather suitcase from the top of the wardrobe. It was heavier than I remembered, hit the floor with a thump, something clattering within. I wrestled open the creaking straps. Inside I saw sackcloth wrapped about a strange shape. I picked it up, shook it without thinking. A heavy object rolled into my lap and I found myself holding a gun.

At first I couldn't move, only knelt there, staring at the wooden grip, at the oily black barrel against the fabric of my skirt. Outside, it was raining, cold droplets spattering the windowpanes. My hands were shaking as I touched a fingertip to the thin, metal muzzle and I felt a rush of fear, familiarity. I knew this gun. It had been my grand-father's — a carbine he had used for hunting, lighter and smaller than other men's rifles. I had even fired it a few times, many years ago. Instinctively, I shifted my hand until my finger rested on the trigger. The wooden grip had a warm glow, darkened in places with the oils from my grandfather's hands. I remembered his arms surrounding me, his rough shirt scratching the back of my neck as he placed his finger over mine, and squeezed.

Abruptly, I let go. When grandfather died,

Papa had hung the carbine on the wall by its strap, and there it had stayed, a home for spiders, until the order came from the Italians that all weapons must be surrendered, on pain of imprisonment. Leon had been the one to lift the gun from the wall, wrap it in a sack, and take it to the *capitano*.

Yet here it was. Almost without meaning to, I reached for it again, pushed the lever up, slid it back, the way I remembered Grandfather doing. In the dim light, something glimmered deep within the casing, like gold in a tooth. It was loaded.

I shoved myself backwards. The gun tumbled off my lap and struck the floor with a *clack*.

'Ceci?' my mother called from the next room. 'What are you doing?'

'Packing,' I shouted. I kicked the gun out of sight beneath the bed just as the door creaked open.

My mother's face appeared. 'Don't stay up too late.' Her eyes drifted to Leon's belongings, exposed by the curtain. 'Thank you, Ceci,' she murmured.

As soon as she was gone, I retrieved the gun. Looking in the bottom of the suitcase, I found five shining, new bullets. Leon *must* have had a reason for keeping this secret. I smoothed the worn wood, repelled and fascinated in equal measure. Why hadn't he told me? I couldn't turn it in now, couldn't tell my parents that Leon had hidden something like this from them. He'd never forgive me. They'd never forgive him, not with everything else that had happened of late.

Quickly, I packed the rest of his things: shirts, underwear, vests, kerchiefs, socks that were more darn than wool. I rolled his razor and comb up in his washcloth, stale with old soap as it was. I even untacked the poster of the busty woman, laid it in the case on top of his best suit. Everything fit. Everything except the gun. I wrapped the bullets in an old rag, tied it firmly and pushed both into the darkness beneath the bed.

I could hear my parents preparing to go to sleep next door, the creak of springs as they lay down. I lay down too, though I was fully dressed, my eyes wide in the dark. Across the room, the gun was a shadow. The room vibrated with its presence.

I listened to the church bells ringing across the rooftops. They struck eleven while I lay there, then half past, then midnight. I must have slept after that, for the next thing I knew, the alarm clock was making a dull *thunk* beside me. I grabbed it, turning it off before the blood-curdling ringing began.

Two o'clock in the morning. Ordinarily, I hated leaving the warmth of my bed for the cold floors of the bakery. I would yawn and bury myself under the blankets until Papa came to shake me awake. But today I pushed back the covers, knelt and dragged out the gun.

The main room of the apartment was dark, but from the alcove where my parents slept, I heard my father's muffled groan as he levered himself on to an elbow, heard the rasp of his palm on his unshaven cheek. Heart thudding, I crept past, even though I knew he would hear me unlatch the door, knew the stairs would make loud, wooden complaints with every step. I hugged the weapon to my chest, praying he wasn't yet awake enough to call out a question, to flick on the light or to follow.

Downstairs, the bakery smelled of ovens turned cold and yesterday's flour. I kept moving, not stopping until I had stepped into the dark storeroom. The gun and the bullets had to be hidden, and not where anyone else might find them. There, at the back, on the top shelf. A dark corner never used. Out of sight, into shadow.

My legs were shaking as I climbed on to the shelving, clinging awkwardly to the sackcloth-wrapped package with one hand. Behind me, I heard the door to the apartment close with a soft *click*, heard Papa's footsteps trudging unevenly downwards. Hurriedly, I moved aside some old, dust-covered tins on the top shelf to reveal a long, thin niche; one of the original stone shelves, from when this was a pantry. I had found it once, during a game of hide and seek, and didn't think anyone else remembered it was there. I pushed the carbine into darkness, hastily dragged the tins in front of it, then some more old sack-cloth, for good measure.

Papa appeared at the same moment I dropped back to the floor. He looked surprised to see me standing there. I was breathing too hard, I knew, could feel the air whistling in and out of my nose.

'What are you doing?' He frowned.

'Nothing.' What if the gun had left streaks of

37

oil on my clothes? What if Papa knew about it, what if he had *asked* Leon to hide it?

He grunted. 'Thought you were sleepwalking. Normally I have to threaten you with yesterday's washing water to — '

'I couldn't sleep.'

As I moved past him, back into the kitchen, he stopped me, palm on my shoulder and stared into my face, as if looking for a lie. I stared back, trying to keep the gun at arm's length in my mind. After a moment, he let me go.

'Let's get to work,' he said.

A night of baking always began with a spark. Cold ash was raked, new wood stacked high into the oven and then, tinder, smoke, flame; bark caught bark until the oven was a cavern of heat and light, driving away the dampness of the early hours, waking us, so that we could bring the bakery to life.

We worked on the *frasage*, the first mixing, in comfortable silence, elbow to elbow at the troughs. I opened one of the sacks of flour and a cloud of powder rose. My fingers sank into the smooth coolness, creaking like snow.

Next came water. It waited by the back door in its pail. I had scooped it from the *gargouille* before I went to bed, my breath misting in the cold air, the sound of the mountain stream filling the silent street. The mountain itself was in our bread, snow and ice older than imagining.

Then came the *levain*, the ingredient that — to me — was the most mysterious of all. *Grandfather dough*, Papa called it, and so it was: a strange substance that was always and never the same. Every day we mixed it into the dough, and every day we pulled off a piece and set it aside to use for the next day's bread. It brought the flour and water alive, made the bread rise, grow, swell with promise.

That practice, that tiny piece of life-giving dough, had been passed down to Papa by his father and his father's father, and his father before. Four generations of Corvins. They were in the stone troughs and the blackened shelves of the oven, in the flour dust that never settled and the foot-worn flagstones. There was a memory of them in every loaf we baked.

With flour and water and the past we began, and with it we fed the life of the town. But there was one more thing: a fourth element, without which our bread would live but would not sing.

If flour and water were man's flesh, then salt was his soul.

Before the war our bread had been the envy of the region. Our flour was the best that could be had, perfect, powder pale. The air would be heavy with it, and the thick, sweetness of proving dough would fill the kitchen deep into the night.

The shelves of the larder were always full then. The hot, salt, caramel scent of freshly baked bread would mingle with the woodsmoke that fired the ovens, until I knew that my hair and skin would smell of warmth and wheat and pine for days. They called to my teeth and my tongue, the memory of those loaves . . .

'Ceci?' Papa said, for I was dreaming.

I pulled a trough of dough towards me, tipped it on to the counter, a rippling, thigh-soft mass,

39

ready for the *rabat*, the *degas*, the *pliage*; the time to stretch and turn and punch and fold the dough, again and again and again. Every night, it made my muscles burn and my arms ache, made me catch my breath until the clean, bright sourness of the dough found its way into my lungs.

They were gone, those rich, soft breads, those decadent crisp loaves, eaten for enjoyment rather than hunger. Now, even decent flour was hard to come by, let alone butter or spices or sugar.

In the cities, *boulangeries* were closing. There, with so many mouths to feed, and the Germans siphoning off supplies, the flour that reached bakery kitchens was little better than floor-scrapings mixed with sawdust. The bread they turned out was not bread, but choking loaves of ash, dry and hard and grey with want.

Here in the mountains, things were a little better. Mountain people looked after their own, Papa said, but even so, the bread we baked now was different. It had a bland, dutiful quality, like everything else. It was hard-working, could be sliced very thin. *Pain bis*. Gone was the silk-pale flour, now we used bran and buckwheat, mixed with whatever else we could find. And if the resulting bread was dense, and the crust hard, people had to admit that it was better than no bread at all.

I did not mind it. I had grown up on whatever the customers did not want. To me, that bread tasted of wheat husks at threshing time, of my grandfather's home-brew beer, foaming in its bucket. To me, it tasted like home.

I glanced up at the clock, blinking. The night had slipped away. Soon, the scent of baking bread would escape through the wooden shutters into the street. There was something unstoppable about it, more powerful than a cockcrow: it told people that the day had begun.

I watched, my back soaked with sweat from the kneading and the ovens, my hands tingling with exertion, as Papa took out the *lame*, the razor that had been his father's. Skilful as a barber, he moved along the loaves, scoring them deftly, opening cuts in their delicate surface. I loved to watch him work; in hands less confident the bread would tear, would fail to rise just so. But the *grignes* on Papa's loaves, the crust like an upturned lip, were always perfect.

Together, we carried the first trays to the oven, loaded them in, and latched the door. Red from the heat, floured from the evening, we smiled at each other. Papa patted me on the shoulder as he walked to fetch the next batch. In moments like these I was glad Leon had lost interest in the bakery, glad that Papa and I had these close, quiet hours together.

Dawn leapt upon us between one glance at the clock and another. The church bells were clanging six. I walked slowly through to the shop. My muscles were fizzing, skin cooling as rapidly as the loaves in my arms. I stacked them into their waiting baskets, and began to take down the shutters. As soon as I sat down behind the counter, tiredness ambushed me, and I let my head fall on to my flour-streaked arms to rest, just for a few moments . . .

41

The door burst open and I sat up, knowing that Papa would scold me for falling asleep when I should be serving. But it was only Paul, struggling to button his jacket, blond hair sticking up like hay.

'They're here,' he gasped before I could ask, cramming the gendarme's cap on to his head. 'The first Jews from the coast, they've arrived.'

Cheshire

April 1993

I spend the rest of the morning glued to the computer monitor, trying not to think about Mum, or Iain. Instead, I work methodically through the pages and pages of data that have to be entered to make this new computer catalogue work. I still can't wrap my head around it, not really. I know how to connect to a thing called a server, know how to type in basic commands, thanks to a training course at work, but the whole concept still leaves me confused.

What about card catalogues? I think, as I punch in yet another file reference number. What about librarians, archivists, like me? Is this our future? Clacking at keyboards, never curating, never touching the pages we work with?

I glance over at Kai. He's at his desk, headphones on, sludgy rock music leaking around the edges of the foam. He's a grad student, seconded here, like the rest of us. For him, this is just a summer job. But for me . . .

I sigh. I use the mouse to click on a new entry. *Real* archives are what I love; artefacts of human existence, handwritten pages, preserved for future generations. The files on the computer have no presence beyond the flashing cursor, the blocky green letters.

'Annie?'

Startled, I look up to find Kai staring at me. The office is quiet, I realize now. Marta and Iain must have gone for lunch.

'Sorry?' I stammer.

'I said, want one?' He's brandishing a bag of crisps at me. 'Pickled onion.'

'I — ' I remember Iain's comments, outside the fire exit. 'OK.' Awkwardly, I scoot my chair out from behind the desk, reach over to take one. 'Thanks.'

'No problem.' Kai slides his headphones off. I can tell he wants to chat. We've never really talked about anything other than cataloguing before. Perhaps because the others were always listening. 'Your phone call earlier . . . ' he starts.

'It was an exception,' I say quickly. 'I don't normally use the work phones like that.'

Kai gives a snort. 'Don't care if you do.' He fishes another crisp out of the bag. 'I was just surprised. I didn't know you spoke French.'

I nod, before remembering the waitress this morning, her despairing look at my one-word answers. *Try*, I tell myself.

'Yes,' I say. 'I am French. Sort of.'

'Sort of?'

He holds out the crisps again. It gives me time to think: to find the simplest answer.

'My grandmother was French,' I tell him after a while, 'my mother is too. At least, she was born there. They came to England after the war.'

'And your dad?'

I swallow. All at once my mouth feels dry, the taste of the crisps too sharp. 'He was Algerian,' I

44

say quietly. 'My mum met him on a posting.'

Kai's face creases. 'I'm sorry,' he says, 'is he . . . ?'

I shake my head, trying not to let the discomfort show, but it's there, always, the same stab of shame, frustration, that I can't answer like everyone else. 'I never knew him. He left before I was born.'

Kai makes a face. 'Sorry.'

'It's OK.' I try for a smile. 'Mum brought me up. And my grandma, when I was little. I've never known anything else.'

'My granny looked after me and my brother too,' he says, scraping the crumbs from the bottom of the crisp bag. 'After school, every day.' He smiles back. 'Yours still alive?'

I stare at him, wondering how much he understood of my conversation on the phone.

'It's complicated,' I murmur, heat creeping up my cheeks.

Kai frowns at me. 'What?'

'We haven't seen her for a long time. I'm not sure — ' I stop, not knowing how to go on.

Kai is staring in disbelief. A few crisp crumbs are caught in his long black hair. 'You're not sure whether she's alive or dead?'

'No. Yes. I mean, I told you it was complicated.' I look down at my hands. 'Mum and Grand-mère had this huge fight when I was seven or eight. About me, I think. They stopped talking. Eventually, my grandmother moved back to France.'

I shift uncomfortably, wondering why I've let the conversation get this far. This is something

I've only ever talked to a handful of people about.

'And you never heard from her again?' Kai's asking.

I shrug, still staring at the floor. 'We did. She sent birthday cards for a few years. But Mum and I were moving around a lot then, for her research positions. They just lost contact and never picked it up again.'

Kai shakes his head. 'Families,' he says, turning back to his monitor.

'I'm going to look for her, though,' I blurt out. I don't want this conversation to be over, not yet. The telephone call with my mother has been repeating in my mind ever since I hung up. It's a relief to talk about it. 'Mum asked me to. She's not been well. I think it's made her realize what's important.'

Kai makes a speculative face but nods. 'Where're you going to start?'

'I don't know. I did start to look for her once before, when I first got the job at the Public Record Office, without telling Mum. She was furious when she found out. I didn't get very far anyway.'

'Well, good luck this time.'

Smiling a little, I swing my chair back towards the computer. I manage to input another two entries before I lose concentration and my brain starts whirring off on its own. I didn't get far looking for Grand-mère last time because she and Mum were both born in France. That meant no birth certificates in the archives. They only moved here when my mother was a toddler.

'Kai?' I call abruptly.

I hear him pull one headphone off. 'Eh?'

'Do you know — have the Home Office archives from the 1940s already been catalogued? From the war era?'

He scratches his chin with the end of a highlighter. 'Yeah, think so. They were some of the first to be done. Most popular, I guess.' He puts his headphones back on. 'Why?'

'Just wondering.'

My hands hover over the keyboard. Mum and Grand-mère were both French citizens when they arrived in this country, which would make them immigrants. And if they were immigrants, the Home Office must have documented them at some time or another . . .

I shouldn't do it. I'm here to work, not to use this expensive new computer catalogue for my own ends. But what harm could it do? Kai is working, lost in the noise from his headphones; Iain and Marta are still at lunch. Swiftly, before I can think twice about it, I click on the icon that will connect me to the Internet. The computer buzzes fiercely, the connection squalls and hums and pings. My heart begins to thud as I wait for the modem to respond.

There: it's live. I load the new catalogue, just a blank screen, and carefully, tap out a series of commands:

```
SELECT *
FROM    Home Office Records: Immigration
WHERE Name= PICOT, C.
ORDER BY year < 1940;
```

I hit enter. The screen flickers as the program scurries off to search through the thousands of records on the system, many of them organized and collated by us over the past few weeks. I sit back, letting out a long breath. *It probably won't find anything,* I tell myself. *Even if the immigration files have been catalogued, who's to say they'll all be there?* And yet, something is flickering in my chest, filling me with warmth: an unfamiliar thrill that comes with breaking rules.

After five minutes, I can't stand the suspense any more and get up from my chair.

'Want anything from the drinks machine?' I ask Kai, but he can't hear me over his music. In the corridor, I take my time, slowly slotting in coins, pressing the button for a hot chocolate I don't really want.

I watch the steam spouting from the grill. If the search produces a result, should I tell Mum straight away? Or should I check it out first myself, so I don't get her hopes up? What if it's a dead end or, worse, if Grand-mère wants nothing to do with us? I can't bear the thought of putting Mum through that.

I'm still standing there when the door swings open: the others, coming back from lunch, cheeks pinked by the breeze. Marta's talking loudly about her bank holiday plans. They both ignore me.

I try to stay calm, but even so, I can feel the thin plastic cup trembling in my hand as I walk into the office. As I reach my desk, Iain lets out a noise of disgust.

'Is someone using the Internet?' he says, the

48

phone hanging in his hand. 'I've got to call London. It's important.'

'Sorry,' I mutter, hot liquid slopping over my fingers. 'I'm just — '

I stop. The computer has finished its search, and on the screen, a block of text is waiting:

```
FILE MATCHES --- 1
```

Saint-Antoine

February 1943

Mama came hurrying down the stairs. She must have heard Paul and me talking, or else leaned out of the window to hear the gossip from our neighbours. She was dressed for housework, apron on, kerchief tied around her head.

'Ceci, I want you to go down to the hotel to see the *capitano*. Tell him that we have rooms to rent here, to respectable people who can pay. Understand? Ceci?'

After the quiet night's work, alone with Papa and our family recipes, Mama's sudden frenzy was bewildering, made me yearn for stillness. She had picked up a basket, was rapidly packing it with bread, five *boule* loaves, hard and floury and wider than my handspan, perfect for cutting into plate-sized slices to make a meal. She hesitated, then loaded in three dense bricks of *pain bis*.

'If people have travelled all night,' she muttered, 'they'll be hungry. They'll want breakfast and the hotel will need to serve more than usual —'
She tucked a napkin over the top. 'Take this down there now. Tell Madame Gougeard I'll put it on her account.'

Wordlessly, I took it. Paul was standing near the door. His face was bright, hair tousled beneath his cap, at odds with the neat gendarme uniform.

Abruptly, I resented him. *He* was the one who had brought this news from the streets. My head was swimming from a lack of sleep, but Mama was pushing my jacket into my hands, trying to untie my baker's smock at the same time.

The night-cold jacket brushed the back of my neck, made me shudder.

'Mama,' I tried to protest, 'we don't even know how many have come yet.'

'It will be fifty this morning.' That was Paul, the eager bearer of news. 'The Italians received a call, at the gendarmerie, before dawn. Father overheard it all. They're planning to send *another* fifty later, and more tomorrow. They're registering every foreigner at the hotel.'

'A hundred?' Mama gasped, shoving me in the back. 'Go quickly, Ceci, before everyone has the same idea. Try to speak to the *capitano* himself.'

I dragged the kerchief from my head, damp with sweat and clinging flour. My hair fell past my shoulders. I felt Mama's eyes lingering over the tangled strands, the too-small blouse that pulled across my chest.

'Paul . . . ' she said uncertainly.

'I'll escort her, Madame Corvin.'

'*Merci.*' She gave him a smile. 'That's very kind of you.'

I turned and strode from the shop as fast as I could. Outside, the narrow streets were clogged with morning mist, like steam trying to find its way out of a pipe.

'Ceci, slow down,' Paul laughed, hurrying beside me.

'You don't need to come,' I said. 'I'm not a child. I'll be fine.'

'Exactly, you are *not* a child. That's why your mother is worried. Those Italians are shameless, the way they chase after girls.'

'They're not likely to chase after me.'

'Of course they are. You're — ' He stopped abruptly, as if he had something stuck in his throat.

'I'm what?' I demanded. For some reason, I felt nervous.

'You're an attractive girl.'

Something had started to shift between Paul and me since Leon had been arrested; there were moments when he would linger, as if he wanted to do or say something more. I gripped the basket's handle, walked on.

'They'll have eyes for this bread, not me,' I said.

Despite the cold, Paul's face was red, cheeks taking on that cherry-juice flush, like Leon's when he'd had a drink.

'Ceci — ' he started.

'Look!' I grabbed his elbow, stopping dead at the edge of the square. Two buses had pulled up outside the hotel, accompanied by Italian army trucks. Even as we watched, people were climbing out of the vehicles, more than seemed plausible. They must have been sharing seats, sitting on the floors, crammed into the aisles. The floating mist made everything seem insubstantial: the people who stood together in tight groups or wandered here and there looked like shadows that might disappear if we got closer.

'They look lost,' I heard myself say.

'I know,' Paul replied softly.

Beneath the bare plane trees, a few other early-risers had paused to watch. Paul and I advanced a few paces. I had never seen so many different-looking people. Old men all in black and women in city clothes lowering themselves to sit on the edge of the pavement, or on to suitcases or bundles. Families gathered, holding on to each other, the children fidgeting, goose-pimpled in shorts and despite the weather. Men with several days' worth of beard were trying to talk to the soldiers, women in fur coats and felt hats were pushing their way to the front, past others who stood with nothing but a blanket around their shoulders.

And there were young people, my age, younger. A girl with blonde plaits; a boy clutching a photographic camera to his chest, as if it were his last possession in the world, a pair of children who were painfully thin, their hair clumsily cropped, raw red patches on their faces. There had been rumours about residence camps further along the coast, about escapees who arrived in Nice half-mad with hunger or illness or both.

'Come on,' Paul murmured, nudging me forward. We walked into the crowd of people, and I felt afraid, without knowing why. Their voices swelled around me like the noise of the river. Accented French, outbursts in German, English, Russian, a woman crying in a flowing, rasping language I had never heard before.

For a moment I wanted to peer into each face

53

and ask, *Where are you from? What have you seen?* But fear caught me up: what if they decided to put everyone back on the trucks, and bundled me in with them? I stepped away, gave them a wide berth.

A line was already forming in front of the hotel, spilling down the steps and back to the square. As we approached, a shutter clacked open above, and I saw the Gougeards' daughter Marie throwing open the windows to air out long-empty rooms. I kept my eyes ahead, didn't look left or right at the people waiting to enter the hotel.

'*Arrêtez!*' a voice was saying, a body blocking my way. 'You, go — back in the line.' An Italian soldier was standing in the doorway, pointing. He looked harassed, his uniform too big, his boots muddy. He was missing his hat, and his ears were red with cold. He couldn't have been more than twenty. 'You hear?' he said impatiently, giving my arm a push.

'No, we live here,' Paul said loudly, pulling his gendarme uniform straight. 'We want to see the *capitano*. *She* does.'

'Eh?' The soldier frowned down at me. 'Why, little girl? We are busy here.' Beyond him, through the doors, I saw soldiers carrying a table up from the dining room, as if they were preparing for a dance.

'I want to tell the *capitano* that we have rooms to rent,' I said as firmly as I could, 'to those who can pay for them.' I was aware of the people who were standing near by, who were listening.

But the soldier only laughed. 'I'll pay you for one, *carina*.'

54

Paul's jaw tightened. 'You — ' he started.

'*Caporale*,' came a shout from the dining room, cutting him off. A man was looking at us. The captain. He was older than the soldier at the door, smarter, his uniform worn and fraying, but mostly clean. He was saying something in Italian, pointing at us. The soldier answered immediately, holding his hands up as if innocent.

'What do you want?' The captain threw the words at us, gestured me forward with a jerk of his head. He spoke good French, I knew.

'*Excusez-moi*,' I said, over the sounds of furniture scraping and Italian voices calling to one another, 'but my mother asked me to tell you that we have rooms to rent, in the village. For the . . . ' I couldn't help but a stammer. 'For the visitors.'

A table had been pushed to the side of the door, and a chair: a makeshift registration desk. A soldier came back in from the crowd outside, his hands full of papers. I saw identity cards and letters, travel documents of all colour and quality. As he shuffled through them, a photograph of a man caught my eye. He was young, his eyes pale and calm, his name partially obscured by four huge, red letters, stamped across the page.

JUIF.

'What is your name?'

The captain looked at me, his pen poised. Cold spines prickled my neck. I had no choice but to tell him.

'Mademoiselle Celeste Corvin. My family runs Boulangerie Corvin, on Rue du Marché.

That is where the rooms are.'

The captain's face brightened. 'Then you are the little baker who feeds my men.' He sat back, apparently forgetting about writing my name down. 'You know, your bread is much better than what they have in Nice.' He smiled. 'It is almost as if you have access to better supplies than our armies.'

I kept silent. After a moment of holding my gaze, he let out a laugh, went back to writing.

'However,' he said, not looking at me, 'I do not care much for your *pain bis*, little baker. When will you make us some *baguettes* or *cornetti*?'

The soldiers near by laughed and I felt heat rising in me again, just as it had in the square when the soldiers had stopped me in my path and made me squirm with embarrassment.

'We'll make those things when you return the butter and sugar your friends the Germans have stolen,' I snapped before I could stop myself. 'Until then, you will have to make do with this.' From my basket I snatched a loaf of *pain bis* and threw it down on the table before him.

For a long moment the captain stared, not moving. But then he laughed.

'*Merci, mademoiselle*,' he said, tearing a chunk from the loaf and saluting me mockingly. 'I was worried I would miss breakfast.'

He dismissed me with a jerk of the head and went back to his writing.

Marie had come down from her chores upstairs; she stood watching me, eyes wide with shock. I shoved the basket of bread into her arms and hurried away, past the line of foreigners.

None of them looked at me. Many simply gazed ahead; some even had their eyes closed, as if they might fall asleep right there.

But after a few paces, I realized that someone *was* watching me. I turned, and found my gaze caught by a stranger, a man with dark red hair that fell over his forehead. He was staring at me intently through a pair of horn-rimmed glasses. For a second, I stared back, frowning. Then, his lip quirked into a smile and he inclined his head, as though we knew each other already.

I turned and ran down the steps.

Cheshire
April 1993

'Annie?'

Someone's saying my name, but I can't answer, I'm staring at that series of numbers and letters, my mind barrelling along at a hundred miles an hour.

```
FILE MATCHES --- 1

NAME: Picot, Celeste
YEAR: 1946
RECORD: HO12/389/C/42b/6d
STATUS: Declassified (CLOSED)
```

'Annie!'

Kai has pulled off his headphones; he's staring at me. They all are. I'm half bent over, I realize, frozen in position. I let myself drop into the chair with a thump.

'Everything OK?' Kai asks.

'Yes,' I stammer, aware that Iain and Marta are listening, are looking at me as if I'm mad, as usual.

I duck my head, scribble the file name on one of my colour-coded Post-it notes before disconnecting from the Internet. Iain goes back to his phone call, Marta to sorting through an archive box.

I stare at those biro letters, wondering what on earth to do.

HO12/389/C/42b/6d.

Home Office 12. Record 389. Cheshire. Room 42b. Shelf 6d. Whatever it is, it's *here*, one of the thousands of boxes of files moved from the old Public Records building in London.

Status: Declassified (closed). Declassified by the government, but still a closed file, not available to the public; kept safe, under lock and key, deep in the mine. Sighing, I stick the note to my monitor. Iain will never give me clearance to go down and look. Perhaps I can apply for permission when I'm back in London.

Nerves still jumping, I turn to the ring binder, pick up the highlighter pen and try to work. The pen is a lurid yellow colour, reminds me of the foam banana sweets I used to eat as a child. Grand-mère would always let me choose something from the sweet shop at the start of our outings. I would chew happily as we walked around the British Museum, looking at the mummies. I didn't realize at the time that we went there so often because it was free, a way to keep me entertained while Mum was at work.

When we came to the Reading Room, Grand-mère would lift me up so that I could see into the immense dome, circled by thousands of books, desks fanning out from the centre like the rays of the sun. It was the grandest, most wonderful place I had ever seen. I told Grand-mère that I wanted to work in a place like that.

'Then you will, *chérie*,' she had said.

I drop the highlighter to the desk, blinking hard. The hurt that comes with memories of Grand-mère is old but always there; every time I think of the Reading Room, or catch the smell of cigarettes and musky perfume, or remember the taste of *madeleines*, baked in Grand-mère's ancient, creaking gas oven.

There's a sound from across the room, and I look up to find Iain peering at me. 'Wakey wakey,' he says sarcastically. 'Are you going to do *any* work today?'

Swiftly, I reach forward and pull the Post-it note from the computer monitor. I hear Iain huff and drop back into his chair, but I'm not thinking about him any more. I'm thinking about a file, somewhere beneath my feet, and about a question unanswered for too long.

Marta stands up, taking out a packet of cigarettes, waving them at Iain. Even if I did manage to sneak down to the mine, I think, watching them, I'd only get as far as the holding bay. To get into any of the archive rooms, I would need a security card. I don't have one, neither does Kai. Marta does, though. She hardly ever uses it, says the mine creeps her out.

The second the office door closes behind them. I stand up, the Post-it note clenched in my hand. Would I really . . . ? The access card is on Marta's desk, white and gleaming. Kai isn't looking, rooting through his bag for a can of coke. My palms are clammy as I walk past, as I reach out and touch the plastic with my fingertips.

A moment later, it's in my hand and I'm pushing my way out of the office, walking briskly across the yard, half-expecting to hear someone yell my name. For the second time that day, I press the lift button repeatedly until the doors open and I can rush inside. I feel myself plummeting, hundreds of feet below the surface of the earth. The doors open on the holding bay. *It's not too late*, I think, staring into the mine ahead, my breath coming fast. If I turned back now, they'd never know.

They wouldn't, but I would. I'd sit there, day in, day out, typing endless numbers, knowing that I had let my fear get the better of me, once again.

Clenching my teeth, I walk into the mine, down the huge, central tunnel, archive rooms branching off to either side. What if someone's watching on the CCTV? Would any of the security guards try to stop me?

I quicken my steps as the room numbers rise, 38, 40 . . . 42. I stop outside a cage-like door. All around, the mine is silent, a deep, enormous silence that makes me feel like an intruder. I suck in a breath and taste salt, lung-deep, before I take out the access card.

My hands are sticky with sweat as I slide it through the lock. A light flickers, then flashes green and the door releases, letting me in to room 42. I flick a switch and strip lights begin to clang and ping. They illuminate a long, low space, metal shelving stretching into darkness.

I count the stacks, passing box after box, all of them identical. They remind me of plaques in a cemetery wall, hiding the remains of life. The reference numbers rise, edging closer to the one

I want, and then I see it, printed on a label: HO12.

Stack 6. Shelf d, the lowest one. I drop to my knees and peer along the row, looking for the box I want. There, records 248–400. Carefully, I shuffle it towards me, not wanting to rip the card, until I can heave it from the shelf. It hits the salt dust with a thud.

I lift the lid. Inside are row upon row of files, tatty green cardboard jackets. I feel as clumsy as a child as I reach in and lift out the first one, staring at the label.

HO12: Foreign Aliens: Residency Permits: 1939–1947.

Foreign Aliens. Of course, that's exactly what my grand-mother was: a single French woman with a child, arriving on the shores of a country not her own. Slowly, I begin to turn through the files.

Orfino, Luca, HO12/352
Orlowicz, Agata, HO12/353
Orschel, Jakob, HO12/354

The smell of must and soft, yellowing paper rises. I touch each cover, marred by staples and pin holes, the inked tattoos of bureaucracy. I forget everything as they pass through my hands, like threads on a loom, each one bringing me closer to the name I want . . . *Perlman*. My pulse is beginning to race. *Pfeffermann, Philippe, Picardo, Picot.*

I stop dead. Above me, the strip lights seem to flicker. I make myself blink, and peer down at the file again.

PICOT, CELESTE, HO12/389

I grip the cardboard. It's slimmer than some of the others, feels almost empty. I hold it there, half out of the box, paralysed by thoughts of Mum, of my job, of all of the rules I'm breaking.

In a sudden movement, I pull the file. It's the work of seconds to replace the lid and shove the archive box back into place on the shelf.

I walk rapidly. Behind me, I hear the strip lights flickering off, as if I was never there. The holding bay is deserted, lift doors still standing open. I step in and stab at the button.

Only as it begins to rise do I finally allow myself to sneak a look at the front page:

Name: PICOT, CELESTE MARIE
D.O.B.: 11 JANUARY 1925
Place of birth: SAINT-ANTOINE, NICE, FRANCE

'Grand-mère,' I whisper.

Saint-Antoine

February 1943

'Ceci, wake up.'

Mama's voice drifted into my hearing. There had been dreams, but now they were nameless, ragged things.

'Celeste!'

I opened my eyes. The light from the window was dimmed by blackout paper, but I could see that Mama's face was red with exertion, that the sleeves of her blouse were rolled back, businesslike.

'The news is all over the town,' she said, as soon as she saw I was awake. 'The hotel is full and still more are coming.' She pulled the blankets off me, nudged me upright. 'Some can only afford a single room,' she was saying, 'but there are others with money, they are asking about renting the empty villas in the valley. I am sure someone will want this place, central as it is.' She rolled the blanket in her arms. 'It is just as well we are almost packed.'

Shivering, head a fug of daytime sleep, I stood up from the bed. The moment my weight left the mattress, Mama began to strip it, shaking the pillows out of their slips, hauling off the worn sheets and placing them with the still-warm blanket. I stared at her. It felt so sudden, this

64

turning-out. It hurt, like a jab with a hat pin that didn't leave a mark.

'You told the *capitano*?' she said, puffing with effort.

I nodded. I found I couldn't speak, words knocked out of me by the strange violence of it all.

'If you are still tired,' she said, 'you can go and sleep at your grandmother's. But take the suitcases with you when you go.'

She was treating the situation as if it was normal; as if these were the old days, when we'd pack up and camp at Grandmother's creaking old house for the tourist season between May and August. I had tried to argue that we should bring Grandmother *here*, rent her house instead, but Mama had refused. Grandmother's house was old, she said, it was dirty and decrepit and would take an age to make presentable. We would get a pittance for it. The apartment, at least, was clean and tidy and right in the middle of town, just what visitors would pay for. But the people in the square were not visitors . . .

'I'll be downstairs,' I said shortly. 'There's work to finish.'

It was only half a lie. There was always work to be done in the bakery. Papa was only too glad to let me take over scrubbing down the workbench, so he could go for his rest. *Good luck*, I thought, picturing Mama trying to strip the bed from around him as he slept.

My head felt heavy as I swept the uneven stone floor, restacked the baskets as bread was sold. Customers came and went, bringing waves of gossip with them: the church alms collection was empty already, the curé was trying to find places for people to sleep, a wealthy family from Montpellier had rented one of the largest villas on the hill. When Madame Blanchi stopped by for her loaf of *pain bis*, she slid an old pasteboard box across the counter, whispering that we should all look to ourselves now. I opened it once she'd gone. Inside were two brown eggs, nestled in straw. It seemed she intended to keep her money and coupons to herself.

Mademoiselle Louise, my old schoolmistress, came to trade half a bottle of ink for a *pain de campagne*. The Rocher boys came tumbling in the moment she was gone, grubby and grinning and truant as always. Everyone knew they only went to school to collect their government-issued vitamin biscuits. They were doing a brisk trade: bartering the tough, flavourless things for boiled sweets and cocoa and cigarettes from the Italian soldiers with a fervour that left the grown-ups of the town shaking their heads and muttering about the way they had been raised.

As I watched, they emptied their pockets on to the counter, sending walnuts rolling in every direction.

'Where on earth did you get these?' I asked, picking one up to shake, in case they were tricking me with empty shells, glued together.

'Forest.' Nino Rocher grinned.

'Not in February you didn't.'

His brother Alfio shrugged. 'You want them or not?'

66

I sighed. Someone must have left their cellar or their shed unlocked. 'How much?' I asked.

The boys jostled out through the door, shoving a loaf of *pain bis* into a satchel, tearing at a *boule* like half-feral things. Abruptly, I wished I was a child again, too young to understand or care about the war or the violence spreading through the country, sending people fleeing towards us.

For a moment, the shop was empty. Without knowing why, I turned my back on the counter and made for the dark storeroom. My toes found the bottom shelf and I stretched up, up, until, with a thrill of fear, my fingertips found the alcove and I touched cold metal: the mouth of the gun.

The doorbell jangled, echoing through the shop, and I snatched my hand away.

'*Un moment*,' I called, hurrying out through the kitchen, 'I am just — '

Light from the window flashed on a pair of spectacles as the man turned. Before I saw the rest of his face, I found myself looking into a pair of blue eyes — the same pair that had caught mine in the vestibule of the hotel, the same pair that had watched me turn and run.

'*Bonjour*,' he said slowly, pushing the dark red hair back from his forehead. He was unshaven, and there was a dull pallor to his skin that I recognized as a sign of sleeplessness. A frown creased his forehead. 'Have you hurt yourself?' he asked, pointing.

I was clutching my fingers to my chest, I realized, the two fingers that had touched the gun, as if I had burned them.

'No.' I let my hand drop.

He smiled, warm, familiar. 'I am sorry to bother you,' he said, 'but I was at the hotel this morning and I heard what you said to the *capitano*.'

'About the *cornetti*?' I asked without thinking.

He laughed, a quick sound. 'No, not about the *cornetti*, although I must admit, I found that amusing.' His French was perfect, but there was a lilt to his words, a slight accent that gave him away as a foreigner. 'No, I am here to enquire about the lodgings you mentioned.'

He was resting a hand on the counter. His fingers were smooth and pale. Not a worker's hands. A wide, gold band wrapped around his wedding finger. And then there were his clothes, crumpled but tailored, his overcoat, his horn-rimmed glasses. He clearly was, or had once been, a wealthy man.

Looking at him, my own clothes seemed to squeeze and itch. My skirt was old and flour-streaked, my feet jammed into ugly work clogs. And he was asking if he could rent our apartment upstairs.

'Are there no rooms left at the hotel?' I watched his expression shift into a frown, as though I'd said something rude. 'It's just,' I stammered, 'well, the rooms upstairs are not very big.' If only I could wipe the heat away from my cheeks. 'They are probably not what you are used to.'

He was staring at me, his lips twisted. '"What I'm used to",' he repeated.

'Ceci?' Mama's voice rang out, her feet tramping down the stairs. 'I need you to — '

She stopped dead at the sight of the man. Her face went taut, and I saw her tongue meet her teeth in the shape of an 'L'.

'This gentleman is asking about the rooms upstairs,' I rushed, to stop her fears in their tracks. 'I was just telling him that they are . . . a bit small.'

'They are perfectly well proportioned,' Mama said. She summoned up a smile, though I could see the agitation still bubbling beneath the surface. 'We are just preparing them,' she told the man. 'But I can show you around, if you'd care to see?'

The man was reaching inside his coat, taking out a wallet. 'That will not be necessary,' he said. 'I am sure they will be fine. And the size of the rooms does not matter.' He was looking at me again. 'There will be only myself. And my wife.'

My mother's eyes widened at the sight of that leather wallet, and even she seemed to quaver. 'Are you sure you would not like to see them first?' she asked. 'They are good rooms, but compared to the hotel — '

'We do not wish to stay in the hotel,' the man snapped. In that moment I saw the way the shadows pooled beneath his eyes, collected in the lines of his forehead. He swallowed hard. 'I am sorry, what I mean to say is, my wife and I would prefer to have a small place to ourselves. We have had a hard few months and the hotel will be . . . busy.'

Abruptly, I understood. 'Busy' meant the

tramping of Italian army boots, the presence of soldiers, the scratch of a pen on a registration list.

'Besides,' the man's look softened, 'my wife is a writer. I should like to find her somewhere quiet to work.'

'A *writer*?' I said, before I could stop myself.

'Yes.' The man smiled at my surprise. 'I left her resting at the hotel. She is not well, right now.' I was too tongue-tied to reply, but that didn't seem to bother him. He took up the wallet again. 'So,' he said, 'how much for the month?'

His name was Daniel Reiss, we learned. He and his wife were from Belgium. They had arrived in Nice from Marseille only a few weeks before. He showed Mama his papers, and she looked at them while he counted out money. I glanced across. Sure enough, there it was, the letter 'J', stamped in red across every page, the colour glaring in the daylight. I stared, my stomach tight with unease.

Of course we had heard the stories: Jews in the cities and larger towns rounded up, arrested and taken away to holding camps. But all of that was happening in other places, far from Saint-Antoine. Most of the people who got arrested were refugees, the news on the wireless said, in France illegally, without papers. They were being sent back east, where they came from, or to work in Germany's factories and mines and fields. But I knew there was a lot that went unsaid, too. I wondered why Daniel Reiss, with his money, had not bought himself new papers, ones without a 'J' upon them.

70

Then he was gone, and Mama was rushing about, emptying drawers and finding the good linen in the cupboard. I could not avoid helping her now, and as I worked, I seemed to see that letter everywhere, in the dust on the shelves and the pattern of the wood grain, couldn't help wondering how it would feel to have a letter stamped across my own papers.

Mama was making the bed with the linen that had been her trousseau. I didn't say anything about that, only straightened the blanket. I could see Daniel Reiss's head sinking on to the pillow with relief, his red hair wet from washing, and found myself smoothing the cotton there.

He had arranged to return within the hour, but the minutes seemed to drag. I found reasons to linger in the shop, so I could watch the street through the window. We had not had strangers staying above the bakery for a long time. What would they be like, elegant Daniel Reiss and his wife, the writer?

I was so lost in thought, I didn't see the couple approaching until they were almost at the door. They were huddled together, soaked by the fine, icy rain that had begun to fall. Monsieur Reiss was carrying two suitcases, but even so, he had one arm around the woman at his side, as if he was supporting her. She was bent almost double, shuffling like a grandmother. Her face was almost completely obscured by a black shawl, wrapped around her head, revealing only a pair of dark-lensed glasses, despite the weather. I had been expecting someone young, poised, as attractive as Monsieur Reiss himself. The bell jingled as they stepped over the threshold.

I stared into those opaque, black lenses and saw myself reflected there. A shiver went through me, and for an instant, I couldn't move, couldn't breathe, couldn't even look away. Part of me wanted the woman to take off the glasses, so I could see her face. Another part wanted to turn, to hide my head and forget about everything, the war and the gun and Reiss's papers stamped with red.

'Myriam, this way,' Monsieur Reiss was saying softly. The woman looked away from me, gripping her husband's arm in silence.

'If there is anything you need, please just ask.' My mother's voice filtered through my thoughts. 'I should have mentioned before that we work down here, at night. Ceci and her father will use the back door, and do their best to be quiet.'

'That will not be a problem, Madame,' Monsieur Reiss said over his shoulder. 'Thank you.'

His eyes met mine for one fleeting moment, and then the door was swinging closed behind them. Mama and I stood, listening as they climbed the creaking stairs, and I could tell we were both thinking the same thing, both wondering who we had let in to our lives.

Cheshire

April 1993

The security card seems to burn in my pocket as I push open the office door, arms about my stomach.

Iain looks up as I walk past.

'Everything OK?' he asks, but what he means is, *Where have you been?*

'Sort of,' I mutter. 'I'm not feeling well.'

He makes a noise, but seems to believe me, looking back to his work. Marta is at her desk, whispering into the phone. From her smile, I can guess she's talking to her boyfriend. Which means they haven't noticed anything is amiss, at least not yet.

But someone is watching. Kai is frowning at me. When I sit down awkwardly, arms gripping my middle, his frown only deepens.

'Are you all right?' he says loudly, over the noise of his headphones. The others glance up.

'Yes, I . . . ' I stutter. I need Kai to be quiet; I need to get him out of the office before he mentions our earlier conversation. 'Actually, I was wondering if you had any aspirin,' I say, trying to think of an excuse. 'Did you say you had some? In your car?'

It comes out strained and awkward sounding. I'm sure the others will notice, but they don't seem to. Perhaps they think I'm always this awkward.

Kai looks bewildered. I stare at him hard, trying to make him understand, and jerk my head towards the door.

'Oh!' He stops, looks at the others. 'Yes. I do. Right.' He's levering himself up from his desk. 'Er — in my car.'

'I'll come with you,' I say, trying not to wince at our unconvincing performance.

'Oh my God,' I hear Marta mock-whisper to Iain as the door swings closed behind us. 'I think they're trying to flirt.'

Right now, I don't care. She can think what she likes. I'm just glad to be away from them, safely outside, my heart thudding beneath the cotton of my shirt.

'What's going on?' Kai asks, as soon as we're out of earshot.

'Not here,' I whisper.

Kai's car is battered and purple, caked in grime.

'Sorry about the mess,' he says, pushing an empty can of coke on to the floor. Gingerly, I sit down, pull the door shut. My feet rest on a carpet of empty crisp bags, crumpled cigarette packets and ticket stubs. The back seats are cluttered with clothes and what could be a sleeping bag.

'So,' Kai says, 'are you going to tell me what the hell's going on?'

Slowly, I uncross my arms, and reach under my shirt. There, warm from my skin, is the thin green government file.

74

'You know I told you earlier,' I stammer, 'that I was going to look for my grandmother . . . ?'

Kai swears when he sees what I'm holding. 'You brought that *out* of the archive?' He peers a little closer at the label. 'It's a closed file! Jesus, Annie — '

'I had to! I have to read it properly, and I couldn't stay down there any longer.'

Kai only stares.

'How did you get in?' he demands. 'We don't have clearance.'

Embarrassed, I take Marta's card from my pocket and place it on the dashboard.

Kai lets out a laugh when he sees it, shakes his head. 'I never had you down for something like this.'

'Me neither.' I manage a smile. In my lap, the cardboard file sits, dog-eared and ordinary-looking. 'I wouldn't have but . . . I don't know. This is important.'

'Important enough to risk pissing off Iain for good?'

'I think so.'

Kai shakes his head again, but leans over to see. 'What is it?'

'An immigration record,' I tell him, holding it out, 'for my mother and grandmother, when they first arrived in this country. I've only looked at the first page so far.'

He takes it with gentle hands, smoothing the bent corners, the wilted fabric ties that hold the file closed. I can't help but smile at the care he takes.

'May I?' he asks, one hand on the top cover.

I nod. Out in the daylight, the file looks fragile, the papers within thin as moth wings, covered in precious dust. I feel a stab of remorse when I think of how I carried it here, crushed against my chest.

But then I see it, my grandmother's name in a black ink scrawl, my mother's name in the gap labelled *dependants*. When Kai turns to the page, I feel myself take an involuntary breath. There, pasted on to a form, is my grandmother's photograph.

She's staring straight at the camera, her dark hair parted down the middle, pulled back in a plait. She looks solemn, almost severe, but her face is smooth and rounded with youth.

'Is this her?' Kai says quietly. I nod, unable to look away from those clear eyes. 'She looks so young.'

'She was.' My voice is husky. 'If this was taken in nineteen forty-six, she would have only been twenty-one.'

'And already a mother and a widow,' Kai says, finger hovering over the column that reads, *Evelyne Picot, Age 2*. He looks up at me, eyes flicking from my hair, pulled back just like hers, my nose, cheeks. 'You look like her,' he says.

'You think so?' My brain is whirring, taking in the dates, the knowledge that my grandmother was a teenager when she had my mum; bearing a child during the war.

'It says here their previous address was in Paris.' Kai squints, trying to make out the clerical scrawl. 'Square de . . . something. But this front page says 'Nice'.'

'She was from the South of France, I know that much.' I look to where he's pointing. 'I have no idea about Paris. Neither of them ever mentioned it.'

'Could you ask your mum?'

'I could, but she was probably too young to remember.'

Kai sighs. 'We should get back before Iain goes spare,' he says, handing me the file. 'What are you going to do with this?'

'What do you mean?' I pocket Marta's card, clamber out of the car.

'I mean, are you going to use it to look for her?'

I hesitate. *If she's alive, it means she's out there somewhere, that she's been alone, all this time. It means she might not want to have anything to do with us, with me. Knowing that might be worse than not knowing anything at all.*

But it isn't my decision, not really. It's Mum who made the choice.

'Yes,' I say, looking down at the file in my hands. 'I think I have to.'

Saint-Antoine

February 1943

All through that first night and into the morning, I'd heard her crying. In quiet moments, when I closed the oven door, or rested from kneading the dough, the sound of her sobs had drifted down the stairs, seeped through the floorboards. Several times I'd heard voices, too low to make out words: Daniel Reiss trying to comfort his wife. Now, at the edge of evening, everything was quiet. Perhaps she too was exhausted.

I let my half-numb fingertips slide over the chickpeas. It was cold, sitting out on the back step. Just as mornings came slowly to the village, nights came on fast. The mountains swallowed the sun, so that even when the peaks glowed gold, the streets were plunged into shade, deep enough to chill stone, to reach the marrow.

I dragged the sack closer, pulled out a handful of chickpeas. Ever since I was a child, this chore had been mine, and no one else's. They were sorry things, the peas, small and hard as marbles, and the job was painstaking, picking out fragments of stone and grit. The good peas went back into the sack, the debris on to the step beside me. Sometimes, to stave off boredom, I'd pick up a handful of stones and take aim: flinging them across the street so that they clattered against the cobbles like hail, bouncing and tumbling all the way to the *gargouille*, which whisked them away. It was a ritual, a secret game of my own.

'That sound . . . ?'

I leapt, so fiercely that I almost upset the sack. Madame Reiss was leaning out of the upstairs window, half in shadow. I hadn't even heard the shutters open.

'I am sorry,' I said, 'I didn't mean to wake you.'

'You didn't wake me.' Her voice was low and raw. 'What are you doing down there?'

'Sorting chickpeas.' I was unable to think of anything else to say.

The woman let out a noise, a strange sort of laugh that seemed to surprise even her. 'Sorting chickpeas,' she repeated, 'what does that mean? I have no idea.'

Of course you don't. 'The merchants,' I told her, looking up awkwardly, 'they mix things into the chickpeas, pebbles and things. To make up the weight. Someone has to pick them out or they'll break the grinder.'

She took her hand from her forehead. 'Isn't that illegal?'

I shrugged. 'So what if it is? Everyone's doing it.'

There was a squeak, a thump, as the window above was pulled closed. I looked up at it, guilt gripping my stomach. I hadn't meant to be rude. I dropped back down to the step with a sigh at myself, dragged out another handful of peas and stones. The light was on the verge of disappearing, swimming grey. It made me blink, made the edges of things hard to distinguish.

The next moment, I heard footsteps, and the woman was standing behind me.

'I'll help,' she said, 'if you show me how to do it.'

I looked at her, astonished. Yesterday, she had crept along, swathed in a shawl, clinging to Monsieur Reiss's arm like an old woman, but now she stood tall, wearing a pair of neat trousers. She was taking a packet of cigarettes from her pocket, lighting one with a match in a practised gesture. The smoke rose past her face, seemed to coil itself into her black hair, a mess of curls around her chin. I knew that I shouldn't stare, should answer her, but I couldn't think of any words. She took a deep drag on her cigarette.

'Do you mind?' she said, holding it up.

I shook my head, finally looked down, fumbling with the handful of peas again. She had an accent, like her husband's, only hers was different, slower, softer. It sounded like the city. I could imagine it filling a space of its own between other voices, bouncing from cocktail glass to coffee cup, people leaning in to hear it. I glanced up again to find her watching me.

'Your name is Ceci?' she asked.

Her fingers were slim. They brought the cigarette close to her lips and held it there, as if she might have to take a hasty drag at any moment.

'Yes.' My voice sounded clumsy, compared to hers.

There was a rustling of cloth as she lowered herself to sit beside me. She didn't speak again, just squinted out into the alleyway through the smoke of her cigarette. A few flecks of ash had fallen and caught on the dark wool of her jumper. It must have been Monsieur Reiss's because it was too big for her. She had no shoes on, only thick socks, the toes and heels reinforced by extra darning. Even so, she somehow looked . . . right. I fidgeted, hating the itchy, wool stockings I had to wear, the skirt and blouse that had to be beaten free of flour and put back on, rough from soap. I wanted to ask her why she had been crying, but I didn't know how.

'What's your name?' I asked instead.

The woman was reaching the end of her cigarette. She pulled smoke from the very last inch and didn't answer until it was done, extinguished on the back step. 'For the past two years I have been telling people I'm Marie Roux, from Strasbourg.' She glanced over at me. 'But here, it seems we are to be ourselves again. Which makes me Myriam.' She smiled, a tired, self-mocking look. 'Myriam Reiss.'

Her lips were chapped, I noticed, her nose red at the end.

'Monsieur Reiss said that you are a writer.'

Her fingers fidgeted, as if they itched to hold a cigarette again. 'Generous of him,' she said. 'I haven't written a word for a year now.'

'What do you write?' I shouldn't ask so many questions, I knew, but I couldn't help myself.

'Stories,' she said, and her voice was bitter. 'Useless, meaningless things.'

81

She turned her face away, shifted on the step, and I felt a sudden wave of fear that she would stand up and leave me, that I had driven her away with my childish questioning.

'Here,' I said, reaching for the sack of peas. 'This is how you sort them.'

She sat with me in silence after that, each of us sifting through our own handfuls. Madame Reiss soon got the hang of it and worked quickly, almost feverishly, gathering debris even faster than I could.

'Now,' she said, when she had finished, hefting the handful of stones, 'how do we make the noise?'

'What noise?'

'The noise that woke me up.'

'You said I didn't wake you!'

She gave a tiny smile, shrugged. 'Well?'

I sat back. I'd never had to explain to anyone. I scooped a handful of stones and shells out of my pile. 'You just . . . ' I drew back my arm and flung the stones down the alley, instinctively aiming for the point where I knew they'd ricochet off the cobbles, would bounce all the way to the *gargouille*.

Madame Reiss watched them dance and clatter. She hadn't laughed at me, hadn't looked askance the way I thought she might. Instead, she weighed the stones in her hand.

'Why do you do that?' she asked.

I stared at the side of her face, at the corner of her mouth, at her eyelid, slightly swollen.

'Ceci,' I said abruptly, wanting her to look at me. 'It means 'chickpea' in Italian. It's what everyone calls me, rather than Celeste.' I prodded the sack with my foot, felt the peas shift, small and hard and unyielding. 'I hate it.' I told her, realizing the truth for the first time.

Warmth bloomed through my cardigan. Madame Reiss's hand was pressed to my shoulder.

'Then I shall call you Celeste.'

I felt myself smile at her. Then she pulled away, shifted on the step to give herself room to aim. 'So,' she said, closing one eye.

The throw was a good one, and I watched her face brighten at the noise of the stones rushing down the alley.

'Myriam!'

The voice shocked us to our feet. Monsieur Reiss was standing in the doorway, looking from me to his wife in surprise.

'Are you all right?' he asked, going to her, searching her face.

'I'm fine,' she answered, placing her hands in her pockets. 'What is it? You made Celeste here jump like a rabbit.'

'I'm sorry,' he turned to me, 'but everyone's looking for you. Your family are in the shop. They've had a letter. From your brother.'

London

April 1993

I reach London just as Friday evening breaks open. The pubs I pass are bursting, people loosening jackets on a warm evening, a bank holiday stretching out before them. I wish I could be one of them, join the crowds of carefree young drinkers squashed on to pub benches and while away the evening in cigarette smoke and talk of nothing and laughter.

But that isn't my world. I turn from the chaos of Euston towards Bloomsbury, to busy Marchmont Street and my tiny flat with its rattling windows and groaning bookshelves and grubby carpets. By rights, I shouldn't be able to afford to live here, so close to the museums and libraries, but it's owned by an old uni contact of Mum's; she lets us have it for half of what it should cost.

The greengrocer and his nephew shout a hello at me, packing up for the day. I duck my head and smile, letting myself into my building and racing up the banana-and-onion-scented stairs. One lock, two, and I'm home.

I drop my bag, lean back against the door with a sigh. It smells musty in here after two weeks away, and the plants on the windowsill are in a sorry state. I pick them up and wander into the cupboard-sized kitchen to water them. Everything is already tidy. There isn't much, really. A bed that isn't even mine. A wardrobe. A phone. A radio. No TV; I've never owned one. Books are what take up most of the space. They spill from the shelves into neat rows on the mantelpiece, the windowsills, the edge of the carpet. Books in French, English, second-, third- and fourth-hand; liberated from library bins or snatched up from bookshops.

I sit on the squashy sofa and carefully take Grand-mère's file out of my bag. I shouldn't have taken it, and if I'm found out I'll definitely be fired, but I can't help feeling like it's *mine*; like Mum and I have a right to hold these pages, the photograph of Grand-mère from all those years ago. I can imagine Mum now, gazing down at the photo of her own mother as a young woman.

The thought brings another stab of uncertainty. I've wanted to call Mum a dozen times, but what does the file tell us, really, that we don't already know?

```
Place of arrival: Dover
Date of arrival: 12 June 1946
Name: Picot, Celeste Marie
D.O.B.: 11 January 1925
Place of birth: Saint-Antoine, France
Children: 1 (Evelyne Picot, Age 2)
Previous address: 8 Square des
  Peupliers, Paris
```

I slump back, letting the pages fall on to my knees. Nothing new except a date, and an

85

address in Paris from fifty years ago. Sighing, I drag my hair out of its ponytail and shake it to ease my scalp, loosening the frizzing curls. A gift from my absent father.

A bus trundles down the street. The windows rattle in their frames. Outside, the light is yellow and grey. Soon it will be night, and I'll still be sitting here in a silent flat with my brain swimming. What did I expect to do, here in London? All the public archives buildings I could search will be closed for the weekend. I might as well have saved my money and stayed in Cheshire, holed up in the hotel. It all seems a bit silly, risking my job for a photograph and one old address. And yet, I'm glad I have them. Holding the file, I feel closer to Grand-mère than I have for years.

I sit up. When was the last time we heard from her? A birthday, I think. I set the file aside and crawl across the carpet on my knees towards the bookshelf. Where did I put it? There, a slim spine with a torn, grubby dust-jacket.

I turn it in my hands with a smile. Mum's copy of *The Little Prince*, from when she was a girl. It's in French, which makes me wonder whether Grand-mère bought it in Paris before they left. She used to read it to me when I was little.

The cover falls open, revealing a stack of cards in the faded colours of another decade. Birthday cards, Christmas messages, sent by Grand-mère before she and Mum lost touch completely. I take them out, open them one after another. The sight of her handwriting, with its old-fashioned letters, sends a shock of familiarity through me.

All my love, Grand-mère Celeste.

The last card I come to is still in its envelope, the torn edge fuzzed by time. Quickly, I turn it over. There, in her handwriting, a return address:

84 Rue du Tage, Paris, Île-de-France

I pull out the card. It was sent for my tenth birthday. Fifteen years is a long time, probably too long, but it's better than nearly fifty.

I sit back on the carpet. I could write to this address and explain the situation, see if I get a response. But even now I can imagine what might happen: a stranger glancing at the letter, addressed to a person long gone, and shoving it into a bin, or on to a yellowing pile of wrongly delivered mail. I could try for a phone number . . . I reach for the phone on the table behind me before remembering that I can't call French directory enquiries unless I'm actually *in* France.

I let the handset drop with a clatter. Outside, a car honks, someone shrieks with laughter, the windows rattle, the world hurtles on with its business. I stare at the envelope in my hand, facing the prospect of a whole, long weekend spent worrying over the situation.

Unless, for once, I do something. Unless I do the leg-work, so that by the time Mum gets back, we'll know, one way or another, whether there's any point in digging up the past.

84 Rue du Tage, Paris . . .

I make it to Victoria just in time to dash to the booth and buy a ticket for the nine o'clock coach. When it's my turn to board, I stop, one foot raised, ambushed by doubt. I feel like I've split in half: one Annie Picot still sitting alone in her flat, the other here about to do something strange and sudden and exhilarating. Then, someone jostles me in the back and I find myself stepping up into the coach's stale, carpeted interior.

It's packed. I make my way down the aisle, searching for a free seat. There's one near the back, and I cram myself into it. Someone will take the aisle seat next to me but at least here I can watch the journey through the window.

The next moment, I hear the hiss and crack of a can opening, and the group behind let out a huge cheer. A group of young people, students by the look of them, all merry with anticipation. One young man with dreadlocks is brandishing his newly opened cider, others seem to be following suit with their own badly concealed drinks. A girl with long red hair is taking a pull from a bottle of wine. She catches me looking and grins sheepishly.

'*Bon voyage!*' she says. I look away, pretending I haven't heard, but all the same, I can't stop myself from smiling.

Soon, we're on our way. A businessman sits next to me, all knees and evening paper, and I hunch closer to the window to watch London slide by. It's only when we hit the motorway that I feel another stab of panic. What on earth am I doing?

The students let out a flood of laughter, making the man next to me tut and flap his paper. I rest my head on the cool glass and watch the cars overtake, trying to think about the past, trying to forget the present.

Despite the noise made by the students, and the stuffy air of the coach, I must sleep, because when I wake up the sky is dark, bruise-purple above the trees. We've left the city behind and are driving through the country. One of the students behind lets out an enormous yawn, boisterousness dulled by booze and darkness and motion.

'Where are we?' one of them asks sleepily.

'Gone half-ten, probably Canterbury.'

He's right. Soon, signs for Dover start to flash by the coach windows, emblazoned with a picture of a ferry. There's a trembling in my stomach as the fields and houses drop away, replaced by steep white cliffs that mark the edge of the country.

I can't tear my eyes from the dark waters of the channel. Nearly fifty years ago, my grandmother stood here, a mirror image. I think of the night wind, filling her hair with salt spray as she sits on a ship's deck, cradling my mother in her lap and facing the unknown; leaving everything she knew behind her.

Then we're rolling forward, the front wheels bump over the gangplank and the chance to turn back disappears in a clang of metal and the deafening roar of engines.

Saint-Antoine

February 1943

The envelope lay open on the counter. They were all standing around it, Mama, Papa, Paul. Mama was crying.

Paul saw me. He rushed forward and caught my hands. 'He's alive. It's all right, he's alive.'

Ordinarily I would have pulled away, but now I returned his grip, grateful for the strength in his body, something to cling to.

'Where is he?' I looked at my father. 'What's happened to him?'

Behind me, I heard Monsieur and Madame Reiss entering the kitchen. All at once I wanted to free myself from Paul, to step away and stand on my own.

'This letter was sent from Toulon,' Papa was saying, 'outside the Italian zone. Leon says — '
He stopped. He was looking over my shoulder, I realized, at Monsieur and Madame Reiss. 'He has joined the *milice*.'

The words seemed to slide across my mind. I did pull away from Paul then, took the letter from Papa. The writing was familiar, hurried and ordinary.

'I don't . . . ' I heard myself murmur.

'The *milice*,' Paul said, misunderstanding my confusion. 'The civilian military that the state set up to arrest,' he too was trying not to look at the Reisses, 'wanted persons,' he finished.

I know what they are, I wanted to shout, *I know, and Leon isn't one of them; he can't be.*

'They're scum.'

All of us turned. Madame Reiss was gripping the wooden workbench, her chapped lips thin.

'The *milice*, they are worse than the Gestapo, arresting, executing their own people, friends, neighbours they've known all their lives. They were in Marseille, we caught the train while they were raiding the synagogue, they took *children* . . . ' Air was rushing in and out of her nose. Her husband took her arm but she ignored him. 'They're scum,' she said, 'inhuman scum.'

There was a choke, a stifled noise as Mama continued to cry. I stared at the woman before me, who only moments ago had touched my arm and smiled as though she understood. Now she looked like a stranger, her pale face twisted with hate.

'No.' My voice shook. I heard the doubt in that word and hated myself. 'No, Leon isn't like that, something must have happened. They must have forced him to join. I know he's hotheaded but he wouldn't do this on his own.' I couldn't meet Madame Reiss's eyes, looked down at the letter instead. 'He wouldn't.'

From the corner of my eye, I saw her sag, as though someone had removed the bones from her body. Monsieur Reiss was waiting; he caught her, held her up, the way he'd done when they first arrived.

'Please excuse us,' he murmured.

My father hurried to open the door to the apartment for them. I stared at the black curls that fell against Madame Reiss's neck, at Monsieur Reiss's horn-rimmed spectacles, and I wanted one of them to turn, to look at me. And at the same time I didn't, because the fear remained, the thoughts of Leon, and the trembling in my gut that I didn't know how to name.

'Ceci,' Papa said, and I dropped my gaze, afraid he would see too much. 'Go down to your grandmother's.' He took the letter away from me and, with it, any further talk about my brother.

The next morning dawned with vast blue skies and a cool, dazzling sun, as if the world was mocking the heaviness that Leon's news had brought upon us; as if it was determined to prove that, despite everything, the seasons would roll on, and soon the burned-out carcass of winter would be pushed aside by a thousand, green shoots of spring.

Perhaps it was the effect of the new residents, maybe it was the weather, but that day, the whole of Saint-Antoine seemed to be awake and outside early. Children were congregating on front steps and street corners. Some belonged to the village, others were strangers from the buses that kept arriving from the coast. As I stepped out of the bakery, the Rocher twins came running down the alleyway with some other boys, all of them shouting swear words in German and French. When they saw me they yelled and rushed off, laughing and hooting, down towards the river no doubt, to throw things into the raging water, the way I had as a child.

I tried not to be envious, watching them run so free, while I had to haul a basket through the streets, make the morning delivery to the hotel kitchen. It was busier there than it had been for years, filled with steam and the smell of weak cocoa and boiling milk. I handed the bread over to Marie. She looked frazzled, her apron unironed, a cloth slung over her shoulder. Every room was full, she told me, even the old servants' quarters under the eaves that they'd been using as storage for years. She couldn't stop for long. I left her cutting the bread into wafer-thin slices, to stretch it as far as it would go.

Outside, I looked up at the dour old place, bursting at the seams with life. Voices drifted down from every floor, babies crying, women shouting, windowsills and balconies strewn with towels and wet linen.

It was comforting, that hubbub, after the silence of the bakery. I hadn't heard a sound from the apartment the previous evening, as we worked in the kitchen below. For some reason, that silence had weighed on me. *Are they sleeping up there?* I had thought, time and again, as I sprinkled flour and stretched dough through the night. *Are they lying awake, their eyes open in the darkness?*

I turned from the hotel, took the back way through twisting passages and narrow alleys. They smelled old, of shadowed stone that never dried, that hadn't had the sun on its face for more than half a millennium.

I shivered, walked faster. Ahead I could see the

little square in front of the church, where sunlight fell bright and made the old yellow stone glow. I stepped into it gratefully. All around, moisture seemed to be seeping from the village's damp-clogged walls, like honey.

'Mademoiselle Corvin!' I heard someone call.

Monsieur Reiss had emerged from the opposite street, a scarf wrapped around his neck, satchel over his shoulder. 'Good morning,' he said, as he approached. 'Or may I call you Celeste? I have never asked.'

'Celeste is fine,' I said. 'Good morning, monsieur. You are out early today.'

He smiled. 'It is Shabbat. Your church has given us a room to use, for prayers.'

A murmur of voices was coming closer, and I saw people begin to emerge from the street behind him. Women wearing shawls, couples holding hands. A small group surrounding an older man. He had a beard, a heavy black overcoat, was carrying something under his arm.

'Is Madame Reiss with you?' I heard myself ask.

He watched the people as I did. 'No,' he said after a moment. 'We were never very observant in Brussels. But now, I find it gives me comfort.'

'And she . . . ?'

'She feels differently.' His smile was soft at the edges. 'As she does about so many things. She used to attend to please her parents but since . . . ' He shook his head and in that gesture I saw her silence, I saw her hands, clinging to his arm, like a person drowning.

'Celeste,' Monsieur Reiss spoke suddenly,

94

'what my wife said about your brother . . . ' He looked past me, as if he'd find the words he wanted written on the old stone walls.

'It's all right,' I said, as if it really was. 'It's all right.'

He found my eyes again, and his face relaxed, making him look younger. 'It was good to see her up yesterday. What did you two talk about?'

'Chickpeas,' I said quietly, although in truth, I barely knew.

'Chickpeas.' He shook his head. 'Well, I'm glad she was talking.' I nodded, turned to go, but he put his hand on my elbow to stop me. Beyond his shoulder, people were watching us. 'Will you talk with my wife again?' he asked. 'I think it would be good for her. She should try to make some friends here.'

Something fluttered in my chest. 'Of course,' I told him. 'I'd be happy to.'

Throughout the rest of the morning, I found myself glancing at the door to the apartment again and again. I didn't have the courage to knock on it and in any case I didn't get the chance. The bakery was busy, as if people had emerged from their winter hiding places, ravenous for spring. At lunchtime, Papa glanced into the half-empty bags of flour and sighed.

'I don't know what we will do after we get through this,' he said, flipping the sign on the door to read 'fermé'. 'I can't trade bread we don't have.'

'What about the coupons?' I asked, peering down at the stacks of them that had begun to fill the money drawer.

He snorted. 'We can only exchange them in Nice, and you know what the flour is like there.' He untied his apron. 'It would be different if we could hunt. We would have something else to barter with, then.'

The words beat through me, the knowledge of what I kept hidden from him on the top shelf in the storeroom.

'Hunting's illegal, Papa,' I murmured.

'I know.' He rubbed at his eyes. 'Did you sort the chickpeas?'

'Yes.' I paused. 'Madame Reiss helped.'

'You had better make some of your famous *socca*,' he said, as if he hadn't heard me. 'Then at least we'll have something to offer if the *capitano* or the Gougeards come calling.'

I watched him leave, trudging off down the street, his head lowered. He wouldn't go straight to my grandmother's, I knew; he'd go to the bar on the square, knock back a Pernod for distraction. I could be trusted, he obviously thought, with something as easy as *socca*.

Outside, the bright afternoon taunted. Girls — my age and younger — clacked past the shop, their cheeks pink. I saw mothers shoo their children out to play, so that they could wash the floors while the day might dry them. The sun streamed through the bakery windows, caught on the flour that always hung in the air, making it seem as if the whole place was filled with fine snow.

Alone, I got to work. I lit the stove beside the ovens, stacked it with wood, to get it hot. Then, I began to turn the handle on the old, iron grinder, listening to the chickpeas being crushed until they emerged as flour, fine as sand and yellow as a rock daisy. It was hot work, with the stove going, and soon I had stripped off the threadbare cardigan. By the time I was finished, my blouse was clinging to my skin, perspiration beading my forehead. I wiped it away.

I went and scooped water from the *gargouille*, so cold still that it stung my skin. I took our secret bottle of olive oil from the pantry. It had been smuggled into France, I knew, given to us by the *capitano* as payment, to keep his men fed. Last came the salt. I lifted down the earthenware pot from its high shelf. In the sunlight, the crystals glittered in a thin layer across the bottom, like frost. I drew my fingers through it, scraped up a scant pinch. Before the war, we'd used salt without regard, like a rich man scattering coins. We'd thrown it into dough and sprinkled whole handfuls over *focaccia*, crushed it with herbs and oil to slather on to loaves of *fougasse*.

Not any more. It was hard to get, even on the black market. *White gold*, Papa called it. It seemed absurd that for thousands of years, men had crossed through Saint-Antoine bringing salt from the coast, taking the old roads over the pass and into Italy, and yet now, we couldn't buy a single bag . . .

'Hello.'

My fingers contracted in surprise, the crystals crushing between them. Madame Reiss was standing there, at the foot of the stairs. I hadn't heard the door creak open; it was as though I'd

97

summoned her, through some spell of sunlight and salt. Carefully, I set the pot on to the work surface.

'What are you doing?' she asked, leaning against the wall.

I let a pinch of salt fall into the batter, feeling strange.

Today she wore the large jumper again, untucked over her trousers. Her feet were bare. All at once I felt intensely conscious of my body, of the blouse that clung and the sweat between my breasts.

'Come on,' she smiled, when I didn't answer, 'I'm interested.'

'Why?' I asked her.

She waved a hand through the flour drifting in a beam of sunlight. 'You feed people, every day. I feel so useless in comparison.'

'It's only bread,' I mumbled.

'Bread is important.' She watched me stir the mixture. 'It isn't only food. It's life. Bread and salt, it binds people.'

'Is that what you believe?'

She nodded, meeting my eyes. 'I do.'

'I saw your husband this morning,' I said, after a moment. 'He was going to pray at the church. Didn't you want to go with him?'

'No.' She sounded impatient, and I glanced up, only to be caught in her steady, searching gaze. 'I'd rather know what you're doing, what you're making.'

I gave the batter a swirl. 'I'm making *socca*,' I said. 'We're running out of bread, and the *capitano* sometimes comes in to get extra rations

98

for his men . . . ' I trailed off, not wanting to say too much about Papa's agreement with our occupiers. Instead, I looked into the foaming, yellow mixture. 'It's made from chickpeas,' I said.

Her smile grew. 'Your favourite.' I found myself smiling back shyly. 'How do you make it, this *socca*? Like bread?'

I left her stirring the batter as I heaved the huge, black skillet on to the stove. Sweat began to coat my skin once more as I worked, trickling down my back as I got the pan hot. Behind me, Madame Reiss looked after the batter, and we talked of this and that; little words that disappeared as soon as they had been spoken. When I took the bowl from her and ladled some of the mixture into the pan, she let out a noise.

'Like *matzos*,' she said. 'My mother used to make them.'

She used to attend to please her parents. In a flash, like sun on a shaded pool, I thought I saw into Madame Reiss; I thought I saw the pain that waited, always, just beneath her skin. She had fallen silent beside me, staring into the pan, at the batter, bubbling with heat. I wanted to touch her, bring her back to the kitchen.

Instead, I flipped the flatbread in the pan. The edges were charred, a smoky, toasted scent rising from the surface. Within moments it was done, and I was sliding it out, straight on to the work surface, I was reaching for the bottle of oil, letting it dribble past my thumb into a golden-green swirl, I was taking up the precious pot of salt, pinching it, throwing a reckless, shining scatter across the bread.

'Here,' I told Madame Reiss. 'This one is for you.'

Slowly, she turned away from the stove to look at the crisp, blackened edges, at the pools of oil, the sparkle of salt.

'It is?' she said, a trace of her smile returning. 'How do I eat it?'

I cut the *socca*, nudging a slice towards her. Her pale fingers gathered it up.

'You should eat too.' She was wearing an expression I couldn't follow.

I took a piece.

Salt; that was the first thing I tasted. Powerful, resounding on my tongue. The crystals broke against my teeth, dissolved in my mouth, and then that smooth peppery oil, the sweet earthiness of ground chickpeas that we had sat and sorted together, the charred edges like embers, like the smoke from a hearth fire late at night. It felt secret, indulgent, after weeks of hard bread and watery stews.

Madame Reiss's eyes were closed. A few drops of oil had caught on her top lip and slicked it bright. At that moment something thundered through me, like a pulse in the ears after running, like a flash of nerves after slicing skin, before the blood and pain.

She opened her eyes, looked straight into mine. Something shifted and for a moment, the entire world was crushed into that one, tiny kitchen.

Dover–Paris

May 1993

Midnight comes and goes somewhere between swells. I can just see the white tips of waves in the darkness from where I sit, huddled outside on a bench, arms wrapped about my knees. The adrenalin of the trip has worn off and now all I feel is sick and tired and uncertain. I'm about to stand up, go and change some money at the little booth inside, when the door squeals open and four people stagger out. The students from the coach. I sink back, not wanting to walk through them.

They huddle near the railing, trying to light cigarettes, but it's too windy; the lighter's flame won't catch and one cigarette even gets stolen from the lips of a girl, carried out to sea on a gust of cold air. After a minute, they give up and hurry towards my bench, out of the wind behind one of the bulkheads.

'Thank Christ,' a girl with short black hair groans, sinking down on the floor. 'How long have we got, Gabe?'

The guy with the dreadlocks checks his watch. 'Another hour before Calais,' he catches me looking, and though I glance away hurriedly, the damage is done. 'This is the long bit, huh?' he says to me, smiling.

I look down, pull my bag towards me. I'll get Grand-mère's file out; then I can pretend that I'm reading.

One of the girls gives a snort of laughter and murmurs, 'Don't think she speaks English.'

I stare down at the file, thankful for the darkness.

'*Pardon.*' The young guy says, looking at me again. '*Parlez-vous français?*'

I open my mouth, but the sea air seems to whip all the moisture away. I nod again instead, wishing I could drop into a conversation as easily as he seems to.

'Oh,' he says, looking a bit lost. 'Right. Er, cigarette?' He brandishes a packet at me.

'*Non, merci,*' I mutter, before realizing the ridiculousness of the situation. What if they think I'm French, then see my passport? I clench my toes in my shoes and try to summon up some nerve.

'I, um, I speak English too,' I say. They all stop talking and turn to look. 'I mean, I speak both, sometimes. Sorry.'

'You travelling alone?' asks the other girl. She's holding a cigarette in her lips while she wrestles with a scrunchie.

I nod. 'Yes, I'm on a . . . research trip.'

'Us too,' the fourth student, a guy with huge glasses, tells me. 'We're researching life.'

'Just finished finals,' Gabe declares, sitting down on the lap of the red-haired girl, who yells. 'And now . . . ' He waves his hands, taking in the sea, the coastline, hidden by distance. 'Who knows? Paris seems like a good place to start.'

They're happy to chatter among themselves without much input from me; something that I'm grateful for. I listen to them run through artists and writers, and people they know who have done stupid things at parties, occasionally turning to include me in the conversation.

I sit back and let it wash over me, like the smoke from their cigarettes. It must be strange, I think, to be so carefree, to set off for France on a whim, not thinking about tomorrow.

And you? I ask myself. *Is that not what you're doing?*

Soon the boat starts to slow, lights appear on the sea and a crackly loudspeaker tells us all to get back inside our vehicles. I excuse myself, rush inside to change some money before the booth closes.

It's gone two in the morning now, and by the time the coach rolls off the boat and out into the darkness, almost everyone is asleep. I listen to the gentle murmur of the coach driver's radio, the sleeping breaths of the other passengers, and let my eyes drift closed.

'Hey!'

Someone is shaking me. For a second, my heart lurches with fear.

'Huh?' I murmur, blinking hard. My eyes feel gritty with tiredness.

'Hey.' A girl's face comes into focus, the red-headed student. 'Wake up, we're here.'

I frown at her before remembering what she means: where I am. I grab at my watch. Five thirty a.m. Outside the coach windows the sky is pink streaked with blue, like veins beneath skin.

All around there's activity, people sitting up and stretching out cricked necks. I fumble my bag from the rack above and stagger from the coach with the rest of the passengers.

For a brief moment, everyone looks lost, breathing in the chilly dawn air and staring around as if in doubt that this is actually Paris. The yard of cracked tarmac where we've been deposited certainly doesn't look much like the city of light. One by one, passengers gather up their things and wander away, towards taxis or buses or trains that will take them into the Paris of their expectations.

My hair has come loose from its ponytail. I twist it out of the way into a bun, trying to wake up. The students seem a bit shell-shocked too, huddled in a group, searching their pockets for cigarettes. Up ahead, a grimy sign tells us that this is *Porte de la Villette*, points the way to the metro. When the students start to walk, I follow them, needing something familiar to hold on to, just for a moment.

I try to figure out where we are, try to bring to mind a map of the city. I've visited a few times before, usually with Mum for academic conferences. They were always whistle-stop tours, never longer than a day or two, never rolled into a holiday. *Because of Grand-mère?* I wonder, thinking of the address in my bag.

84 Rue du Tage. I take a breath.

'Excuse me?' I call to the students, hurrying to catch up with them. 'Do any of you have a map?'

Saint-Antoine

March 1943

After that day, nothing was the same. It was as if that one afternoon of sun had been enough to shake winter loose once and for all.

It didn't go quietly. The *gargouille* and the fountains sang with snowmelt, blue and cold. Bursts of rain and sun made the houses glimmer, like perspiration on flesh, and the town sloughed off its winter grime, leaving everything fresh and tender and new. At this time of year, the river was at its fiercest, swollen and tumbling through the valley. The sound was inescapable; I heard it in my dreams, couldn't even separate it from the sound of the blood in my veins.

Amongst such fever, I couldn't rest. When I wasn't working, my legs would twitch and dance, my eyes would stray towards the bakery windows. When I took my afternoon nap, in the attic room at my grandmother's house, I pressed my head into the scratchy pillow, my thoughts a mess of olive oil and cigarette smoke and an earnest voice asking, *Will you talk with my wife again?*

'Ceci, what is wrong with you?' My mother's voice broke into my thoughts. They were all looking at me, Mama, Papa, Grandmother . . . my knife hung limply in my hand, the bread and jam uneaten on my plate. Their plates were empty.

'Nothing,' I muttered, smearing the tiny amount of plum jam across the slice of *pain bis*. 'I was just thinking.'

My grandmother made a noise through her few remaining teeth. 'Spring sickness,' she said, the deep lines of her face growing deeper with amusement. 'Happened to me when I was a girl. Jumpy as a colt, I was, every spring, until I married your grandfather.'

'I was saying,' my mother ploughed over her, 'we don't see much of our . . . guests.' She took a sip of her coffee, and winced. 'Madame Clermont has rented her downstairs to a family who don't speak a word of French, and *they're* out and about all the time. You know, she saw them doing their washing in the fountain, the way you used to, Mother.'

They're not guests, I wanted to say, *they didn't choose to come here*. Instead, I filled my mouth with bread so that I didn't have to answer.

'Madame Reiss, in particular,' my mother continued. I looked up at her, but she was talking to my father. 'She stays holed up in that apartment all day. I have barely seen her.'

'I've seen her,' Papa said slowly, dabbing at crumbs with his finger. 'I've seen them both, walking to register at the hotel in the evening.' He nodded my way. 'And Ceci has seen her, too. She helped you with some chores, didn't she?'

'*Vraiment?*' Mama raised her eyebrows. 'I thought she wasn't fit for housework, it is

106

Monsieur Reiss who does it all. He is the one who queues for coupons, and Marie told me the other day that it is he who brings their laundry — '

The knife fell on to the edge of my plate with a clatter, the sudden noise breaking the flow of my mother's gossip. She tutted at me, mouth open in rebuke, only for her words to be swallowed by a knocking at the door.

I scrambled up, chair scraping against the tiles, but Papa made a gesture, went to answer it himself. We were silent, even Grandmother, as we stared at that panel of wood, hearts tight as fists, wondering who might be behind it.

'Ah,' Papa's shoulders dropped, 'Paul. Come in.'

Paul stepped around the door. His cheeks were pink with cold, his eyes bright. He was not in his uniform for once; instead, he wore his old, brown Sunday jacket.

'Hello,' he said, unaware of the tension he had broken. I frowned at him. He knew we always had a *goûter* at this time, like children. Until a few years ago, that had meant a long piece of baguette, crammed with chunks of chocolate or squashed full of apricot jam, eaten with a glass of milk, but now, it was usually just bread and coffee, no butter, and whatever preserve we were eking out, tart and runny from a lack of sugar. I'd always found it embarrassing, that *goûter*, eaten not long before other people went to the bar to take an aperitif, but Papa and I were usually tired, and needed the strength.

'Paul,' my mother smiled, 'sit down, we have just finished. Would you like something to drink?'

107

'No, thank you, Madame Corvin.' He stepped towards the table, but didn't sit. 'I was just wondering if you might spare Ceci for an hour or two? Mademoiselle Louise has organized a social for all the young people, so that the newcomers can make some friends in town.'

'A social?' My mother's voice was uncertain. Even I remembered Marshal Pétain's ban on dancing, his call for decency and dignity, his solemn rebuke to the people who made merry while France's young men were held in camps and factories. 'But — '

'The Italians have given permission for it to go ahead,' Paul told us. 'They said that we are under their laws now.' He smiled, a little bitterly. 'It is in the hotel, so it will be chaperoned.'

'Well . . . ' My mother still hesitated. I could see her running through every possible scenario in her mind. Then she caught my father's eye and her expression changed. 'If you are going, I don't see why not.'

'I have no objections,' Papa said, clapping Paul on the shoulder as he walked past. 'You two should have some fun. So long as you're both back by nine, and Ceci isn't too overexcited to work later.'

I stared at them all. Not one of them had asked me if I wanted to go; they had talked about me, right over my head, as if I was a child with my hair in ribbons. No one would talk to Madame Reiss like that.

'No.' I said, but it sounded childish rather than courteous. 'Thank you, Paul, but I'm afraid I am too tired.'

He looked down at me, surprised. 'We need not stay long.'

'That's right.' All at once, my mother had switched positions. 'Don't be rude, Ceci. It's very kind of Paul to ask, and it will do you good. You've been bad-tempered all afternoon.'

'Spring sickness,' my grandmother chuckled, pulling the jam jar towards her.

After that I had no choice but to go. I dragged a comb through my hair, pulled off my stained work cardigan and replaced it with a clean blouse. Paul waited for me at the bottom of the stairs, talking in a low voice with my father.

'Back before nine,' Papa told us when I emerged, my Sunday cardigan over my arm. He laughed at my sour expression.

Outside, we walked a few steps in silence. The late afternoon was clear, cold, filled with the sound of running water.

'What's wrong with you today?' Paul said after a moment, shoving his hands in his pockets. 'You look as cross as a boar.'

'Better than pretending to be a priest,' I retorted, hands beneath my arms for warmth. 'Why do you talk like that around my parents?'

'Just being polite.' He shrugged. When I didn't reply he glanced over and slowed to a halt on the street. 'Ceci,' he said, 'if you really didn't want to come — '

I cut him off with a sigh, dropped my neck. My hair fell forward to hide my face and behind it, I screwed my eyes closed. I didn't know what was wrong with me, but whatever it was, Paul wasn't to blame, nor was Mademoiselle Louise and this newly legal social.

'It's all right,' I told him. 'It's just . . . all of this.' I shook my head.

'I know,' he said softly. In the dull light his face was comfortingly familiar, with its round cheeks and reddish-blond hair. I smiled, feeling a wave of affection.

'Come on, then.' I linked my arm with his. 'Let's see what this gathering of yours is about.'

He didn't let go of my arm, even when we walked up the steps at the entrance to the hotel. Outside, as always, an Italian army truck was parked, soldiers milling about. They watched us pass, but said nothing.

Mademoiselle Louise had commandeered the hotel's lounge. The old-fashioned chairs, with their creaking, horsehair padding, had been pushed to the sides, the rugs rolled back, leaving an insurmountable stretch of tiled floor in the middle. Two girls huddled together in the furthest corner by the chimneybreast, speaking in whispers, while Mademoiselle Louise talked loudly and earnestly, using signs, to three boys. They were wearing shorts, despite the cold weather, watching her, wide-eyed.

'Paul?' I murmured warningly.

'There'll be more people coming,' he whispered back. 'Annette and Lucie promised they would come too.'

Mademoiselle Louise spotted us. Her face lit up, that stretched-eyebrow look she used to wear when we struggled through passages of reading at school.

'Paul, you came! And Ceci too. Oh I am so

pleased,' she rushed. She had made an effort to dress up and was wearing heeled shoes rather than her usual stout ones, with a bright scarf tied at her neck, tucked in to hide the threadbare edges. 'I think it's so important you young people get to know each other, don't you? We must try to love our neighbours, especially when times are hard . . . '

I didn't hear the rest of what she said. Mademoiselle Louise was a churchgoer, and so it was likely something about the Lord and charity — the sort of thing that I'd heard a hundred times before. The two girls were looking over at me. I smiled. Tentatively, they did the same.

'Here, let me introduce you.' Mademoiselle Louise was propelling us towards the three boys. 'This is . . . but oh dear, I've forgotten already. Wolf, was it? And Claude? And — oh, Annette!'

With that she hurried off towards Paul's cousin Annette and her friend Lucie, who were standing in the doorway, wearing the same expressions that Paul and I had worn a moment before. The boys looked at us and shuffled their feet and nodded shyly.

'*Bonjour*,' they said, one after the other. Paul and I murmured in response.

They weren't as young as all that, I realized. It was the shorts that made them seem so. In fact, one of the boys, the one she'd called Wolf, looked only a year or so younger than me.

'What's your name?' Paul asked the youngest boy, the one Mademoiselle Louise had left un-introduced. He had dark hair, a thin face with a strong chin. In fact, they all had that chin,

111

but on the youngest it was more pronounced than the others.

He looked at Paul, mouth open, then back at the other boys.

'*Parlez-vous français?*' I asked.

They understood that, and shook their heads.

'*Non,*' said the eldest. '*Pardon.*' There was a soft shadow of facial hair on his upper lip, his cheeks, and another shadow around his eye, strangely yellow. A fading bruise, I realized.

'*Polonais?*' Paul was asking. '*Russe?*'

All three of them shook their heads.

'*Deutsche,*' the youngest said.

German. For a while we all stared at each other. I didn't know much German; at least, none beyond 'hello' and 'goodbye' and what I'd heard on the radio. How strange it must be for those boys to hear that, in a country not their own.

'*Parlez-vous italien?*' I asked in a burst, so quickly that Paul looked at me, surprised. I knew a little Italian from my grandfather. '*Parli italiano?*'

Their faces brightened, the oldest especially.

'*Si! Si un po!*' he said, beaming.

Their names were Wolf, Claude and Benjamin. With a mixture of Italian, French and German we discovered that Wolf and Claude were brothers; Ben, as they called him, was their cousin. Their aunt had married an Italian man in Turin, they said, which is why they knew some Italian. They had been trying to learn French as well.

'They say they are from Stuttgart,' I translated

for Paul. 'But they left there over a year ago. They have been in a '*kinderheim*' — what is that?'

Claude, the middle one, caught my confusion. His jacket was far too small for him, ripped at the armpits. '*Kinder*,' he said, and pointed across the room, to where one of the Rocher twins was inspecting a bowl of wax fruit on the sideboard. 'Er . . . *bambini?*'

'Children! Oh, a children's home. They have been living in one, somewhere near le Puy, I think?'

'*Si.*' Wolf nodded. 'But we not stay there.'

'And your parents?' Paul asked the youngest. 'Where are they? Mama, Papa?'

The boy shook his head. One of his shoes was tied with string, instead of a lace. At first I thought he didn't understand, but then he shrugged, shook his head again and I understood.

'He doesn't know,' I said softly. Wolf tried to explain what had happened. I couldn't follow all of it, only that Ben's parents had been taken six months ago, sent somewhere in the east, along with his little sister.

'And yours?'

Wolf and Claude either didn't know or didn't have the words to explain. By now, there were more people in the hotel lounge. The volume had increased, conversations like ours taking place all over the room, a babble of different languages. Marie brought in a tray of glasses, filled with weak blackcurrant *sirop*. Groups of young people were forming, shaking hands, clandestinely swapping cigarettes, leaning in to peer at a dog-eared fashion magazine. Someone else had put a lively song on the gramophone, swing music. Annette was laughing, blocking Mademoiselle Louise from changing it to something more spiritual. The sounds, the conversation with Wolf and Claude and Benjamin, the dozens of unfamiliar faces, the squeals of the Rocher boys as they were ejected by Monsieur Gougeard; all of it made my head spin.

Beside me, I could feel Paul's body begin to jig to the music. As Claude and Ben went to fetch drinks for themselves, Lucie beckoned to us from the dance floor, her hand on the shoulder of a boy with too-long, curly hair.

'Do you — ' Paul started.

'Wolf doesn't have a partner,' I said quickly. 'It would be rude of us to leave him.'

'Annette can dance with Wolf. Annette!'

Leaving someone else to guard the gramophone, Annette wove her way through the dancing figures.

'Yes?' she said brightly. 'Hello, Ceci.'

'This is Wolf,' Paul told her. 'Wolf, Annette.' He turned to me with a smile as they began to introduce themselves to each other shyly. '*Voilà*. Now will you dance with me?'

Lucie grinned as we joined her in the middle of the room. Others were also joining, laughing, moving their hips and shoulders towards and away from each other in the cramped space. Paul loved to dance. He was a good partner, and he made it easy to slip into the rhythm, and turn and step and forget my reluctance of a moment before. The song ended, and another began, this one faster, with a melody that hopped through the growling and squalling with trumpets. The boy with Lucie let out a whoop and spun her around, dancing more wildly. If it weren't for the Italians, Paul and his father would have been forced to put a stop to dancing like this, and I couldn't help but grin as he span me around with abandon, our clasped hands growing hot.

'What's this song?' I asked breathlessly.

The boy dancing with Lucie heard me, smiled my way. 'It is name 'Zazou-Zazou',' he said, 'I bring it with me, all the way from Paris.' He jerked his head at Mademoiselle Louise, who was looking pale. 'I do not think your teacher likes this!'

I laughed then, and let my feet move faster, matching Paul's pace. It felt good to dance after so long, not to think about anything but the music. Encouraged by the curly-haired boy's recklessness I danced harder, turned faster, my hair flying out around me, my blouse coming untucked from my skirt. The song was coming to an end and I didn't want it to; I wanted to dance and dance until I had no breath left. I threw myself into another turn only to trip, catching my toes and crashing into Paul.

He caught me, arms closing around my back. We were both panting, and I could feel his shirt, damp with sweat, against my neck. For a moment, he looked down at me, his mouth slightly open, and I felt his grip tighten. Then, over his shoulder, I saw her.

Madame Reiss was standing at the top of the stairs, in the lobby of the hotel, her head turned away from the queue of people in front of the registration desk. She was wearing her neat trousers, a beret crammed over her dark curls, hands in her pockets. She was watching me.

I found my feet, pulled back from Paul, but she had already turned away, leaving me to wonder whether that look had been real, or if it had just been a trick of the light.

Paris

May 1993

At Châtelet, I say goodbye to the students, wishing them luck with their stay. They grin and chorus back the same as they bundle on to the platform. The metro doors clatter shut behind them, and I feel a pang of longing, wishing I could be like them, here for no other reason than to wander and soak up Paris.

But that's not what I came for. The thought of the envelope in my bag pushes me on; a fine, fragile thread of hope. If I can pick it up here, follow it to its end, what might I find? Something or nothing? My skin prickles as I watch my reflection, ghosting on the glass above the black tunnel walls. Pale face, dark hair, just like the photograph of Grand-mère. I can't shake a strange feeling that the moment I step off this train, everything will change. Whatever happens next, good or bad, might alter my life in some way for ever.

I ride the metro almost to the end of the line, to Maison Blanche, deep in the 13th arrondissement. This is where I'll find the Rue du Tage; not in chic Opera or the buzzing Marais, but in the former workers' district of the city, bounded to the east by the Quartier de la Gare. A hundred years ago, the students told me, it would have been all smoke and smog from the sprawling Austerlitz station, as goods arrived and men hammered out rails to knit the city together. According to them, it's now a quiet place, not much there except houses and hospitals.

My hands are clammy as I step from the train, and my head feels light. I emerge from the metro to find Paris fully awake: shutters clattering, cars zipping past, people on mopeds performing daring feats of traffic dodging.

I find the Rue du Tage easily enough, though for long minutes I can only stand on the corner, staring. It's a small, residential street, running like a calm inlet off the busy Avenue d'Italie. This is where Grand-mère lived fifteen years ago. This is the pavement she must have walked every day, perhaps to buy a birthday card or take it to the post office. I begin to walk forwards, watching the house numbers rise, just as I did down in the archives; only behind these doors I'll find real people. I'll find life.

Number eighty-four. It's a three-storey house with window boxes on the sills, containing spring flowers. Hesitantly, I climb the steps. There's an old buzzer system by the door, with name plaques in different hand-writing. I look closer.

JONAS, M & Me
MOREAU, Me
GEUSSENS, Mlle

My heart slows its pace, a strange mixture of disappointment and relief coursing through me. Of course, she wouldn't still be here. And at least

118

now I know that our letters would have gone unanswered, had we written. I look at the buzzers again, wondering if I should ring one, ask if anyone remembers her. The plastic cover doesn't fit very well, the edges of the name tags sticking out, disintegrating from the weather. I look around. The street is quiet, no one watching. I grab at the edge of the first name tag and pull gently.

It comes out, just a piece of card, nothing underneath. Quickly, I slide it back in. The second one is stuck, looks older than the others, as if it has been there a long time. But the third one comes free, just like the first. I peer at the old label beneath it, at the letters, half-scratched off:

PI T, Me

Picot. Madame Picot.

I touch a hand to the buzzer, wishing I could slip back through time, five years, ten, to when I could ring the bell and hear her footsteps, hurrying towards the door.

'*Excusez-moi?*' A young woman is looking up at me from the street, a bag of shopping on her arm, keys in her hand. 'Can I help you with anything?' she asks, frowning.

I shove the name tag back into its holder, hoping it isn't hers.

'I — sorry, I — ' I stammer, dropping back down the steps. 'I was looking for someone who used to live here.' I pause, trying to catch my breath. 'An older woman, called Madame Picot?'

The girl shakes her head, her face impassive. 'I've never heard of her.'

'Oh.' I can feel embarrassment creeping up on me. 'Is there anyone here who might remember her?'

The girl makes a noise. 'Madame Moreau on the second floor might know. She's lived here for years. But she's on holiday at the moment, with her son. The Jonases are newer than me, so . . . ' She shrugs.

'Oh,' I say again, hopelessly. 'Well, thank you anyway.' I duck past and walk quickly down the street. Behind me I can hear her letting herself into the building, but I don't turn back, not until I'm out of sight.

Only then do I slow, letting my shoulders drop, rubbing at my eyes. All at once I feel bone-tired. A dead end, but I'm not ready to turn around and go back to London, not yet. There are answers here. There have to be.

I let my thoughts drift as I walk, setting one foot before the other. The morning is at its height now, the city displaying itself proudly. The neighbourhood I wander through is nice; small roads and squat little houses, old people wheeling trolley bags, children squealing in a play park in the middle of a square. It doesn't feel like Paris at all, more like a village, very different to the place where Grand-mère lived in London. She had a flat above a bakery there, on a busy road in Islington. She lived there for years; the man who owned the bakery let her stay, even when she retired and only helped him work the till on busy Saturdays. *Did Grand-mère prefer it here?* I wonder as I walk. *Did she feel freer, back in her home country?*

Finally, I come to a café and sink down on to one of the little tables outside with relief. The waitress is brisk, unsmiling, and does not attempt to make small talk. She brings an espresso without fuss and leaves me to it. I'm grateful. My head is swimming, with tiredness, with memories, with fevered thoughts of what to do next. Quietly, I pour in half a sachet of sugar and drink the coffee, letting the conversations and the buzz of traffic wash around me.

When it comes to paying, I take out a note, knowing that I'll have to wait for change. As I lay it on the table, the name of the café, printed on the receipt, catches my eye.

Café des Peupliers.

I stop, gripping the flimsy paper. *Peupliers.* I've seen that name before, and recently. I haul my bag on to my lap and take out the file of papers stolen from the archive.

Where is it? I carefully turn through the pages, searching for the original landing form.

8 Square des Peupliers. The address where my grandmother lived at the end of the war, before she left for England. She came back, I think, staring around me. She came back here, to the neighbourhood she knew.

The waitress has reappeared, looks impatiently at the note on the table, and begins to fish through her apron for change.

'Excuse me,' I ask, forgetting my nerves. 'Do you know a place called Square des Peupliers?'

She nods, and jerks her chin at the opposite

road. 'It is that way, and left.' She drops a handful of change on to the table, oblivious to my stunned expression. '*Bonne journée.*'

Saint-Antoine

March 1943

The moment the song finished, I shrugged out of Paul's arms and stepped away, so quickly that he made a noise of surprise. He was blushing.

'That was a great dance,' he said.

But I wasn't listening. I didn't want to be there any longer, in that room with the laughter and the black-currant *sirop*. I didn't know what I wanted. Paul followed my gaze to where the Reisses were shuffling forwards in the registration line.

'Is that . . . ?' he asked.

'Monsieur and Madame Reiss, our lodgers.' I made an effort to tuck in my blouse, to straighten myself. 'I must say hello.'

'But they are registering — '

I ignored him, stepped away from the dance floor, where Mademoiselle Louise was trying once again to put a stop to the jazz.

In the lobby, some of the older foreigners were looking down the stairs, watching the young people dance, their faces a mixture of sadness and relief. Some weren't looking at all, just staring straight ahead or down at their shoes. The cold air from the front door brushed my rapidly cooling skin and made me shiver.

Monsieur and Madame Reiss had reached the

front. The *capitano* saw me and winked but I didn't respond. I watched as Monsieur Reiss printed his name neatly and passed the pen to his wife. She scrawled hers, threw the pen down with such disdain that the *capitano's* assistant frowned at her. Monsieur Reiss took her arm and steered her away before anything was said.

'*Bonsoir*, Celeste,' he greeted when he saw me. 'That looks like quite the party you are having down there.'

'Yes. Mademoiselle Louise, the teacher, organized it.' I looked over at Madame Reiss, but she didn't meet my eye, looking instead into the lounge with its dancing figures.

'Well, I'm glad you young people have found a way to have fun.' He too glanced into the room. 'It's important.'

A new dance was just starting up. I looked over at Madame Reiss again. There was a greyness to her skin, a look of exhaustion. Finally, she met my gaze.

'I didn't have you pegged as a lover of jazz,' she said softly.

'I haven't heard much before,' I admitted.

'Then you should visit us, upstairs.' Monsieur Reiss sounded pleased. 'I have just bought a wireless. The English stations play jazz sometimes.'

I couldn't put it into words, but the idea of visiting the Reisses upstairs made me feel unsteady. I just gave a quick smile in reply.

Madame Reiss's eyes flickered over my shoulder. Something about her shifted. 'And this is your dance partner.'

I felt a touch on my elbow. Paul was there, smiling politely. They hadn't yet been introduced. 'Yes,' I said. 'Paul, this is Monsieur and Madame Reiss.'

'*Bonsoir*. I'm Paul Picot.'

Monsieur Reiss lingered over the handshake. 'Picot — then your father is Monsieur Picot, of the gendarmerie?'

'That's right,' Paul said quickly, but he looked uncomfortable.

'Well, please don't let us interrupt you.' Monsieur Reiss smiled. 'I think you might be wanted for another dance, Celeste.'

'I . . . ' I looked at Madame Reiss but she had turned her face away.

'*À bientôt*,' Monsieur Reiss was saying and they were walking away, both of them, without a backward glance.

'They seem nice,' Paul said when the doors had swung closed behind them. 'Ceci, Annette was wondering — '

All at once the hotel was too warm, too fogged with breath and voices and faces.

'Can we get some air?' I said, already turning back to the lounge for my cardigan.

Paul looked surprised, but nodded. 'Yes, if you like.' He paused. 'We could go and look at the river.'

Outside, the light was fading from the sky. We walked in silence through the deserted streets, down past the old town walls towards the little bridge over the water. In the houses, lamps were beginning to glimmer through blackout paper. From some buildings came the smell of cooking or woodsmoke. I felt some of the agitation drain from my chest. Paul knew me well enough not to try to speak just then, and I was grateful.

When we reached the bridge I stood closer to him, so that he could hear me over the noise of the water.

'Thank you for asking me to the dance,' I said.

He looked down at me and smiled. There was something sheltering about the sound of the river at this time of year; the rushing water was so loud, so constant, it seemed like you could say anything and the words would be washed clean away, leave no trace.

'I'm sorry for dragging you out,' he said. 'But I'm glad you came. I . . . I like spending time with you, Ceci.'

The light was on the brink of disappearing completely, a gentle smoke-pink that wouldn't last a moment longer. Somewhere in the valley a bird was singing, one of the first of spring, alone in the evening. Its song trilled and questioned, trilled and questioned, and that light, that sky, that bird brought a yearning to my chest so powerful that it hurt.

'Ceci . . . '

I felt Paul turn, angling his body towards mine. His hand brushed my face and I looked up. His gaze was intense; it seemed the mirror of the feeling in my body. He bent his head, and I let him gently touch his lips to mine, place a trembling hand on my neck. And all the while, the pain in my chest, the bird's song, the dying light . . . I felt as though they were going to rip me apart. I wanted to scream, wanted to run, wanted to do anything to prove that I was living, blood hot, heart beating.

And so I pushed myself forward, pressed my lips hard against Paul's. He faltered and lifted his mouth a fraction, but I gripped his waist and held him there. He took the invitation, arms tightening around me, breath growing fast as his kiss spread from my lips to my cheek, my chin, the side of my neck, still damp beneath the collar with sweat from the dance.

He pressed a fraction closer. I felt hardness through the cloth of his trousers and he made a strangled sort of laugh, his breath warm on my throat. 'You taste like salt,' he whispered.

I opened my eyes. The smoke-pink light had vanished, the singing bird gone too; there was only the noise of the river, roaring, rushing. And all at once I smelled Paul's sweat through his cologne, tasted the sickly tang of blackcurrant *sirop* on his breath and it was all wrong, his hands on me, the wetness of his kiss on my neck. I didn't want it.

I must have tensed, because he stopped.

'Ceci, what . . . ?'

'I have to get to back to my grandmother's,' I told him, pulling my cardigan about my chest, suddenly self-conscious.

For a second, he didn't answer. Then he straightened. 'Of course,' he said, though his voice shook. 'Of course, I'll walk you there.'

We didn't speak as we made our way uphill, though I knew he wanted to. I didn't look at him, didn't trust my face not to show something that I couldn't explain. We cut through one of the old alleyways, cold with shadow, and as we passed the bakery, I stopped. All I wanted was to be alone; I didn't want to walk back into my grandmother's house where they would all be waiting and watching, with the feel of Paul's kiss still on my lips.

'You can leave me here,' I told him. 'I left my jacket inside. I want to get it before we come back for work later.'

He stopped with me, looking lost. 'I'll wait while you get it. Your father said I should have you home — '

I made a noise, turned away. 'I'm not a child, Paul. And it's still early. I will be fine.'

He caught my arm. 'Ceci,' he said miserably, 'I'm sorry.'

I stood still for a moment before I felt myself sigh. It was impossible to be angry with Paul.

'It's all right,' I told him, summoning a smile. 'I'll see you tomorrow.'

I thought he'd leave it at that, but after a moment he pulled me closer, kissed me again. This time, I felt nothing, just dampness and the pressure of his lips. I stepped away as soon as I was able and let myself into the bakery without a word.

Inside, it was quiet. It would stay that way until Papa and I arrived back here for work, in the early hours of the morning. I stood against the closed door, as if bracing it. I was shivering all over. Perhaps Marshal Pétain had been right to ban dancing. It was too much, the movement and the closeness and the wild music carried by foreign young people who did not know where their parents were or when they might return home. Boys like Wolf and Claude, only a handful of years younger than my brother . . .

Tears flooded my eyes and I choked on a hasty breath, pressed my cold hand to my lips, acutely aware of Paul's kiss. I swiped at my face, rubbed my sleeve across my mouth, wanting to rid myself of what had happened on the bridge, wanting to be me again, whole and separate. I pushed away the door and made for the storeroom. There was one thing I had that was mine and mine alone.

It wasn't calm I felt when I held the rifle; it was something else, something I didn't have words for. It made me feel grim and cold and yet, it was real. It had a power I had never felt before.

My tears subsided as I stared at it, the memory of Paul eclipsed by its presence. *It would be different if we could hunt*, Papa had said. My finger traced the curve of the trigger. Did I dare . . . ?

Before I could answer that question there was a noise, footsteps on the stairs and I spun around, my back to the door, had to climb on to the shelves in a rush and push the weapon out of sight.

'Daniel?' a voice murmured in the corridor.

I stepped out. Madame Reiss stopped when she saw me, and for a moment, we only looked at each other. How could she be both the last and the only person I wanted to see, right then?

'I thought you were Daniel,' she said awkwardly.

129

'He's not here?'

She shook her head. 'He is often out.'

'Even at night?'

She shot me a look. 'Especially then. Why do you ask?'

Those words would have sounded defensive, were it not for the gentle mockery that crept into her voice. I gave my best shrug.

'I have been thinking of going out at night myself.'

'Have you?' She moved a few steps closer. 'To meet with your beau, I suppose.'

'No,' I retorted. She heard the petulance in my voice and smiled, and I felt myself smiling too. I couldn't help it. 'Anyway, he isn't my beau.'

'Indeed.' She was looking at me with that strange, twisted expression of hers. 'So, you have other secrets?'

I hesitated. I had time to spare before I needed to be back at my grandmother's. And I wanted to do something, wanted to share something with somebody who wasn't my family, wasn't Paul; a secret like the clattering of stones in the alleyway, the first slice of *socca*, the taste of salt. I turned back towards the storeroom, towards what I knew was hidden there.

'I want to show you something,' I said.

Paris

May 1993

The street sign for Square des Peupliers stops me in my tracks.

It's mounted high on the wall above a cobbled alleyway that runs into shadow, broken by shafts of sunlight. An old-fashioned gas lamp rises ahead, and for a moment, I'm convinced that if I step on to the street, I'll find myself walking into a different time, into a city still occupied by a foreign army, where the sound of military boots and terse wireless announcements can be heard, where propaganda posters scream down from the walls and ration tickets worth little more than the paper they are printed on are clutched in fists as people queue outside empty markets . . .

I take a deep breath and step into the past.

The buildings rise above me, shrouded by trees and green, climbing vines. As I walk further, the sound of the city drops away, and I'm encased in the cool, shadowed silence of these secretive houses. A bird sings, and I feel I could be somewhere far away; a provincial town in the south, sleepy with dusk.

Some of the houses are in bad repair, glass awnings broken, rails rusting, vines straggling and woody, but others look perfect. How much would it cost to live here, in this odd, green oasis? Or are these houses treasured heirlooms, irreplaceable, once bought never sold? I'm so entranced that for a long minute I forget why I've come, but then a house number catches my eye.

8 Square des Peupliers looms above me. It's in better condition than the others; looks recently painted, with a high manicured hedge to keep out prying eyes. If anything, it looks a little *too* clean.

What now?

Ordinarily, I would cringe at the idea of opening a stranger's gate, of walking up the steps and ringing the bell unannounced, knowing that I would trip and stumble over my words as soon as they opened the door. But today is different; I feel as if I'm in a dream as I push open the metal gate, as I climb the steps and reach for the shiny gold bell.

Inside, a dog starts barking and I feel my nerves return. Someone may actually answer. And what then? I stare at the front door, dry-mouthed, tempted to run away, but it's too late: I can hear footsteps approaching, the dog yapping and my heart clenches at the thought of who might be on the other side.

A woman, a stranger, is staring out at me. She looks elegant, intimidatingly so, a pair of rimless glasses balanced in her blonde hair, a long, draping cardigan over her shoulders. She frowns at me, taking in my wrinkled shirt, my clumpy shoes.

'*Oui?*'

Never have I heard a question sound more like a dismissal. Behind her a fluffy white something is barking its head off at me, claws skittering on the vinyl floor.

'Stop that, Bibi,' she tells it, before turning her gaze back to me.

'I'm sorry to disturb you, but I'm — er — I'm looking for someone who used to live here.'

The woman's frown deepens.

'Here? I do not think so. This house has been in my family for generations.'

I blink at the woman, can't think of anything else to do but plough on. 'Well . . . it was a while ago, during the war.'

'I'm sorry, but you have the wrong house.' The woman is already closing the door.

'Wait!'

It comes out louder than I mean it to, echoes around the tiny street. It does me no good. The door is shut, the dog yipping and growling on the other side.

Frustration and embarrassment twist my stomach. I raise my hand again, to knock, to insist that the woman listens. But as I do, a horrible thought occurs to me: what if my grandmother lied on the landing form? I have nothing to prove that what she told the immigration official was the truth.

I turn away, disappointed with myself for being so caught up in this absurd search, as if it was a game, make-believe. I'm just relieved that I haven't told Mum anything about it, that I didn't get her hopes up for nothing.

I haul my bag on to my shoulder. Back to

England, I'll go back to the archives and keep my head down and do things *normally* until Mum returns. No one ever need know that I came.

As I pass the gate of the house opposite, I hear a noise, like air being released from a valve. I stop. Eyes are looking out at me through an ivy-covered gate. They're pale blue, sunk deep into wrinkled sockets, filmed over with cataracts. For a second, I think I'm seeing things, but then they move, and the face of an old man appears.

'You don't want to be talking to *her*,' he says. 'She's crazy.'

Part of me is tempted to smile and hurry away. I don't want to get stuck here, talking to a senile old man, but then, it's not exactly as if I have anything else on.

'*Pardon?*' I say, half-turning back.

'Number eight,' he gestures to the house. 'Crazy, the pair of them. Them and that mop they call a pet.'

The description of the small white dog makes me smile. 'Well,' I tell him awkwardly, '*bonne journée.*'

'Who are you?' He's looking at me intently, gnarled hands clasping the bars of the gate, as if I'm the most interesting thing to happen for months. *Perhaps I am*, I think, looking up at his neglected house, the overgrown garden.

'I'm . . . I came here to look for someone,' I say, feeling sorry for him. 'Someone who used to live at number eight, a long time ago. But the woman there said it has always belonged to her family, so I guess I must be wrong.'

'Maybe not.' The man grins, revealing

134

toothless gums. 'Maybe not.' He falls silent, and I'm about to ask him what he means when he speaks again, his voice cracked and lisping. 'During the war, was it?'

'Yes.' I step closer. 'How did you know?'

The old man laughs, taps his nose. 'I know. It might belong to herself now, but during the war that,' he jabs a shaking finger towards number eight, 'was a boarding house.'

'A boarding house?'

He bobs his head so hard I'm worried his neck might snap. 'Yes, yes. But you can't ask her, she wouldn't have a clue about it.' He sniffs. 'None of you young folk do. Her old aunt filled the place with lodgers to make ends meet. Six to a room they were, sometimes, poor souls.' His eyes are watering with mirth. 'She'd make them hide in the attic when her friends came to tea, told them not to make a sound, so she could pretend she wasn't renting rooms at all, and that she wasn't just as hungry and desperate as the rest of us.' He wheezes out a laugh.

'You're sure?' I'm close to the gate now. I can smell the mixture of liniment and old pipe tobacco on the man.

'Of course I'm sure.' He grins again. 'I was here. Working with my papa at the tyre factory.' I catch a waft of stale brandy on his breath. 'Who are you looking for?' he whispers conspiratorially.

He doesn't seem all that sane, I think, staring at his wide eyes, his eager grin. But what do I have to lose?

'My grandmother,' I tell him. 'I'm trying to

135

find her. This was her address in France, before she emigrated to England.'

'Find her?' he repeats, and starts laughing, a noise like rusted gears. 'You mean you lost her! That's a shame; then again, *my* grandchildren know exactly where I am, can't wait to lose me. They want to throw me in a home so they can have this place — '

'I think she was here,' I interrupt, desperate not to let this opportunity slip, 'some time before nineteen forty-six. She had my mother with her, a very small child. Her name was Celeste, Celeste Picot.'

The man clucks his tongue at me. 'No, no,' he says, eyes fixed on mine. 'Too many to remember names, always coming and going they were.'

He must see the disappointment in my face, the frustration, because abruptly his smile loses some of its mockery.

'Nice-looking girl, was she?' he says, shifting in his slippers. 'Like you? I'd remember that.'

Of course you would, I think, but I don't say anything. 'Here . . . ' I pull the file out of my bag, leafing through it to find the photograph of my grandmother. 'Here, that's what she looked like in nineteen forty-six.'

I hold it up to the gate. The old man reaches out nicotine-stained fingers, brings it close to his face, then far away, then close again, as if the details will change with distance. He makes a thinking noise, low in his throat.

'Perhaps,' he murmurs. 'What did she do, this grandmother of yours? We swapped things sometimes, you know. There was one woman,

136

worked as a cleaner in one of the grand hotels, and *she* could swipe almost anything, soap, butter, even got me a bit of steak once on my birthday.'

'She was a baker,' I say quickly. 'At least, I think so. I'm not sure.'

'Wait.' His milk-filmed eyes fix on the picture again. 'There *was* a girl who brought bread. Pretty little thing, but fierce. She pushed my cousin off those steps when he tried to get too friendly with her.' He breaks off into chuckles again. 'From the south, she was. They make them wild down there — '

'That's her!' I grab the bars of the gate, much to the old man's surprise. 'That would be her, she was from Nice, or somewhere near by.' I feel myself smiling with excitement. 'Do you remember anything else about her? Why she left for England? Where she worked? Did she know anyone else in Paris who she might — '

'No.' The old man shakes his head, a flicker of unease crossing his face. 'No, it was all so long ago.'

'Please.' I reach through the ivy-covered gate to touch his hand. 'Please, is there *anything* you can tell me?'

He stares at my fingers, resting on his wrinkled skin, and his face seems to crumple. For a moment I think it's going to be too much for him, that he'll collapse, but then he clears the phlegm from his throat.

'I think . . . I once traded her some rubber, so she could fix up her shoes. She gave me some bread in return.' A ghost of a smile creeps back on to his face. 'Good stuff it was too. Not the usual grey rubbish.' He frowns. 'She worked at a place in the sixth, I think — can't have been so far, she walked there, but then, everyone walked in those days — ' He breaks off. 'It was a hard time, you know. Afterwards, we all tried to forget.' He stares at me from behind his rusting gate, a look in his eyes that's almost pleading. 'What happened to her, that girl? Did she live?'

'She did,' I say gently. 'She went to England, raised a child there.'

'But you said she was lost.'

'Only to me,' I tell him, 'only for now.'

Saint-Antoine

April 1943

I waited for Madame Reiss all morning. It had been three days since I'd shown her the gun, and yet she had not sought me out again. Not like Paul. He had started to appear at lunchtimes, to walk me from the bakery to Grandmother's house. He did not try to kiss me, not there in the bright, busy streets, but he did take my hand. Once, I'd shaken him off, feeling irritable. Another time I gripped his fingers in return, had even pulled him into the shadow of a doorway, wanting . . . I didn't know what. Not the kiss he gave me. It left me feeling guilty and more confused than ever.

I was not the only person who seemed unsettled. It was as if the whole town had been thrown off balance. Every morning or afternoon, or whenever the bus had fuel enough to reach the top of the mountain, another twenty or thirty refugees would be deposited in the town. Many had nothing with them, only the worn clothes on their backs. Others were better off and had suitcases and sewing machines and portable gramophones strapped to the roof of the bus. Some looked thin and frail, others were sick from the journey, from the twisting switchback roads and the fumes and the uncertainty.

At first, the Italian soldiers had been nervous and short with people, standing on guard with their guns, their unkempt uniforms buttoned. The town was now a supervised residence, we were told, and the foreigners were supposed to stay within its limits at all times, and register their presence twice a day. In reality, as more and more people arrived, the task of counting them all grew harder, and the Italians became lax in their checks.

For one thing, there was nowhere else for the foreigners to go. From Saint-Antoine, twisting footpaths led east to the neighbouring villages, west to the sanctuary of the Madonna, at least a couple of hours' hike away. To the north there was nothing but mountain: slopes and scree and ice. South was the road to Nice, but there were few motor cars, apart from the Italians' trucks. The bus was really our link to the world; the only viable way down.

Most of the newcomers looked too exhausted to try to run from Saint-Antoine, and seemed willing enough to turn up to the hotel in the evening to register, to sign or call out their names without trouble.

Little by little, like snowmelt trickling into a pool, the town began to fill up. People moved into apartments, rooms unoccupied for years, even into some of the grand villas outside the town, built before the war by rich families and left to stand empty. It was strange to see smoke rising from those chimneys, to see linen drying over sills, children playing on the roads. It was as if the old tourist season had come early, like a spring bulb fooled by a warm day into pushing through the soil too soon.

We sold as much bread as we could make, and still we had to turn people away. Every morning, while the town was still cold with the shadow of night, a line began to form outside the bakery. We took everything in exchange for bread: coupons and money, vegetables, matches, tins of condensed milk, even reels of cotton and paper. The townspeople of Saint-Antoine fared the best. They grumbled that there was not enough to go around, but many of them were from farming families. After four years of war, they had mastered *le Système D*, and always had something to barter or trade. It was the refugees who went short.

I saw Wolf with his brother and cousin outside the workshop of Monsieur Lebrun, the carpenter. He was holding up offcuts of wood to the boys' feet, to make soles for their ruined shoes. They waved to me as I passed, and I waved back, though it filled me with shame to remember that I'd once complained of my sturdy work clogs, or a single hole in my well-made walking boots.

They came into the bakery later that morning, their new wooden soles clattering on the cobbles.

'*Bonjour*, Mam'selle Corvin,' Wolf greeted me with a grin, 'how are you today?' As the designated leader of the group, his French was improving quickly.

'*Bonjour*,' I replied with a smile. 'Ben, Claude.'

They smiled and nodded back, but their eyes kept straying to the huge round, floured *boule* loaves, the few precious *pain aux noix* studded with walnuts, even the dense *pain bis*. Abruptly, the scent of freshly baked bread, as familiar to me as my own skin, seemed overwhelming, luxurious. Wolf took three coupons from his pocket and handed them over.

I stared down at those little squares of paper. Four ounces, I was supposed to give them in exchange. Hardly enough for one meal, let alone three. I thought of Leon when he was a boy, as I reached for a knife to cut the meagre portions. He had always been hungry, even before the war. Behind me, I could hear Papa in the kitchen, the swish of the linen *couche* on the floured counter as he shaped another set of loaves. I could smell the latest batch beginning to brown in the oven, and I knew that they would be replaced by another batch, then another; the pantry was already heady with the sourness of proving dough.

Rapidly, I seized a whole *boule*, bigger than my outstretched hand, and flattened the tickets to the bottom of its floured crust.

'*Alors*,' I told Wolf briskly. 'Have a good day.'

For a second he frowned, staring at the bread and the tickets. Then he met my eyes and smiled wide.

'*Merci!*' he said, holding the loaf to his chest. '*Merci beaucoup!*'

I turned away to fetch the loaves for the next customer only to stop. Papa had emerged from the doorway of the kitchen and was staring out of the bakery window. I followed his gaze. Outside, Wolf, Claude and Ben were crowded around the loaf of bread, each tearing off great chunks, flour clinging to their hands and chins.

I braced myself, expecting a rebuke, but Papa didn't say anything. He only looked at me, and I knew we were thinking the same thing: that though we were hungry, we had never starved. We had a trade. We had wood and ovens and raw ingredients and an ancient skill that provided food for many people. We were the lucky ones.

Papa gave me a sad sort of smile and shook his head, before disappearing back into the kitchen, to eke out the dough as far as he possibly could.

Ordinarily, Paul would call for me at lunchtime to accompany me back to Grandmother's house, but today, the thought of sitting silently at the table in the cramped, dark kitchen was too much. It was a glorious day, the sky blisteringly blue. Not a day to be inside. Even Madame Reiss had gone out; I had heard the door to the apartment open and close while I worked in the shop.

'Papa,' I said quickly, taking off my smock, for I knew Paul would arrive at any moment, 'do you mind if I have my lunch later?'

He looked up from the bench, wiping his hands on a cloth. The earlier incident with Wolf and his brothers still lingered between us.

'Why, Ceci?'

'It's such a beautiful day,' I said, as casually as I could. 'And it's warm now. There might be mushrooms down by the river. I wanted to go and look.'

He was watching me closely.

'All right,' he said after a moment. 'But be

back in time for *goûter*. We are going to have another long night later.' As I stepped past him, he caught my shoulder. 'Remember yourself,' he said.

Those words rang in my mind as I let myself out through the back door and ran down the narrow alleyway, towards a patch of sunlight at the end. *Remember yourself.* Did he think I was going to meet Paul for a tryst? A strange, wild laugh broke from me and I swiped a hand through one of the fountains as I passed, sending water flying in a glittering arch.

Although it was a weekday, the square was busy, and I had to stop to marvel at the change. The cafés were in business again, and had dragged their tables and chairs out into the sunlight. It didn't seem to matter that they had nothing much to serve beyond the rough, locally made wine, acorn or chicory coffee, home-made *sirops* and perhaps some fiendishly expensive spirits. It didn't seem to matter that it was Lent, and that the people of Saint-Antoine, sober at the best of times, were looking on disapprovingly. People had come, regardless, and the little square was as full as on any market day. Voices echoed back from the cobbles, bounced from the walls, were carried downstream by the *gargouille*; words in half a dozen languages, talk, debate, jokes, questions, news.

It was not only men sitting there, I saw with surprise, it was women too. I even saw a few young women, my age, sharing a cup of coffee between them. I had never been allowed to visit the café on my own, was only permitted to wait

144

for my father outside while he knocked back a drink at the bar.

I was about to turn away, cowed, when I heard a familiar laugh that snatched at my attention. I looked closer. There, at a table near the edge of the square, sat four men and a woman. Madame Reiss.

She was wearing her dark glasses again, but this time they seemed elegant, defiant of the hot, bright sky. There was a tumbler of wine at her fingertips, a cigarette in her hand, as always, and I watched as she stopped with it midway to her lips to listen to what someone was saying, before answering back with short, sure words.

I found my eyes lingering on her cheeks, flushed from the sun, the corner of her mouth, stained by the wine. She was beautiful in that moment, animated and assured, and yet for some reason I wanted to grasp those busy hands in mine and breathe with her, until she saw that even just by breathing, by being, she was beautiful too. I turned away, feeling strange, wishing I could sit with her, knowing I couldn't.

'Celeste!'

Too late. She had half-risen from her chair, had pushed the sunglasses on to her forehead to see me. I stared back, trying to show her that I couldn't join them, that I was too embarrassed, but she beckoned and I had no choice. My face burned as I stepped up to the table.

Monsieur Reiss was there, and three other men I didn't recognize. They were speaking a language I didn't know, but stopped politely as soon as I appeared.

145

'This is Mademoiselle Corvin,' Madame Reiss said in French, leaning back in her chair, a strange half-smile on her face, 'the baker's daughter.'

Two of the men nodded across to me, smiling. The third leaned in towards Monsieur Reiss, who translated, before he smiled and nodded too. I murmured hello in return.

'Would you like to join us?' Monsieur Reiss was saying, pulling out a chair.

I did want to, desperately, but I knew that if I lingered among these odd, city types, it would get back to my mother, my father . . . Maybe.

'Thank you,' I said. 'I cannot. I have things to do.'

'Always busy,' Madame Reiss said. 'Not like us wastrels.'

'Wastrel?' one of the men said good-naturedly. His accent sounded Russian. 'I resent that. You know I would be working if I could.'

'We all would,' the other man answered. Of the four of them, he seemed the least at ease.

'Please excuse me,' I said hurriedly. 'I must go. It was very nice to meet you all.'

'Where are you going?' Madame Reiss's voice stopped me.

I frowned at her slightly, trying to fathom what she meant by keeping me there.

'To the river,' I said. 'It has been good weather, there might be some things to pick, plants, herbs, some mushrooms.'

Madame Reiss pushed back her chair. 'I'll come with you,' she said, crushing her cigarette beneath her shoe.

My gaze snapped towards her face, confused, elated, even as her husband frowned. 'My dear,' he started, 'are you sure?'

'Of course I'm sure,' her eyes were bright from the wine. 'The fresh air will do me good. And you men have business to discuss anyway. That is, if Mademoiselle Corvin does not object to my company?'

'Of course not,' I replied, wondering why my stomach had started trembling so. 'You are most welcome, Madame Reiss.'

Paris

May 1993

The old man's voice lingers in my mind as I walk the streets of the Left Bank. I feel as if I'm drawing closer to Grand-mère, and yet, every time I find some trace of her, she seems to disappear, leaving me alone. I don't know much more than when I left Cheshire, and the few details I have gathered about my grandmother's life are wispy and fragile.

It's almost lunch, and I find myself wandering through Saint-Germain: the 6th arrondissement that the old man spoke of, the heart of the Rive Gauche. Ordinarily I'd gawp like a tourist at the illustrious cafés and dozens of patisseries, but now, I find myself wandering in a daze. This is where my grandmother spent the end of the war. I half-expect to run into her as a young woman, hurrying home to my mother after a long shift at a bakery, flour caught in the dark plait of her hair.

The streets are bustling. There must be a market near by, because people keep walking past me, laden down with vegetables and fruit and paper-wrapped packages. I can't help but stop opposite a *boulangerie*, watching customers come and go. It looks as if it's been here for a long time. The sign is weather-worn, the interior dark and poky. Grand-mère might have worked here, or in another place like it. The door swings open and the hot, toasted scent of freshly baked bread wafts out, calling to me, beckoning me inside.

The wooden racks behind the counter are stacked with loaves of all different shapes and kinds. Flour hangs in the air, and the smell of sweet, soft dough. I order a *tartine* and take a seat at one of the tiny tables crammed into a corner.

For a while, it's enough just to sit and soak up the sounds and scents of the bakery, imagining my grandmother working in the kitchen out the back, pushing her hair from her forehead with one hand, the way she always did. Then the *tartine* arrives, and I realize how hungry I am. One long slice of dark bread, piled with a soft cheese and roasted ham smeared with primrose-yellow mustard. It's delicious, so much so that I almost feel guilty, eating so well for a handful of francs, when my grandmother must have struggled to feed herself and my mother during the war years.

I dust off my hands with regret. I should probably make my way back across Paris to the coach station and buy a ticket for the long journey home. I don't want to; it feels too much like defeat. All I've found of my grandmother are faded signs of her presence in the world, vague memories. I stand up and shoulder my bag. As I hand the plate over to the girl behind the counter, I see a payphone standing on a leaflet-strewn shelf, a well-thumbed copy of the

Pages Jaunes next to it.

I stare. I'm such an idiot. I was so obsessed with the old address that I didn't even *think* to try the most obvious place of all: the telephone directory. Hurriedly, I drop my bag. There's a *Pages Blanches*, a residential directory, underneath the leaflets. *P*, I turn the pages rapidly, trying not to rip them in my haste . . . *Picot*. I read down the list. None of the first names begin with a 'C'. I close it with a thump of frustration. Of course it wasn't going to be as easy as that. If Grand-mère is in Paris, then she must be ex-directory. Unless she isn't in Paris at all. Or . . . a shiver runs through me. What if I'm already too late?

Feeling a little ill, I place the directory back on to the shelf. Perhaps she truly is lost to me, like I told the old man in the Square des Peupliers. At least he has his family.

. . . my grandchildren know exactly where I am, can't wait to lose me. They want to throw me in a home so they can have this place.

I stop, one hand on my bag. A home. I hadn't thought of that. Grand-mère would be sixty-eight, too young for a home really, but if she was ill, perhaps . . .

This time I reach for the *Pages Jaunes* and start to thumb through it. What would it be under? *Health? Hospitals?* I turn past pages of dentists and chiropodists and specialist doctors. I'm turning so fast, I almost miss it, the words 'Maisons de Retraite' halfway down a page. I run a print-stained finger down the listings.

There are over twenty of them.

'Excuse me?' I ask the lady at the counter, pulling a note from my purse. 'I don't suppose you could give me some change?'

Outside the window, the afternoon begins to lengthen. After listening curiously to my first five phone calls, the lady behind the counter asks me what I'm doing. Hesitantly, I explain that I'm looking for my grandmother, trying to make that sentence sound as normal as I can. She looks surprised, but after a while she nods thoughtfully.

'Don't bother with the homes in the first and second arrondissements,' she tells me, going to serve a customer. 'If she was a baker she'd never be able to afford them, trust me.'

That gets rid of another four from my list. Still eleven to go. I try two more, only to come up with nothing. I'm starting to get tired of saying the same thing, asking if they have a Madame Celeste Picot resident there. The lady from the counter brings me over a slice of *tarte aux pommes* they haven't sold, whispering that they'll be closing for the afternoon in ten minutes, but that I can keep using the phone while they tidy up. I thank her, take a bite of the sweet, sharp pastry to bolster my nerves as I dial yet another number.

'*Résidence Les Jardins d'Automne*,' a male voice answers, sounding distracted.

'*Bonjour*,' I say wearily. 'I'm wondering if you have a resident there by the name of Celeste Picot, Madame Celeste Picot.'

There's a pause before the voice says. 'We don't have anyone by *that* name, I'm afraid.'

151

There's a strange inflection in his voice, an emphasis on the 'that'. It makes me press on.

'She would be around sixty-eight, now,' I say, trying not to sound too desperate. 'I'm afraid we lost touch with her a few years ago. She used to work as a baker here in Paris and . . . ' I trail off, listening to the silence at the other end of the phone. '*Monsieur?*' Nothing. I sigh, lowering the phone.

'*Mademoiselle!*' The voice catches me. 'One moment, we don't have a Celeste *Picot* here, but we do have a Celeste *Corvin*. Mademoiselle Celeste Corvin. Might she be the person you are looking for?'

I clutch the phone. *Corvin.* Why is that name so familiar? Did Mama mention it once, did I see it on a card or hear it spoken? My grandmother's maiden name?

'Is she — ' My voice dries up. 'Is she there? I mean, is she there right now?'

'Of course,' the voice says, as if it's the simplest thing in the world. 'Might I ask your name? Hello? *Mademoiselle?*'

I can't speak. It's too much, too real, the fact that my grandmother is no longer a memory or a distant phantom, but a living, breathing person, here in this city. Confined to a nursing home . . . What's wrong with her? She wouldn't be there if she was healthy. Guilt and fear prickle down my neck when I remember the urgency in my mother's voice, her obvious need for forgiveness, to forgive, while there is still time.

I just pray we're not already too late.

Saint-Antoine

April 1943

'Do you truly want to come with me?'

My hands were tingling, my body fizzing with excitement, as Madame Reiss and I walked through the town.

She shrugged as we stepped over the *gargouille* and into the shadows of the old streets. 'I said, didn't I?'

'And on Sunday?'

She nodded. 'And on Sunday.'

I fought back a smile. After showing Madame Reiss the gun, I had told her of my plan to go out hunting, to try to catch something that could be bartered or traded for what we could not get by ordinary means. She had been interested in that, had made me promise to tell her when I was planning to go, so that she could come with me.

Sunday, I had told her, *early, before church. It will be quiet then.*

She had smiled wryly. *Won't you be working?*

Not on the day of rest. Even God spares bakers once a week.

Quickly, before anyone saw us, I led the way down some steps, through an archway and out on to the path that marked the edge of the town. It led down towards the river, then up again into the trees that covered the slopes. Beneath their protective canopy, I felt lighter than I had for months and my spirits rose like the birdsong echoing around us, living, questioning.

Madame Reiss was quiet. I didn't try to talk, only led the way. Finally, we came to a place where the trees parted around a pile of huge, grey rocks that looked down over town, its roofs a jumble of terracotta shards on the mountain. The sun fell bright; the air was quenching and clean.

'I can breathe,' Madame Reiss murmured, sinking down on to the rocks and taking off her sunglasses. 'Out here I can breathe.'

She lifted her face to the sun and closed her eyes. I couldn't help but stare, taking in every pore of her skin, the soft down on her cheek.

'You can't breathe in town?' I asked. It sounded so stupid that I bit my lip and hoped she hadn't heard.

'I find it hard here,' she said. 'You must have noticed.' When I didn't answer, she sighed. 'These mountains, they make me feel trapped. Like this place is the end of the line . . . ' She trailed off, gave me her practised, clever smile. 'You must think me terribly ungrateful.'

I shook my head, even though her words stung as much as they made sense. Saint-Antoine was *my* town; I had seen its peaks so often that they were etched on to my eyes, like a design scratched into glass. I barely saw them any more, rather felt them, always watching. To us, the mountain was protection. The snows kept us isolated and safe in winter; the long, steep road held trouble at arm's length, even in summer.

I thought of Leon, who'd left our refuge and been snatched up by the war, in a city somewhere far below. Perhaps Madame Reiss was right. Perhaps the world could find us, even here.

I found myself staring at her, my eyes tracing the line of her jaw, the shape of the bones beneath her skin. 'Where are you from?' I asked after a while.

'I thought Daniel told you.' Her eyes were drifting closed against the sunlight. 'Brussels.'

'But before there?' It didn't seem possible that she had come from anywhere real.

'Before?' She opened one eye a fraction to look at me. Her irises were the colour of water today, the soft grey of the sea in winter. 'How do you know there was a before?'

I shifted, thinking of the men she had sat beside in the café, that unfamiliar language they had shared. 'You were speaking something else earlier.'

She half-smiled. 'You heard. Yes. I don't speak it very well. Daniel does, though. He's quite the linguist. French, Yiddish, Flemish, even English. We talked about moving to London, but by the time we tried to leave Brussels . . . ' She opened her other eye to look at me. 'I was born in Budapest,' she said abruptly. 'If that's what you are asking. Do you know where that is?'

'Of course,' I said, though I didn't really. Only that it was to the east, somewhere.

Madame Reiss sank back on her elbows, legs stretched out before her. 'I don't remember it at all. We left when I was still a baby.'

'And Monsieur Reiss?' I shifted so I could see her face better, all thoughts of mushroom picking abandoned for now. 'Reiss is your married name, isn't it? What was yours, before?'

'All these questions.'

'I feel like there is so much I don't know,' I murmured.

'You are a young woman. You are allowed not to know.'

'I'm not that young,' I insisted. Madame Reiss could not have been more than twenty-six or twenty-seven.

'Only a young person would say that.' I must have frowned, because she let out a sort of laugh. 'Fine. Beck was my maiden name. Myriam Liza Beck.'

I looked across at her. 'Can I call you that? Myriam?'

Strange, how that name had changed shape in my mind over the past few weeks. Now, its meaning was her and only her.

'Of course,' she said, and met my eyes. 'Now it is *my* turn to ask a question. That boy, the gendarme. Is he your sweetheart?'

I sat up, dizzy from the sun, from being too close.

'I have to get on.' I clambered to my feet, gathering the basket. 'Once we lose the sun it will turn cold.'

'Celeste!' She sat up too. All at once she looked frightened, pale in the sunlight. 'Wait for me.'

We didn't talk as we took a path down towards

156

the river but I felt a gentleness in the air, her apology, breathed if not spoken. As the canopy thinned, I began to see flecks of colour on the loamy ground, until I couldn't keep a smile down. It felt like years since I had seen anything growing.

Violets had sprung from the damp, winter mulch. I knelt down and brushed a petal to get its scent: sweet as boiling sugar, delicate as blossom and just as soon lost. Myriam and I gathered a few handfuls, and soon the smell was all around us, clinging to our skin, finer than any perfume.

Down by the river, where the water met the rocks in clean white crests, Myriam stopped and plunged her fingers into a pool.

'It's like ice,' she said, wincing.

I let it run over my own hands. 'It is ice, or was, not long ago. It has only just changed.'

The water left my hands chilled to the bone, but nevertheless, I made a cup of my palms and drank. Myriam did the same. That water tasted ancient, like a secret, a draught from a stone bowl made by forgotten hands. It was pure and neat and somehow reminded me of drinking wine unwatered for the first time. We filled our stomachs with it and Myriam splashed her face, droplets collecting in the strands of her hair.

Remember yourself, my father had said, and suddenly his warning made sense, because in that moment I didn't want to think about obligations or duties or the fact I was expected home for *goûter*.

I looked over at Myriam, wiping her face on

her sleeve, and thought again about the sound of her sobbing deep into the night, Monsieur Reiss's quiet voice saying, *My wife is not well.*

'We should go back,' I said softly.

I left her at the door of the bakery. The scent of the forest still lingered on us, crushed stalks and floral sweetness, mixed with earthy loam that clung to the soles of our shoes. Our fingernails were stained green from picking violets. Madame Reiss held a bouquet of them, but with her other hand she caught my sleeve, the cuff of her jacket still damp from the river.

'You'll let me come out with you again?' she asked.

My heart leapt. 'Of course.'

'Sunday?'

'Sunday.'

She smiled, a fragile expression in the gathering evening, a look I felt instinctively was just for me. 'Then *à bientôt*, Celeste,' she said.

Paris

May 1993

The retirement home is almost back where I started, on the edge of the 13th arrondissement. It seems unthinkable that I might have passed within a few streets of my grandmother and never known she was there, were it not for a few chance words from a stranger.

Visiting hours are apparently almost over for the day, but the nurse I spoke to on the phone promised me he would try to get an evening pass sorted. The closer I get to the home, the more uncertain I feel. Should I be doing this without Mum? My steps slow as I turn on to the Rue de Tolbiac. Shouldn't I wait until she's back in the country, so we can do this together? But I'm here now. And so is Grand-mère, after all this time. I can't just turn around and go back to England, especially not if she's expecting me. I walk on resolutely. At least this way I can prepare Mum for the worst, if I have to.

I stop beside a flower stall, for distraction more than anything. I don't have enough money for a bouquet, but the florist offers to make me a posy. I point out colours that catch my eye: white marguerites, green bay leaves and delicate spring violets.

Minutes later, I'm standing before a building,

trying to work up the courage to go inside. *Résidence Les Jardins d'Automne*, the sign tells me. It's a dull-looking place with a grimy grey façade and a ramp instead of steps. It seems impossible that Grand-mère is inside.

The paper of the flowers sticks to my palms as I push open the glass door to the reception. It's too warm in here, the air thick with the smell of disinfectant and unidentifiable savoury food. Families are milling about, children smartly dressed to visit their elders. Some of them glance at my rumpled appearance with disapproval. I approach the receptionist, mouth dry with nerves.

'*Bonjour*,' she says briskly before I can speak. She's wearing a white uniform, a cardigan over the top. 'Visiting hours are over, I'm afraid.'

'I know that, but . . . the nurse I spoke to said he would get me a pass, an evening pass to see my grandmother?' The nurse raises an eyebrow at me. 'Her name is Celeste. Celeste Corvin,' I stutter, the name feeling clumsy in my mouth.

The nurse's expression clears. 'You're the one that Alain spoke to? The girl who telephoned?'

I nod, and she claps her hands together, smiling. 'I will go and tell him. He'll want to come and see you. In the meantime, here, you may see your grandmother.' She slides a plastic VISITEUR badge across to me.

I pick it up with trembling fingers. She has no idea about the enormity of that statement. *You may see your grandmother.* In a daze, I clip it to the edge of my shirt.

'Where is she?' I hear myself ask. 'Where do I find her?'

'That way.' The nurse points down the corridor. 'In the lounge, on your left.'

The smell grows stronger the further I go from reception: a stale stuffiness that makes me want to shove open a window and let the cool spring air flood into the building like water. The soles of my shoes squeak on the lino. Finally, I see a room labelled *lounge*, and slow to a halt outside. It's filled with round tables and high armchairs and seems empty, apart from one old man, parked in a wheelchair in front of a television. I'm about to turn away, tell the nurse that she must have been mistaken, when I see her.

She is sitting at the window, so still that she almost disappears into the shadow of the curtain. She's looking out at something, staring with such intensity that I know it isn't the drab, paved courtyard outside she's seeing. She's somewhere else, far away; another time, another place.

I walk towards her on hesitant feet, my throat tight. She doesn't look up, even when I stop within arm's reach.

'Grand-mère?' I whisper.

She doesn't move, doesn't even blink.

'Grand-mère,' I repeat, louder, in case she hasn't heard me. I kneel down by her chair and look into her face. It is perfectly calm, still as a pool hiding life beneath the surface. Her eyes are the same bright brown that I remember, rich as cherry bark, and I feel a sharp pang of familiarity. There are deep lines on her face that I don't remember, lines that look as if they have been caused by pain. Her hair is long, the way it always was, no longer peppered brown but completely grey, twisted into a low bun.

The Grand-mère of my childhood was a small, tough woman, strong enough to lift me up. Now she looks thin, almost fragile. What has happened to her? A flock of pigeons whirrs past the window, reflected in her unmoving gaze. There is a tissue clenched in one of her hands.

'Celeste,' I try, and touch her arm.

She blinks, as if waking. 'What did you say?' Her voice is slow, vague.

Oh no. I blink back tears, lift my face towards the light.

'It's me, Grand-mère. It's Annie. Your granddaughter.'

'Annie?' The word is drawn out, a long breath. 'Little Annie? My Evie's girl?'

'Yes.' I want to put my hand on hers but can't summon the courage. 'Yes, that's right. I came here to look for you, from England. We wanted — ' I have to push down emotion. 'Mum wanted to find you.'

'England,' she repeats, searching my face. 'Then Evie . . . ?'

'She's fine,' I lie. 'She's travelling, working. Somewhere in the Pacific, right now.' I feel tears rising again when I think about what this means, when I imagine the conversation with Mum, the joy, the shock I'll hear in her voice, when I say, *I found her.*

'The Pacific,' Grand-mère repeats the word carefully. Her eyes slide closed, a smile stretching the corners of her mouth. 'My little vagabond.'

I reach out, grip her hand.

162

'Grand-mère?'

With a start, she straightens. She stares at my hand, before looking up to meet my gaze. For the first time, her eyes seem to clear. The lines in her olive skin shift, like crinkled fabric being straightened. 'You found me,' she says.

Am I imagining it, or does she sound afraid?

'Mam'selle Picot?' I leap to my feet. A young man is standing in the doorway, tall, with a shaved head, a single earring. He's wearing a nurse's uniform. 'I'm Alain Moussa,' he says, 'we spoke on the phone.' His gaze shifts to my grandmother. 'I'm going to have to steal your granddaughter away for a moment, Celeste,' he says. 'Not for long, I promise.'

'Oh, all right, Alain.' Grand-mère's words seem strangely automatic. 'Did you get me my bread?'

'*Mais oui*,' he smiles, 'it is in your room.'

'You're an angel,' she says, turning back to the window.

'Here,' I whisper, holding out the flowers. 'These are for you.'

She doesn't take them, doesn't even look up. I lay them gently in her lap, and follow nurse Alain out into the hallway, emotion kicking at my chest.

'She won't eat the bread we have here,' he says as we walk. 'Says it's rubbish. I have to go and get hers from a real bakery — '

'What's wrong with her?'

He puts a finger to his lips, motions me towards a fire exit. 'She can hear more than she lets on,' he murmurs, shoving open the door,

163

wedging it there with a brick. He turns to me then, his face serious. 'You must know,' he says after a moment, 'I was very surprised by your call. Why haven't you come before? She has been here for three years and this is the first time anyone has visited.'

'I didn't know she was here,' I say, trying to get control of my voice. 'My Mum — they had a fight, the two of them, and lost touch. This is the first time I've seen her for almost twenty years.'

He watches me for few seconds. 'I always wondered,' he says. 'She is a proud woman, Celeste. And very private. It doesn't surprise me that she would have secrets.' He smiles. 'But I am glad to meet one of her relatives at last.'

I smile back a little. 'You were going to tell me what's wrong with her?'

He nods, solemn. 'Your grandmother has been suffering from a series of strokes. The first one was what brought her here. They are not too severe, compared to others I've seen, but they slow her down.'

I watch his face, still serious. 'There's something else, isn't there?'

'There is.' He looks me in the eye. 'She's suffering from dementia. It's early stage, not too advanced yet.'

I can't answer, and have to look away to fight down the tears. He puts a hand on my shoulder.

'I am sorry, Mam'selle Picot. But you should know that your grandmother is a strong woman. She may yet surprise us all.'

When I get back to the lounge, the chair by the window is empty, the flowers gone. I look about in alarm, but the only other people in the room are the old man and a young female nurse, preparing to wheel her patient from the room.

'Excuse me,' I stumble, 'do you know where my grandmother is? She was here.'

'You mean Mam'selle Corvin?' The nurse smiles. 'She said her granddaughter was visiting.'

That name again . . . When did she stop using Picot?

The nurse straightens from tucking a blanket around the old man's knees. 'I helped her to her room. She said that you were taking her out for dinner. Reception will give you a pass, but please have her back promptly by nine.'

I stare at the nurse for a second, wondering if she's made a mistake. The woman I just saw didn't seem capable of making dinner plans. I mumble a few words of thanks and follow her directions to my grandmother's room.

When I get there, the door is slightly ajar. I knock lightly and step inside, not wanting to startle her.

'Grand-mère?'

The room is plain, almost bare. A single hospital-style bed stands against the wall next to a dull wooden chest of drawers, a bookshelf filled with paperbacks and a chair, positioned by the long window. I can see the back of Grand-mère's head over the top of it, her knot of grey hair.

'Grand-mère,' I say again, as gently as possible. 'I'm back.'

I walk around to see her. She is dressed for the outside in a dark coat and a soft, pale scarf; sturdy lace-up shoes on her feet. She's holding the posy I brought her.

'These flowers,' she murmurs, passing the petals of the violets through her brown, knotted hands, 'they remind me of home. Flowers of the mountain, that grew in the spring.'

I go to her side. 'Grand-mère,' I whisper, 'I'm so sorry it took us this long.'

She covers my clammy hand with one of her own, cool and dry as paper.

'Stop it, girl,' she says, 'there's nothing to be sorry about.'

The words are so fluent, so articulate, that I look up, startled. The vague expression on my grandmother's face is gone. Her eyes are clear and almost amused. As I watch, a smile twitches into being, the exact smile that I remember from childhood.

'Let's get out of here,' she says.

Saint-Antoine

April 1943

False dawn had just begun to seep across the sky, like ink on silk. The kitchen door scraped softly behind me as I left Grandmother's house; no locks or keys to jangle and betray, just a twist of old, faded rope and a wooden bolt, worn smooth by decades of use.

The garden was thick with darkness and damp. Trees gathered the mist, their branches starred with new blossom, just about to unfold. I stopped. Above the sound of the river, I could hear a lone bird singing. Was it the same one I heard on the bridge? The sound trembled, soft and hesitant, as if the bird couldn't quite believe that it would hear a reply, that others might exist, out there in the valley.

Overgrown vegetation stroked my knees as I walked and left wet streaks on the worn trousers. They were Leon's, an old pair that he only ever wore for work in the bakery. Every day, we expected word from him, in every knock on the door, every time someone walked past the bakery holding a telegram, but so far, we had heard nothing. People in town told us not to worry. They said he would be safe with the *milice*. I couldn't say out loud what I was thinking: that it was the *milice* he should be kept safe from.

167

There were no lights in the town yet, not even at the hotel. That was good. I knew how to walk so as not to make noise. I knew which cobbles were loose, where puddles collected, which rooftop guaranteed a wet head when it rained. It was strange to be out so early. On any other day, I would be working at this time, sweating at the door of the oven with Papa, our arms and hands floured to the elbow, oblivious to this huge sleeping silence, just beyond the door.

But today the bakery was shuttered, Sunday-sober. I let myself in through the back door. The clunk of the lock was loud enough to make me pause, but nothing stirred. I slid in through the gap and turned to close it gently when I heard footsteps.

I turned and reached out into the dark corridor. Someone caught my fingers.

'It's me,' Myriam whispered. The feel of her hand tangled with mine took my breath away, sent heat rushing through my chilled skin.

'Did anyone see you?' she said.

'No.' I let go abruptly. 'I don't think so. It's so quiet out there.'

We stood, letting our eyes adjust to the darkness.

'Monsieur Reiss?' I asked.

'Asleep,' she said. 'Like a log. He was out until a few hours ago. He'll probably sleep till noon, at least.'

In her voice, I heard the hours that lay ahead; two, three, just for us.

'Let's go,' I whispered. 'I have to be back before Mass.'

She held my bag while I retrieved the gun from the storeroom. I didn't need to turn on the light; I could've found the weapon in my sleep. Its wooden grip was cool in my hands. I slung it over my arm by its leather strap, the way Grandfather used to, until it rested on my tailbone.

Outside, the day was lighter by a few inches. There was something quickened about it; every droplet of mist seemed alive, like bubbles in champagne. I had drunk it only once, at a cousin's wedding in Nice. I remembered the way it had scattered across my tongue, like tiny pinpricks. That was how my body felt, as we walked in silence down the narrow streets. I glanced at Myriam once, twice, then hastened my steps as the alleyway sloped uphill until we were both running, racing to the top, soft on the balls of our feet.

Where the alleyway ended, I lurched to a halt and caught her arm to hold her back. We had reached the chapel. Inside the priest would be awake, preparing his sermon, the grumbling of his stomach echoing from the stone walls.

Myriam's breath misted in small clouds. She was wearing her husband's jumper again, with dark trousers and a short jacket that might have once belonged to a suit. Her hair hung around her face. I had never seen anyone so beautiful.

'What are we waiting for?' she whispered, casting a glance around the square. 'There's no one here.'

Soon we were hurrying again, and around us the streets began to rise. The *gargouille* grew steeper, the water louder in its song. At the top of the street, I could see the school building with its iron fence and stained walls. Past that were a few villas and then the meadow: an expanse of rocks and new grasses and no one but us.

The moment the town dropped out of sight, something broke free of my chest. It was relief, I realized, like I'd never felt before. I closed my eyes and raised my head to the sky. In that almost-light I wanted to jump and scream, I wanted to fall into the long grass and spread myself out until I dissolved into the earth and roots and brittle snakeskins; I wanted to push off from the ground and feel my body come apart at the edges, fray into the air until there was nothing left except pure feeling . . .

I opened my eyes, and found Madame Reiss watching me. The coming day caught the brightness in her eyes.

'Look at you,' I thought I heard her whisper, but I wasn't sure, it could have been the wind, carrying the distant noise of the river, that sound of the lone bird, singing in the valley.

Our boots crunched in the cold mountain dirt. We followed a ridge high above the river, its sound split by distance. Myriam looked down, and stopped. The valley below clung to night and held its cold shadows close.

'Come on,' I murmured, touching her elbow. 'We're almost there.'

Beyond the curve of the hillside, I saw it. It was exactly as I had remembered: a stone hut, with a doorway on one side, built into a tumble of boulders. I leapt the last few feet towards it and sat down at its entrance. Myriam was slower to climb the final few steps. She looked tired now, but perhaps that was just the light growing stronger.

'What is this place?' she asked, staring around.

Carefully, I slid the gun from my shoulder and laid it across my lap. 'The goatherds use it during storms. It's where we always came to play, as children.'

'It must have been here a long time,' she said, lowering herself to sit on the rocks before it.

I looked up at those stone walls, beaten by weather, the leaning timber roof. It was a fixture of my world, so familiar that I'd barely given it a thought.

'It has always been here,' I said.

She laughed, that quick, breathy sound that I knew now wasn't the same as a real laugh. 'Always,' she repeated softly.

It tripped me, that noise, made me feel foolish and thick-tongued. 'Well,' I said awkwardly, 'we should make a start.'

I turned the gun upright on my lap, trying to recall the lessons from long ago, when my grandfather had taught Leon to shoot, and let me try as well. I fumbled a little, but remembered how to work the mechanism, to check the bullets. Gold gleamed back at me.

'It is loaded?' Myriam's voice was hushed in the dawn.

I nodded. 'We need to go over there.' I pointed to where a stand of trees straggled and clung to the ridge, as if peering over the lip of the ravine. 'That's where you see them, sometimes.'

Up here on the mountain, rosemary grew in clusters, alongside woody, wild sage, only just putting out new leaves. I would gather a few handfuls later, to explain my absence, if I had to. The plants released their scents as we brushed past. I could *feel* Myriam behind me, as if she were another part of my body. Near a boulder, I knelt down, almost shuddered when I felt her do the same.

I readied the gun and hunkered down to wait. Minutes passed, ten, twenty. I had no way to keep track of them, but we waited for what felt like hours. My legs began to turn numb beneath me, but I didn't want to move in case I startled anything away. After a while, a hare hopped into sight, and I tensed, my finger on the trigger. But he was nervy and stretched up on his hind legs, nose twitching. He knew we were there and before I could aim he was gone, disappearing in a rustle of grass.

I felt Myriam shift behind me, and almost turned to tell her to be still when, between one blink and another, it appeared. Not six feet away from us was a partridge, strolling pout-chested from the undergrowth, eyes roving over the ground as though it had lost a pocketwatch. My eyes filled with moisture as I raised the gun to my face, rested my cheek against the wooden grip. One squeeze, a hair's breadth of pressure on the trigger would do it . . .

Thunder exploded, jolted my body backwards. For one inexplicable moment I thought I had been shot; I thought that the crash through my body had been the force of a bullet. But then I heard Myriam's voice, calling my name. My ears were ringing and the pungent smell of hot metal and powder was all around, the noise of the shot fading into the air. I just hoped it was still too early for anyone to be awake enough to hear.

'Celeste!' Myriam was at my side, pulling my arm. 'Celeste, I think you hit it!'

'Where?' I asked stupidly, staggering to my feet.

She pointed. Down at the edge of the undergrowth was a flurry of movement. Irregular wing beats, frantic and jerking; those of a creature trying to hide itself. I walked towards it. In that clammy dawn I felt sick. The partridge must have heard me coming, because its flapping increased, its clawed feet scrabbled at the ground as it tried to rise.

'What are you going to do?' Myriam had followed me. She was staring down at the dying bird.

Silently, I handed her the gun. There was only one thing to do, and she knew it. Even so, my whole body felt weak as I knelt, and for one terrible moment, I thought I wouldn't have the strength. My shot had hit it just below the wing. It hung limp, while the other one spread and beat at the grass. It was beautiful, with chest feathers scalloped sugar-brown and black, and a fine dark streak painting its eye and neck.

The feathers were soft, clung all over with cold, and as I touched them I swallowed a sob. I had killed chickens before and thought nothing of it, even ducks, when my grandfather used to keep them, but this was different. This was a thing of the mountain and the dawn and its blood was staining the grass that cushioned my head on hot days.

The bird's struggles increased beneath my hand and I heard Myriam make a noise. 'Can you not just shoot it again?' she whispered, pleading.

'I only have five more bullets.' Tears were clogging my eyes, my nose, as I closed my hands around the bird's soft neck. I felt its life fluttering beneath my palms. I shut my eyes, gripped hard, and twisted.

I don't know how long I sat there, holding the bird's limp body, smelling the grass and the mud and the clang of fresh blood on the clean air. I was crying, I knew that, and I knew it was stupid to cry, but I couldn't stop. Then Myriam was next to me; she was making me let go of the bird, she was taking my hands in hers and holding them to her chest, she was putting her arm around my neck. She was crying too.

We clung to each other in the grass. My hands were holding hers so tightly I thought she might complain but she didn't, she only held me all the closer. My head was against her cheek, and I could feel her breath ruffling my hair, I could feel her tears, slick where my face was pressed to hers.

I felt her shift, felt a welcome warmth as, for an instant, her lips touched my forehead, right at the edge of my hairline. If I raised my head an inch or two now, would her lips find mine?

Clang, the church bells rang out, filling every inch of the valley. *Clang*, the distant bell of the

174

sanctuary answered, and it broke the moment between us, like a thread being cut. Myriam pulled away. She was pale and trembling, her eyes huge. I looked at her, my hair stuck to my face with tears. I wanted to ask her so much, wanted to *know* her, but she was taking a deep breath, and blotting her cheeks on her sleeve.

'A fine pair of hunters,' she said, but her smile shook.

I wiped my nose on my hand and turned to gather up the partridge, small in death but precious, all the same.

We were silent on the walk back. I had wrapped the gun and the remaining bullets in an old piece of oilcloth and hidden them in the darkest corner of the hut. The ridge outside was in sunlight now, the lone bird's song over-whelmed by other calls, so many they were almost raucous. I could see smoke rising from the town, could hear the church bells clanging intermittently. To the rest of the village, this was another ordinary Sunday.

Just as we were about to leave the meadow and step out on to the road, Myriam caught my hand.

I turned, expecting her to say something, but she only smiled. It was a gentle smile, and sad, not like the bitter humour that sometimes crossed her face. She placed her other hand on mine too, and squeezed.

I held on tight, as I would to a boat that was drifting away from the shallows, out into the current.

Paris

May 1993

'*Mon dieu.*' My grandmother turns her face to the sky, letting the cool, evening air fall across her skin. 'Thank God for that.'

I push the wheelchair on, mind reeling. Yesterday Grand-mère was a childhood memory, a name inside a faded birthday card, a ghost, existing only in traces of regret and hurt. Yet now here she is, sitting before me as if this were nothing more than an ordinary weekend stroll.

I have to call Mum, I have to tell her . . .

'Would you stop here, Annie?' Grand-mère asks as we pass a newspaper kiosk. I drag the chair to a halt, still tongue-tied, wanting to ask so many things but not able to put them into words.

'A copy of *Le Monde*,' she tells the newspaper seller, 'and a packet of *Gitanes*. Do you have a lighter?' She is craning her neck around to look at me.

'No,' I stutter, 'I don't smoke.'

'And a lighter, please.'

As I watch, she opens the enormous handbag that sits on her lap and extracts a leather purse. Inside is a wad of cash. She peels off a note to pay for her purchases.

'*Bon,*' she says, and tears the plastic wrap from the packet as soon as the man hands them over.

She gestures down the road. 'Shall we go?'

Speechless, I push the wheelchair forward once again. After a moment, the smoke from her cigarette coils up, catches on the cold air and fills my nostrils.

'Grand-mère,' I make myself ask, 'why didn't you *tell* us that you were here? If we had known you weren't well, Mum and I, we could have — '

I stop, my hands tightening around the plastic handles of the wheelchair. In all honesty, I don't know what we would have done. Until recently, healing the rift between Grand-mère and Mum seemed impossible. If it hadn't been for Mum's illness, her brush with death, would I even be standing here?

I hear Grand-mère sigh, the cigarette held close to her lips. 'Shall we find somewhere to eat?' she asks. I can tell she is trying to sound composed, but her voice trembles. 'I don't want to talk to you from this chair.'

I push her onwards, wondering if she's buying time, preparing her reasons, her excuses for remaining absent so long. *And what are yours?* I have to ask myself.

Half a dozen times I swallow back questions before they come tumbling from my lips. *Where have you been?* I ask the back of her head silently. *Why did you cut us off?*

'Turn right here!' she says abruptly, pointing down a side street. *Rue de l'Espérance*, the sign reads. Road of Hope.

I wheel the chair around, out of breath. Even with Grand-mère's slight frame, it's hard work. 'What's down here?' I ask.

She knocks the ash from her cigarette, and I see the side of her face raise in a smile. 'A good meal, I hope. I owe you that, at the very least.'

The road slopes gently upward, turning from tarmac to cobble. The wheelchair rattles and bounces, but Grand-mère doesn't complain. She's looking about. 'I used to like coming here, of an evening,' she murmurs.

Soon we come to a restaurant, with tables on the pavement and a burgundy awning. It's elegant and busy, even the outside tables are crowded with people enjoying aperitifs beneath the heaters. I push the chair inside, feeling scruffy amongst the smartly dressed diners.

'Hello,' I murmur to the waiter, who appears. 'I don't suppose — '

'We'll take that table.' Before I can move, Grand-mère is pushing herself out of the chair. Automatically, the waiter catches her elbow.

'*Merci*, young man.' She smiles at him. 'And you can take the chair away. Throw it in the Seine, for all I care.'

The waiter laughs, and soon another one appears to help me fold the chair and wedge it behind the coat rack.

Sitting opposite Grand-mère with only a small, round table top between us, my skin prickles. Is this what I thought I'd be doing, yesterday afternoon, as I stared down at her file, surrounded by salt dust?

Her eyes are taking in my face, my pulled-back hair, frizzing at the edges now, my nose, my cheekbones.

'Annie,' she says. 'Little Annie. Look at you.'

Abruptly, her face changes. 'Do you mind that I call you that? Or should it be Anna?'

'Everyone calls me Annie,' I say quietly.

'But which do you prefer?' She leans towards me, her eyes serious. 'What do you like to be called?'

'Annie is OK,' I tell her. 'It's . . . what you used to call me.'

She turns her head away, her eyes swimming with moisture.

'Excuse me,' she calls to a waiter, who is hurrying past. 'Do you have any *génépi*?'

He smiles. 'I believe so, Madame.'

'Bring us two, please.'

I have no idea what she's ordered, but something tells me not to interrupt as she takes out a cigarette, lights it with difficulty. Her hands are shaking, not just with age. She is as nervous and confused about this meeting as I am.

The waiter returns with two small glasses of liqueur. It's a golden-green colour, like expensive olive oil. Slowly, Grand-mère picks hers up, raises it to her nose to smell it. I do the same. It smells spicy, a sort of herby greenness with a hot slap of alcohol. It's for courage, I realize. It's to give her the strength to sit here and talk to me.

'Shouldn't we drink to something?' I ask awkwardly, as she raises the glass to her lips.

She stops. 'What to?'

I think of the archives, of the file in my bag and an old address, a photograph and the story of a man in the Square des Peupliers.

'To the past?'

My grandmother watches me for a moment,

179

her brown eyes thoughtful. In her other hand, the cigarette is burning down to ash. 'The past,' she repeats. 'Yes, I suppose we must.'

She raises the glass without touching it to mine and drinks it down in one. I take a sip. The liqueur is strong, makes me cough. Grand-mère laughs a little when she sees that.

'Artemisia,' she says, rescuing her cigarette. 'Wormwood. It grew wild on the mountains at home. We used to pick the flowers in the summer, and my father would wrap them in muslin and steep them in alcohol for the winter, when we needed the fire of the sun in our blood.'

'It's bitter.' I take another cautious sip.

'Yes,' she says. 'It is.'

Before I can ask any more questions, the waiter is back, and we have to pretend to be normal once again. Grand-mère orders extravagantly: onion soup and sea bass in a rich sauce and potatoes and good wine and bread. I nod along, ordering what she does, unable to consider anything else at that moment.

'Can I ask a question?' I say, once the wine has arrived, before I lose my nerve.

My grandmother nods once, motioning for me to pour. 'Of course you can.'

I swallow. 'You mentioned home, the mountains. Do you mean Saint-Antoine?' I remember the name from the file. 'Is that where you're from? If so, why didn't you go back there? Why did you leave in the first place? Did something happen?'

'No.' The word is sharp, so vehement that the people at the next table glance over. My grandmother works her mouth, attempts to smile. 'That is not a question for before dinner.' She's trying to be casual, but it isn't working. She takes a gulp of wine. 'Let me ask you a question instead please, Annie.'

I reach for my glass. 'Go ahead.'

She's watching me intently, studying my face. 'How did you find me?'

Steadily, we work our way through our carafe of wine. I forget all of my tiredness as I talk, barely paying attention to the soup when it arrives. I'm still talking when the waiter clears the plates, brings the main course. The smell of wine and herbs and butter rising from the dish makes my stomach rumble.

Grand-mère is shaking her head. 'You really went to the old square?' she asks. Her eyes are bright with interest.

I nod, mouth full.

'I remember that man, I think.' She closes her eyes. 'He was an irritating fellow. But he helped us, a few times, I seem to recall.'

'He said you worked in a bakery.'

She nods. 'At the *Boulangerie du Marché*, in Saint-Germain. The owner's son had been killed in the fighting, so they needed an extra pair of hands.'

'I don't think I would have found you, if I hadn't stopped in a bakery,' I say. 'They made the most wonderful-looking bread there — '

Her chest hitches and I see wetness glistening on her lashes.

'Grand-mère.' I lean across the table and reach for her hand. She squeezes back, but then pulls

181

away, swiping at her eyes with her napkin.

'Stupid, stupid of me,' she mutters. She takes a long, ragged breath. 'And what of your mother?' she asks. Her face is etched with longing. 'You haven't told me about her. How is she?'

I stare at her. *Do I lie? Evade the question?* But I can't, not with her.

'She's fine, now,' I say, staring at the tablecloth.

'*Now?*' Grand-mère goes still. 'What do you mean?' When I don't answer, she leans in, tries to catch my eye. 'Annie, what haven't you told me?'

'She was ill,' I whisper. Tears flood my eyes, and I'm crying, the way I haven't for months, the way I never let myself, around Mum. 'She was really ill, and I was so scared that she might not . . . But the treatment worked,' I try to smile, 'and she's got the all-clear for now, so . . . '

I can't go on, have to clench my hands in my lap until I can get myself back under control.

'I haven't told her that I've found you yet,' I murmur, when I can speak again. 'She's the one who asked me to start looking. She wants to say that she's sorry, that it's time we were a family again.'

There's silence from the other side of the table. When I look up, I see that my grandmother has her hand pressed to her forehead.

'This is my fault,' she says, voice broken. 'I was always a bad mother, I never knew what to do.' She looks up at me and her lined face is wracked with guilt, pain. 'How can either of you ever forgive me?'

I push back the chair. The next moment, my arms are around her. She clings to me, and I can feel the dampness of her tears through my shirt. 'It's already forgiven, Grand-mère,' I tell her, 'everything is forgiven.'

She pulls back, shaking her head. 'No,' she tells me, and her eyes are haunted. 'It isn't.'

Saint-Antoine

April 1943

The day I shot the bird, I became a liar. Not that I hadn't lied in the past, but those had been small lies, the lies of a child. The ones I began to tell that day were different, dangerous.

Myriam wanted to come with me when I took the bird to trade, but I told her no. It was risky enough for me to go alone, me, who knew the town and its people. I left her at the door of the bakery. We stood there for a long, silent moment, the town awakening around us and the toes of our boots almost touching. Paul had kissed me here again, a few days ago, and all I'd wanted was to step away from him. How different this felt.

'Will you come and see me again soon?' she asked. There was a hint of uncertainty in her voice, as if I might say no.

'Of course,' I told her. 'Of course I will.'

I couldn't watch her go back inside, knowing that she would creep up the dark stairs, perhaps even slide back into bed next to Monsieur Reiss. Instead, I turned and ran downhill, following the water that tumbled headlong through the gutter.

Instead of taking the street towards my grandmother's house, I struck out along the main road. The people I was going to see lived outside the town, in every sense, even though they were as old a family as any. They never came to church, rarely involved themselves in local business, and yet, somehow, they knew everything that went on in Saint-Antoine. On the surface of things, they were farmers, with a flock of goats on the mountain. But if they produced milk or cheese, we never saw it. The town gossips said that the goats were just a cover, a reason for being up so high, near the pass into Italy; that the Rochers had been smuggling and poaching for years now.

I wiped sweating hands on my trousers, hitched the satchel a little higher. Up ahead, at the top of a steep slope, I could see the Rocher house. It was almost hidden, but what was visible was in a sorry state. Its walls were green with mildew, the broken windows mended scrappily with wood.

I walked as quietly as I could through the trees towards it. There were sounds from the house: a baby crying, a snatch of conversation, a fuzzing voice that must have come from the wireless. At the edge of the mud-churned yard, I hesitated.

Something clicked near by, and my heart locked in my chest. I turned my head a fraction to see the dark length of a rifle pointed at me from the trees.

'What do you want?'

I didn't recognize the voice.

'I . . . ' My throat was dry from walking. 'I just — '

'Mam'selle!' someone cried. To my relief the Rocher twins came skidding around the side of the house. 'What're you doing here? Bring us any bread?'

'Not today, boys,' I managed, though my hands still trembled uselessly at my sides.

'Mam'selle?' the voice with the gun said, and I was finally able to turn. Beyond the barrel was a young man, heavyset, with pale eyes and a beard that covered his face from chin to cheekbone. Carelessly, he lowered the weapon and laughed. 'Ceci,' he said, eyes travelling over my trousered legs, the belt cinching them to my waist. 'You've grown.'

'*Bonjour*, Michel.' I spoke carefully. 'I didn't know you were home.'

Michel was older than me by a few years. He was one of the only people Leon had ever been afraid of. Rumour had it that Michel had deserted the French army during the surrender like a rat from a ship. People said he had been living wild since then. He was a criminal, said some, like the rest of the Rochers. He was *Résistance*, said others.

'Not going to tell our Italian friends I'm here, I hope?' Michel said, tapping his boot with the gun. 'Heard some of you girls have been getting too friendly with them of late.'

'Not Mam'selle,' Nino Rocher piped up. 'She threw a loaf of *pain bis* at Capitano Rossi the other day.'

Before I could answer, or smile, the door creaked again.

'What is going on?' Madame Rocher was standing in the kitchen doorway, staring at me. She looked thin, hair streaked with grey, but I

186

knew she was as tough as any of her sons. 'What are you doing here?' she said.

I fumbled open the satchel and pulled out the dead bird.

'Have you anything to trade?'

Madame Rocher jerked her chin. Michel came forward to take the partridge from me. I felt a strange rush of loss as it left my grip, as if it still retained the feel of Myriam's hands in mine.

'For this old thing?' Michel asked, but I could tell he was interested, checking the bird's wings. 'Where'd you get it?'

I put my hands in my pockets, so he wouldn't see them shaking. 'That's my business. Can you trade or not?'

He exchanged a look with his mother. 'What did you have in mind?'

'We need salt at the bakery. We have contacts for flour and oil but we can't get salt.'

Michel shrugged. 'For this? A little, maybe.'

'There'll be more.' The words sounded desperate, but all at once I didn't care. 'More birds; maybe rabbit or hare. I'll give you first pick.'

'Salt.' Michel nodded mockingly. 'Anything else?'

Sweat prickled cold beneath my arms as I stared him down. There were dozens of other things I could ask for: honey for *pain au miel*, cinnamon and currants and butter for *brioche*, sugar even. But my thoughts were treacherous. 'Cigarettes,' I said, thinking of Myriam: 'Women aren't allowed to buy them any more. And bullets, for a rifle, if you can get any.'

'You're a surprising little thing,' Michel laughed. 'Does your gendarme know about this?'

187

I felt my jaw clench. The Rochers always did know everybody else's business. 'No,' I said. 'And he doesn't need to. Are you going to tell him?'

He looked at me, lips curling beneath his beard. 'No,' he said.

'*Bon*,' his mother announced briskly from the door. 'You bring us more meat and we'll see what we can do. No promises.'

No promises . . . She couldn't have known that there was only one promise I was interested in keeping; the one I'd made to Myriam, to see her again.

And yet, as the days went on, she seemed to disappear into one of her long absences. Two days became four, and still I didn't see her. Paul continued to call by the bakery every day. Mama made a fuss whenever she saw him and sometimes Papa would clap him on the shoulder and wink. I tried not to notice.

Frustratingly, I saw Monsieur Reiss regularly enough. He sometimes returned to the bakery very late, when we had already begun our night's work.

'It is Passover,' he told us, sliding out of his sodden coat at nearly three o'clock in the morning one night, shaking the water from his hat. 'I've been at a Seder.'

'Passover?' I asked, pushing the hair back from my sweaty forehead, wondering if that was why Myriam had locked herself away.

'A special festival,' he said with a smile. 'I'm afraid you might have fewer customers this week. We don't eat leavened bread on these days. I had quite a few questions to answer from the old folk

188

about our staying in a bakery.'

Papa only grunted a laugh. 'Don't let the Italians catch you out so late. They don't like it.'

'They gave their permission for the Seder,' Monsieur Reiss said easily. 'The *capitano* has been quite understanding.'

He soon disappeared upstairs, and though I listened to the creak of footsteps, strained my ears to catch a murmur of voices, I didn't hear anything, and I had to get back to work. It was a welcome distraction. The act of baking was in my blood, had shaped my muscles. Papa and I rested when the bread did, taking our own *repos*. We drank acorn coffee while the mixture drank cool water. When it was time to turn the proving loaves, we turned too, switched positions between the ovens and the counter. Sometimes I wondered, as we shaped the bread, whether we weren't shaping our own thoughts; deep, silent thoughts that rose slowly like leavening, that could only exist while other people slept.

Moment by moment, the long night turned into another long morning. Despite what Monsieur Reiss had said, we still had plenty of customers. I supposed that people were too hungry to be strict about religion, these days. I knew for certain that none of the townspeople in Saint-Antoine were observing Lent. If a chocolate éclair were to fall from the sky and land in their laps they would have eaten it in one ecstatic gulp, no matter what holy day it was.

It was on Good Friday, almost a week after I had last seen Myriam, that the rain began. It fell ceaselessly, battered the bakery windows in gusts. I hated it. It felt as if the new spring that Myriam and I had shared — tender, green and fragile as blossom — was being drowned, trampled into mud by that pitiless fall of water.

The morning rush had been and gone, and now was the quiet time, after lunch. There was a lot to do. Papa had caught the bus down into the valley, to see about getting some more flour; he had left me to shape the last of the dough we had made earlier that day, so we could take some to dinner with Paul's parents that evening, as Mama had arranged.

For some reason, however hard I tried, I couldn't get the shape of the loaves right. No matter how deftly I twisted or how hard I punched the dough, they all looked wrong.

I swore, squashed the dough back into a ball and threw another handful of flour on to the counter. It rose into the air and got into my eyes, making them sting. I swore again and dragged the hem of my blouse from my skirt, to wipe my face. Over the sound of the rain, I didn't hear the stairs creak. All I saw was the door to the apartment swinging open.

I looked up.

She stepped down into the corridor and came forward to stand by the ovens; not an idea, not an impulse or a fevered thought, but real, wrapped in a fraying wool cardigan. Her hair was flattened on one side, as if she had been lying down, her nose red at the tip. Something tender pulled in my chest.

'Are you all right?' she said, though I should have asked her.

I didn't know. Everything felt different in her presence. I became aware of myself, of my heart thudding beneath the cotton of my blouse, my arms covered in flour.

'I missed you,' I said, unable to stop myself.

'You did?'

'Yes.'

I wanted to reach for her. Maybe it was the memory of her hand catching mine, or her lips pressed against my hair. I risked a look into her eyes. Today, they were grey-blue, shifting between the colours like clouds on a distant peak of ice.

'I missed you too,' she said.

Two steps separated us, no more than two, a small movement across the worn stone floor, and yet it might as well have been a chasm. I imagined striding over to her but what then? I wiped my hands convulsively on my apron.

'Could you . . . ?' I asked, voice a husk in my throat. 'Could you pass me that cloth?' A scrap of linen lay on the counter next to her.

'This?' she asked, as if she knew I didn't really need it.

I watched as she picked it up and crossed the distance between us.

'Here,' she said, but I'd already forgotten about it, all I could see was how perfect the dark sweep of her eyebrow was, how flushed the skin over her cheek.

Her eyes were on me. I felt them lingering over the corner of my mouth, my ear. Almost absent-mindedly, she raised a hand and brushed my forehead.

'There's flour in your hair,' she whispered.

I didn't think any more. My body moved as if it knew what to do without me and I was leaning forward, touching my lips to hers. For a moment, she didn't move. Then with a rush of breath she was kissing me back. Her hands reached up and found my neck, my hair, and nerves were shooting through me, gathering at my core, making me shiver with heat, like a bath that scalds.

She leaned in and my back met the counter, our bodies were pressed together breasts against breasts, hip to hip, hers slim and angular, mine rounded by muscle. Her hands were cool on my neck. One of them slipped down my throat to brush my collarbone, the curve of my breast, and I couldn't help the noise that broke from me, hushed almost immediately by her mouth, finding mine once more, as I reached for her waist —

A noise cut through our breathing, reaching our ears a second too late. The sound of the bell above the door: someone stepping into the shop. We froze, separated from whoever it was by only a thin wall and the doorway to the kitchen, our eyes wide, lips inches apart.

'Hello?' someone called, a man's voice. It was the *capitano*, I realized, here to collect some bread for his men.

'Just a moment,' I called, pulling at my chemise with shaking hands, swiping at my face.

Just before I reached the door, Myriam snatched at my arm, pulled me back.

'Sunday,' she whispered, and pressed her lips to mine.

Paris

May 1993

'Is everything all right?'

The waiter is leaning over the edge of the table, a concerned frown on his face. Around us, people are trying not to stare.

'Fine.' My grandmother raises her head and looks at the waiter, though I can see how grey her skin looks suddenly, how her neck is straining. 'We are fine. Perhaps you could bring us some coffee?'

'*Bien sûr*,' the waiter says, clearing our plates.

I go back to my chair, shaken. Grand-mère has taken a tin from her handbag and is fumbling it open, spilling a few pills on to the tablecloth. I watch as she swallows two of them with the rest of her wine.

'Grand-mère,' I ask carefully, 'what happened to make you leave France? What happened in Saint-Antoine?'

She doesn't meet my gaze. 'It is a long story.'

'We have an hour and a half before you have to be back at the *Résidence*.'

An expression flashes across her face, a touch of anger and defiance.

'Wait,' she says, 'I want to show you something.'

From her bag she takes two envelopes. One

looks old and thin, brown paper with worn edges. The other is new and stuffed full of something. She hesitates, then hands me the thicker one.

'Open it,' she says, putting the other envelope away.

I do. Inside is a wad of banknotes. 'What . . . ?' I ask, looking down at all those francs. 'What is this?'

'I've been saving for years.' Her hands are folded tightly around her almost empty wine glass. 'I can pay for the trip, and more besides.'

'The trip?' All at once the conversation with nurse Alain comes back to me, the dreaded name of her condition. 'Grand-mère, are you all right?'

'As soon as I saw you, I knew it was time. I have been too afraid to go on my own.'

'What are you talking about?' I ask, as gently as I can.

'Saint-Antoine.' Her voice cracks on the name. 'I have to go there. There's a sleeper train that leaves from Gare d'Austerlitz at ten o'clock on Saturdays. We can be in Nice before morning.'

I stare at her, dumbfounded.

'You can't . . . ' I stutter. 'You can't just go to Nice, you're not well.'

'I know that.' She meets my eyes. 'I can feel it, Annie, I can feel it all starting to slip away. I have to go back there while I'm still myself, before it's too late. And now you're here.' The strange look of fear crosses her face again. 'I have to go.'

I don't know what to say, can only stare at her. Is this rational or some delusion? If I knew her better, as an adult, I might be able to tell.

I look away, trying to think. Catch-22. I can't let her run away from the nursing home and get on a train to the South of France by herself when she's obviously unwell. And I can't go with her either; I can't enable . . . whatever this is.

It's only Saturday, a treacherous voice whispers, *you don't have to be back at work until Tuesday.*

'Annie.' I look back to find Grand-mère watching me, her anxious expression replaced by a sad smile. 'Let's go for a walk, shall we? The way we used to.'

Outside, evening has fallen. The streets are busy, headlights and tail lights glimmering in the dusk, the noise of engines and car horns mingling with the music that spills from bars. I push the chair along the grand boulevards in silence, broken only by Grand-mère's occasional quiet directions. Perhaps each of us is trying to decide how to convince the other that they are wrong.

When we reach the Boulevard Raspail, Grand-mère gestures for me to go straight.

'Grand-mère,' I murmur, wheeling her chair to one side to avoid a group of tourists, 'where are we going?'

She doesn't answer. I sigh. The effect of the wine and the coffee and the nerves are wearing off and the chair is getting harder and harder to push. Every café we pass, every table beneath a heater, begins to look more tempting, even though I know I'll soon have to take Grand-mère back to the *Résidence*.

'Are we going anywhere in particular?' I try again, as we reach yet another crossroads. There's no response. I drag the chair to a stop. 'Grand-mère?' I ask.

Her face is pale and set, her eyes staring straight ahead. At first I think she hasn't heard me, but then she raises a finger and points.

'We're going there,' she says.

Up ahead there's a grand building, wrapping around the corner of the boulevard. Huge, gold letters adorn the front.

'Hotel Lutetia,' I read. 'Grand-mère, I can't go in there, I'm not dressed for it.'

'Please, Annie,' she says softly. 'I want to. It is important to me.'

Reluctantly, I wheel her towards the carpeted entrance. I can't look at the uniformed doorman, and duck my head, waiting for him to take one look at the state of me and sneer, *Je suis désolé . . .*

'*Bonjour, mesdames,*' he says politely, and opens the door, allowing me to push the chair into the lobby.

It's even grander inside, with a black-and-white tiled floor and lighting that makes everything seem golden. The place smells of lilies and fine leather. Grand-mère's eyes are wide, her hands gripping her bag so hard that her knuckles are white.

'Two for the bar, please,' she tells the concierge.

The man nods courteously, though not, I see, without a sideways glance at my attire. We follow him into a room filled with deep-red velvety armchairs and polished tables. Without a word, he helps my grandmother out of the wheelchair.

'Would you like to see our wine list?' he asks her smoothly, ignoring me entirely.

'No,' Grand-mère says. 'We'll have champagne. Your best. Two glasses.'

Although my grandmother's face looks calmer than before, I can see her agitation in the way her eyes flick constantly to the walls, the door; in the way her fingers work against each other.

'What's going on?' I whisper, once the waiter has left.

She smiles a little fixedly. 'You wanted to drink to the past. That is what we're doing.'

The waiter returns with two coupes of champagne, straw-gold, the bubbles catching the light. Grand-mère touches the glass with her fingers but doesn't lift it.

'I used to come here every day,' she tells me, 'when we lived on the Square des Peupliers. Sometimes twice, morning and evening.'

'How could you afford it?' I frown. 'The man in the square said no one had any money.'

'I didn't come to drink. I came to wait. And to look.' She lifts the glass, holds it towards me. 'This is the first time I have ever drunk here. I'm so pleased that it is with you, Annie.'

She touches the glass to mine. It rings, softly, clearly.

To the past.

The champagne fills my mouth, prickling my tongue, my lips. It must be the tiredness, because it goes straight to my head. Grand-mère is also blinking rapidly, half her glass empty already.

'Oh dear.' She smiles slightly, sits back in her chair. 'I never was much of a one for alcohol. I remember, on my wedding day, I drank too much . . . '

Her eyelids flicker, and she presses a hand to her forehead. 'Grand-mère,' I lean forward, 'are you feeling all right?'

'I am fine.' But her voice sounds vague, her hand tremoring. She opens her eyes, summons the waiter with a smile. 'Just the champagne. Perhaps you could point the way to the bathroom, young man?'

The waiter smiles back and offers his arm. 'Of course, Madame.'

He helps Grand-mère out into the lobby, towards the large golden door of the ladies' toilets. I wander behind, feeling awkward.

'Do you need any help?' I ask.

'No, no.' She waves a hand. 'I will not be long.'

I walk back across the tiled floor, feeling as if I've swallowed something far more than champagne, something fitful and shadowy, too big to fit inside my skin. The maître d' is watching me, a telephone receiver pressed to his ear. It gives me an idea.

'Excuse me,' I whisper, 'is there a telephone I can use?'

He points towards the rear of the cavernous lobby with his pencil, where a bank of payphones is tucked discreetly out of sight.

I walk towards them, digging through my pockets for change. Now or never. The coins stick to my hands as I slot them into the phone, and I have to force myself to dial a series of familiar digits: my mother's mobile telephone number. It won't be working in the Pacific, but I know she checks the voicemail every day. It's our arrangement. The dialling tone gives way to a long silence, as the call travels huge distances over oceans, over continents, to send this message plummeting to earth like a falling star.

A crackle, and then I hear a voice, asking me to leave a message. I clutch the phone to my ear.

'Mum,' I say and have to clear my throat. 'Mum, it's me. Everything's fine but . . .' There are too many words, not enough time. 'I don't know how to start this. Mum, I've found Grand-mère. I know you only asked me to look yesterday, but I checked the files at work, and I found a record for her and now — ' I gulp back tears, abruptly forgetting all about breaking the news to her carefully, about managing her expectations. 'I found her, Mum. She's alive. She's in a nursing home in Paris. She's not well, the nurse told me that she has dementia, and now she has this crazy idea about going south, about going home, she says, to Saint-Antoine, while she still can.'

The phone starts bleeping, my money running out too fast. Frantically, I shove in my last centimes.

'Mum, I don't know what to do. I can't leave her on her own. I'm going to try and persuade her to wait, until we can plan this better, until you're back, but I don't know if — '

The bleeping starts up again. I almost yell in frustration, searching my pockets uselessly for money.

'I'll call again soon. I'm so sorry to tell you like this, Mum.' The beeping increases, I have only seconds. 'I love you — '

Too late. The phone cuts off; I'm left with the flat, empty tone. Shakily, I drop the handset back on to the cradle. For a long time, I stare at it. It must be almost nine now, time for Grand-mère to be back at the home. How long will it be before they realize something is wrong? *They won't, I tell myself, because she's going back, right now. All this talk of the past, it's my fault for showing up unannounced. I shouldn't have stirred things up like this.*

Resolutely, I turn towards the bar. As I do, a plaque on the wall catches my eye. I glance up at it as I pass, only to stop, the words holding me fast.

From April to August 1945, this hotel was transformed into a reception centre to receive a large number of survivors from concentration camps . . . The joy of those returned could not erase the anguish and the pain of the families of the disappeared, who waited for them in this place in vain.

The breath catches in my throat.

I didn't come to drink. I came to wait. And to look.

I stumble into a run, back towards the toilets. I feel so stupid; it all makes sense now. My mother never knew her father, she always said he'd died soon after she was born, but I never put two and two together, I never thought . . .

I wrench open the door, ignoring the maître d's incredulous stare. The toilets are empty, and I race back across the lobby, into the bar. I have to tell Grand-mère that I know why she's afraid to go back to Saint-Antoine, that I understand.

The waiter who served us looks up in alarm.

'Mademoiselle?' he asks, but I don't hear him because past his shoulder, the table where Grand-mère should be sitting is empty. Her bag is gone.

'Where is she?' I demand in English, forgetting to speak French in my panic. 'Where did she go?'

The waiter's eyebrows shoot up.

'Madame requested a taxi,' he says, looking bemused. 'I believe it has just arrived.' He indicates a door on the other side of the room, leading out on to the street.

I trip forward, grabbing my bag from underneath the table, sending the wheelchair flying. I don't care, my eyes are fixed on the doors, on the glowing taxi sign and what looks like a driver, opening his door, climbing inside . . . I push past a doorman and stumble out on to the pavement just as the car pulls away.

'*Arrêt!*' I scream, slapping my hand down on the back of the cab. 'Stop!'

To my amazement, it does, brake lights flaring. The driver's head appears, yelling, but I ignore him and yank open the back door.

Inside is a small, hunched figure, her bag at her feet.

'Grand-mère,' I burst out. 'What are you doing?'

Her eyes find mine. 'I thought you were calling

the *Résidence*,' she says, lips trembling. 'I can't let that happen, Annie. I'm going back, while I still remember.'

'I know, Grand-mère,' I say, sliding in next to her and taking her worn hand in mine. 'I know. I'm coming with you.'

Saint-Antoine

April 1943

I laboured up the hill in the early-morning light. The knapsack was heavy, and sweat was already beginning to prickle my shoulder blades, though the sun had barely risen over the ridge of the mountain.

I smiled to myself. Soon, the church bells would start ringing for the Sabbath. Easter Sunday. I hitched the bag up higher as I took the path towards the meadow, pushed my hair off my face and hurried on, wanting to squeeze every last blink and breath out of the morning.

When I reached the hut, I slid the knapsack from my aching shoulders. Everything looked exactly as I had left it, even the gun, but I wasn't here for that. Not today. Propping the bag upright in the corner, I checked I had a kerchief in my pocket then set off back down the path at a run, my boots skidding on the stones, my skirt flapping around my legs. Out of sight, I sat and waited for her to arrive.

Sunday. As the sun crept over the peaks, soft as the paws of a stalking cat, I turned my face to it. To think, that most of the village would soon be buttoning itchy church clothes, walking the shadow-cold streets to Mass, to sit in the chilly darkness and hear their sins read back to them.

None of that for the foreigners. On most Sunday mornings they did their washing, the women calling to each other, bringing pots of bitter root coffee to share, while the men gossiped in the square and the young people went for hikes, or played football, or paddled in the river, too cold still for swimming. *That* was a Sunday. But ours would be even better.

The sun seemed to seep into my skin and I imagined how it might feel to lay my forehead against Myriam's, warm in sleep. Then, I heard a scraping on the path, the sound of feet and I leapt up, tumbled out in expectation and joy.

Myriam gasped when I appeared, but a second later she was smiling.

'You made me jump,' she laughed. 'I thought you were a wild animal.'

Her cheeks were pink from exertion, but she looked fresh and bright, her eyes clear, sunglasses pushed back into her curling hair. For a few breaths, I could only stare at her, hardly daring to believe that she was here, that this day was ours.

'How did you get away?' she asked. 'Aren't you supposed to be at church?'

I felt a smile tug at the corners of my mouth. 'I said I was walking to the sanctuary of the Madonna, to take the monks some Easter bread. And to pray for my sins on this holy day.'

'You're a devil.'

'And what about you?' I asked. 'What excuse did you give?'

'None at all. Daniel was fast asleep when I left.'

Was he out again, late into the night? I wanted

204

to ask, but I pushed it aside.

'Come on.' I held out my hand. She took it.

A little way along the path was a grassy bank. 'Here,' I said, bending down. 'What do you see?'

She frowned, but it was a smiling frown, as she peered where I was pointing. 'Leaves,' she said.

'And?'

'And more leaves. Is this a trick?'

'No.' I leaned forward to push some of the leaves aside and show her what she had been missing.

Wild strawberries were clustered on the green stems; they were tiny, some no bigger than a pea, but I knew how they deceived, how they would burst on the tongue. They weren't quite ripe, flushed pink rather than red, but still, the sight of them filled me with joy.

Myriam let out a laugh and leaned closer. 'I would never have known,' she said.

'Here.' I pulled the ripest from a stem and hesitantly held it to her lips.

'My God,' she murmured after a moment. 'It tastes like . . . sour apples and sherbet.' She looked at me. 'I am amazed I can even remember what sherbet tastes like.'

'Pick a few,' I said, handing her the kerchief. 'They'll go with breakfast.'

'Breakfast?' she asked, but I was already running back towards the hut.

Hauling the knapsack on to my back again, I called to her and she followed me, past the hut, deeper into the meadow. It had grown in the past week, thanks to the beating sun, the bursts of rain. The grass was now almost waist-high, a green sea that rustled around our knees and caught at our clothes. It was studded with flowers, too, cow parsley and yellow-eyed marguerites just opening, waxy buttercups and bright, pink clovers. When we were in the centre of the meadow, far enough so that no one would happen upon us, I dropped to my knees and slid the bag from my back.

'What are you doing?' Myriam asked, catching her breath.

'Don't laugh,' I commanded, then dropped to my front and started to roll back and forth, crushing the stems beneath me, wrinkling my nose at the feel of patches of mud. By the time I had finished, a flattened circle was formed in the grass and Myriam was shaking her head, smiling.

'You are the strangest girl I have ever met.'

I didn't answer, only reached up, my heart beating fast from the movement and the excitement. I took her hands and pulled her down beside me.

'But look,' I said, 'now we're safe.'

The grass and flowers rose all around, shielding us, enclosing us in green walls.

Myriam's eyes found mine. Then she was reaching out, and our lips were meeting, breath disappearing into skin. My mouth grazed her cheek, her chin, her hair before finding her lips again. Her hands were gripping my blouse as she pulled me closer, exhaling my name. She tasted of wild strawberry and smoke and *her*, something indefinable, too wonderful for words.

Finally, we pulled away, and she put a hand against my cheek.

'My girl,' she whispered, and I reached for her again, but she sat back, a wry smile on her face. 'You promised me breakfast.'

I couldn't ignore that, and so I tried to collect myself, tried to stop my mind from racing, to cool the heat that was pulsing through me as I unpacked the knapsack. Myriam watched as I took out the packages, wrapped in muslin and newspaper, as I spread a scrap of old sack on the ground. First, I laid out the few strawberries we had picked, then a tiny amount of soft goat's cheese, so fresh and pale it barely held together, bartered yesterday from a farmer on the outskirts of the town. The last package I didn't open, but offered up to her.

'This is for you,' I said, blushing despite everything.

She smiled questioningly, but didn't speak as she loosened the ties on the cloth. Inside was a loaf of bread, one that I had made the day before, in the hush of a late Saturday afternoon when no one else was around. I had stolen an egg from grandmother's chickens to make it; I had scavenged the last few drops of precious orange blossom essence from the old, sticky glass bottle, the one with Arabic writing upon it. I had added the flour and water from the *gargouille*, had let it trickle through my fingers into the mixture, remembering our day in the forest, the smell of violets and the taste of old stone.

I had folded and turned and watched the dough with care as it rose, timing it by instinct alone. Now, I looked down at the small loaf of bread in her hands. It wasn't perfect, nothing like it should have been, but it was something just for her.

'It's supposed to be a *fougassette*,' I told her. 'They used to be my favourite. We haven't made any for a long time now. The ingredients are too expensive.' I looked down at it. 'It's not very good. It's supposed to be white, not dark and heavy like that. And it should have sugar, and almonds, but I couldn't get any. I . . . I just wanted to make something, for you.'

Myriam was staring down at the bread, her face so still that for a moment I thought she didn't understand.

'I thought I'd find nothing but death in this town,' she whispered, face twisting.

I kissed her lips then, trying to make her see how I felt, even when I didn't know how to say the words.

Eventually, we sat back and ate. It was so different from the meals of the town below. Everything there tasted weak and eked out. *Sirops* that were nothing but a ghost of flavour in the water, chicken stew that was all strands and no substance, potatoes cut to pieces to avoid the green or the mould; bitter, black acorn water instead of the richness of coffee.

But this meal was simple, it was raw and right. It tasted of summer to come, when the fruit trees and vegetable patches would put colour back into our cheeks; when the earth would bloom and life would spring despite the fear and chaos.

Around us, the day grew warmer, but we were protected, surrounded by high grass, its scent as sharp as a June apple. No one could see us here, only the shy creatures of the mountain and the birds, who called out *huit-heure, huit-heure,* as if to remind us of the time.

Myriam's skin was so pale in the sunlight. My hands looked coarse and brown in comparison, tangling with hers before she let go to release one button of my blouse. I had felt bold earlier, but now I trembled as the garment slipped from my shoulder.

'Celeste,' she breathed, lips lingering over my neck, my collarbone, until I couldn't keep my eyes open any more, because I thought I might break apart.

So this is what it means, I thought wildly, as her lips returned to mine, and her hand brushed my legs beneath my skirt, my thighs. No one had ever touched me like that before; not even myself. For endless, glorious minutes, nothing else existed, nothing but breath and skin and her.

I lay with closed eyes, listening to the breeze rustle the stems. In the town below, church bells were clanging out their strange, raucous rhythm. Myriam's head was resting against mine, our hands entwined, and I could see the edge of a smile on her face.

'Have you ever known others — like me?' I asked, though it sounded clumsy.

'I've known no one like you.' Her hand smoothed my hair, coming loose from its plait. 'I promise you that.' Her eyes met mine. 'But you are asking if I've been with other women?'

I nodded, marvelling at how she could speak so calmly, so directly, with no shame.

'Yes,' she murmured, her fingers tracing the

shape of my nose, my lip. 'Yes, there have been others.'

'And what about Daniel?' I almost didn't want to ask, wanted this time to be for us alone, but there was so much I was desperate to know.

'What about him?' I heard the touch of defiance in her voice.

'Does he know, about . . . ?' I trailed off, wishing I had the words.

'He knew me before we were married,' she said, propping herself on to an elbow. 'He knew my friends. So yes, he knew that our marriage was never going to be a conventional one.' Her eyes fell from mine. 'Of course, so much has changed. Before, in Brussels, it somehow made sense, but here . . . When so many people see you as one thing, it is hard to remember what you were before.'

'Do you love him?' It came out as a whisper.

I watched the thoughts shifting behind her grey eyes, as if she was trying to decide what to tell me.

'There are different kinds of love,' she said in the end. 'I care for Daniel deeply. He's a good man, a good husband.' She met my eyes again. 'But he can't give me everything I want.'

Compared to her, I felt hopelessly inexperienced. And yet, as we reluctantly packed up and left our protective grass circle, the memory of her lingered, the feel of her, our hands tangled together, the sound of her voice as she whispered to me, clear and unashamed into the warm spring air.

On the path below the hut, she tidied my hair,

pulling seed pods and bits of grass from the strands. I did the same, combing out her curls with my fingers.

'There's a grass stain on your shirt,' I said, unable to stop smiling, even though I knew we'd soon have to leave each other.

She craned over her shoulder. 'So there is. No matter. I will say I stopped and took a nap beneath a tree, like someone in a fable.'

The happiness of that morning filled me to the brim, even as anxiety and fear bubbled beneath it. It seemed impossible that I should feel so much at once. Even the prospect of spending another evening with Paul and his parents couldn't dim my mood.

We approached the bakery from the main street, following the *gargouille*'s course. I had intended to leave Myriam at the back door, steal a last, hurried moment with her, but the second we stepped into the square, something stopped us in our tracks.

A man was standing outside the bakery, peering through a gap in the shutters. A uniform; a navy jacket and a gun belt, a revolver jutting from it, oil-black. Terror washed through me and I couldn't speak, even when I heard Myriam's sharp intake of breath beside me, even though I wanted to push her away and tell her to run.

But it was too late. The man was turning, shielding his eyes against the light. My heart froze. Beneath the dark blue beret I saw my brother's face.

'Ceci!' he called, and he was hurrying forwards, opening his arms. Eighteen years of habit made me step towards him in disbelief. Then, he was sweeping me into a hug, lifting me off the ground, the way he always had. My cheek was pressed hard into the shoulder of his uniform, into the smell of damp wool and ingrained sweat, into cold metal buttons that stung. He dropped me back to the floor and I staggered, my mind a mess of his embrace and Myriam's touch.

'Where's father?' he started to say. 'Is he — ' He noticed Myriam standing beside me and stopped, a frown darkening his face.

'Myriam . . . ' I said, unable to stop my voice from trembling. 'I mean, Madame Reiss, this is Leon Corvin. This is my brother.'

Paris–Nice

May 1993

I lie in the darkness of the train carriage, listening to my grandmother's voice as she tells me of her childhood in the Alpes-Maritimes, of growing up surrounded by mountains, their peaks like the blind eyes of a god, always watching. As the train leaves Paris far behind, she tells me of the bakery she was raised in. Of how she began to help in the kitchen as soon as she was old enough; of how, as children, she and her brother would scrape seeds from exotic vanilla pods or scoop honey from combs into dough, or steal morsels of dried fruit and candied nuts meant for the baking.

She tells me of how her brother grew less interested in the bakery, how he had no love for the long, taxing nights, no ability or deftness with the bread. How it was she, at sixteen, who went to work with her father full time, while her brother took other jobs instead: as a guide for the tourists in the summer, or with the local mechanic, or as a delivery boy for the bakery. How by eighteen, she was already an expert in the ancient techniques of the *boulangerie*, easily able to keep up with her father.

'Tell me about the mountain,' I ask sleepily. 'Tell me about Saint-Antoine.'

Saint-Antoine, she says; a place of granite and wild-flowers, of trees that cling stubbornly to the steepest slopes. A place where marmots cry their warnings, where goats wander, belonging to no one but themselves, and elusive chamois look on from impossible heights. It's a place where the wind blows from the peaks, tasting of ice even in summer. A place where larches turn the mountainside gold in the autumn, like the candlelit hair of the church's ancient Madonna. Where the water tastes of wild violets and stone.

I lie there in the swaying darkness, breathing in her descriptions. She brings alive the world of her youth, when she climbed the slopes and drank the streams, before the world found her, before she left it all behind.

'We didn't know.'

I must have fallen asleep, because my eyes are closed. Grand-mère's voice scuds across the surface of my mind and for a moment, I wonder if I'm dreaming.

'Mmm?'

'We didn't know,' she says again.

I open my eyes a little. I have no idea how many hours have passed. Beyond the train windows, there is nothing but rushing blackness. In the few centimetres of light coming under the compartment door, I can see the glint of an open eye, looking up at the ceiling from the opposite bunk.

'Didn't know what?' I ask groggily, hauling myself on to an elbow.

'We were so sheltered from it all,' Grand-mère whispers, her voice almost lost to the noise of the

214

train on the track. 'We kept our heads turned away, safe in our mountain refuge. We didn't act. We only waited. Until they came.'

'Who?' I ask, knowing that this darkness might coax out more truth than daylight ever could.

'Them,' she repeats, as if it were obvious. 'They brought the war to Saint-Antoine. They brought the world. Everything we had been trying to ignore.'

'What happened?' I whisper, hardly daring to speak.

'Some terrible things.' There's a ghost of movement from the opposite bunk as she looks towards me. 'Some beautiful.'

I want to reach out to her in the darkness, but I'm afraid that I might break this fragile moment of remembering.

'Why did you never talk about it?'

Her head moves from side to side. 'I couldn't. I had to live, for Evie's sake, and in order to live I had to forget. Until now. Now I don't want to forget. I want to remember it all, while I still can.'

'Tell me, then.'

Silence fills the compartment, broken only by the sounds of the high-speed train hurling us across France. Then I hear movement, the rattle of a tin. Grand-mère taking pills from her handbag, swallowing.

'It all began in February of nineteen forty-three,' she says, soft and hesitant, 'when I was just eighteen. That's the month when I met the person who changed everything.'

'Who?'

There's no answer. I don't say anything, waiting for her to gather her courage in the darkness. Then, after a long while, so long that I am half-lost in sleep, I hear one, whispered word:

'Myriam.'

Saint-Antoine

April 1943

I took a sip of the *génépi* Papa poured from his secret supply. The liqueur flooded my mouth, sweet and cloying, hot with alcohol and finally, unbearably bitter. I set it back down. It was meant as a treat. Grandmother had already over-indulged, Mama had been forced to put her to bed for a nap.

I picked up my fork and looked down at the thin slice of veal on my plate. I knew I should be thrilled to see it. We hadn't had any meat but chicken for a long time, but for some reason, the glistening fat on its surface repelled me. Leon had brought it with him as a gift. A perk of his new job, he said. I watched as he ate noisily. He reached for the bread, cut himself two, three thick slices. Despite my mother's happiness that he was home, I saw her face tighten at his thoughtlessness.

'Well,' he said, piling the bread at the edge of his plate, 'seems like a lot has changed since I was last here.'

We all knew what he was referring to. My mother was the one who rallied.

'Yes.' I could see her eyes flicking from Leon's lean, tanned face to his close-cropped brown hair, to his military beret, sitting proudly on the

217

armoire. 'It was rather a shock at first, so many new people, but things have settled down now. And it has been good for business. Isn't that so, Yves?'

My father nodded, eating methodically. 'We're selling bread as fast as we can make it. We'd be doing well if flour weren't so expensive.'

'What about the money from your lodgers?' Leon said, ripping a piece of bread in half. 'I saw one of them earlier, at the bakery. A woman.' He pointed the bread at Mama. 'They *are* paying you?'

'Of course,' she stammered. 'Of course they are. They pay in advance, for the whole month.'

Leon laughed. 'They all have money, you know, don't believe them if they say they don't. Most of them are smuggling jewellery. We found one man, in Fréjus, who had hundreds of francs hidden in the heels of his boots.'

He looked up at us, expecting us to laugh. I stared at him, thinking of Wolf and Ben and Claude, of their ruined shoes, mended with wood because there was nothing else to be had.

'This is what we get with those macaronis in charge,' Leon carried on. 'Defying official orders and letting all the scum of Europe into our streets. Nice is full to bursting. And it's not only Jews, there are communists and Poles and gypsies too.' He ripped apart another chunk of bread. 'We should take back the streets from them. France for the French. The Germans would let us govern ourselves, if Pétain wasn't surrounded by so many useless people.'

'The Germans are far worse than the Italians.'

218

The words were out of me before I could stop them.

'How would you know?' my brother shot back at me. 'You've hardly left Saint-Antoine, you haven't seen some of the cities. They're overrun.'

The milice, they are worse than the Gestapo. They took children . . .

'I've heard news,' I said, looking him in the eye. 'I've heard what happened in places like Marseille.'

'We only arrest people who are here illegally,' he said defensively. 'If they don't register, then they're breaking the law.' He raised his chin. 'Just like Paul and his father would, if they had any power. Do you know some of your precious Italians killed a gendarme, up near Digne? Murdered him, after he caught them poaching — '

'Please, let's not talk politics,' Mama said, her voice overly bright. 'We were having such a lovely meal.' She touched Leon's arm. 'Whatever has happened, we're just happy you're safe.'

Leon's eyes were still on mine.

'Ceci doesn't seem happy,' he said. It was meant to be a joke, but I could hear the hurt behind it. A distance had rushed between us ever since I stepped back from his first embrace, and we could both feel it.

'Of course I am.' I looked down at my plate, knowing that I was about to break some silent family agreement. 'But, Leon — the *milice*?'

I heard my father's chair creak, my mother's gulp of breath. By the time I risked a glance up, Leon's jaw was tight. He knocked back the rest of his *génépi*.

219

'They offered to bail me out,' he said, gripping the tiny glass as if he could push it through the wood. 'They're recruiting people like me — patriots — in return for pay, rations. So I said yes. Otherwise, I might have been sent to one of the work camps. Or to a prison in Italy.' He looked at me again. 'Would you have preferred that? Would you have preferred me to be sent away, to work like a slave in some factory?'

'No,' I whispered, 'of course not.'

'Then stop acting like I've done something wrong.' His own eyes were bright, but he blinked rapidly and reached for the bottle of *génépi*. Papa didn't stop him. 'Anyway, I care about my home,' he said, splashing more into the glass. 'The *milice* are loyal to France. I wanted to protect you all. If I'd known that *this* would be the welcome I'd get then I never would have come.' He drank down the liqueur.

'Leon,' Mama placated, 'Ceci didn't mean anything by it.'

'Really? Because she seems on very friendly terms with your foreign lodger.'

My skin turned cold, even as my lips burned, the shape of Myriam's mouth imprinted all over them for everyone to see. I stared at Leon, not daring to breathe.

'You should have seen them,' he said, a note of spite in his voice. 'Smirking like children together. You shouldn't let her fraternize with them.'

Suddenly my lungs were filling again, relief rushing into my chest. He hadn't seen anything. He thought of me as a child still, a foolish girl.

Mother was frowning. 'Ceci?'

'I saw Madame Reiss on my way back from the sanctuary,' I said, thinking rapidly. 'I was telling her about the cakes we used to make for the May celebrations, that's all.'

Papa made a noise. 'We'll be lucky if we can even make bread. We're almost out of flour again. I don't know where it goes. It will mean another trip to Nice — '

'We can take you,' Leon said quickly, proudly. 'The *milice* have vehicles. They are coming to scout this area in a few days. They want me as their guide.'

While they talked and planned, I helped Mama clear the table, grateful for something to do. Her jaw tightened when she saw the half-eaten meat on my plate, but she said nothing, wrapped it carefully in some wax paper.

'I would come and help you in the bakery tomorrow,' Leon was saying when I came back into the room, 'but I want to meet with Paul and his father officially while I'm here, see what we can do to help the gendarmerie.'

'Ceci, go and get changed,' my mother called, untying her apron. 'We are due at the Picots' in half an hour.'

Gratefully, I made my escape up the rickety stairs, walking quietly so as not to wake Grandmother. I slept in the attic, in a bed wedged beneath the eaves, surrounded by dust and dead flies and long-forgotten boxes. Remnants of childhood remained up here, a broken spinning top, a stack of yellowing baby linen folded neatly into a basket.

I had just finished changing, tying back my hair, when the stairs behind me creaked. Leon was standing there, staring around the room. He hadn't thought to knock politely, he never did. My fingers slipped on a hairpin. I tried to remember how I would usually act, swamped by the strange feeling of being tongue-tied around my own brother.

'I can't believe we both used to sleep up here every summer,' he said. 'Do you remember how you'd cry and cry unless I checked all the corners for bats?' He looked over at me, half a smile on his face. 'It seems like yesterday.'

'Yes.' I gathered up my cardigan. Leon waited, obviously hoping I'd say more.

'Mama said that you packed my things from the bakery,' he said at last. 'Where are they?'

'In Papa's old room,' I moved towards the stairs. 'I'm sorry if they are creased — '

He grabbed my arm as I tried to step past. 'Where is it, Ceci?'

For a second, I frowned at him, wriggled my arm to free it before I realized what he meant. The gun. It came back to me in an echo of thunder, a gleam of dull gold in the darkness, the colour of damage and death.

'I don't know what you're talking about,' I whispered, but he knew I was lying, he could see the barrel of the gun in my eyes. His face hardened.

'What have you done with it?'

'Nothing, I — '

'Stop lying!' he hissed. 'I know you found it. Where is it? Did you tell anyone?'

'No,' I gasped, 'I don't . . . '

I could see his temper rising. Leon had always been hotheaded, but usually it would fizzle out quickly, be laughed off even quicker. Now, the anger in his eyes scared me.

'I threw it in the river!'

I didn't know where the lie had come from, I only knew that with it I was breaking something, cutting the threads that connected us as brother and sister.

Leon went still. 'You did what?'

'I threw it in the river,' I said again, buying time. 'When I found it . . . I was scared. They said that anyone with a gun would be arrested or worse, and I thought they might take Papa.' I stared at the floor, throat burning. 'I'm sorry, Leon, but I didn't want to get you into trouble. I didn't know what else to do.'

In a burst of movement, he pulled me against his chest, held me tight. He was trembling with ebbing rage, but with something else as well: fear of what was happening to us, of the parts that we had almost played against one another.

'It's all right,' he said. 'Of course you were frightened, I see.' He let me go, held me at arm's length. 'You shouldn't have thrown it away, though. I could have used it to hunt. I'm allowed to now. But I suppose you weren't to know that.'

I shook my head.

'It's a good job they gave me a weapon, then, isn't it?' he said, making his voice brash, the way he did when he was unsure.

I nodded and stepped past him, wanting to

escape. 'We should go,' I said. 'The Picots are expecting us.'

'You should have told Paul about the gun,' he murmured as we walked. 'He's one of us. We French have to stick together.'

Paris–Nice

May 1993

Myriam.

The name has a rhythm of its own, a bringing together of the lips, a falling away into breath. That was how Grand-mère said it: carefully, fearfully.

Who was she? I had asked.

She came to Saint-Antoine in the spring and lived above the bakery. She was like no one I had ever met.

I had waited for more, waited for my grandmother to start talking again but she had fallen silent. I had dropped questions into the darkness, but they returned nothing but rushing silence. Eventually, I had fallen asleep, that name echoing through my dreams.

The train's intercom wakes me a few hours later with a crackle of static, a blared announcement that almost makes me roll off the narrow bunk.

Mesdames et messieurs, in approximately twenty minutes we will arrive at Gare de Nice Ville. Please make sure . . .

Blearily, I sit up. Outside the window I see a flash of blue. It's enough to make me scramble from the blanket, to press my forehead to the window. Outside the train, so close that I could run across the shore towards it, is the Mediterranean. The sun has barely risen and the water is pearlescent and hazy, edged by tiny white waves. I peer along the track past the palm trees and into the distance. There are the Alpes-Maritimes, smudges on the horizon that hide the town of Saint-Antoine.

'Grand-mère!' I call. 'I can see the mountains.'

'Then we are nearly there,' she murmurs. Slowly, she pulls her bag towards her and takes out her pills.

Over the next few minutes, I help her to get ready, handing her pins for her hair, helping her on with her cardigan. Whatever the pills are, they start to kick in, and by the time the train slows, she looks steadier.

'One last thing,' she says. From her handbag she takes a shiny gold cylinder and a pocket mirror. Lipstick. She applies it carefully to her feathered lips, pausing when the train jolts. It's a deep crimson, almost shocking in its vividness. She turns to me.

'How do I look?'

I can tell that she's scared, that this bright, red lipstick is armour. It comes back to me then, the reason we're here: the fact that Grand-mère is preparing to confront her past, after fifty years.

I grasp her hand. 'You look wonderful,' I tell her.

Ready, we stand by the door of the carriage, watching the buildings of Nice slide past.

'How long has it been since you were here?' I ask.

'A lifetime.' She looks at me, her hand

tightening on my arm. 'Thank you, Annie. I don't think I could have done this alone.'

Together, we step from the train, part of a crowd of yawning, rumpled passengers. I'm so busy staring about, at the elegant arched glass ceiling, at the palm trees growing inside, that I don't notice how Grand-mère is struggling until she stumbles, and I have to grab her arm to keep her from falling. The wheelchair was left behind at the hotel.

'Can you make it to that bench?' I ask.

All at once, the red lipstick looks garish, a mask instead of make-up. She nods, lips pressed tight.

Just hold on, I want to tell her, *we've come this far.* As she lowers herself to the seat, I feel a stab of guilt for not being more responsible, for not insisting that she returned to the home; for not realizing she was too weak to travel.

'Are you sure we shouldn't go and find a doctor?' I ask, kneeling in front of her.

But she's shaking her head, her eyes fierce. 'No,' she says, fumbling in her bag for her cigarettes. I light one for her, against my better judgement. She sucks on it as if it will give her life. 'I shall be all right,' she says. 'Why don't you go and find out about buses? It's really the only way to get to Saint-Antoine. There will be an information desk somewhere.'

I hesitate, one hand resting on her knee. I can feel the weakness in her muscles, see the fabric on her long skirt trembling, like a pulse in the belly of an animal.

'Go,' she says gently. 'I'll be fine. I promise.'

Sighing, I shoulder my bag, set off into the comings and goings of the station. It's a busy bank holiday Sunday, and there's a queue at the information booth, tourists with suitcases and neon bumbags looking lost. When it's finally my turn, I ask for a bus timetable to Saint-Antoine, trying to be quick, only for the woman to give me a blank look.

'Saint-Antoine?' I ask again, feeling my cheeks start to burn with embarrassment. 'It's a village, in the mountains?'

'Which direction?'

I have no idea where we're going. Didn't Grand-mère say something about the Italian border? 'I think, towards Italy?'

The woman rolls her eyes. From beneath the desk, she pulls out a bundle of timetables.

'*Alors*,' she says, lifting her glasses on to her nose. Laboriously, she begins to look through them. She's nearing the bottom of the pile when her brows contract and she pulls a thin strip of paper free. '*Voilà*,' she says, slapping it down on the counter. 'Saint-Antoine.' Her biro is pointing to a dot at the end of a sparse-looking route. 'There are two buses a day,' she tells me briskly, circling things with her pen. 'The next leaves at ten fifteen from the front of the station.' She jabs her pen across the concourse. 'Is there anything else?'

All of my nervousness seems to be returning under the gaze of this stern, official woman. 'Um,' I stammer, gathering up the timetable, 'I don't suppose I could borrow a wheelchair?'

I race back across the station, pushing a

228

rickety chair before me, PROPERTY OF NICE VILLE GARE stamped on it. There is only one return bus from Saint-Antoine to Nice every day, at half past six in the evening. If I'm to stand any chance of getting back to England in time for work on Tuesday . . . I shove the thought aside. One thing at a time.

To my relief, Grand-mère is where I left her, sitting on the bench, her head bent. At first, I think she might be asleep, but then I see that she's reading something, a single sheet of paper, held protectively close to her body.

'I borrowed a chair!' I call. 'And there's a bus that leaves in a couple of hours.'

She looks up and I almost stop, astonished. The weakness is gone from her face, the frailness too. She looks younger than before and her eyes are bright, her jaw set.

'Well done, *chérie.*' She smiles, hurriedly folding the paper and sliding it into the old brown envelope. 'Now, how would you like some breakfast?'

I can't help but frown at this change in her. What is she hiding? But she only gives me a smile and pushes herself to her feet.

'Shall we?'

Saint-Antoine

May 1943

I waited for Myriam on the back step. The day was bright, the air fresh as only a day in late spring can be. Beyond the town — just beyond — the mountains were beckoning. Snow clung to the peaks, but the slopes were downy green. Even the ancient pines looked new, as if they'd cleaned themselves up for a wedding. My feet itched to run free of the town, although I knew that before the day was out, I would have to stain the clean air with the smell of blood, and kill another creature.

Michel had been as good as his word. Twice, I'd given him a hare or a partridge from my hunts and twice the Rocher twins had waylaid me in the street with little muslin bags of salt. I added the contents to the pot in the kitchen without a word. If Papa thought it was strange that our supply never seemed to run out, he didn't comment on it.

I turned my face to the sun as it needled its way between the buildings, thinking about the mountain meadow, about drowsing with Myriam, her arm across my chest —

'Ceci!' I snapped my eyes open. Paul was walking down the alleyway towards me. He was wearing his full gendarme uniform. I had only ever seen him wear it on special occasions. He'd had his hair cut too, close to the ears, like Leon's.

He stopped when he saw my face.

'It's strange, I know,' he said, tugging sheepishly at the jacket. 'But Leon insisted. One of his group has a camera. He wanted a photograph of the pair of us together, in uniform, before they went out on patrol.'

'I like yours better than his,' I said, unable to keep the bitterness from my voice.

'He told me that you didn't approve of him joining up.' He tried to smile again. 'But Leon isn't like the rest of them, Ceci. I know it was rash but . . . At least this way he is out of jail.'

'He seems different.' My voice was quiet.

Paul shook his head. 'War changes things. Nothing will be the same as it was before.' His eyes found mine, searching. 'But some changes might be good. Don't you think?'

I gripped the handle of the basket. I knew where this was going, and I didn't like it, not when Myriam might step from the back door at any moment. 'I don't know,' I said, looking down.

But Paul was moving closer, and I could smell the starch that his mother must have used on his uniform, the blood-tang of polished metal. I had to look up.

'Well, *I* know,' he said, raising a hand to my chin. 'Won't you believe me, Ceci?'

My stomach gave an empty thud. I felt trapped in that alleyway, with the sun in my eyes and Paul's tall, uniformed body and his lips,

231

lowering towards mine. Then there was a clack, a latch lifting, and Paul jumped back so rapidly he almost fell.

Myriam!

But it wasn't her. It was Daniel Reiss, with his burnished hair and his neat spectacles. He was carrying a brown-wrapped package.

'*Bonjour*, Celeste,' he said, closing the door behind him.

'Monsieur Reiss,' I said, knowing that my face was burning. 'You remember Paul Picot?'

His eyes took in the smart uniform. 'Of course,' he said. 'I barely recognized you.'

'Monsieur Reiss.' Paul shook his hand, looking proud.

'Well,' he glanced between the pair of us, 'I'm afraid I must get on. I'm catching the bus to Nice.'

'Is Madame Reiss at home?' I asked quickly. 'I . . . I wondered if she might like to go for a walk.'

'She is,' he spoke carefully. 'But I'm afraid she is not well today, Celeste.'

I stared at him. There was something behind his words; something he had left in the shuttered rooms upstairs, that he was not going to bring into the light of day.

'What's wrong with her?' I asked, even though I knew it was rude.

He smiled tightly. 'She is just not feeling herself. I am going to see if I can get some medicine while I am in Nice.'

Questions, anxiety rolled through me. *Did she tell you about me? Did she say what had happened? What have you done to her?*

'Monsieur Reiss,' Paul was saying, through my taut silence, 'please, do not let us keep you.'

He was nodding, raising the brim of his battered hat.

'*À tout à l'heure.*'

We watched him go.

'He ought to be careful in Nice,' Paul murmured. 'The Italians might be in charge but . . . ' He trailed off and I knew he was thinking about Leon, about the *milice* with their oath of patriotism and their black cars, which seemed to swallow people whole. 'Is it true,' he said abruptly, turning back to me, 'That you threw away Leon's gun?'

'It wasn't *his* gun,' I said distractedly. 'It was Grand-père's.'

'Ceci.' Paul's hands were on my shoulders, squeezing them, giving me a gentle shake. 'Why didn't you say anything to me? I would've helped.'

You would have taken it from me, like a knife from a child.

'I don't know.' I sighed. 'I'm sorry, Paul.'

'Well, it's done now.' His hands were still on my shoulders. 'Anyway, I was coming to ask if you would eat supper with us again this evening? My mother would like to talk with you.'

The words brought another wave of that sick inevitability. 'I will have to ask Papa.'

'I just saw him in the square, he gave his permission.' He smiled at me, searched my face. 'So I will see you later?'

'Yes,' I said, just wanting to be away from him. 'Yes, I'll see you then.' I turned, pushed through

233

the back door and shut it firmly behind me, not caring what he thought.

The bakery was empty, the shop closed. My feet took me straight to the stairs, to the door that I had opened unthinkingly so many times. Now, it seemed like a barrier, impossible to pass. I raised my hand and knocked.

'Myriam?'

There was no answer; no creaks even. Was she truly up there?

'Myriam?' I tried again, louder.

The silence only grew more deafening. I stared at the ceiling, holding my breath. Then, I couldn't stand it. I pulled the door open and ran up the stairs two at a time, the way I always had done.

'Myriam,' I called, opening the door to the apartment. For a moment, the strange reality of seeing that place with someone else's possessions in it stopped me in my tracks. An unfamiliar photograph of an old-fashioned couple was propped on the side table, a stack of books sat on the windowsill, and a jumper — the dark one that Myriam sometimes wore — was draped over the back of a kitchen chair. I peered into the alcove where my parents' double bed was. There was no one there. Then I turned, and saw that the door to my room was closed.

'Hello?' I called, softer now, touching the handle. There was no answer. Hardly breathing, I opened the door a crack.

The room was dim, the shutters latched tight over the blackout paper. In the bed, *my* bed, a shape was huddled. As I stepped forward, I felt a strange tremor, as if I was looking at myself, months ago, hiding from the war and the winter.

'Myriam?' I whispered. 'It's me. What's wrong?'

Why was it so hard to reach out and touch her, when that was the only thing that mattered? My fingertips brushed the blanket near her hair, pillow-tangled. There was no response. I sank on to the bed and leaned over to see her face.

Her eyes were open. She was staring dully at the wall. I had never seen that expression on anyone's face before.

'Talk to me,' I begged, reaching out to touch her cheek.

She didn't move, didn't even look at me. 'I'm going to die here,' she said.

The words chilled me, and I gripped her through the blanket. 'Don't say that.'

'It's true.' Her voice was flat. 'There's no way down. I'm trapped. If I could get down again, if I could reach Nice, I could end this. I could live.'

I had never been so frightened, not even when the German planes had droned high overhead. 'You're living now,' I whispered, 'you're safe here.'

'Safe?' she choked. 'Nowhere is safe, there's nowhere left, they've backed us into a corner.'

I saw her face contract, eyes squeezing closed. It took all of my courage to lean down and place a kiss on her cheekbone.

'I'll keep you safe.' I barely knew what I was saying. 'I'll be here, I promise.'

Tears were pushing beneath her lashes. 'Don't,' she said. She coiled in tighter on herself.

'I can't see you, Celeste.'

I froze. 'You don't mean that.'

'How can I even look at you?'

The words came out as breath, gathered on the plaster wall before her, their meaning lingering long after the sound had faded.

'What?'

'You love him.'

'No, not like that, never — ' But this wasn't about Paul.

This was about my brother. This was about Leon, about the people he might have taken by the shoulder and led away; about the children he might have lifted into trucks and driven to the nearest station. About the families he might have broken, sending them into the unknown . . . I had loved him once, that much was true. But could I love him now?

I lifted my head from hers a fraction. 'He didn't have a choice.' My voice was weak.

'He did. We all do. And yours is to love him.'

I clutched hopelessly at the blanket. 'That isn't a choice,' I said. 'He's my brother, Myriam. He's my *brother*.'

Silence.

'Please — ' I choked, but she wouldn't speak to me again. She only lay there, coiled and hard as a bud in earliest spring; one that would die if pulled apart.

Nice

May 1993

'Saint-Antoine?' the bus driver says, loosening his sweat-damp collar. 'Single or return?'

'Single,' Grand-mère says, handing over the money with something like defiance.

Watching her, I feel afraid, I want to drag her away from there, find some comfortable hotel and make her rest, tell her that it's all right to forget, that she doesn't need to relive events that happened decades ago. But I can't. All I can do is help her along the bus to a seat.

I'll tell you everything, Annie, she promised, back at the café where we had breakfast, *I will tell you. Only please, get me to Saint-Antoine first.*

To anyone else, this bus is just a dusty single-decker, chipped and faded. But to my grandmother, it's the final step: the gateway to the past.

When we pull away from the station, sliding out into traffic, I see her grip the seat in front of her, eyes fixed on the window. She watches the buildings and streets intently, as if searching for traces of the city she left fifty years ago. We drive along the Promenade des Anglais, full of tourists and dog-walkers, all enjoying the sun. I try to imagine it as it must have been during the war,

237

with the beach off-limit to civilians and the seafront amusements torn down to make way for military defences. But I find that I can't. The wounds of that time might still run deep, but five decades have plastered over any outward scars.

Eventually, the grand buildings drop in height and become industrial as we leave Nice behind. The bus takes us away from the coast and into the foothills of the mountains. We pass by a few nameless suburbs, sprawling from the edges of the city, and then, on either side, the land is rising, all pale rock and pines dark as sun-shadows. There's barely anyone else on the bus: an old woman, and a middle-aged man in overalls. We make a stop in a dusty village, where the man gets off. The houses here look dilapidated, sun-beaten. Up ahead, a faded sign reads *SAINT-ANTOINE: 41km*, and before I'm ready, the bus veers into a canyon.

Rock shade falls over us, the hot, tarmac smell replaced by stone and water. There's a tunnel approaching and I feel an odd sense of foreboding, as if this is the point of no return. Beside me, Grand-mère shivers.

We emerge on to a road barely wide enough for the bus. It twists up the mountain like a flat ribbon, dropped carelessly from the sky. A few times the bus makes sudden stops that have me gripping the edge of my seat in horror.

'How far does this road go?' I ask Grand-mère, as the bus squeezes into the rock wall to let another car past. I can't take my eyes from the sheer drop beside us.

'It ends in Saint-Antoine,' she says vaguely.

'You can't go further than that by car. Only on foot to the next villages. Or over the mountain, by the old salt road.'

'The salt road?'

She nods. 'They brought salt from the coast this way, for thousands of years.' Her eyes are fixed ahead. 'The paths are still the same, over the summit.'

Salt brought me here, I want to say, looking down at that ancient landscape, but when I glance over at her, she is lost in thought.

We begin to pass through villages balanced like goats on rocky outcrops. The houses here are crumbling, their paintwork peeling away. I feel as if we're entering another world, a forgotten place, a thousand miles from the glamour and bustle of Nice. Without a car, without this bus, Saint-Antoine would be almost inaccessible. The thought brings a tremor of anxiety to my stomach when I wonder how I'm going to get down again, let alone in time to catch a train or a flight.

The slopes become steeper, the trees wilder, until at last the mountain peaks appear: towering and snowcapped, bleeding streaks of ice.

Grand-mère's eyes are fixed upon them. 'We're almost there,' she says.

Finally, the bus rumbles around a corner and a town comes into view. It's perched on a hilltop, old medieval walls still visible in places. Around it spreads a narrow green valley, dotted here and there with villas and houses. Below, I can see the glint of water; a river, tumbling busily from the mountain in clouds of white froth.

The bus swings around one switchback, then another, before pulling to a stop in an empty dirt yard. I peer out of the window at a faded wooden sign: *SAINT-ANTOINE GARE.*

I look back to find Grand-mère climbing out of her seat without my help, making for the doors.

'Grand-mère!' I call, hauling our bags down from the rack.

I catch up with her at the edge of the pavement. She's staring about, her eyes huge, as if she'll see herself as a girl come striding around a corner.

'It's barely changed,' she breathes. 'I thought it would have changed . . . ' A second later she sets off, faster than she's moved since I found her yesterday.

'Where are we going?' I ask, hurrying after her.

She laughs, as if it's a foolish question. 'The bakery, of course.' She stops for a breath, and points into the valley. 'My grandmother's villa was down there,' she says. 'I think it went to Leon. It's probably long gone.'

'Leon? Your brother? Did he stay here after the war? Why didn't he look for you?'

'The hotel!' Grand-mère is craning her neck as we pass a large stone building with alpine eaves and wooden shutters. 'It's still here. It's where they had to register every evening, at twilight.'

'Who?'

'Myriam hated it. She always sent Daniel to register without her.'

I have so many questions, but Grand-mère is determinedly walking on. Ahead, I can see a small square lined with trees and café tables, empty in the heat of noon except for a few old men, drinking glasses of Pernod in the shade. But Grand-mère doesn't stop. She skirts the side of the café, into a shadowed alleyway. It's so narrow that I find myself looking up fearfully. Wooden balconies and walkways cling between the buildings, brittle as old bones.

Suddenly, we come upon a stream, a stone gutter, running right down the centre of the street in front of us.

'What is this?' I ask, as Grand-mère steps over it.

'The *gargouille*.' She doesn't look at me. 'Water from the mountains. We used to use it every day, in the bread. We — '

She stops. Her eyes seem to cloud and flicker. I catch her arm as she reels.

'Grand-mère,' I tell her, feeling a pang of concern, of responsibility. 'You're overdoing it.'

'Yes,' she mutters. 'I just . . . need to catch my breath.'

Up ahead, there's a small square. In one corner, a bleached telephone box stands next to a bench and a noticeboard. I propel Grand-mère forwards.

'Sit,' I say firmly, dropping the bags, half-wishing she would admit defeat. 'You have to rest.'

'All right,' she breathes, dragging her handbag towards her. 'I will. Just for a few minutes.'

My eyes stray to the telephone box. Was it only yesterday evening that I called Mum? It feels like months ago. My stomach churns when I imagine her, listening to my frantic message, to the words: *I found Grand-mère, the nurse told me that she has dementia . . .*

'I'll be right back,' I murmur, pulling out some change from the bus. 'Will you be OK?'

She nods, breathing deeply.

As the sun beats down through the clear plastic window, I feed coins into the payphone. My hand hovers over the keys. I could try Mum's mobile telephone, but I have no idea if it will be working. Hastily, feeling like a coward, I punch my own number instead, dialling into my answering machine at home in London. If she wanted to get in touch with me, she'd leave a message there.

You have one new message.

Shit. Grimacing, I press the '1' key.

'Annie!' My mother's voice breaks in straight-away, as though she couldn't wait for the recording to finish. All of the relief, the homesickness that comes from hearing her voice is eclipsed by guilt when I hear how upset she sounds, how confused.

'I can't believe you've . . . have you truly found her? I know I said I wanted to look for her but I never thought, I didn't mean — oh, Annie . . . ' I hear her gulp, and my heart clenches horribly. 'Is she all right? Where are you? I can't believe this.'

For a few seconds, all I can hear is rushing static, as if she's holding the phone away, giving herself time to catch her breath. *Please don't worry!* I want to shout down the phone, *She's OK, we're both OK.*

'Annie, does she . . . ? Is she coherent, when she talks about wanting to go to Saint-Antoine? She would never tell me anything about it, only that she couldn't go back there. She can't be in her right mind if she wants . . . Oh, Annie, please tell me you haven't done anything stupid.'

My eyes are burning with shame, for being so irresponsible, for causing Mum to worry when all I wanted to do was protect her. I squeeze them closed.

'*Call me* as soon as you get this,' Mum is saying, 'day or night. I'm seeing what I can do to get back to France as soon as I can. This is more important than work. Tell Grand-mère,' her voices shakes, 'tell Mother that I love her. And you too, *chérie.*'

I listen to the end of the message, to the answerphone bleeping. *Why* didn't I wait until she was back? I could have talked it over with her sensibly before rushing off on my own.

Because she would have got cold feet, a quiet voice reminds me, *like she has for fifteen years. Because you wanted to do this on your own.*

I slam the handset down.

'Grand-mère,' I call, stepping away from the phone. 'That was Mum, she — '

I stop. The bench is empty, our bags abandoned on the ground. A groan of frustration breaks from me. Not again. I search the square but there's no sign of her. *She can't be in her right mind . . .*

'Grand-mère?' I shout.

No answer. I grab the bags and head back the way we came. After a few steps, I change my

243

mind. *The water*. I turn and break into a run, following the gargling stream up the narrow, medieval street.

'Grand-mère?' I call, my voice echoing back from the houses, shuttered and sleepy in the noon sun. I catch a glimpse of an old man with a broom, a cat's tail whisking around a corner, but apart from that there's almost no one around, no one to ask.

Then the street is growing lighter, opening into another little square.

'Grand-mère?' I call, blinking in the sudden brightness. She can't have made it much further than this. The square has shops on three sides, all of them closed: an ice-cream parlour, a gift shop, and another one that looks as if it hasn't been open for years. Heavy wooden shutters barricade the front windows beneath a peeling painted sign:

Boulangerie Corvin, Est. 1846

The bakery. Feeling sick, I hurry towards it. Up close, I can see the front door is ajar, gaping into darkness beyond. As I step over the threshold, my shoes crunch on something: broken glass. The door panel has been smashed. Lying there, amid the shards, is a loose cobble-stone.

'Hey!' someone yells, splitting the silence of the square. A thickset man has emerged from the street opposite, is staring at me in obvious anger. 'What are you doing?'

I dash inside, the man's shouts echoing behind me. I blink, sunblind, and make out some shelves, an old wooden counter as I rush past, stumbling into the corridor. To one side, I see what looks like an abandoned kitchen. To the other, a second door, hanging open.

I step around it. A staircase leads up into the gloom. The man's shout echoes again, closer, and I have no choice but to run up, taking the steps two at a time. They groan under my weight, so much so that I'm worried they're going to collapse. At the top, another door stands ajar.

Beyond is an apartment, decorated in the style of another era. The air feels heavy with decay, stale, except for a faint disturbance, coming from somewhere off the main room.

I approach on careful feet. The smeared windows only let in a yellowish half-light, but through it I can see a figure, standing in the middle of the second room.

A board creaks under my weight, and my grandmother turns, eyes wide.

'Myriam?'

'No, Grand-mère,' I tell her gently, my voice shaking. 'It's me. There's no one else here.' But even as I say it, the hairs are standing up on the back of my neck. There's *something* about this room and for a moment, I think I'm going to hear other footsteps hammering up the stairs, a young woman calling out . . .

Grand-mère gasps, as if in pain. She's crumpling, her knees giving way, and it's all I can do to catch her and lower her clumsily to the floor.

'Grand-mère, what's happening, what's wrong?' I can feel myself panicking.

She doesn't answer. Her mouth is hanging open, the muscles on one side of her face twitching, tremors wracking her body.

I grip her hard. 'Help!' I shriek. 'Please, someone, help!'

Saint-Antoine

May 1943

'Ceci, where are you?'

Mama's voice broke into my thoughts. She was looking at me disapprovingly across the table. 'Agathe asked you a question,' she said.

Paul's mother was holding up a slice of cake, a crumbly thing, flavoured with saccharine. 'A little more?' she said.

I dragged my mind back, and nodded. I had eaten to be polite, but it had been like swallowing sand.

'Thank you, Madame Picot.' I held out my plate. Anything to give me an excuse not to speak.

She tsked at me. 'Ceci, how many times have I asked you to call me Agathe?'

'Of course, thank you, Agathe.' If I sounded wooden, they didn't seem to notice. They were too busy gathering up the crumbs of their cake. Sometimes, a plume of smoke crossed the window and a snatch of laughter; Paul and Leon, sat outside in the darkness, smoking on the Picots' front step.

You love him.

I pressed my fork on to the china plate, wanting it to shatter.

'What is wrong with you today?' Mama said, exasperated.

Had they asked me another question? I scooped up a mouthful of cake. 'This is very good,' I murmured, to cover my lack of attention.

Agathe smiled. 'Thank you, my dear.'

'Ceci,' my mother said, in her severe voice, 'we were talking about you.'

I looked from one of them to the other, hoping this was not the conversation I had been fearing for weeks. 'Oh.'

Mama laughed, a little too quickly. 'Oh? Is that all you have to say?' She shook her head at Madame Picot. 'Ceci, you are eighteen now.'

She was looking at me meaningfully. They both were.

'I know,' I said. I knew it was rude but I couldn't help myself, couldn't be meek and quiet then.

Mama opened her mouth to reprimand me, but then there were voices outside: male voices, raised in panic. All of us stood, ready to grab at each other or cry or dig in and fight. I thought at once of the dark bakery, of Myriam sleeping there, and I would have run for the door had Daniel Reiss not burst through, flanked by my father. He looked dreadful, his red hair matted with rain, eyes like two dark holes behind his glasses.

'What — ' Agathe managed to say, before Monsieur Reiss saw me.

'Where is she?' he demanded. 'Celeste, where is she?'

Everything seemed to stop: my blood, my nerves, even my heart for a moment. 'What?' I whispered.

'Madame Reiss is missing,' my father sounded exasperated. 'I'm sorry for bursting in like this, Agathe, but for some reason, Monsieur Reiss seems to think that Ceci might know where his wife is.'

'She isn't at home,' Daniel Reiss was saying to me, as if he hadn't heard my father. 'She was supposed to meet me for registration, but she wasn't there, and now . . . '

I couldn't help it. My eyes slipped towards the open door, towards Leon in his *milice* blue. It only took a second for Monsieur Reiss to follow my gaze.

'You!' he said, turning on my brother. 'What have you done with her?'

Leon's face was pale with anger. 'I haven't done a thing,' he spat. 'I've been here all evening, you filthy kike.'

Monsieur Reiss raised his arm, only for Paul to appear from nowhere, pushing him back. My father wedged his large body between the pair of them.

'Enough!' he barked, as Leon's hand clenched into a fist. 'Monsieur Reiss, I see you are upset, but I will not have my son accused. Now,' he held the two of them apart, 'what exactly has happened?'

Daniel was shaking. 'I am sorry,' he said, breathing hard. 'I am sorry, but Myriam is missing. It is most unlike her. You cannot blame me for fearing the worst.'

'Have you checked the hotel, the church?' my mother asked.

'Of course I have!' Monsieur Reiss lost control

of his voice again. 'I've looked everywhere!'

'Might this not be a misunderstanding?' Agathe's face was twisted with worry. 'Perhaps she is visiting one of the other . . . one of her friends.'

'She doesn't visit anyone,' Daniel said tautly. 'Except . . . ' His eyes found mine, and in that moment, I saw that he knew far more than he had ever let on. 'I thought she might be with you,' he said.

'I haven't seen her since this afternoon.' I spoke as calmly as I could, but still, my voice was tight with guilt. 'After you left for Nice.'

'You called on her?' It sounded like an accusation.

'Yes,' I murmured. 'She wasn't . . . herself.'

Monsieur Reiss let out a noise, almost of pain, but my mother spoke over him, in the maddeningly soothing tone of someone who doesn't understand the situation.

'If she was feeling poorly, perhaps she has gone to Dr Brion — '

'You don't understand,' Daniel cut her off. 'My wife is not 'poorly'. She is with child.'

Shock pitched through me, taking hold of my limbs. Daniel was answering my mother's questions but I couldn't listen. All I could hear was Myriam's voice, that terrible, featureless tone as she told me, *I'm going to die here.*

I braced myself against the table. *With child* . . . How long had she known? How long had she been planning on keeping it a secret?

I'm trapped. She didn't mean Saint-Antoine, I realized, she meant her own body. She was

250

trapped by the future that was growing inside her, even as her world crumbled, as every door to safety was slammed in her face. In that moment, my heart burned for her, my whole body ached, and I wanted to go back to this afternoon and comfort her so badly that I couldn't stop a noise from escaping my throat.

'Ceci?' my father asked, frowning.

If I could get down again, if I could reach Nice, I could end this. My skin went cold. She couldn't be planning . . .

The next moment I was moving, striding over to Paul. He was still wearing his fine uniform, with its holsters and pockets.

'Give me your torch,' I demanded.

He blinked at me. 'What?'

'Give it to me!'

The urgency in my voice must have done something, because he was unclipping it, handing it over, and I was making for the open door.

'Go to the Italians,' I told Daniel over my shoulder. 'Get the *capitano*, tell him what's happened, say that you need one of their jeeps.' I turned, only for my brother to catch my arm.

'What the hell are you doing?' he said. 'You can't just run off after one of them!'

Rage coursed through me and I shoved him, hard enough to break his hold, hard enough that he stumbled back against the wall.

'Head for the road out of town,' I yelled to Daniel. 'Drive slowly!'

His questioning shout was lost as I ran down the steps, on to the steep, cobbled street, slick

251

with rain. Footsteps sounded behind me, boots on stone, and for a moment I thought it was my brother, or my father, come to rip the torch from me.

But it was Paul. I risked a look back and saw a chaos of bodies spilling from the Picots' house, crowding the front step. 'Ceci!' Paul was running after me. 'What are you doing?'

'I know where she is,' I gasped. 'Paul, I have to go to her, she'll listen to me.'

'But Monsieur Reiss — '

'Go with him, make sure the Italians help him.' I staggered to a halt at the edge of the square, next to an alleyway that led away from the town. 'Paul, please!'

His eyes were wide in the torchlight. He looked into my face and nodded once.

'I'm trusting you, Ceci!' he yelled, but I didn't wait to hear more, just turned and ran down the dark alley, so narrow it snagged the wool of my cardigan. The voices dropped away as I emerged on to the steep slope that led to the road out of town.

The roar of the river filled my ears as I ran. Overhead, the sky was growing darker every moment, like an eye closing. The torchlight swung wildly back and forth, back and forth, and I prayed no sentries were watching. As I reached the road, I slipped and went down heavily, but I picked myself up, and staggered on, my eyes searching the way ahead.

The mountain pressed close on one side, a rock face soaring upward. On the other side was blackness. One badly placed step, one foot sliding in the wet, could mean disaster . . . I staggered on, chest heaving, torch needling the mountain darkness.

If I could get down again, if I could reach Nice . . .

Please Myriam, I begged silently, *please don't have done something stupid.*

I rounded a corner, where an overhang of rock made the road even narrower. As I swung the torch, something pale caught in its beam, so quick, it might have been a moth fluttering. But there were no moths out here, not in the rain. I swung it again, blinking water out of my eyes, and this time it caught on a pale hand, and a face, and wet hair, plastered to skin.

'Myriam!'

I don't know where I found the breath to shout, because I could barely run to close the distance between us. She was crumpled by the edge of the road, a bicycle lying on its side near her, its front wheel bent out of shape.

She was shaking with cold, soaked with rain, wearing only her thin jacket. Her trousers were torn, and in the torchlight I saw blood and grit on her knee, staining her palms. She was crying uncontrollably, and I held her tight, swiping away the tears of relief that streaked my own face. It was only when I propped the torch against a rock and dragged the wet cardigan from my own shoulders that she even seemed to notice I was there.

'Celeste?'

'Yes.' I hugged the wool around her. 'Yes, I'm here.'

In the torchlight, her eyes found mine. 'I was trying to get to Nice,' she shuddered. 'I'm . . . ' I watched her curl in on herself, the way she had in the dim bedroom.

'I know,' I told her, trying to take her hands. 'Myriam, I know.'

'I can't,' she sobbed, 'I can't have it. Not when there's nothing but death.'

I had no answer to give, could only wrap my arms around her and try to keep her from breaking as she cried, her mouth shaking with grief against my face.

'You won't die here.' It was the only thing I could think of to say, and I repeated it like a litany, echoing back from church walls. 'I promise, I promise you, Myriam. You won't die here.' I took her face in my hands, tried to make her look at me. 'I won't let you.'

She sagged against my side, arms locked around my neck. A moment later, the roar of the river grew louder, until I realized it wasn't the river at all, but the Italians' jeep, hurtling around the mountain. I raised my head, but I didn't let her go, not even when brakes squealed, when headlights dazzled my eyes and I saw Daniel's terrified face through the windscreen.

'Don't leave me,' she cried as boots ran towards us. I held her as tightly as I could, whispering that I wouldn't, until hands lifted her away, and I was left alone, repeating my promise into the night.

Saint-Antoine

May 1993

The doctor sits back in his chair, unwrapping the blood pressure band from around Grand-mère's arm. 'Well, she seems to be stable. That's about all I can tell you, I'm afraid.'

I nod vaguely, covering her hand with mine. Lying on the crisp white pillow, she looks older than before, and smaller, her grey hair wisping about her face. In the doorway, the hotel proprietor and his wife stand watching. I blink hard. I feel exhausted, unable to concentrate properly or think of the right questions to ask.

The past hours are all a blur: shouting myself hoarse when Grand-mère collapsed on the floor, until the angry man from the square came stomping up the stairs. He'd yelled about breaking and entering, until he had seen the state Grand-mère was in. I had begged him to call an ambulance, a doctor, anyone. He'd returned with the best he could manage: a member of the mountain rescue team, with a portable stretcher.

'I've called the doc,' he'd told me gruffly, 'he's two villages over right now, up in Belvedere, but he's on his way.' He had looked around, at the damp-stained walls of the apartment. 'Let's get her out of this place.'

I hadn't wanted to move her, but he'd insisted.

'She'll be better off at the hotel,' he'd said. 'My brother runs it. It's what the doc would want. What the hell are you doing here, anyway? Why'd you smash up the door?'

I hadn't been able to answer. Instead, I had helped to strap her in and held her hand while he and the mountain rescue man carried her down the stairs and a short way across town, to the hotel. I had been aware of people staring, but at the time, I hadn't cared. All I could see was her face in that room, the pain in her voice as she'd called out.

Myriam.

The doctor is talking to me again. I drag my mind back.

'Sorry?'

'I asked if you are sure you do not want me to call for an ambulance?'

'Would it — ?' I have to clear my throat, dry from dehydration and shouting. 'Would it take her back to Nice?'

'That is the nearest hospital, yes.'

What do I do? Tears creep in my eyes. I can hear my mum's voice telling me that I've been stupid and thoughtless.

'No,' I whisper, feeling as if I'm condemning Grand-mère. 'No, she was desperate to come here. She'll never forgive me if I let you take her away.'

'With all due respect, Mam'selle . . . ' The doctor pauses. 'I am sorry, I don't know your name.'

'Picot,' I tell him shakily. 'Anna Picot.'

There's a flash of movement from the doorway, as if the hotel owner has given a start. I glance up at him, but he only shuts his mouth hurriedly, staring between my grandmother and me.

'Mam'selle Picot, I would have thought that your grandmother's health was more important than a holiday,' the doctor says.

'We're not on holiday.' I don't even have the energy to be indignant. 'We're here . . . ' I trail off hopelessly. 'She's not been well. She was born here. She said she wanted to come home.'

I hear a noise from the doorway again, the hotel owner whispering rapidly to his wife.

'I see.' The doctor sighs. He sounds sympathetic. For the first time, I force myself to look at him properly. I'm surprised by what I find. Although his brown hair is peppered with grey, and his wire-rimmed glasses make him look grave, his face is young. Beneath his shirt, his neck and arms are tanned, the careless sort of dark-and-light tan of someone who spends a lot of time outdoors. Abruptly, I become aware of how grubby I must look, with bags beneath my eyes and crumpled clothes from my hastily packed bag.

My cheeks are growing hot, and I have to avoid his gaze when he looks up. 'She has tablets in her handbag, from the nursing home in Paris, if that will help.'

'You've come all the way from Paris?'

I nod, feeling as if every crazy decision I've made in the last three days is being laid bare. 'On the overnight train. We arrived in Nice this morning.'

He shakes his head. 'No wonder she's

exhausted. I'm amazed the home discharged her, she's clearly in a weakened state.'

I press my lips together, hoping I won't have to admit that she wasn't discharged, that instead we absconded. 'I'll get the tablets,' I mutter.

As I search through her bag, my fingers brush the worn, brown envelope that contains the page she was reading at the station. I resist the urge to pull it out.

'Here,' I tell him, handing over the bottles, as well as the tin I've seen her shaking pills from. 'This is what she's been taking.'

As he reads the labels, his frown grows deeper. 'Fluoxetine, olanzapine, lamotrigine,' he mutters, peering at the doses. When he opens the tin and pokes at the tablets, his eyes widen.

'I'm sorry, Nino, Aline,' he says suddenly over his shoulder to the hotel couple, 'would you mind leaving us for a few moments? Any discussion of medication should be confidential.'

'Of course!' Nino, the owner exclaims, 'of course, Doc. Call if you need anything.' With a last glance at my grandmother, he closes the door.

The doctor's smile disappears as he gets up from his chair, comes to kneel beside me on the other side of the bed. 'They are probably listening,' he murmurs. This close, I can smell the clean cotton of his shirt, dried in the sun, and something spicy that might be cologne, as well as a faint breath of coffee. There are tiny seed pods stuck to the leg of his trousers, I see in a daze, as if he's walked through long grass to get here . . .

'What?' I ask, aware that I haven't been listening, have been studying him, as if he was a page full of secrets.

'I said, were you aware she was taking these?' He's speaking softly, but even so, I can hear a hard note in his voice.

I look down at the tin in his hand. 'Yes, I thought they were just her medication. Why, what are they?'

He hands over a small, white pill.

'Dexedrine,' he tells me. 'Amphetamines. They're illegal.'

I almost drop it in shock. 'She's been taking *amphetamines?*'

All at once I remember Grand-mère's strange bursts of energy: this morning at the station, yesterday in the restaurant, the difference between the first time I encountered her and the second.

The doctor takes the pill back, drops it into the tin. 'They are probably what got her here. Otherwise, it is my guess that she wouldn't have had the strength.'

'Oh God.' My hands go to my mouth when I realize that by letting myself get caught up in Grand-mère's determination, I might have hurt her, perhaps fatally. 'What have I done?'

'If you didn't know, it is hardly your fault.' The doctor lays a sympathetic hand on my shoulder.

'The other pills,' I ask him. 'Do they tell you anything about her condition? The nurse at the home said she has early-stage dementia, but I don't know what that means for her, exactly.'

He takes his hand away then, walks around to

the other side of the bed. My shoulder seems to be tingling. I resist the urge to touch it.

'Not much,' he says, picking up the bottles once again. 'One is used as an antidepressant, the other to alleviate muscle spams.' He shakes his head, takes out a notepad. 'I'll make a note of them and investigate. If you won't allow her to be admitted to hospital in Nice, then with your permission, I'd like to take a blood sample, see if there are any other substances in her system?'

I nod, and watch with an ache of conscience as he takes a sterile needle from his doctor's bag and draws a sample. My grandmother's blood shines in the tube.

'There,' he says, taping a cotton ball in the crook of her elbow and laying her arm back down.

'Will she — ' My voice gives out. 'Is there anything I can do for her?'

When he looks up, his eyes are kind. 'Let her rest for now. She should recover before long, though she might be a little groggy, especially without these.' He smiles ruefully, rattling the tin. 'I'm going to have to take them away with me, I'm afraid. Or you'll be in trouble with the gendarmerie.'

I manage to smile at that. 'There's a gendarmerie here?'

'No town is too small for trouble,' the doctor says, closing his bag. From outside the door there's a muffled scraping, the sound of feet hurrying away. He rolls his eyes. 'Trust me.'

In the corridor, I hold out my hand, feeling awkward. He shakes it firmly. 'Thank you,' I tell him. 'Will you come back? To check on her, I mean?'

'Of course. I'll come tonight, at the end of my rounds. If you need anything else — ' He lets go and searches through his bag for a card. 'Here is the number for the surgery.'

I take it. 'Thanks.'

He looks more closely at my face. 'Get some rest, Mam'selle Picot,' he says. 'You will be no help to your grandmother if you're so tired you can't see straight.'

Before I can answer he turns, striding off down the wood-panelled corridor. When he's gone, I turn over the card in my hand.

'Dr Matteo Sala,' I murmur to myself.

Saint-Antoine

May 1943

I didn't see it coming. I walked into Grandmother's kitchen before Papa, my mind a mess of fear for Myriam and fear for myself. I would tell them it was nothing, I decided; I would tell them I had just been comforting her. When the door slammed closed behind me, rattling on its hinges, I turned.

The blow caught me square across the mouth.

For a second, I only stood there, stunned. Then came the pain, a wash of hot blood where my teeth had sunk into my lip.

'Yves!' I heard Mama cry. Through watering eyes, I saw her blurred shape as she stepped into the kitchen, her hands over her mouth.

'How dare you run off like that?' Papa shouted, his voice trembling with anger. 'How dare you put yourself in danger for one of them?'

I wanted to protest, but the blow had knocked the words out of me. Papa hadn't laid a hand on me for years. Not since I was a child. From the corner of my eye I could see Leon standing in the doorway, his face was pale, his uniform rain-spattered.

'I didn't think . . . ' I managed to whisper.

'No, you didn't!' Papa grabbed my arm. 'This isn't a game, Ceci! We're at war. The Italians have orders to stop the Jews leaving town. They are armed, they could have shot you.' He shook me. 'Do you understand?'

I nodded, staring at the floor, feeling tears well in my eyes, and not just from the pain.

'What's got in to you?' Papa barked, but I could hear the anger going out of him.

'It's that woman,' Leon said from the doorway. 'That Reiss woman, putting ideas into her head. They don't share our values, you know — '

'Enough, Leon,' Papa said. Finally, I looked up and met his eyes. I saw weariness there, and desperation. 'I am just trying to keep you safe,' he told me.

'She knows, Yves,' my mother said quietly, before looking over to where I was standing. 'Ceci, I think you should go to bed. Leon will help in the bakery tonight.'

Leon began to protest, but my mother cut him off. 'You might have a uniform now,' she snapped, 'but you are still a member of this family.' She jerked her head. 'Go and change. And don't wake your grandmother.'

We walked up the dark stairs together, the way we once had as children.

'Ceci . . . ' Leon started to say, but I ignored him, kept climbing the second set of stairs up to the attic, to the creaking, dusty darkness where I could be alone.

Mama came up later. She brought an oil lamp with her and lit a candle beside the bed so that the wooden space was filled with a warm, old-pine glow. She didn't say anything, only handed me a piece of rag that had been soaked in cold

263

water. Slowly, I pressed it to my throbbing lip.

'You can't blame your father,' she said softly. 'He's right, what you did was dangerous. You frightened him. You frightened us all.'

'I had to help Myriam.'

My voice sounded wooden. I heard my mother sigh. 'Ceci, you should not get too close to Madame Reiss. The time might come when — ' She stopped. I knew she was trying to gather up the strands her thoughts, of the thousand, clinging fears and anxieties and rumours that plagued us, every day. In that tremulous, golden light I saw someone who knew more than they let on; someone who could never — would never — speak it aloud.

'Your father and I talked, before he left,' she carried on, taking the cloth from me, folding it to a cooler side. 'We both think you need some stability, some purpose. It would be best for you and Paul to marry, as soon as possible.'

'Marry?' The word felt wrong in my mouth. 'But — '

'Ceci,' she leaned towards me on the bed, 'you cannot pretend this is a surprise. Others may see you as a foolish little girl, but I know you're not.' Her face was almost pleading. 'And I know you've been expecting this.'

She was right; I had known all along what was intended. I had let it happen, the night of the dance, down by the bridge where the lone bird's song nearly pulled my soul from my chest.

'It's too soon,' I said. 'Why does it have to happen right away?'

My mother shook her head, half sad, half resigned. 'You're eighteen, Ceci. I was married at your age.'

'What about the bakery? Who will help Papa?'

Mama waved a hand, and seemed relieved to talk about such everyday things. 'It's all arranged. You will live with the Picots, but carry on helping your father at the bakery, for as long as . . . as long as you can.'

Until you have your first child, she meant.

'Mama,' I scrabbled for an excuse, anything, 'I can't — '

'Celeste!' Mama sounded stern, even as she blinked rapidly. 'Paul is a sweet boy, and he cares for you.'

I held her gaze.

'Get some sleep,' she said, sitting back. 'Leon will help tonight, but you will have to open the bakery first thing in the morning.'

That night, my dreams were anxious, running things disguised as wakefulness, so that I was never sure if I was truly asleep or if I was calling Myriam's name into the musty darkness of the attic. When the church bells finally woke me at five, my eyes were scratchy and hot, as if I had been crying. I sat up and my head pounded, along with my lip. Tentatively, I explored it with my fingers. It was swollen still, bruised. These lips, she had kissed . . .

'Celeste!' My hand jerked away as my mother's voice echoed up the stairs. 'Wake up! It is past five!'

Grandmother was already up and dressed by

the time I came down, holding her garden basket.

'Good morning,' I murmured, and kissed her on the cheeks.

She caught my hand as I pulled away and stared at my lip with an unusually clear gaze.

'Oh, my dear,' she said softly. 'Here,' she reached into her basket, 'look what the girls laid.' She placed an egg into my palm, a perfect buff oval, still warm from the coop. 'You can have it for your breakfast.'

I didn't feel like eating, but couldn't disappoint her, not when eggs were so scarce. Mama soft-boiled it, and put it before me in a china cup without a word. I ate it carefully while they watched, trying not to brush my bruised lip.

'Oh, my dear,' my grandmother said again, when I patted my mouth with a kerchief, and winced.

'Here,' Mama murmured. She was holding out a little shining cylinder. For one, heart-stopping moment, I thought it was a bullet, one of the few remaining tooth-gold shells from Leon's gun, but it wasn't. It was lipstick, the expensive lipstick that a lady from Monaco had once given Mama as a gift for delivering bread to their villa all season. She rarely wore it, and certainly had never let me, despite my asking. Now, here it was, in my hand.

'You said I couldn't,' I murmured, turning that gold tube. 'You said it wasn't seemly for girls my age.'

'It wasn't,' she said, taking it from me and removing the lid with a soft click. 'But now you are a woman, soon to be a wife.' Her smile was strained as she handed it back. 'Today, you may wear it.'

In the little hall mirror, I touched the red to my lips. It was strong, so strong a colour that it took over the rest of my face, until all I saw was that red. I winced in pain as I dragged it over my bottom lip, but it hid the small bruise, covered it like it wasn't there at all.

'Let me see,' my mother murmured. Her face looked odd in the dim, cold hallway. 'Yes,' she said, 'you're quite the woman.'

I could feel that colour, thick and stiff on my lips.

'Papa won't like it,' I whispered.

Her jaw tightened. 'Papa will say nothing, nor will Leon, not today. Now,' she handed me my cardigan, still damp from the night before, 'off you go.'

By the time I reached the bakery, there was already a queue forming outside. I kept my head down as I walked, and swiftly let myself in the back door. I could hear activity in the kitchen, the dry, sandy shunting of loaves on to racks to cool, the squeal of the heavy oven door, the clank of trays. Today, the scent of baking was almost overpowering, toasted and rich. I was not used to smelling it as an outsider; by this time of the morning, I had usually long stopped noticing it. I took a deep breath, trying to let that comforting, familiar scent fill me up. To me, that scent was home, even if my family felt like strangers today.

Leon was the first to see me. He looked exhausted, working at the oven in his vest, sweat streaking his arms. He opened his mouth to make some remark, but then his eyes flickered to the corner of my lip, and he shut it again.

'I burned myself,' he said a moment later, holding up his wrist, wrapped in a rag. 'Out of practice.'

He was trying to be friendly, to make a joke. I twitched my lips, but couldn't smile. 'Are these ready?' I asked instead, lingering near a tray of *pain bis*.

Papa's gaze caught on the red of my lips too. 'Yes — ' His voice cracked. 'Yes, take them through.' He paused. 'Thank you, Ceci.'

I opened the shop, letting in the waiting crowd. Some of our neighbours exclaimed and said that I looked like a starlet, others eyed me closely, no doubt already gossiping over last night's events. I saw Myriam and Daniel's friend from the café, Monsieur Jacob, I knew his name was, now. He looked paler than ever as he handed over his coupon. For some reason, that little pink ticket filled me with rage. Recklessly, I picked up a whole loaf of *pain bis* and placed it in his hand.

'You shouldn't have done that,' Leon murmured behind me, as I watched him leave, 'you can't let them take food out of our mouths.'

Through the bakery window, I could see Wolf, talking animatedly with Andre, the curly-haired boy from the dance. I could see women dressed in black who spoke no French, or Italian or even German, their hair wrapped in faded scarves. I could see those who had once been wealthy, queuing now for bread, their jewellery pawned, their businesses and lives left behind.

268

'Shut up,' I snapped.

Leon froze with shock, on his way back into the kitchen. 'What did you say?'

'I told you to shut up.' It was as if those bright lips belonged to someone else, someone braver than me. 'What do you know about any of it?'

He rounded on me then, nostrils flaring with anger. 'You little — '

'Leon.' My father appeared in the doorway. His eyes went from the pair of us to the customers, waiting at the counter. 'Back to work.'

Paul came for me at lunchtime. He couldn't have known that I had been planning to sneak up and see Myriam, but still, I resented him for stopping me. I wanted so badly to see her, to take her hand in mine. I wanted to know whether the terrible fractures that had rushed across her soul were still there, and whether, if I held her, I could try to knit them back together.

But there was Paul, waiting by the back door, no gendarme uniform today, no empty gun holster, just Paul, sweet Paul, with his rumpled blond hair.

'Well, Ceci,' he said, smiling, 'I hear there's been some gossip about us.'

I looked into his eyes, searching them for a sign of understanding, for any doubt in me, any inkling that I had changed so deeply and irrevocably. But there was nothing, only a flash of surprise as he took in the red of my lips.

'Why are you wearing — ' he started, before his cheeks flushed. 'I mean, it makes you look different.'

'I am different.'

'I know.' He sounded so serious that I looked up in hope. 'You're not just Ceci any more, my friend's little sister.' He reached out, gathered up my hands. 'You're Mademoiselle Ceci Corvin, a beautiful woman who I have long admired, who I'm asking to be my wife.'

I can't love you, I cried inside, *not the way you want, not any more.*

'Ceci?' he said softly. 'Will you? I promise I'll make you happy.'

As I stood there, everything seemed to contract. *There's no way down,* she had said, *I'm trapped.*

I felt the tears slide from my eyes.

'Yes,' I said. 'I'll marry you.'

Saint-Antoine

May 1993

By the time I wake, the day has rolled into evening. For a second, I'm bewildered in that strange, shadowy light. I roll over, expecting to see the peach wallpaper of the hotel in Cheshire and the grey car park outside the window. Instead, I see mountains, their peaks brushed with gold. Deep green forest covers every crease and ridge of the slopes, like the wrinkled hide of a creature at rest.

I scramble from the bed and push the windows wide, letting the crisp mountain air flood into the room. The sound of water rushes up to greet me, white and busy, the same snowmelt that pours through the veins of the town. Here, the thought of Cheshire or London or even Nice is incomprehensible. I lean my elbows on the sun-warmed, peeling wood. How could someone leave here and never return? Turn away from all this beauty?

A sound rings out across the town, merging with the early-evening birdsong. The church bell, striking the half-hour. I check my watch. Half past seven. So much for the evening bus. I wouldn't have taken it anyway, not until I know Grand-mère is safe and cared for. I told Mum as much in my latest message, giving her the

271

number for the hotel. Every time I look at the phone, I keep expecting it to ring. Perhaps she's out of range, on her way back to the coast of Australia.

I close the window with a sigh. I'll have to think of something to tell work, too. Right now, they seem a million miles away, as insubstantial as ghosts.

The hotel owner let me have the room opposite Grand-mère's, so I can check on her. They didn't have many guests, he said, it not being tourist season quite yet. Slowly, I creep across the landing and open the door to her room.

She lies still, her chest rising and falling almost imperceptibly. I sit down and touch her hand, wanting her to know that she isn't alone. From her bag, I unpack a few things: her toiletries bag, her pill bottles, a miniature photograph album. I can't resist flicking through it.

The first pictures are of my mother as a child, grinning, gap-toothed, in front of a zoo enclosure, sitting on a flour-covered work surface, posing in a school uniform before the window of a bakery. There's a photograph I recognize: the two of them on the beach. Grand-mère is smiling, Mum beaming, her brown hair wild with salt. Gently, I turn the page. Next is a picture of a baby in a hospital crib, the colours those of a different decade. I flip it over. *Anna*, it says, in my mother's handwriting, *18 October 1968*.

Me. I stare at the tiny shape in the picture, pink and frowning beneath a blanket. Mum was younger than me when she got pregnant, a grad student on a research placement in a foreign country, who met a handsome musician twice her age, and it being the 1960s . . . Once, when I was a teenager, we'd argued about it. I'd accused her of severing a link to who I was by not keeping in touch with my father. *He did not want us, chérie,* she had told me firmly. *I found out later, he already had a family of his own.*

And what about Grand-mère? I had demanded. *What about her?*

Grand-mère . . . My mother's face had flickered, sadness and remorse replacing frustration. *She never understood why I wanted to raise you alone. She never had that choice.*

I flip past other pictures of me — at birthday parties, school performances — to the final pages of the album. Tucked into the back pocket are a few loose photographs. I shake them out. The first one is of a woman. I don't recognize her. It looks like an old picture, clumsily developed. The woman is sitting in a café chair, wearing a man's jumper and a pair of dark glasses. She's smiling at something beyond the frame, a lively expression, caught by the camera, unaware. On the back, there's a date.

April 1943

My heart gives a squeeze. Is this Myriam? I shiver when I remember the way my grand-mother called out that name, as if she was trying to summon a spirit from the walls of the old apartment. Carefully, I set the picture aside and

273

pull out the other photo, in case it holds more clues.

It is creased down the middle, as if it has been folded in half for a long time. It shows a wedding party standing before a church. Mountains are visible above the roofs. *Saint-Antoine.*

I scan the faces of the party until, with astonishment, I realize that the bride looking back at me is my grandmother. I peer closer. She looks so young, her dark hair coiled beneath a veil, a loose white dress in the cut of another decade and a bouquet in her hand. But her face: I recognize that expression. It's the one I saw as she sat in the taxi outside the Hotel Lutetia, hunger and defiance and guilt all mixed up together, as if at any moment she might turn and run. And next to her . . .

My fingers tighten on the card. A young man, his fair hair combed back, a smile on his face like any groom. A person I have never seen before. My grandfather.

Saint-Antoine

May 1943

We were married within the month.

It seemed that as soon as I had said 'yes' to Paul, the wedding left my hands. It was not my event, but something that belonged to the whole town. In the weeks that followed, Saint-Antoine rose to the occasion. Cellars and attics were raided for anything that could conceivably be of use, until the kitchen at Grandmother's house began to resemble a junk shop: table linen and spare chairs mended with rope, tarnished centrepieces, paper flowers. Mama made me visit our neighbours with the barrow, stuffed with straw, so that we could borrow wine glasses and crockery and cutlery for the wedding dinner, none of them matching, most of them chipped.

Papa called in favours from far and wide. His friend the wine-grower smuggled a few bottles of a decent vintage up to the village, hidden beneath bundles of kindling. A distant relative in Nice donated three pots of apricot jam. Paul's mother even 'found' a quart of sugar in her pantry and handed it over to my father with great ceremony. It was to be an almond cake, she declared, sweetened with the jam and a little brandy, wrestled from old Madame Gougeard at the hotel.

Ordinarily, I would have been overwhelmed by such generosity; instead, all I felt was guilt. I let the preparations happen, as if it were someone else getting married, not me.

The night before the wedding, Papa worked even longer hours than usual. I knew he was preparing food for the wedding breakfast, and I would have helped him, if only to give my mind a rest from dwelling. But I wasn't allowed. I had to sit at the kitchen table with Mama and Agathe and Grandmother instead, as they took up Mama's wedding dress, sewing lace cut from a curtain on to its hem and cuffs to hide the places where it had yellowed.

As they sewed, they drank a *tisane* made from mint and nettles, and prepared me for what awaited the following night: a wife's duty to her husband. I listened, my head bent over the cup so they would not see my expression. How could I tell them that I knew already what it felt like, that fire and ache at my very core, the way a person's hands could touch me in a way that made it seem as if all of my skin was pink and new and leaping with nerves? How could I tell them I feared I would never — could never — feel that with Paul?

He had become bolder over the days between the announcement and the wedding, and would kiss my cheek openly now, or hold my hand in the street. Sometimes, when we were left alone for a few minutes, he would pull me into the shadow of a doorway and kiss me, his hands awkwardly brushing and squeezing at my waist, my breasts. I let him. Part of me hoped that I

276

would grow accustomed to it, the way Mama and Agathe said I would. Part of me wondered whether the thoughts of Myriam would fade away, and not sting me with guilt and longing at every waking moment.

I had seen her twice since the night on the road: once holding Daniel's hand to walk slowly to registration, once at the upstairs window. She had peeled away a sheet of the blackout paper and her face had been a pale oval, so still it could have been my own reflection. I had opened my mouth and taken a step towards the back door, only for her to disappear.

I tried everything I could think of to see her. Daniel had stopped going out so much, and so I couldn't simply walk up the stairs. Instead, I lingered near the hotel at registration time, pausing to talk to Wolf or Andre or Marie, trying to catch sight of her. I began to take walks up the road, to the villa where some of the Jews held their prayers. I watched the twinkle of candlelight through the shutters, listened to the low, rhythmic murmuring, and once I thought I heard Daniel's voice exclaim something. I had raced down to the bakery, hoping to find Myriam alone, and had almost burst through the door to the apartment before I heard voices, women's voices, speaking French and the language I didn't understand.

I had waited, hidden in the storeroom, until finally Daniel had returned, his head bent in the twilight. A minute or so later, the three women had left the apartment. They were matronly, gossiping, fussing, all of them. They had obviously been there to keep an eye on her. I knew how much she would hate that.

The day before the wedding, I even went up to the mountain hut, saying I would pick flowers for my bouquet. I had waited there for a long time, hoping beyond hope that Myriam would be there. I had even found one of her cigarette butts in the dirt, had picked it up, run my fingers over the end that had touched her lips and touched it to my own. But she didn't appear.

Before I went, I had taken out the gun and sat with it on my lap, letting the wood warm under my hands, weighing out the three remaining bullets. It did something to calm the awful, crushing anxiety in my belly, to know that I had this powerful secret; that I wasn't only little Ceci, the baker's daughter, the reluctant bride. I had snatched up flowers from the meadow with the scent of gun oil on my hands.

On my wedding morning I stood and stared out of the tiny attic window at Grandmother's house. The whole valley seemed to be glowing green, trees surrendering the last of their blossom. At the edge of the meadow, *our* meadow, wild irises were opening, their petals a deep, sodden blue, as if they had been soaked in the sky.

There were a few in the bouquet beside me. Agathe had made it. She had taken the frothing cow parsley and yellow ragwort that I had picked and twined them together with buds of eglantine roses and summer savory, 'for desire', she had said with a wink.

What if I spoke to Paul? I thought desperately.

What if I tried to tell him the truth, that I couldn't be the wife he wanted . . . ? But I knew he wouldn't hear it, not now.

'Ceci?' My mother climbed the creaking stairs. 'Are you hungry? It will be a few hours until we eat.' She stopped when she saw me, and her eyes turned bright. 'Oh Ceci,' she said, coming forward to fold me in an embrace.

She was wearing perfume, a heavy, powdery scent that filled my nose as I pressed my face into her shoulder. Soon this would no longer be my home, even a temporary one. I would be living with another woman who I would have to call 'Mother'. I would have another life.

'Oh dear,' my mother laughed, wiping her face, 'crying already.'

Downstairs, Papa and Grandmother were waiting. They were all dressed up, Papa in his brown suit that no longer fitted him so well. Mama wore her blue dress, the rare lipstick. Even Grandmother had risen to the occasion, in a dress as old as mine, and a hat that looked even older.

She cooed when she saw me. 'Like a crocus,' she declared. In her lap was a hat box. Waiting among layers of tissue paper was the veil that she had worn on her wedding day, the veil that would now serve its third generation.

I stood still as Mama fixed it to my hair. Papa lingered by the armoire, and I knew that he was pouring himself a glass of *génépi*, for strength.

'There.' Mama lowered the veil, and the world became a fine, white fog that smelled of cedar and age-old tradition. I was lost in it, as thoroughly as if it had rolled down from the mountain and caught me where I stood.

'Well,' Papa cleared his throat, 'I suppose it's time.'

The square outside the church had been decorated, the crumbling yellow stone hung with garlands of branches and scraps of white ribbon that blew in the breeze. Although the day was warm, I could feel the cold air billowing out from the church doors. It was always freezing in there. Perhaps it was because of the crypts, or the water that rushed through the rock far beneath.

Mama and Grandmother disappeared inside, and soon it was just Papa and I, standing in the doorway, waiting. We didn't speak, just stared ahead into the darkness. Then the throat of the church organ opened and we were walking. Sunblind, I tried to make out faces in the crowd, but saw only disjointed features: cheeks and eyebrows and hats, until I realized that I was searching for Myriam.

I wanted her to be there. I dreaded seeing her, but hated every face that wasn't hers. I looked down instead at the cracked tiles beneath my feet. Just before the altar, I stopped, the pale dress swaying over my shoes. I had seen those tiles almost every Sunday of my life. This was the last time I would see them as Celeste Corvin.

My father gave my arm a tug and I was walking again, taking a few last steps to where Paul was waiting, his blond hair combed to his head. Next to him stood Leon, returned from his patrols for the occasion, every button on his *milice* uniform shining. Papa lifted the old veil from my face, and stepped away.

Just as my eyes had failed to take in the crowd, my ears couldn't adjust to the pressure in the room, or the pressure in my head.

'Dearly beloved — '

A smile in the twilight.

'Join these two people — '

Oil on lips, the taste of salt.

'Under the eyes of God — '

The sound of grass in the breeze, laughter echoing across the meadow.

'Do you, Paul Arthur Picot — '

Her mouth on mine.

'I do.'

Don't leave me.

'Do you, Celeste Marie Corvin — '

Paul was looking at me, waiting for me to answer. He seemed a hundred miles away. I stared into his eyes, and in that moment I saw his face flicker, saw the first hint of uncertainty appear, like a hairline crack across the ice.

I won't.

'I do.'

And it was done.

★   ★   ★

It was over so quickly. Paul had kissed me chastely and taken my hand, I had found a pen pushed into my fingers to sign the register, the ink splotching as I wrote the new, unfamiliar surname. My mother was crying. Paul's father stood proud and puffed as a wood pigeon in his ceremonial gendarme uniform. I looked around for my own father, saw him shaking hands near the door, exchanging pleasantries, but his shoulders looked lower than usual, somehow cowed, and his neck showed ropes of strain.

There were petals and leaves for confetti — no one could waste rice or paper — and a photograph, taken by the mayor's assistant. The new Madame Ceci Picot let herself be pushed and posed and admired, while inside, Celeste Corvin cried out in panic. I did not know which one of us the black eye of the camera lens would capture.

The square looked festive. I knew people had worked all morning on it, under the watchful eye of Agathe. The cafés had lent their tables and chairs, and borrowed linens glowed in the sun, overlapped to hide stains and worn edges. Bunches of wildflowers, picked by the children of Mademoiselle Louise's now vastly expanded class, had been arranged in bottles and jars. Onlookers came out to watch the wedding party crowd and jostle for the seats. I saw the two dark-haired girls from the dance at the hotel, and the Rocher twins lurking near by, ever ready to swipe an unattended drink or a piece of bread. Ben, Wolf's young cousin, came running across the square as Paul led me to the top table, a bunch of daisies in his hand.

'Many congratulations,' he said stiltedly and grinned, before sprinting back to where Wolf and Claude were waiting in the shade of the town hall. I smiled over, wishing that I could watch all of this happening to someone else. It was only

282

after every seat had been filled that I realized what I had known all along: the Reisses had not been invited.

But still I looked, hoping to catch a glimpse of her at the edge of the square, or passing along the street. Madame from the café began to bring out the glasses of wine from Papa's friend and a great cheer went up. The whole town had truly thrown themselves behind the wedding.

'Of course they have,' Paul answered when I murmured this aloud, 'people are glad to have something to celebrate.' He smiled down at me, touched my face. 'And it's rare they see a bride as beautiful as you.'

I smiled back, turned my cheek for him to kiss, sadness chipping away at my heart.

The wine in my glass was yellow, almost green. It had a raw edge, like grass, but I drank it down as soon as it was poured. Paul just laughed and poured me a little more.

'I'd be doing the same,' he murmured, 'if your brother hadn't insisted on making so merry last night. Same old Leon.'

I sipped the new glass, resisting the urge to drink that down too. It was burning my throat, my stomach.

'Where is he?' I asked, using it as an excuse to look around, to try to find one face amongst the many.

'At the bakery, with your father,' Paul answered, a secretive look on his face. 'They have a surprise for you.'

I didn't have to wait long to find out, though I had already finished the second glass of wine. A shout went up from one table then another, as my father appeared around the corner in his shirtsleeves, a white apron slung over his good trousers. Leon walked behind him, a tray of loaves on each arm. But Papa was carrying a different tray, and as he drew closer, I couldn't believe what I was seeing. It was a loaf of *fougassette*.

As he lowered it to the table, the morning in the meadow came back to me. I had tried to bake *fougassette* for Myriam because it was my favourite, something that reminded me of better times, when life had seemed sweet. Papa couldn't have known what it meant to me, that the taste would forever be linked to the memory of her, that morning. I felt myself trembling as he stood back.

It glimmered with honey, still warm from the oven, the scent of orange blossom filling the air around me.

'How on earth did you make this?' I heard myself ask. It looked just like the ones we used to bake. The cost of the sugar, the orange blossom water, the eggs and the pale, fine flour he must have used made my head spin.

'I know, it is extravagant. But Leon managed to get some credit down in Nice.' He shifted from foot to foot. 'I remembered how much you used to like them,' he murmured.

I looked up at this man, who only a short while ago had struck me in anger and fear.

'Thank you, Papa,' I whispered, and broke the bread.

The *fougassette* was only the beginning. There

were platters of crayfish, one for each person, caught from the river's pools by the boys of the town. They had been boiled with wild garlic and tarragon and were brought out steaming from the pot. All around me, people were laughing, breaking the tails from the bodies to get at the juicy, white flesh, sucking at the heads.

There was boiled chicken, and I did not want to dwell on where it had come from, though I suspected Leon must have had something to do with it. And if the slices were cut as thin as wafers to make them go around, no one seemed to mind, because there were tiny, new green peas too, tasting like the sap of the earth, and round onions, cooked to sweetness in a sauce that had *definitely* seen a knob of butter.

And though I ate with the rest of them, I drank too. One glass of wine after another, filling my glass when Paul wasn't looking. Things started to become hazy as the sun slipped towards the edge of afternoon, and people gave their speeches. I tried to smile and blush when I was supposed to.

Last, there was the cake that Papa had made, filled with jam, and acorn coffee served in mismatched cups. It was a modest meal by pre-war standards, but now it seemed like a feast.

I hadn't tasted anything as sweet as the cake in a long time. It seemed to rush through me, tingling in my blood. But rather than comfort, it only frayed my nerves, until I couldn't keep that other Celeste in, and she was insisting loudly that some of the cake be saved, so we could give it to the young people at the hotel.

Mama flicked a worried look my way, but Paul's family only laughed, saying that I would regret my generosity tomorrow. Anger heated my already warm cheeks. I tried to cool them with the backs of my hands.

'Ceci,' Paul was touching me, leaning in close, 'are you all right?'

'Fine.' I resisted the urge to jerk away. 'Look, it's time for the toasts.'

That distracted him, as Madame from the café started to pass around the tiny glasses of *génépi*, donated by almost every family in the town. I wanted to stand up and tell them to take their liqueur home and save it for another wedding, one that was not a masquerade. But it was too late for that. Instead, I finished the last of my wine.

The sun was sinking by now, rays lingering at the edge of the mountain like the fingers of a drowning man. Soon the foreigners would fill the streets, to gather outside the hotel and to take the air; to talk and gossip. Daniel and Myriam would be among them. Yet Paul and I would have to walk in the opposite direction, towards his parents' house, which tonight would be ours alone.

When the toasts came around, I knocked back my glass of *génépi* with tears burning my eyes, and panic threatening to claw its way free of the bridal white. When they were done, I pushed my chair backwards.

'Ceci?' Paul looked concerned.

'I must . . . I need to take a moment.'

'Do you need help, Ceci? With the dress?' His mother was already half out of her seat.

'No, no, thank you,' I muttered, feeling beads of perspiration spring out on my forehead. I turned and made for the café as fast as I could.

I had not used the toilet in there since I was a child. Madame smirked at my flushed cheeks, my clenched hands.

'It's all right, chicken,' she said, as I let myself into the dark, rank space, 'the first time is usually over quick.'

I was shaking so hard that I thought I would vomit, right down the hole in the floor. Outside, I heard Madame chuckle to herself, and walk out, leaving the café empty.

A moment later I was opening the door, gathering up the hem of the dress and stumbling through the curtain that led to the kitchens. There was a boy in there I didn't recognize: one of the refugees, his arms in a sink full of dishes. He looked up in alarm as I ran past, but I didn't stop, I just took the greasy back steps and fled into the crooked streets. Down one passage, through a dark courtyard, I ran like an animal released. I had only a minute, perhaps not even that before I had to be back . . . I was almost crying by the time I saw the back door of the bakery.

'Myriam!' I shouted, not caring who might hear.

I scrabbled for the door handle and couldn't seem to make it work. A cry of frustration escaped me, but then, beneath my hands, the door was swinging open. In the twilight, I saw that familiar jumper and that perfect, untidy hair.

'I'm sorry,' I burst out. 'Myriam, I'm sorry.'

She reached out and a second later I was in her arms. I clung to her, breathing in her scent, never wanting to let go.

'Don't apologize,' she whispered fiercely. She was leaning in to look at me. 'You have done nothing wrong.'

'I married him.' The words came out muddied by wine and tears. 'I can't love him. And tonight . . .'

I didn't need to say more. Myriam pulled me to her, wrapped her arms around me. 'Oh my girl,' she murmured, and I heard her voice shake like mine had.

'Myriam?'

It was Daniel. I heard the floor creak, footsteps coming down the stairs.

'Listen to me,' she was saying rapidly, 'don't be afraid. Whatever happens, it is only one piece of you.'

'But — ' I pulled back an inch, until I could see her pale face.

'What's going on?'

Monsieur Reiss had stopped in the corridor. Over Myriam's shoulder, I met his gaze and everything was there; everything true, everything unacknowledged.

'Not now, Daniel,' Myriam said, but I could feel how tense she was, how she was easing away from me. There was a voice in the street, someone calling my name.

'Myriam,' he started, but she turned on him.

'I said not now!'

His face flashed white. A second later, to my amazement, he closed his mouth. 'Be careful,' was all he said.

'Celeste,' Myriam's hands held my face, 'it is your wedding night. You will have to go.'

I searched her eyes. *I won't leave you*, I tried to tell her silently, thinking of the unknown future she carried in her body. *I promise.*

A moment later, I heard feet hurrying across the cobbles, and her hands fell.

'Ceci!' Paul's face was flushed. 'Are you all right? What's happening?'

Monsieur Reiss stepped forward, but before he could speak, I swiped away the tears, and turned.

'I am fine,' I told Paul, clasping my hands. 'I thought — I just wanted to see the bakery, on my wedding day.'

Paul's face relaxed into a smile then. 'As if it was a member of the family,' he said teasingly, and put his arm around me. 'If you'll excuse us, Monsieur Reiss, Madame, I think my new wife may have had a little too much to drink.' His arm squeezed my shoulders. 'It is time for us to go home.'

Saint-Antoine

May 1993

I don't know how long I stare at the photographs, side by side: the dark-haired woman, the fair-haired man. Where are they now? I wonder, staring into their faces. I fear I already know the answer. Grand-mère makes a noise, stirring in her sleep, and I drop the photo, feeling bad, as if I have disturbed her rest by probing into the past. Quietly, I replace the photographs and close the album. There's been enough trouble for one day.

I'm shutting the door to her room when someone calls my name. I look around to see Dr Sala coming up the stairs. I push at my hair, frizzing from a lack of products. *Stop it*, I tell myself sternly. *You are not here to flirt with doctors.*

'*Bonsoir*,' he says when he reaches me. 'I was just coming to check on your grandmother.'

'That's very kind . . . ' I stammer, feeling all useful words slip away from me. 'She's sleeping.'

He nods. 'Most likely the effects of the amphetamines as much as the attack. She should feel better by the morning.'

'And her condition?' I force myself to ask.

His face creases. 'I am still not certain, to be honest. Dementia can be tricky.' He stops, gives me a kind smile. 'I can't be sure without speaking to her.'

'Could . . . ' I hesitate, wondering whether I should share the real reason we are here. 'Could the attack have been brought on by emotion? By an upsetting experience, say?'

To my surprise, he nods. 'Of course. The brain is a strange and fragile thing.' He looks at me through his glasses. 'Why do you ask? Is that what happened?'

I nod. 'This is the first time she's been back to Saint-Antoine for fifty years. I think it might have been the shock of seeing it all again, especially the bakery. That place belonged to her family. She was desperate to go there.'

The doctor's eyebrows shoot upwards. 'Was it her who smashed the window?'

'Yes.' I want to cringe with embarrassment. 'You heard about that?'

'Of course. The whole town knows.' He rubs at his chin, where a shadow of stubble is just starting to emerge. He looks tired. 'Listen,' he says, rather stiltedly, 'were you planning to eat downstairs? Only, I often take dinner here. Nino and his wife have been trying to fatten me up ever since I arrived. We could perhaps . . . eat together, carry on talking there?'

I stare at him. Three days ago I would have turned as red as a tomato, mumbled some incoherent excuse and stayed in my room all night, making do with free hotel biscuits and cursing myself for being so hopeless.

'Yes,' I say before I lose courage, so quickly that Dr Sala looks a little taken aback. I smile to cover my nervousness. 'Yes, thank you. That would be nice.'

'Good.' He waves his bag. 'Well, I will check on your grandmother, and be right down.'

The hotel's restaurant takes up the whole of the ground floor. There's a huge alpine-style fireplace with a faded rug before it, and an outside terrace perched on the edge of a slope, overlooking the valley below. Apart from an elderly couple in hiking gear, we have the place to ourselves. It's a mild evening, and the doors are open to the mountain air.

'*Bonsoir*,' the proprietress says, plonking a carafe of wine down on the table. Her eyes linger on me as if I'm some rare bird that has wandered into her restaurant.

'I have to say,' Dr Sala murmurs once she has bustled away with our order, 'you and your grandmother have caused quite a stir in town.' He pours the wine and nudges a glass over to me. 'I've never seen Nino so quick to offer help. As if he knew her already. You said she was born here?'

'Yes. Her family ran the bakery.' I take a sip of the wine. 'She has a brother here, I think, or had one. Do you know him? Leon Corvin, I think his name is.'

The doctor shakes his head. 'I only came here last winter. I'm learning about this place and the people,' he smiles, 'but they are slow to give up their secrets.'

My skin prickles, thinking about how Aline and her husband looked at me when I said my name. 'Has anyone mentioned anything to you, about Grand-mère?'

'Not to me, other than to ask questions, but I have seen them talking.' He reaches for the bread basket, rips a large chunk of baguette in half. 'Do you know when she left the town?' he asks, chewing unselfconsciously.

'During the war or just after. Before nineteen forty-six, anyway. That's when she and my mother moved to England.'

Dr Sala stops eating for a moment, looking at me thoughtfully.

'The war,' he says slowly. 'Yes, that would make sense. People here don't like to talk about it. It's the same in a lot of places. It seems that people would rather forget.'

Aline brings our first course — buttered crayfish in their shells, fresh spring asparagus — and while we eat, I find myself telling Dr Sala about my mother and my grandmother, about how I didn't even know where she was three days ago.

'She must have lost people during the war,' I say, thinking of the Hotel Lutetia. 'I assumed it was my grandfather, but recently she's been talking about someone else as well, a woman she knew. A Jewish woman, I think, who came here as a refugee. Grand-mère said that the Italians were occupying this part of France then.'

I look over at him cautiously. *Matteo Sala*. An Italian name. What if he's offended? But he doesn't look offended, just nods.

'I'm familiar with the history. My grandfather lives not far from here, over the border in Italy. It is why I took this position, to be near him.' He sits back as Nino appears, bringing our second courses, an apron over his clothes. 'But the Italians only occupied this region until the September of nineteen forty-three. Once they signed the Armistice,' he shrugs, 'they left. Then in rushed the *Wehrmacht*, the Gestapo, the *milice* — '

Nino drops one side of the plate, spilling sauce on to the tablecloth.

'Pardon!' he rushes, dabbing at the stain with a napkin, taking his time over it. I get the feeling he's trying to eavesdrop.

'Nino,' Dr Sala smiles, 'you might know the answer to Mam'selle Picot's question. She was wondering about her grandmother's brother, a Monsieur Leon Corvin?'

Nino looks between us, eyes wide. 'Monsieur Corvin?' he asks. 'Yes, I knew him.'

Knew him. Past tense. He must see the disappointment on my face because he grimaces. 'I am sorry, Mam'selle Picot,' he says, 'I thought you would have known.'

I shake my head. It's too much to explain that even though I've only just become aware of Leon's existence, it still stings to hear that he's dead. Another family member lost. I swallow down a wave of regret that we didn't find Grand-mère sooner.

'When did he die?' I ask quietly.

'About two years ago.' Nino wipes his hands on his apron. 'He was in a home at the end. Couldn't look after himself any more. I'm sorry,' he says again, after a pause.

'Do you know what he died of?' Grand-mère's

condition comes back to me. Leon couldn't have been much older than her.

Nino shakes his head, shrugs. 'He was old, and never in the best of health. I'm sorry I can't tell you more.'

I try to smile. 'That's all right.'

He turns away, when something else occurs to me. 'Wait,' I call, stopping him. 'You said he died two years ago. Was his funeral here, then, in Saint-Antoine?'

He nods, and I can tell we're thinking the same thing. That Grand-mère didn't come back, not even for her own brother's funeral.

'Monsieur Corvin — ' Nino stops and shakes his head. 'Your grandmother had her reasons.'

I knew it, this man knows my grandmother, knows more about what occurred here than he's letting on. 'What reasons? What happened between them?'

But he's shaking his head more forcefully now, holding up his hands. 'You will have to excuse me. It's not for me to tell. And anyway, I was just a kid then. I wouldn't want to get it wrong.' He looks between us. '*Bon appétit.*'

Dr Sala fills up my wine glass. 'I'm sorry about your grandmother's brother,' he says, after a moment.

'Thanks,' I murmur. 'But it's her it affects, really. I barely knew he existed.'

A wave of sadness rushes through me at the thought of an old man, alone here at the end of his life. Whatever happened between Grand-mère and him, they never had the chance to talk about it together, face to face; they never had the chance to try to put it behind them, after all these years.

But perhaps it would not have been that simple. I remember Grand-mère's expression in the restaurant, when I told her that everything was forgiven.

No, she had said, *it isn't.*

Dr Sala touches me lightly on the arm, calling me back to the table. I sigh and pick up my fork. 'I suppose I'll just have to wait for Grand-mère to tell me about it herself.'

Dr Sala smiles and dives in to the home-made gnocchi before him, fragrant with a fresh *pistou* of basil and pine nuts and oil. I do the same, but a minute later, I pause. Something he said, before Nino appeared, has been prickling at me, like a thorn lodged in cloth.

'When the Italians left in nineteen forty-three,' I ask, looking up at him, 'what did the refugees do? Do you know?'

He puts down his fork, finishes his mouthful before answering.

'I am not sure. But Saint-Antoine would not have been safe for them. The Germans knew they were here.' His face is serious. 'They wouldn't have waited long before coming to hunt them.'

Hunt. My chest turns tight.

'So what happened?' I ask, the food forgotten. 'Where did they all go?' *Why did my grand-mother call out Myriam's name?* I can't contain the emotion in my voice.

'I am not certain, I'm afraid. Mam'selle Picot, are you all right?'

296

I take a gulp of wine. 'I'm fine,' I say, trying to get myself under control. 'It's just that I can't help feeling something terrible must have happened here, to make my grandmother run the way she did.'

Saint-Antoine

May 1943

The bedroom door creaked closed. Paul and I hadn't spoken during the short walk to his house. A basket of my clothes sat on the wooden floorboards near the bed. The brass bedstead had been newly polished, and looking at it, I felt a tremor of fear. In that moment, I wanted to peel off my skin along with the wedding gown and slip out into the street, a nameless, naked thing.

I looked out of the window. Night was dripping into the sky. Rapidly, I pulled the shutters closed, then the heavy blackout curtains, not wanting to see any of it, when all of it made me think of her.

I turned around to find Paul watching. He had brought out a bottle, two glasses. 'Brandy, from father's secret supply,' he said, face pink. 'I'm sure he won't begrudge us a glass.' He was trying to sound calm, but I could hear how tight his voice was, I could see the way his hands shook as he poured. He was as frightened as I.

A fine pair, Myriam's tear-choked, mocking voice came back to me, and I had to close my eyes, trying to banish it from my mind.

'Ceci?' I opened my eyes. Paul was holding out a brandy glass towards me.

298

I took it, gripped it tight. 'Celeste,' I said, looking up at him, my head swimming. 'Will you please call me Celeste?'

He smiled. 'Why? You'll always be Ceci to me.' He raised the glass. 'To us,' he said.

I tried to say the same, but I couldn't form the words, could only raise the glass to my lips and drink the brandy down in one.

'You look so beautiful,' Paul whispered, placing a hand on my cheek. 'I can hardly believe that you're my wife.'

I felt tears gather beneath my eyelids as he kissed me, felt one drop, but Paul didn't notice, or if he did, he didn't say. The brandy was doing its work, raw in both our mouths, and his kiss grew harder, his tongue finding its way between my lips.

I let him take the glass from me. My hands were stiff, like the claws of a frightened bird. Perhaps he will be too nervous, I thought wildly, perhaps it will not be tonight . . . But his breath was hot in my ear, and his hand was gripping me through the dress and I knew that his nerves were ebbing away. They only returned when he looked me in the eye. What did he see there, to make his face flush, his mouth shake a little?

'Shall I . . . ?' He cleared his throat. 'Shall I help you undress?'

I closed my eyes, turned my back to him. Anything to delay. One by one, his fingers released the fabric-covered buttons of the dress, until it slipped and sagged and fell to the floor, leaving me in only my cotton slip. Without that dress, I felt as if every emotion, every secret thing, would come seeping out of my pores. I turned away, made for the bed with its stiff, starched sheets. I wrapped myself in them, trying to find the warmth that coursed through me at the thought of Myriam's touch. If I could find that, if I could think of her, I would be able to pretend.

★　★　★

The day after the wedding, Paul's mother greeted me with a sly look in her eye, said she hoped I'd slept well. Paul, to his credit, did not let on that anything was amiss, although I knew he'd felt me crying silently, my face pressed into the sheets, far into the night. Early this morning, he had tried to put his arms around me once more, but I had got up from the bed swiftly and turned my back on the confusion, the hurt on his face.

'I don't feel well,' I had muttered, and fled to the bathroom. It wasn't a lie. I felt nauseous, wanted to scrub myself all over. But no matter what I did, no matter how much of the Picots' soap I used, the night remained, and with it another fear, newer, sharper than all the others.

This was how people got with child.

Leon laughed when he saw me at grandmother's house later that morning. I knew I looked pale, with dark circles beneath my eyes. 'Overindulged yesterday, Madame Picot?' he asked. I nodded. It was easier than admitting the truth.

'Cheer up, Ceci,' Mama had whispered in my

300

ear, giving me a hug. 'It gets easier.'

Leon soon left again to rejoin his *milice* group. They were patrolling the valley and the local mountain villages, looking for members of the *Résistance*, who had stepped up their activities lately. And though my mother cried, and Papa clapped him on the shoulder, I watched his departing back and was glad that he had gone.

There was no slack in our lives to allow for such things as honeymoons, and so two nights after the wedding, I found myself slipping out of bed at two o'clock in the morning. Paul was sleeping, snoring softly after another awkward, fumbling encounter. I dressed quickly, thankfully. There was a freedom, I realized, in a baker's life. We worked when others slept, and claimed the quiet hours as our own. *A reprieve from the marriage bed*, I thought with a humourless smile, as I let myself out.

Perhaps it was the strangeness of the previous days, the unfamiliar nights spent sleeping, but I grew tired faster than usual, sweating as I heaved soaked bricks into the oven to create the steam essential for a proper crust. When I slammed the door closed, I sagged. Papa saw and laid his hand on my shoulder.

'Take a break, Ceci,' he said gently, 'get some air. We need more water anyway.'

Outside the back door, it was growing light. The night had been cold, but now I felt the barest breath of warmth, a hint of the long, hot season to follow. I let my head fall back and listened to the sound of water rushing through the gutters. I breathed it in, knowing that

301

Myriam would be hearing it too, that sound, from the apartment above. I had just opened my eyes when I heard a tiny sound, scrabbling, like bird claws on tiles. I looked up.

She was at the window, her face barely illuminated by the pale sky. Her cheeks were pink with sleep, her hair ruffled, and I ached to be beside her in the dawn, to be able to roll over in the blankets and hold her to me. For an endless moment, we only looked at each other. Then a smile was touching her lips and she was leaning forward, breathing rapidly on the window so that it misted up. She began to write, frowning over the backwards letters.

D . . . I . . . M . . . ?

Dimanche. Sunday.

Heat and happiness flooded through me as I realized what she had already known: that no wedding night, no husband, would make the slightest bit of difference to what there was between us. We were unstoppable, inevitable as the seasons.

Saint-Antoine

May 1993

Huit-heure, a bird is calling, as if reminding me of the time. *Huit-heure*. I roll over in bed and check the clock. Half past eight in the morning. The bird isn't much of a timekeeper.

I flop back on to the pillow, enjoying the quiet. My eyes linger over the telephone that stands on the bedside table. I should call work and leave a message. And yet . . . it's the strangest thing. Despite everything that's happened, all the guilt and the worry and panic, I feel as if I'm outside of time, as if Saint-Antoine exists in a different place, where all of my old responsibilities and anxieties mean nothing. It's an intoxicating feeling.

Smiling, I roll away from the phone, and go to have a shower.

In the steamy bathroom mirror, I fight a comb through the wet curls of my hair. Ordinarily, I'd just leave it, maybe shove it back in a ponytail, but today feels different. Perhaps it's being here, where my grandmother was a young woman, but I begin to plait it until it hangs over my shoulder, just like hers did in the photograph from the file.

Grand-mère's room feels stuffy with the curtains closed. Moving quietly, I open the windows to let in the fresh mountain air. As it brushes across her face she stirs, opens her eyes.

'Grand-mère?' I ask softly.

'Mmm?' she asks, but it sounds groggy, and soon her eyes are sliding shut again. I sit beside her. She looks a little brighter today. Her skin is a better colour, no longer waxy pale. I rearrange the blanket, then scrawl a note on the hotel paper, saying that I'll be back in a little while. Perhaps she'll be properly awake by then. I prop it beside the lamp, where she'll see it. Finally, feeling guilty, I open her bag. The wad of money is still inside. Would she mind if I borrowed a bit? I don't have any more of my own. After a second's hesitation, I peel off a couple of notes and shove them into my pocket.

'I won't be long,' I whisper.

Saint-Antoine seems busier today. It's a bank holiday Monday and the café is open, old men already ensconced in the plastic chairs, watching the world pass. Children are playing in the stream, families gossip outside the *tabac*. A moment later, the smell of freshly baked bread stops me mid-stride, and I see a *boulangerie* — an ordinary-looking one with tiled walls and a shiny glass counter. I smile, remembering nurse Alain's words about Grand-mère's bread snobbery.

'*Bonjour*,' the woman behind the counter greets me briskly when I step inside. I'm just a stranger to her, I realize with relief. She doesn't already know me as Mam'selle Picot.

I buy a loaf of *brioche* for Grand-mère, as well as a *ficelle*, a thin, crusty baguette, in the hope that she'll find them comforting. For me, I order a *pain au raisin* and a coffee. I perch on a stool in the window of the bakery to eat, and watch the town pass. The caramelized, custardy pastry doesn't last long, and leaves me licking my fingers, wishing I'd bought two.

'Excuse me,' I ask the woman as I leave, 'I was wondering . . . How long has this bakery been here?'

The woman makes a thinking noise. 'Well, my husband's family opened it. It must have been in the early nineteen sixties. Why do you ask?'

'No reason,' I try to sound casual. 'I saw the old bakery, down in the other square, and wondered.'

The woman nods. 'Boulangerie Corvin. Bit of an eye-sore, isn't it? It's a shame, really, a lovely shopfront just going to waste.'

'Has it been closed a long time, then?'

'Ooh, years.' The woman tucks her hands into the pockets of her tunic. 'It's why this place opened. The man who ran Boulangerie Corvin just couldn't keep it up on his own.' She shrugs. 'Kept living above the shop, though. Wouldn't let anyone touch the place, though he could've made a decent amount in rent. Don't ask me why.' She shakes her head. 'He died a few years ago, but there must be some problem, because it hasn't been put on the market.'

'Oh. Well, thanks.'

Despite all of my efforts at nonchalance, I catch her watching me curiously as I leave. I wander down the main street, peering through the windows of the shops. Some are closed, but others are obviously hoping to take advantage of a sunny public holiday. There's a gift shop, and a place that sells hiking gear, but finally I see what I'm looking for, a sign that says '*LIBRAIRIE*'. Summoning my nerve, I walk up the steps and push open the door of the bookshop.

It's tiny inside, crammed with shelves, bending under the weight of books. At first, I think there's no one here, until I realize that a pair of eyes is blinking back at me. A birdlike older woman is peering over her spectacles.

'Oh,' I say awkwardly. 'Hello. I . . . Do you have a local interest section?'

'What are you after?' the woman asks coolly, laying her book aside and standing up, her necklace clinking.

'Anything about the area, really.' I pause. 'And it's history. Recent history, especially.'

Her eyes narrow at me for a moment, but she doesn't say anything, only nods to an alcove, hidden in the back of the shop. 'You'll find what we have over there.'

Thanking her, I retreat to the safety of the bookshelves. Taking down an old paperback, I riffle its pages and breathe in the comforting, autumn-leaf smell of old books.

I don't find anything useful. Most of the books are about the town's medieval history. I can't find anything that deals with Saint-Antoine beyond the turn of the century. It seems that Dr Sala was right: people don't like to talk about the war.

Among the paperbacks, I find an old packet of postcards, probably from the 1920s, all pictures of Saint-Antoine. I smile at the grand old hotels and villas of another era. I'll buy them for Grand-mère, I decide. We can look through them together.

I'm about to step out of the alcove when I hear the bell over the shop door jangle. All of a sudden, there's a clamour of women's voices, speaking at once.

'Lucie, how are you?'

'You'll never guess — '

'Did you hear? Yesterday afternoon.'

' . . . with Dr Sala last night, at the hotel, Aline told me.'

'Who would have thought? Alfio was the one who found them, he said it was as if she had appeared from thin air, after all these years.'

The shop owner hisses something and makes a shushing noise that's lost in the tumult of conversation.

'And what about the girl, have you seen her?'

'Who?'

'The granddaughter, of course.'

'But does she *know?*'

'Shh!' the shop owner hisses. I hear her beads clacking, as if she's making frantic motions towards the alcove, where I stand, hidden.

Face burning, I step out into the shop. Three old women look up, like a gaggle of children caught doing something naughty.

'I'll take this, please,' I say to the shop owner.

'Of course, yes, how lovely.' It's her turn to gabble now.

As I pay, I can feel them staring at me, their eyes boring into the side of my head. I take my change and turn away, dropping the postcards into my bag.

307

'Mademoiselle,' the shop woman calls after me, 'do you — '

But I don't wait to hear more, just yank the door open and clatter down the steps. As I do, I hear the old women burst into discussion behind me.

I stride down the street, eyes stinging. *But does she know?* The people of Saint-Antoine remember very well what happened here; they remember why my grand-mother ran. They're just not willing to talk to me about it. Which means I'll just have to try to find out for myself.

The front door of the bakery has been taped up with cardboard, 'DO NOT ENTER' scrawled across it in marker pen. Tentatively, I push the old-fashioned handle. It squeaks, and the door drifts open.

Yesterday, I was so panicked I barely took a look at the place. I only got the vaguest impression of dust and decay before I ran upstairs to find Grand-mère. Now, as I take a step forward, goosebumps shimmer across my skin. The shop exudes the strange feeling of a once busy place fallen silent.

Slowly, I walk further into the bakery. The scent of the place rises around me, old stone and must and sweet, decaying wood, but something else too, not quite there: the powdery tang of raw flour, a ghost of woodsmoke from the ovens that once sustained the people of this town and more besides.

As my eyes adjust, I make out floor-to-ceiling wooden shelves, baskets chewed to pieces by mice. I see a wooden drawer lying empty, a huge

308

ledger on a shelf, the cover brittle and cracked, pages swollen with damp. I trail my fingers along the counter. They come away stained pale grey, from dust or flour that settled over thirty years ago.

I step into the kitchen.

It's all still here. On the shelves are bottles and jars, thick with dust. There are even paper sacks leaning against the wall, long-split by rodents. As I take a step towards them, something crunches beneath the sole of my shoe. I bend down to look. A tiny, hard sphere, long-shrivelled. A chickpea.

The rest of the downstairs is in an equally poor state. There's an empty storeroom, its walls blooming with mould, a dark closet toilet that's not much more than a hole in the ground, the porcelain cracked and stained. Down a short corridor, there's a stout door, letters piled up against it in a yellowing drift. I pick one up. It's addressed to Monsieur Leon Corvin, with a date of three years ago. It looks like a bank statement or a utility bill. I place it back on the floor.

Once again, the creaking of the stairs is terrifyingly loud. I grip the banister, half-convinced that the door at the top will fly open and an old man will appear, his eyes the same colour as my grandmother's, yelling for me to get out.

But no one does. The apartment is empty, just as it was yesterday. I take a deep breath of the stale air, and look around. There are signs of life here, albeit a lonely one. A tabletop electric hob sits on the wooden sideboard, plugged in with a fraying cord. An ancient waterproof coat sags on a hook. There are a handful of dog-eared adventure novels on a shelf, an old clock-radio, its face dark, and stacks and stacks of yellowing racing papers. In an alcove there's a bed, its threadbare cotton pillows covered in dead flies and grit. Brown medicine bottles clutter the shelf above it.

Gingerly, I take one down. *Monsieur Leon Corvin*, the faded label reads, *twice daily*. Judging by the number of bottles, he must have been ill even before he was moved to a home. I blink back tears for the great-uncle I never got a chance to know. Two years since his death and yet here are all of his things still, undisturbed. No one has come to sort them out.

And Grand-mère? I ask myself, staring down at the medicine bottle. She must have known he was alive. Did she feel sorry for him, alone up here? Did she grieve for him? Did she not consider making the trip even for her own brother's funeral?

I have been too afraid to go on my own.

With a sigh, I place the bottle back on the shelf, and turn towards the room where Grand-mère collapsed. I stop, the toes of my shoes on the very edge of the threshold. I don't know why, but I'm reluctant to go in.

The room looks ordinary enough. There's a bare single bed with a rusted frame, a wardrobe, a few boxes. But there's something about it that makes my skin prickle; it's not creepy exactly, just *charged*. I shut my eyes, and for the briefest moment I think I catch a scent, a wisp of cigarette smoke. I shift my weight to take a step forward.

'Excuse me?'

My eyes snap open and I step back. Someone is in the shop below, their voice echoing up through the floor-boards. A woman.

'Hello?' the voice calls again. 'Anyone there?'

Myriam. Rapidly, I cross the floor, run down the stairs. 'Yes,' I call, breathless, 'yes, I'm here.'

I throw myself round the door and almost collide with someone, standing on the other side.

'*Mon dieu!*' Aline gasps. 'You gave me a fright.'

My shoulders drop, disappointment shooting through me, replaced a moment later by unease. Why did I think of Myriam?

'Sorry,' I tell her, before starting forward. 'What are you doing here? Is it Grand-mère? Is she all right?'

'She's . . . ' Aline tells me. She's looking at me strangely, glancing from my face to the bakery walls and back again. 'Well, you better see for yourself. She's asking for you.'

Saint-Antoine

May 1943

When I woke at dawn on Sunday, it was raining. I could hear it, a slow, soft hush in the streets. I was warm. Paul lay beside me, his eyes closed. For a moment, I watched his face, so calm in sleep, and felt a prickle of guilt. It was becoming impossible to disguise the fact that I did not enjoy sleeping with him. Last night, after he had finished, I had seen a flash of embarrassment and hurt cross his face.

'Ceci,' he had asked, cheeks pink, 'am I doing something wrong?'

I had shaken my head and rolled over, murmuring goodnight. I felt like a coward, but there was no answer I could give him.

Carefully, I slid out of bed and began to dress. Myriam and I would go to the hut, I decided. It would be dry there until the rain passed. My hands slipped in haste as I buttoned my blouse, thinking of the last time we were together, in the meadow.

'Ceci?' Paul called sleepily, rolling over. 'What are you doing?'

'I'm going up to the sanctuary,' I whispered, jamming my feet into boots before he was too awake to stop me. 'To take the monks some *pain bis.*'

'Don't go now. Come back to bed.' I could hear the want in his voice, the way those warm sheets were working on him.

I bundled my hair down my collar, too rushed to plait it. 'No. I want to go and pray as well. To be a good wife.'

A lie, but it worked. I saw him blush. 'All right.' He slumped back into the sheets. I planted a swift kiss on his cheek, pulling away before he tried to draw me closer.

Outside, even the chill rain felt like relief. I hurried up the cobbled street, out towards the edge of town. The path along the meadow was full of puddles, the grass and leaves dripping and bedraggled. By the time I reached the hut, I was soaked to the skin. Luckily, the roof was sound. Inside, I peeled off my wet blouse and my sodden skirt, and hung them to dry on a nail. I pulled the blanket from my knapsack, wrapped myself in it, and sat down to wait.

Morning came slowly, the light lost behind the clouds, but finally, I heard the crunch of feet. I stuck my head outside, praying it was who I needed it to be. She was half-running up the path, her jacket held uselessly over her head. Her shirt was clinging, her trousers spattered with mud from the road.

'Of all the days,' she gasped, stepping inside the shelter and dropping the jacket. A second later we were in each other's arms. I pressed my face into her neck, where her dark hair clung in wet strands. She kissed the edge of my ear, my nose, the crease of my eye.

313

'Let me look at you,' she said, pulling back. 'Are you all right?'

I knew what she was asking.

'I am fine,' I told her, 'though I'm afraid of what might happen . . . ' My eyes strayed to her middle, its roundness showing now, even beneath her loose blouse.

She made a noise and reached into a pocket for her cigarettes. 'Our lot, as women,' she said bitterly. Her hands were trembling as she lit one, and I realized how tactless I had been. I reached for her.

'I'm sorry,' I murmured.

She shook her head and smiled, though there were tears in her eyes. 'Don't be,' she said. 'It is done now.' She took a drag, and shivered. 'Are you going to let me into that blanket of yours?'

Wrapped together, shoulder to shoulder, knee to knee, we sat in the doorway of the hut and watched the day lighten.

'This was a mistake,' she told me, glancing down at her belly. Her voice was soft, over the sound of rain falling. 'We had always been careful before, especially once we had to leave Brussels.' She pulled smoke from the very end of the cigarette, and gave a cough. 'But there was a time, at the end of last year, when I thought I couldn't go on.' The cigarette end smouldered in her hand, but she didn't flick it away. 'It was after Marseille, when my parents were taken. They thought it was safe to go and pray with our neighbours, but the *milice* . . . '

She shook her head and I leaned in closer to her, shame coiling through me.

'They were sent back north,' she carried on, 'to some kind of holding camp outside Paris. The last letter I got from them was in November. They said they'd been scheduled for deportation, somewhere in the east. They wished us a happy Hanukkah, and said they'd write when they arrived.'

I felt her body tense, as if the words were too hardened to speak.

'Then nothing. No news, no letters. It started to eat me up, that not knowing. By December, I couldn't cope. I just needed to feel *something*.' She laughed, a broken sound. 'I never even gave it a thought. I never considered that I would end up feeling too much.'

I wrapped my arms around her, and held her close in the shelter of that blanket, until the hardness began to leave her body. The rain was petering out now, droplets vanishing into the air.

'Myriam,' I whispered, wanting the world below to dissolve into water and leave us here, safe, above the flood, 'I . . . I love you.'

She turned in my arm, pressed her face into the crook of my neck, holding me tight.

'Like this?' I felt one of her hands creep to her middle. The questioning in her voice almost broke my heart.

I shifted on the floor, so that I could see her. Tentatively, I placed my free hand on the curve of her belly. 'This is you,' I told her, wishing I had better words. 'Made of you, and you are here, with me. How can I ask for anything else?'

She kissed me then, and we lost the minutes to

each other. Outside, uncaring of us, the sky began to clear.

'Are you hungry?' I asked as we dressed later, pulling on rain-damp clothes. 'I have some *pain bis* in my bag.'

'I couldn't tell you,' she said, as she buttoned her shirt. 'I haven't been able to eat much, so I suppose I must be.' She smiled. 'I keep thinking of that picnic we had in the meadow. If I could eat like that every day, I'd be fat as a hog. It's the other stuff I can't stand, tinned and powdered and watered down.' She took my arm, pulled me close. 'I want food like you gave me, food that's *alive*.' Her eyes lingered on mine. Today they looked almost blue, like the sheen on river rock. 'I don't have anything to give this child but life.'

I would find it for her, I promised. This land was mine and I knew its secrets. Everywhere there were mouths, and food was scarce, but up here we could keep what we found. We could gorge on it and share it only with each other. I would give her the food of the mountains, I told her: trout caught from the river's pools, tasting of silt and cold water, raised on flecks of ice. Plums and cherries, snatched from trees that clung to the rocks, wild herbs, peppery and green, to feed the life inside her. I'd catch her rabbits and partridges, and she would eat them, nose to tail, beak to foot, so that the mountains would come to see her as their own and protect her.

That day, I led the way through the glistening meadow and down towards the river where the holm oaks grew, making everything green and cool.

'What are we looking for?' she asked, kneeling beside me.

'Whatever we can find,' I laughed, the scent of growing things strong in my nose.

That day, I showed her how to recognize *coustelline*, with its bluish-leaves and sunny yellow flowers. I pointed out a clump of rocket, and we chewed on its mustardy, juicy leaves. Near by, there were wild radishes. We ate those too, until, mouths burning, we had to drink from the river, letting the icy water cool the fiery heat on our tongues. We followed the stream back towards the village, and I used the edge of the blanket to collect nettles, and a bunch of thyme for Papa and me to use in the bakery.

Noon was approaching by the time we reached the edge of the town. We were muddy, both of us, our clothes sodden at the hems, fingernails green from picking leaves and shoots. I stood for a moment, listening to the church bells, to the cough and splutter of an engine, to a dog barking, children squealing in a game. It seemed like another world, one that would burst the simplicity that existed between us up there on the mountain.

I can breathe, she'd once said to me, on the slopes above the village. *Out here I can breathe.* For the first time, I truly understood what she meant.

'Do you know,' she said, coming to stand beside me. 'I think I may start writing again.'

'Really?' I turned to her. 'What about?'

'I'm not sure yet. About this place, maybe. About you.'

317

'Me?'

'Yes, Celeste.' She laughed at my dazed expression. 'You. But do not get your hopes up. I haven't written a thing for ages.' She breathed out, tilted her head back. 'I keep finding words, though, floating about my mind, like pieces of a daisy chain.' She looked at me. 'Especially at night. They always come to me then. When I can hear you working in the kitchen below.'

'Will you let me read it?'

The idea that Myriam might be able to describe what I was feeling — let alone write about it — was incredible to me, intoxicating.

'I might,' she teased and took my hand. 'One day.'

Saint-Antoine

May 1993

My bag thuds against my side as I walk.

'Is she all right?' I ask Aline, jumping the *gargouille* as if I've done it all my life. 'Should we call Dr Sala?'

'I already asked Nino to telephone the doctor, to let him know.'

We hurry across the dusty square, setting a dog outside the café barking. At the hotel, I take the stairs two at a time.

'Grand-mère!'

She looks tiny in the bed, even smaller than usual. But she's smiling back at me, her brown eyes bright.

'Are you all right?' I gasp, dropping down beside the bed. 'I'm so sorry. I never would have brought you here if I had known it would hurt you.'

She is shaking her head at me, an expression on her face somewhere between frustration and amusement. Her mouth opens and closes for a second, fish-like. 'I . . . ' The noise emerges with difficulty. 'Wanted to.' Her eyes crease. 'Stubborn . . . old woman.'

I grip her hand, trying to disguise my horror. Her speech is slow and stilted, nothing like the quick-tongued woman of yesterday.

319

'Your m-mother?' she asks a moment later, eyes fixed on mine. 'Evie?'

'I told her we were here. She's on the other side of the world, but she said she would try to get here as soon as she could.'

'Mam'selle Picot?' someone calls from the corridor. There's the sound of hurried footsteps and a moment later, Nino appears. 'The doctor will be here soon,' he says, before catching my grandmother's eye. He has the strangest expression on his face, one of tentative hope. Grand-mère frowns, as if trying to place him, and he grins; a mischievous look that makes his face seem twenty years younger.

'Hello, Ceci,' he says.

I watch Grand-mère's eyes open wide. 'Nino?' she whispers. 'R-Rocher?'

The man nods, self-consciously drawing himself up. 'Been a long time, Ceci. Sorry. Madame Picot. Or . . . ' His smile wavers. 'I'll stick with Ceci. Like old times.'

I stare between them. *Ceci?* My grandmother is smiling too, her mouth working. 'You,' she says eventually, pointing around at the room, 'own this?'

'Yes,' Nino says, putting his hands in his pockets. 'Who would have thought it, eh? I'm on the tourism committee too. Alfio even ran for mayor.'

Grand-mère makes a wheezing noise and I grab for her hand, only to realize she's laughing.

'And what about you, Ceci?' Nino asks, edging forward. 'I've already met your lovely granddaughter. But . . . where did you go? I'm going

320

to be honest, we all thought you might be dead. Even Leon wondered that, before he died.'

The muscles in Grand-mère's jaw twitch as she stares at the man. I could hit him for asking such a pointed question, for upsetting her, but she's already answering.

'P . . . ' She struggles, and can't seem to get the word out. 'P . . . ' She looks at me, frustrated.

'Paris?' I ask her, and she nods, relieved. 'Paris,' I tell Nino. 'She lived in Paris for a while, with my mum, Evelyne. And after that, London.' I realize for the first time what a huge leap it must have been for her, to leave this tiny, remote place for a huge, chaotic metropolis.

'London?' Nino sounds amazed. 'Ceci Corvin, living in London.' He flushes a little. 'And what about her? Did you ever — '

Before he can finish, there's a shout from the stairs, Aline calling him. 'Ah,' he says, flustered. 'I had better see what that is.' He pauses in the doorway. 'I'm very glad to see you, Ceci.'

I wait until he's gone. 'Ceci?' I ask.

Grand-mère has closed her eyes. She nods. 'What they . . . called me.' She opens one eye, looks at me. 'Hated it.'

I help her drink a glass of water, and get ready for the doctor's arrival. At her request, I lift her cavernous handbag on to the bed.

'My pills?' she asks rather mournfully, after poking through with one hand.

I had almost forgotten.

'Dr Sala took them away,' I tell her sternly. 'Amphetamines, Grand-mère? What were you thinking? Where on earth did you even get them?'

She gives a short laugh at my expression. 'P — porter,' she says. 'At the home. Nice boy.'

She sinks back into the pillows. I watch her face. I don't want to upset her any more, and yet, there's so much I want to ask.

'Grand-mère,' I say at last, 'when Nino said 'her' just now, he meant Myriam, didn't he?'

She blinks her eyes open, looks over at me, and there's such sadness there that I want to bite back the question and swallow it again. But I can't. A moment later, she nods.

'What happened to her?' Now it's my voice that won't seem to work. 'What happened between the two of you?'

Her eyes crease. I watch them fill with moisture. Then she's struggling with her bag, pulling the worn envelope out on to the bed, the one that contains the page she was reading at the station.

'Her words,' she says, looking exhausted. 'The book she never . . . wrote.' She pushes it towards me. 'Read it. Please.'

Saint-Antoine

June 1943

Slowly, summer crept up the mountain. First came the flowers, clouds of honeysuckle, orchids and a rush of green plants that seemed to shoot up in a matter of days.

The sun shone hotter, until I was doubly glad to work at night, and sleep away the baking noons. Summer changed Saint-Antoine, for everyone was equal when it came to the heat.

The townspeople no longer looked askance at the foreign women, washing their linen at the fountains. Our ears were accustomed now to the sound of different languages. Polish and Czech could be heard in the square; Hungarian was spoken as couples took strolls together. Music drifted from windows, songs sung in what I now knew was Yiddish by the families that gathered on Friday evenings. Daniel often visited the villa at the edge of town for prayers. Myriam sometimes went with him, and although I knew she tried to avoid drawing attention to herself or the baby, it was getting harder, as her stomach swelled. On multiple occasions I saw her in the street outside the bakery with other women, smiling uncomfortably as they laid hands to her middle.

The little school had finished for the summer.

I wagered that the children would learn more during those long days of freedom than in any lesson. I heard the Rocher boys speaking now and then in a newly acquired patois of French, Italian, Russian, and whatever other language they could lay their hands on.

With the hungry months of April and May over, we finally had fresh produce again, a relief to mouths tired of old potatoes and powdered eggs. Still, there was never quite enough to eat. Even as we tried to fill ourselves on dandelion and wood sorrel and mustard greens, people could be heard eulogizing over the food we had once taken for granted: dishes of *tartiflette*, rich with cream and eggs and bacon, radishes smothered in fresh, cool butter, the fruit tarts my father used to make, filled with custard and nutmeg. It all seemed luxurious to the point of absurdity now.

But we always had bread, and as chief gendarme, Paul's father had his pick of whatever black market goods came his way. As the weather grew better and the days grew longer, illicit crossings over the Italian border increased. When a *passeur* got caught on the mountain trails, his knapsack and pockets laden with goods from Italy, Paul's father would come home happy. Technically, he should have handed over the contraband to the Italian authorities, but he never did. It was a matter of pride; one of the only ways he could exercise the power the Italians had taken from him.

The first night it happened, I could barely believe my eyes. I watched as he placed a hunk of parmesan on the table, bigger than my hand, and a whole cured *prosciutto di Cuneo*.

Agathe had hurried to close the shutters, and none of us spoke as we set the table, our eyes fixed on the food, mouths watering, blood leaping in anticipation. Almost reverently, Paul's father took a knife to the crumbling cheese, and handed the plate around.

Slowly, I picked up a piece and placed it in my mouth. It shocked me with its richness, warm as hazelnuts, sharp and powerful as seawater on the tongue. I had not eaten prosciutto for a long time, either. It was cut wafer-thin, a transparent rosy pink. I had forgotten how strange it felt, slick as riverweed in my mouth, tasting of the farmyard that made it, the salt of the Mediterranean and the cool, mountain air.

Things were far from easy between Paul and me, thanks to our awkward nights together, but still, neither of us could keep from smiling at one another as we chewed, thrilling at those potent flavours, so long untasted.

For the first time in months, my stomach felt replete, and I wished I could have shared it all with Myriam.

'This is just a fraction of what the man was carrying,' Paul's father told us, when we finally sat back, every tiny crumb scooped up. The rest of the meat and cheese had been wrapped carefully and hidden away.

'You should've seen what else he had. We let him go with most of it, of course. That way, he'll come back, and we can keep an eye on him.' He winked at me. *We can take our cut*, he meant. I

325

smiled back, feeling almost drunk on the food.

'Where do they get it all?' I asked. I wondered if the salt deliveries I received from Michel, via the Rocher boys, were coming from a man like this *passeur*.

Paul's father shrugged, his sunburned cheeks flushed. 'Got their contacts, haven't they? They take what *we* have over there, sugar and cigarette papers mostly, and bring back what *they* have.' He nodded at Paul over his wine glass. 'So it's best we catch them on the way back.'

After that day, cured meats were something of a regular addition at the Picot house. They kept them secret, would share them only sometimes with my parents. Agathe kept a close eye on them, so however much I wanted to, I was never able to steal any for Myriam.

Paul spent less time patrolling the town and more time accompanying his father into the hills, scouting the mountain trails for *passeurs*. There was nothing for them to do in the town, anyway, other than stand around and look for trouble. Some of the young Jewish boys liked to mock Paul, I'd noticed, especially when he walked around in uniform, with his hand on his empty gun holster. They knew he couldn't touch them, no matter what they did, since they were under the protection of the Italians. So even though he often came back from his scouting missions sunburned and empty handed, he seemed glad to get away.

I was glad too. It meant that I had the afternoons to myself. As often as we could, Myriam and I would meet on the edge of town and flee into the shade of the wooded slopes, away from the hot sun and prying eyes. There, we could be alone. There, the taste of skin and sweat became mixed up with the scent of crushed pine and the perfume of the forest raspberries we'd gather to eat.

Myriam's body was changing every day. Her belly was swelling, growing taut and hard as an upturned bowl. A dark line of hair was forming from her navel downwards, like a swipe of charcoal. It was only when I saw her bare that I realized how thin the rest of her body was, why no one had been able to tell she was carrying a child for so long.

'I hate it,' she murmured, propped on her elbows, looking down at herself. 'I don't feel like me. And my breasts,' she sat up, crossed her arms over her chest, 'they *ache*.'

They had grown larger too, until she complained that none of her brassieres fit any more.

'Then go without one,' I had said drowsily, trailing my fingers along her shoulder.

She had snorted with laughter. 'And risk the disapproval of the matrons?' She looked down at me. 'I remember the first time I saw you, your blouse clinging to your back, working there in the bakery. You looked so strong, so *alive*.' She brushed her fingers over my forehead, through my hair, and watched me shiver. 'I wanted you then. I wanted to be you.'

Seeing the thinness of her limbs that day, I swore that I would do everything I could to love her, to make her stronger.

'You're not eating enough,' I said sternly, as we walked back to the town, my basket full of borage and wild chicory.

She made a face. 'The doctor says I should have meat, but the coupons only get us ninety grams, *with* bones. And all we can find are offcuts. I know I should be grateful even for that but I just can't stomach it.' She glanced at me. 'The baby doesn't want that kind of food. Whenever you give me something to eat, it's happy.' She smiled. 'I'm happy.'

'How about an exchange,' I said, pausing for one last kiss, before we had to part ways at the edge of town. 'Food for words. I want to read what you've been writing.'

She groaned. 'I haven't got very far. When you read it, you'll see that it's not a fair exchange.'

'Myriam!'

'All right.' She held up her hands. 'All right. One page. I will write out a copy for you.'

⋆   ⋆   ⋆

It was the strangest thing, but as Myriam's pregnancy advanced, the bolder I grew. Over the days and weeks that followed, I began to care less and less about what people thought of me. I had spent eighteen years being obedient, pleasing people, being quiet, being good. Perhaps it was Myriam's influence, but I found that I was no longer content to be little Ceci, the baker's girl. I was a wife; I wanted to be treated like a woman.

I tried to make Paul understand. Every time I

328

asked him to call me Celeste he would shrug and agree, but it would be 'Ceci' again, a minute later.

He murmured it in my ear one night, sliding his hand beneath my nightgown.

'No,' I told him, pushing him away. I didn't want to play the awful game of our marriage any more. I didn't want to pretend.

'Come on,' he said, reaching out again.

'I said no, Paul!' I sat up in bed, stared down at him. His cheeks were flushed, his mouth open.

'Ceci,' he said, 'we're *married*.'

'What does that have to do with anything?'

Hurt flashed across his face, and anger.

'You're my wife,' he said. 'You're supposed to listen to me.'

I made a noise, turned away.

'You're supposed to listen to me,' he repeated, grabbing my shoulder. When I didn't reply, his face turned hard. 'Other men don't have to ask, you know, they take their wives when they want.'

I stared at him. All at once my nervousness and guilt were replaced by anger. This was *Paul* talking to me, Paul who I'd known for ever.

'Then go ahead,' I snapped, 'go ahead, if you want to make me hate you.'

He pulled back, shocked. 'Ceci — '

'No,' I rounded on him, 'you said that you would make me happy. Do you think that's what you're doing now?'

The heat of my words filled the air between us, collected on those stiff sheets, until there was no room for anything else. Paul looked away, his face contorted.

'This is about her, isn't it?' he said, his voice low. 'That *woman*. She's putting ideas into your head.'

'If she is,' I told him, 'I'm glad.'

Paul did not try to sleep with me again for a while, after that. Sometimes, I would look at his back beneath the sheets and feel sorrow for the sweet friend I had lost, for both of us, trapped.

But at other times, I couldn't help but feel glad of it. When I was not at the bakery, Papa assumed I was with Paul or Agathe. Agathe assumed that I was at the bakery, or my grandmother's. It widened my days, granted me precious stretches of empty hours that — for the first time in my life — were my own, to do with as I pleased.

And so, I gave them to Myriam.

Daniel had begun to stay away from the apartment again, sometimes returning dog-tired in the middle of the night. Papa turned a blind eye, and none of us spoke of it, even Myriam. But I had my suspicions. Paul and his father had begun to talk more about the growing number of 'saboteurs' in the area, about explosives detonated near the Italian barracks in Nice. It was better to say nothing.

As June slipped into July, growing hotter and hotter, I began to spend every moment I could find with Myriam. Her stomach was large now on her slim frame, and she no longer fit any of her clothes, even Daniel's trousers, though Dr Brion told her she likely had two months to wait before she delivered.

'Two months,' she groaned to me, when we

330

escaped the town for the coolness of the river. 'I already feel like a whale.'

In spring, the bank we were sitting on would be covered in raging snowmelt, but now, at the height of summer, it was a sleepy, sandy cove. Myriam lay with her feet in the water, her head cushioned in my lap, dressed in only her thin cotton chemise. Through it I could see the flush of her skin, the curve of her belly, her full breasts.

'You look beautiful,' I murmured, stroking her dark curls back from her forehead.

'Liar,' she said. She reached up, touched the skin of my shoulder. 'Look at you, though, you look as if you've swallowed the sun.'

I smiled. The hours I spent foraging the slopes and forests had burned the skin of my face and arms brown, made freckles come out in a scatter across my nose and turned my hair a straggly gold, like ripe wheat.

'You look like a creature of the mountain,' she said. A moment later her expression turned inward, the way it did sometimes. I didn't interrupt, just sat there in the dappled sunlight, holding her.

'Celeste,' she said, 'do you remember before, what I told you about feeling trapped?'

How could I forget? The memory of her, coiled hard on that narrow bed, haunted me. I twined my fingers with hers, willing it away. 'Yes.'

Her lips twitched into a sad smile. 'It was because I felt that if I were to die here, my soul would somehow be stuck, trapped for ever in these mountains. *That* is what scared me.' She looked up, into my eyes. 'Now, I'm not so afraid. You are part of these mountains, you were born here, you might die here one day, years from now. As long as you're here, my soul will have a place to go.'

I felt my chest filling up then. There was nothing I could do but lean over and kiss her.

'I'll keep you safe,' I whispered, my lips brushing hers. 'I promised you, remember?'

'My girl,' she said softly, 'it might not be your promise to keep.'

Saint-Antoine

May 1993

Before I can open the envelope, Dr Sala arrives and I have to put it to one side, though I'm desperate to read what's written within. *Her words*. Instead, I sit with Grand-mère and hold her hand, while Dr Sala takes her blood pressure, looks into her eyes and talks to her about how she is feeling. He listens patiently to her stilted answers.

When he's finished his examination, I walk him out of the hotel to his car.

'Is she going to recover?' I ask quietly.

'In the short term, yes,' he says, putting his bag in the boot. 'It's likely she had a transient ischaemic attack yesterday. A mini-stroke,' he explains, seeing my face. 'It seems she's suffered from a number of them in the past.'

I nod, remembering what nurse Alain said. 'The home told me that. I completely forgot.' I rub at my eyes. 'What about her speech? Will it get better?'

'It should be back to normal soon enough.' Dr Sala looks at me. 'She's weak still. The bloods I sent off to Nice should tell us more about her general health, but that'll take a few days, I'm afraid.'

I smile, shake my head. 'It doesn't look like

I'm going anywhere for now, does it?'

He smiles back. 'It would be good if you could stay.'

His eyes are a deep hazel, I notice, flecked with gold. Faint laughter lines fan away towards his temples. For a moment we both stand there, with the mid-morning sun all around us.

'Well — '

'I'd better — '

'Thanks.' I step back on to the pavement, tongue-tied. 'Dr Sala!' I call a second later, as he's getting into the car.

He stands up as if he's been stung. 'Yes?'

'Thank you, for everything you're doing for Grand-mère. I really do appreciate it.'

'It is my job, Mam'selle Picot. But I am glad to help. Your grandmother seems like a remarkable woman.'

'She is,' I tell him. 'And please, call me Annie.'

'Annie, then,' he says softly, 'à bientôt.'

Upstairs, Grand-mère is looking livelier. When she says that she would like to take a bath, I help her up from the bed and into one of the hotel's robes. As the water runs into the tub, we talk about little things, easy things, like the new bakery in the town, and the bread I've bought her.

She laughs and thanks me, haltingly says that she will go and judge them for herself soon. Words hang unspoken between us in the steamed-up air. We're both afraid, I realize: afraid to touch the past, in case what happened to Grand-mère in the old bakery happens again. In case the past has the power to hurt us.

334

She lays a hand on my arm as I leave her to have a bath in peace. 'Read it?' she says, her eyes intent.

I nod, try to smile. 'I'll be right outside,' I tell her.

In the room, I rearrange the bed and push the window wide. I sit beneath the billowing net curtain, staring at the envelope in my hands.

Finally, with the sound of church bells echoing through the streets, I lift the flap and slide the page out.

It is handwritten. I force myself to be professional for a moment, to examine the paper. It looks as if it was once cut carefully from a notebook. The ink must have been a cheap kind, and although it has faded it's still legible. The handwriting itself is fascinating, somewhere between old-world elegance and a restless scrawl, cursive loops giving way to hurried slashes and dots that have bitten into the paper, as if whoever wrote this was leaning into the page, pushing themselves through the pen. *Her words.* Did Myriam write this, all those years ago?

They say Lot's wife was turned into a pillar of salt for looking back.

I have tried to write of the future, but I cannot find the words. I have tried to write of freedom, but I can't remember its taste. And so, look back I must, to the beginning of what might prove to be my final summer on this earth. If my punishment for that is salt, so be it.

It's not a letter at all. It's the start of a chapter, the beginning of a story. *Never finished.* A single page; is this all that's left of Myriam?

As soon as I reach the end I begin to read over again, each time building a clearer picture of Saint-Antoine in my mind; not the one I arrived in yesterday morning, but a different one, of fifty years ago, seen through the eyes of someone who was also a stranger here. I can almost taste the burning of bitter herbs on my tongue, feel the chill of snowmelt in my belly, smell crushed grass and fallen wild fruit, filling the air around me.

I reach for you.

I feel my eyes widen. I hear myself asking again, *What happened to her? What happened between the two of you?*

Bread, salt, the writing answers. *Life. Love.*

I stare at that precious page, stunned by the secret that my grandmother must have carried with her for so long.

Saint-Antoine

Summer 1943

It might not be your promise to keep.

No matter how I tried to forget her words in the days that followed, they clung to me. They echoed through my mind at strange moments, like when I was cutting branches of rosemary for Papa and me to use in the bakery, or picking blue-flowered mountain lettuce and chamomile to cool and calm Myriam on hot evenings.

The days were long and languid, but beneath the surface they simmered; not with anxiety, quite, but with a restlessness that made my feet dance when I tried to sit still, that made me want to shriek and run wild like the children, feral with summer.

With her ever-growing bump, Myriam was often too tired to walk all the way to the meadow, so I thought of other outings for us instead. Her favourite thing to do was to go to the river and catch crayfish, using a pair of old nylons I stole from Agathe as a net. Together, we would sit with our feet in the shallows, using whatever scraps we could find for bait. Myriam would wear her dark glasses and smoke and call for the crayfish to come out until my laughter would have frightened any creature away. In the end, we would lie on our backs on the sunlit bank, drowsing until the nets trembled in the stream and we could pull them up, excited to see what we had caught.

I would make a fire and we would cook the crayfish right there on the shore, with water from the river and wild flowering fennel from the banks. We would boil them in an old coffee can the way I had when I was a child, until they were done and we could eat them hot from their shells, like a pair of savages.

Once, a pair of Italian soldiers found us there, after smelling the smoke from the campfire. I thought we would be in trouble, but they had only smiled and asked us what we were doing. Before the hour was out, they had shed their jackets, rolled up their trousers and were splashing through the river, trying to catch crayfish of their own, one of them losing the cigarette from his lip when he yelled in excitement, and all the while us laughing at them, calling words of encouragement.

As the summer wore on, the Italians had begun to act less and less like soldiers. News crept from wirelesses and newspapers, brought up a day late by the bus. The Allies had invaded Sicily, the war was lost, said some, Germany would be sending reinforcements, said others. Il Duce was finished, I heard one soldier declare to another.

If anything, they seemed relieved. They began to drop their pretences of duty, acting instead like the young men they were. More than once I saw some of them playing lazy games of football with the young people, before slumping in the shade at the edge of the field. At first, the *capitano* had tried to keep them in order. He disciplined them for incomplete uniforms, or for lounging or singing rebellious songs, but the day I saw him giving a piggy-back to a little girl with a grazed knee, I knew that even he had given in and was no longer a *capitano*; he was just a man, a father, who wanted to go home to his family.

I didn't know how it made me feel. I should have been happy. They were the occupiers, after all, they had imposed upon our lives in Saint-Antoine, they had taken our sovereignty, people said. If they went home, we would no longer be under their thumb. But, I couldn't help thinking, if the Italians left, what would replace them? I didn't believe Leon when he declared *France for the French*. The rest of the country — outside the slim, Italian zone that surrounded us — was commanded by the Germans. Would it mean a *kommandantur*, to answer to? Would it mean *feldgendarmerie* on their motorbikes, *kettenhunde* as I had heard them called by some of the foreigners: chained dogs. Would that be better?

And what of the Jews in Saint-Antoine? The thought brought a flash of fear. Once the Italians were gone, what would happen to them?

There were no answers. But during those hot days, with change hanging over our heads, everyone seemed to live harder, drink deeper, talk louder, whether to make the most of our current freedom or to distract ourselves from the distant rumble of thunder, I couldn't tell.

Things began to change at the end of a hot

339

July day, like any other. I lay drowsing on the bed at the Picots' house, woken from an afternoon nap. Paul was out on patrol in the hills, and I had the room to myself. Myriam had been suffering from cramps in her back and was resting today. Tomorrow, I would make her a *tisane* of chamomile to try to ease the pain, just as Mama used to do for me, when my time of the month was bad.

Abruptly, I opened my eyes in the shuttered light. Cold prickled down my neck. When had my last monthly course been? It was so hard to keep track, these stifling days. I counted the weeks by Myriam's condition, by the ripening fruit on the trees. Not this month, I realized in horror. It had not come.

Alarmed, I sat up, and propped myself on my elbows, as Myriam had done, to stare down at my belly. I didn't *feel* different, but perhaps it was too early to tell. I pushed down a wave of nausea and rolled over, hands around my middle. I hated the feeling that something might be happening inside me without my knowledge, without my agreement. Was this the source of the restlessness that had been filling my body? It seemed to reach a pitch then, until I felt as if tiny creatures were swimming, scrabbling through my veins. I barely made it to the toilet before I was sick.

I didn't say anything to Agathe. I didn't need to. She had heard me retching and spluttering in the bathroom, and was waiting when I came out, pale and filmed in cold sweat.

'Ceci,' she said, 'are you all right? Do you

think it might be . . . ?'

I looked down so she couldn't see my face, the tears of rage and fear that had reddened my eyes. 'I don't know,' I muttered. 'It might just be a stomach upset.'

She clasped my arms. 'Well, we'll find out before too long, won't we? Back to bed for now, though, you look white as a sheet.'

But I couldn't sleep. Lying on those clammy, twisted bedclothes, I wanted to scream from the not knowing of it all. I needed to move; I had to do *something*. That evening there was to be a concert in the town. Everyone would be there, even the Italians. No one would be watching the hillsides. As late afternoon slid into evening, I pushed myself from the bed and began to dress, hurriedly plaiting my hair. I would go and hunt, I thought wildly, I would go on to the mountainside and shoot, until the thunder and force of the gun took some of the frenzy from my veins.

'Ceci!' Agathe said, when I hurried down the stairs. 'How are you feeling?'

'Better, thank you.' My heart was thudding as I stood there. 'I was thinking of taking a walk to Grandmother's, to eat supper with her before the concert.'

Agathe nodded. 'We will see you there. Paul said he would come too, if he returns from patrol on time.' Her eyes flickered to my middle. 'I'm sure you will be wanting to see him.'

I forced my face into a smile as I fled past.

Soon, I was making for the road out of town. It was early evening and the streets were busy; no

341

one noticed one more person amongst the strolling couples and running children. I walked swiftly, blood beating, trying to stride past the nausea that rose in my throat.

I reached the hut as the bells tolled half past seven. This was the time for hunting rabbits, when they emerged from their burrows after the heat of the day to eat the cooling grass. The moment I unwrapped the gun, I felt calmer, stronger. Agathe might be whispering about my condition already — to Paul's father, to her friends — but she didn't know about this. This was mine. It made me feel reckless, like a criminal. Which I suppose I was.

There was no time to dwell, not if I wanted to get back in time for the concert. Listening for any sign of life, and finding none, I set off away from the town, towards the forested slopes and the steep path that led to the village of Belvedere.

The sun had already vanished from this side of the valley, leaving it cool and dim with gathering dusk. As I walked further, the noises of the town were lost behind me, replaced by the vast quietness of the mountains. Night insects trilled and clicked, birds whirred in sudden flight through the trees. The smell of warm, crushed pine needles rose all around me, until finally, I began to feel calm. This was my mountain. It was in my blood, just as it would be in the blood of any child I carried. That thought let me breathe again.

I stopped when I reached the edge of the Belvedere path, little more than a winding, terraced track through the trees, with grass growing between its curves. I'd seen rabbits here before, and it was far enough from the town that a rifle shot would — hopefully — go unnoticed.

I crept on to the grassy bank and lay down, the rifle pointed upwards, letting my eyes adjust to the shadows. Sure enough, my eyes picked out the dark shapes of droppings, littering the grass. In the distance, I heard the church bells toll eight. I tried to make myself still, waiting in the dim light, my arms aching from holding the gun. I didn't have a watch, but even so, I felt the minutes slide past and began to worry that I would not catch anything, that I would soon have to sneak back to the town. Then, just as I was ready to give up, I heard a scuffling, the gentle, rhythmic thud of paws on earth. Through the grass I saw a flash of white, a bobtail. Six feet above me on the slope, a rabbit was lowering its head to graze.

Silently, I brought the gun to my eye, and fired.

The sound split the quiet, made my nerves screech and my ears ring. I didn't move, just gripped the gun and lay still in the grass. But it soon passed. I was able to climb to my hands and knees and crawl forward to look. The rabbit was dead, the soft fur of its throat bloodied. An almost perfect shot.

As I touched it, a second sound exploded into the silence. A gunshot. It rang in my ears and for a terrible moment I thought the rifle had discharged accidentally, but no, it hadn't. Which meant that someone else . . .

Another shot rang out, then another. Then there were voices, feet running, and I cowered into the grass, my mind blank with fear. Footsteps were coming closer, figures were emerging from the trees, skidding on to the path above, two, three of them, sprinting madly. There was a crash and a scuffle; one of them had leapt from the road to land on the slope beside me, a familiar voice letting out a curse.

It was Michel Rocher. I must have cried out because he looked up, eyes frantic, his teeth red with blood, as if he'd bitten his own lip. His eyes fell on the rifle beside me.

'Idiot!' he swore.

A second later he was on his feet and running, disappearing into the undergrowth, a knapsack thudding on his back.

Run, my brain screamed at me, *run!* But everything seemed to be happening too slowly. I staggered to my feet and took a step away, only to remember the rifle. I turned back for it just as another figure leapt from the path, sprawling into the grass, crying out in pain. I knew that voice. The figure rolled over, spectacles askew, jaw clenched. It was Daniel Reiss.

I stumbled towards him. 'Daniel,' I gasped, 'what's going on?'

His eyes were huge, frantic, as he took in my face, the rifle beside me. 'Celeste?'

From the trees I heard shouts, the crush of boots on branches, the jangle of buckles.

'It's the *milice*,' he hissed through gritted teeth. 'Or something like them. Doesn't matter.'

All of those nights out after dark, the

exhausted, bleak expression he sometimes wore, his trips to Nice with packages: here was proof.

'You're *Résistance?*'

Before he could answer, there was another shout. At any moment, they would find us. If Daniel was caught, he'd be arrested, taken away from here, maybe sent east like Myriam's parents. I seized him by the jacket and pulled him with me.

'What are you doing?' he choked, as I dragged him to the slope where Michel had disappeared.

'Stay down,' I gasped, 'don't move until they're gone.'

I didn't wait for him to answer, but used all of my strength to push him sideways, sending him tumbling, rolling down the slope into the undergrowth beneath the trees. The moment I turned to pick up the rifle, figures burst on to the path.

'Stop!' someone yelled. There were boots, and the smell of men, and hands grappling roughly with my arms. I recognized some of them: young men from the town, boys really, too young to be called up or sent away to the work camps. Others were older, bringing up the rear. They spoke with city accents and held guns, they wore *milice* blue, playing at being police. There was someone else with them, someone in a dark, worn uniform, secured with a belt I had seen a hundred times before. He was bending, picking up the rifle that I'd left in the grass.

All the air went out of my lungs. It was Paul.

★　★　★

I stood and watched, my hands empty, as one of the *milice* picked up the rabbit I had shot and shoved it into his bag. My jaw clenched, but I couldn't stop him. Instead, I stared at Paul's back, as he stood in muttered conversation with the other men. He was speaking earnestly, gesturing at me, but I couldn't hear what he said.

How long had the gendarmerie been helping the *milice* to hunt for *Résistance* in the hills, when they were supposedly looking to catch smugglers? For the first time it occurred to me that Michel Rocher might be both of those things: smuggler and *Résistance* member, criminal and fighter, one and the same. But what about Monsieur Reiss? There was little love lost for the *Résistance* around here; people were too afraid of reprisals. Not necessarily from the Italians, but we'd all heard stories from other villages, of people rounded up, even shot indiscriminately as revenge when a power line had been cut, or a building attacked.

I looked up, unable to stop trembling. The group of men were splitting up, those in *milice* uniform heading back up the hill towards Belvedere, others tramping down in the direction of Saint-Antoine. A few of them looked my way and laughed as Paul came walking towards me, the rifle slung over his shoulder.

'Let's go,' he said gruffly.

I had expected him to haul me away, but to my astonishment, he put an arm stiffly around me and waved to the departing men. We started walking towards the town. I had gone through every excuse I could think of, waiting there, and now a strange, grim calm filled me. There was nothing I could do.

The moment the other men were out of eyeshot, Paul let his arm drop. In silence, we walked the steep, wooded path, taking a different way back to town, rather than cutting through the meadow. At last, the path broke free of the trees and we emerged on to the bridge, the place where — all those months ago — he'd kissed me for the first time, and I'd kissed him back, thinking of Myriam, my heart bleeding out into birdsong.

It was coming up to nine now. The square would be packed with people listening to the concert. The sound drifted down to us over the old walls, brass instruments echoing through the valley.

'I managed to convince them it was *you* who gave us the tip-off,' Paul said finally. 'I told them that you've been working with me, and that one of the men dropped the gun as he ran.'

'One of the men?' I asked, thinking of Daniel, still hidden in the forest.

Paul flashed me a look. 'The saboteurs. Don't pretend to be stupid, Ceci.'

'I don't know anything about them,' I said, as firmly as I could. 'I've been using the gun to hunt, to trade for the salt we need in the bakery — '

'You lied to me.'

It wasn't the rage in his voice that was so terrible, I could have dealt with that. It was the hurt; a deep hurt, right down to the bone. Hurt that would leave a scar. I stared at him, my stomach twisting with pity and anger and the knowledge of what might be happening in my body, even as we spoke.

'Yes.' I said.

'What else have you lied to me about?'

The bright notes of the town band, distorted by distance, filled the space where my answer should have been. Paul gave a strangled sort of laugh. The next thing I knew he was grabbing me by the arms, his fingers digging into my flesh, and was shoving his mouth against mine. I couldn't stop the noise of protest that broke from me as I turned my head away.

'You see?' he said hoarsely. 'You don't even want me.' He didn't let go. 'What's happened to you, Ceci?'

'What's happened to you, Paul?' I wrenched myself from his grip. 'When did you join the *milice*?'

'I haven't.' His voice was low, defensive. 'We are looking for the same people, so we patrol together. I'm just doing my job.'

'They're thugs. Helping them isn't your job. You know it isn't.' I stepped towards him, wanting the old Paul to look at me, with his wide blue eyes and his flushed cheeks. 'Where did the sweet boy I grew up with go?'

Above us, in the town, the band played the final notes of a song. The sound of applause and cheers drifted down to us.

'I protected you,' Paul said, his voice weak. 'I didn't have to do that. I can report you to my father, I can tell *your* father what you've been doing — '

348

'Go ahead,' I threw at him, turning away. 'Show your future child exactly the kind of man you are.'

I heard Paul make a noise behind me.

'Ceci,' he said, voice choked, 'are you . . . ?'

'I think so.' I couldn't keep the fear from my voice, but neither could I let Paul touch me, not then. 'Do what you have to,' I told him, suddenly exhausted by it all. I stepped away before he could reach for me. 'I will be in the square.'

Dazed, I walked into the town, hands limp by my side. I was tired of conflict, tired of pretending, of seeing everything familiar twisted out of shape, until it was unrecognizable and frightening.

I stopped at the edge of the square. People had brought chairs from their homes, and had arranged them in a rough circle. They were watching Wolf and Annette, who stood side by side, playing a duet on violin and flute. I could see Paul's parents sitting with my mother and father. No doubt they all thought I was with Paul. I stared around until I found Myriam, surrounded by the women she called the 'matrons'.

I took a step forward, unthinking, just wanting to speak to her, when a ripple began to spread through the crowd. People were talking, shushing and grabbing each other's arms until Wolf and Annette slowed and stopped, mid-melody. The commotion was coming from the bar.

I hustled forward with everyone else. A group of Italian soldiers were crowded around the wireless, and were waving frantically for us to be quiet, their mouths open.

'*Attenzione*,' came a voice from the wireless, sombre and clear. '*Attenzione*.'

Someone was translating, whispers running back through the crowd that was now pushing at the doors.

'His Majesty the King has accepted the resignation from office by the head of government . . . his excellency Sir Benito Mussolini.'

'Il Duce has fallen!' someone yelled. 'He's done!'

'He's done?' I heard someone next to me ask, as all around people began to murmur, to shriek and clap. 'Does that mean it's over?'

'No, listen to what they're saying.' That was Monsieur Gougeard from the hotel, who spoke Italian. '*La guerra continua. L'Italia tiene fede alla parola data*. The war goes on. Italy will be true to its word.'

'They're just stalling,' someone said. 'It is over for them, it must be, the Allies are invading — '

'We are going home!' I heard one young soldier crow in French.

Everything was confusion and laughter, questioning in more languages than I could count. I searched through the chaos for Myriam, only to see her staring through the crowd, looking for Daniel, one hand laid protectively across her growing belly.

Saint-Antoine

May 1993

I don't know how long I sit staring at the page,
as the afternoon drifts by outside the window.
Love? I think, reaching for the photograph
album again.

The groom looks back from the wedding
picture, smiling, his fair hair slick, his hand
clasping Grand-mère's. Her face is serious,
distant, her dark eyes staring into the lens of the
camera as if she is not seeing it at all. At once, I
feel a strange twinge of sympathy for them both.

Their marriage couldn't have been happy, I
realize. And it was short. By nineteen forty-six,
Grand-mère was a widow, living in Paris. My
fingers tighten around the picture, as I stare at
the grandfather I never knew. He looks friendly,
with round cheeks and an open expression. I
blink away sadness. What happened to him? Did
Grand-mère resent him? I pick up the picture of
Myriam. How must she have felt, falling
pregnant with his child when she was in love
with . . .

A cold thought is creeping across my mind.
What if Grand-mère ended up resenting her own
child? What if that was the real reason why
— thirty years later — they quarrelled and cut
ties the way they did?

I feel my eyes blurring with tears as I look between the pictures. I came here to find Grand-mère, to try to heal the rift between us, to be a family again. I didn't want this mess, this tangle of human emotions that still have the power to wound, even after fifty years.

I throw the pictures on to the bed and stand up, wanting to walk until my thoughts are calm and ordered and tidy.

But the bathroom door opens, and there is Grand-mère, holding on to the wall. With her hair loose and wet over her shoulder, and her skin pink from the heat, she looks younger, more like her sixty-eight years, less like a fragile old woman.

I try to control the emotion rising in my chest, but I can't. I feel horrible for thinking the worst of Grand-mère, but at the same time, I need answers, I need to understand why we've come all this way to raise the past.

'What happened to my grandfather?' I ask. However much I try, I can't keep the sorrow out of my voice. 'What happened to *you*? When are you going to tell me?'

Grand-mère's eyes fall on the photograph lying on the bed. 'Paul,' she says, 'poor Paul.'

'You told Mum he died in the war.'

'He did.' She takes a step towards me, clinging to the wall.

'How? You said that he was a soldier, that he died fighting, but this isn't a soldier's uniform.'

'I never said he was a soldier.'

'But you *implied* it, so that no one would ask questions.' The words are out of my mouth before I can stop them. I'm trembling. Without a father, Grand-mère and Mum are the only family I've ever known. Now, I'm suddenly terrified that everything I thought I knew about them is a lie. Without that, what do I have left?

My eyes are locked on hers. 'Tell me,' I plead.

She shakes her head and looks away. 'Annie,' she mutters.

'You see! It's secrets, always secrets.'

'You don't understand.' Her hand is white on the wall. 'So many terrible things . . . I wanted to spare you and Evie.'

'That isn't for you to decide! We have a *right* to know, Mum and I.'

Grand-mère has closed her eyes, as if weathering a storm.

'All right,' she murmurs. 'All right.' Abruptly, she looks terrified. 'But let me talk, please. I have . . . never told anyone these things. I am frightened of saying it aloud. I'm frightened of . . . what it might do to me.'

I take a breath. The upset that rolled through me is cooling, leaving behind a resolution, a determination to hear my grandmother's words at last, whatever she may have to tell me. I hold out my hand and help her to sit on the bed, before sitting down beside her.

'I'm here,' I tell her, 'I'm listening.'

Her hands are shaking as she gathers up the photograph of the wedding party, and the one of Myriam. She takes a breath.

Saint-Antoine

Summer 1943

Everything changed for good on the day the figs started to fall.

They had been ripening steadily for weeks, their soft, pigskin flesh turning from bright green to reddish purple to black, like a slow-blooming bruise. The best trees hung over the walls of the hotel. On that day, their stems finally began to sunder, sending them thudding to the road, splitting on impact. They were snatched up almost immediately by the townspeople, even though the taste of them was almost too much, now we had gone so long without sugar. Those figs had a savage sweetness that left the blood humming, eaten in quick, furtive bites, like a sin.

My course had never come, and I knew, beyond almost any doubt, that I was carrying Paul's child. I begged my family not to tell anyone. I told them they might jinx it by talking too early. That made them hold their tongues. Although I knew it was foolish, for some reason I did not want Myriam to know. I wanted her to believe that I was hers and hers alone.

So I stayed quiet. It made two secrets that I was keeping from her. I had said nothing of my encounter with Daniel in the forest. It would only worry her, I told myself, when what she needed was peace. When Daniel had returned to the bakery late the night it had happened, I had paused, elbow-deep in the mixing trough. His hands had been scratched and muddy, I saw, as he hid them in his pockets. After he had exchanged a few pleasantries with Papa, he had looked at me. I had held his gaze, and nodded.

I will keep your secret, I told him silently, *for her.*

Paul said nothing more of the night with the gun either. I did not know what he had done with the rifle and I did not ask; that was the bargain between us. Although he tried hard to pretend that we were happy, both of us knew we were not. We were drifting further and further from the friendship we had once shared, until I sometimes felt as if we were two strangers, who happened to share a name and a bed.

Myriam's baby was due within the month, and very often she was tired, her hips aching. Sometimes, she was too exhausted to walk anywhere, even to the river. Then, I would sneak upstairs to the apartment, bringing her slices of bread and runny jam, made from the summer's spoils. We would sit, side by side on my old bed, and Myriam would rest her head against my shoulder. When she wasn't dozing, we would talk gently, dreamily; not of what had happened, but of things that might be.

I imagined the child inside her, a boy or girl, it didn't matter. That child seemed real to me in a way my own pregnancy did not. The baby would have Myriam's dark, curling hair, I decided. It would have Daniel's pointed chin and her tipped-up lip. I imagined us, here in Saint-Antoine, in a summer where there was no war and the grass in the meadows had exploded high in celebration. I saw myself carrying my own child on my hip through the meadow flowers, as Myriam held the hand of hers. Then, we would let go and the children would play, squealing and laughing, and Myriam would look at me and roll her eyes and tell me I was a bad influence, that the children were half mountain goats already. She would place her hand in mine and we would walk, the grass rustling like an ocean, and the birds in the thicket calling out *huit-heure, huit-heure,* as one of the children called out —

'Myriam!'

I sat up, so rapidly that I cricked my neck and Myriam complained sleepily. I had fallen asleep there on the bed, my arms around her, where anyone might have found us. And now someone was calling her name.

'Myriam!'

It was Daniel. I scrambled from the bed, pulling my skirt and blouse straight while Myriam sat up, her hair a mess, eyes puffy from sleep.

'What is it?' she said.

Daniel's feet hammered up the stairs. He threw himself around the doorframe and the moment I saw his face, I knew. It had come, the thing that had been simmering in the summer's heat for so long, the beast-growl that had been building in my chest for weeks: the moment that would change everything.

'The Italians have surrendered.' His face was

pale, despite the sweat that beaded at his temples. 'It's happened. Come to the square quickly. We're gathering there.' He looked my way, unsurprised to find me there. 'You too, Celeste. This concerns all of us.'

'Daniel!' Myriam called after him, but he was already hurrying away, thundering down the stairs and back out of the bakery.

'Oh God.' Myriam's grey eyes had lost their sleepiness, were filled instead with panic. Her hands rested on the ridge of her belly. 'What does this mean?'

I knelt down before her. 'It might be good news,' I said, trying to comfort her. 'Maybe this is the beginning of the end.'

But even as I helped her dress, my mind was racing. I saw German uniforms swarming through town; I saw my neighbours pointing fingers, their faces white with fear, as doors were kicked down, as the families I had come to know over the past few months were dragged out into the street. I saw my brother drawing his revolver as some of the young people tried to run. I saw Myriam caught by the arms and thrown roughly into a truck, with no thought for her condition. I'd protect her, I thought wildly, even though I knew that in other places, people had been arrested, or worse, for sheltering Jews against German orders.

I tried not to let my thoughts show as I helped Myriam into her sandals, but she must have been thinking the same because her face was pale, her eyes terrified.

Outside, every house of Saint-Antoine was

357

disgorging its people. Doors stood wide open, women in slippers and headscarves hurrying out, carrying children still half-soaped from washing, still chewing dinners. There was a strange feeling in the air, like a shriek, jubilant or frightened and no one sure which.

The square was packed, people spilling from the doors of the cafés where the wirelesses were tuned to BBC London, repeating a message in English. Some children ran screaming in a game of tag between the legs of people, more manic than usual. At the front of the square, several of the Italian army jeeps had stopped, the soldiers before them looking dishevelled and lost.

'Celeste!' Mama was calling me. I didn't want to leave Myriam's side, not then. But two of her matron friends were descending on us, and I had no choice.

'I'll be back soon,' I whispered. Nodding vaguely, she let go.

Mama was standing at the edge of the square with Papa and the Picots. After a moment, I saw Paul, in his dark gendarme jacket, threading his way through the crowd.

Mama and Agathe were smiling widely. It stopped me in my tracks.

'Ceci!' Agathe cried when she saw me. 'Oh my dear, it's wonderful news, the Italians have surrendered, they're leaving! We'll be French again!'

Among them, Paul was the only one who looked uncertain, though he summoned a smile when his father clapped him on the shoulder, saying that they'd no longer have to answer to the greasy bastards. He came to stand beside me, and for a moment, everything that had passed between us was eclipsed by this sudden change.

'What will this mean for them?' I asked quietly.

'I don't know,' he said, staring around at the jostling, nervous crowd. I saw his eyes fix on something. It was one of the young men I'd seen him with in the forest. 'I don't think any Jew will be safe here any more.'

There was a stirring in the crowd, rippling across the square, and an army jeep's horn blared into the warm, still evening.

'Please!' It was the *capitano*'s voice, booming over the hubbub. '*Attenzione!*' He was standing on the seat of his jeep. His jacket was hanging open, his shirt sweat-stained. 'Please! We have just received news that Prime Minister Badoglio has signed an Armistice with the British and the Americans. Italy is out of the war!'

His announcement caused an explosion of voices, questions, concerns, almost all of them the same: *What about the Germans?*

The *capitano*'s face was waxy with perspiration. He was afraid. 'The German army will occupy this area within a few days — we cannot say when. We will no longer keep any of you here, you are free to leave.' His face flickered, some of the military manner dropping away. 'And you should. The *Wehrmacht* know you are here. My men and I will leave tomorrow morning for the Italian frontier. If anyone wishes to follow us, we will not stop you.'

He seemed to sag then, and a second later was

stepping down from the jeep, shaking his head.

There was a second of silence, as if lightning had flashed above the square. Then came the thunder. I heard children wailing as mothers seized their arms; I saw old people clutching at their worn jackets and shawls, tears gathering in their eyes. Some of the young people were huddled in groups, talking rapidly, others were already running for their houses.

I couldn't think; it was all so sudden, so violent. I pushed into the crowd without knowing why, though my mother was shouting behind me. *Free to leave*, the *capitano* had said. How? There was no way down off the mountain, except for the bus, the army jeeps. And even if people did get to Nice, the Germans might already be there, waiting. It was then that I heard a familiar voice calling out over the crowd. I looked up to see Wolf, standing on a café table, making a speech in German. I couldn't understand it, apart from one phrase, repeated: *Col de Madone*. He was talking about the pass that led over the mountains into Italy, the old salt road.

I fought through the crush of people around him, trying to reach the other side of the square where I'd left Myriam. But it was Daniel I found first, his voice ringing through the shoulders and frightened faces, speaking calmly, clearly, just as Wolf had done. It was a speech, I knew then, and they had rehearsed it. They had been waiting for this to happen.

'We will take the path to the north of the village,' Daniel was shouting. 'It is around six miles to the sanctuary, where we can rest for the night. From there, the trail leads over the pass and into Italy. We leave in the morning. Dress in warm clothes, and bring only what you can carry . . . '

I stood, listening in shock, watching the effect of his words on the faces before me. Some were shaking their heads, as if in denial.

I knew why. What he was suggesting was impossible. The trek to the sanctuary was hard, even on good legs: six steep miles on a track through pine forest. Then, beyond the sanctuary, it got harder. The slopes turned to scree, into sharp rocks that slid underfoot. There was no shade up there, no comfort. I'd hiked that far only once, before the war, and it had been exhausting even for me. I remembered gasping for breath in the thin air, scrambling on my hands and knees, three steps forward, sliding four steps back. I had given up before reaching the summit.

I looked at the people before me. Some wore only sandals, held together with rope or string, others wore slippery wooden-soled shoes. None of them had clothes suitable for the mountain peaks, where the sun could burn even while the air froze. And then there were the old people, small children, women with babies.

Myriam.

I turned and reached for Daniel, grabbing hold of his jacket. 'She'll never make it,' I heard myself saying. 'Daniel, she'll never make it.'

'We don't have a choice,' he said savagely, stepping out of my hold. 'You heard the *capitano*. The Germans know we're here, they'll

361

hunt us down.' I saw the desperation in his face. 'She can't stay here, Celeste, she'll be trapped — '

He stopped, looking over my shoulder. Myriam was standing behind us, her eyes wild with fear. She'd heard every word.

'Myriam!' Daniel cried, starting forward, but it was too late. Her eyes were rolling back, her knees giving way as she crumpled to the ground.

★   ★   ★

Dr Brion's stout, red face hovered above the moon of Myriam's belly, his ear to the end of a wooden listening horn. Daniel sat beside her on the bed, stroking the hair away from her forehead, wiping the tears that ran silently from her closed eyes. I stood in the doorway, feeling sick, trying not to grip my own stomach. On the floor by the bed was a bowl of bloodstained water.

No one had stopped me from coming to the bakery, rather the opposite; the room behind me was full of people. My mother and Agathe had come, and one of Myriam's matronly friends, even Paul and my father. It was as if Myriam's condition was somehow tied to the news of the Armistice, something that affected us all.

Dr Brion was smiling, patting Myriam's belly, pulling the blanket up over her, but as he turned away I saw his face fall, his lips turn downward. Fear rushed hot into my throat.

'What's happened?' I asked, the moment he closed the door to the room behind him.

Dr Brion stepped past me with a sigh. 'May I?' he asked my mother, indicating the sink. Nobody spoke as he washed his hands, dried them on a kerchief from his pocket.

'Both she and the baby are fine,' he said, though his voice was uncharacteristically flat. 'The bleeding is part of her body preparing for labour.' He shook his head. 'It is early, probably brought on by the shock, or the fall.'

I saw my mother and Agathe exchange looks, faces creased with worry.

'Labour?' I repeated stupidly, and I saw Paul glance at me, at my middle. 'She's having the baby? Now?'

The doctor made a sound that wasn't a laugh. 'Not right now. But soon. It could be hours, or days. There is no way of predicting.'

For a moment, all of us were silent. I could tell from the faces that we were thinking the same thing. Tomorrow. The next day.

'Celeste?' Daniel had come to the door. His face was dry but it was clear that he had been crying. 'She'd like to see you.' He looked beyond me to the room, to my parents, Agathe, Paul, Myriam's friend, all standing there.

'We will leave you in peace,' my mother said, and blushed, as if realizing the ridiculousness of those words the moment they were out of her mouth. 'Let us know if we . . . if there's anything.'

Daniel only nodded, stepping aside so that I could go in. I walked past him and shut the door behind me without a backwards glance.

'Celeste,' Myriam cried, holding out her hands towards me. The next second I was on the bed beside her, holding her, kissing her face, her hair, the both of us crying. 'I wish this had never happened,' she sobbed, her head buried against my arm. 'It's going to kill me — '

'It won't.' The words I made were little more than noise. I squashed any thought of my own baby down then, though in truth, the same fears haunted me. It was Myriam who was important now.

'I have to leave.' She was frantic. 'I have to get out. I have to get down off the mountain.'

'You're safe here.' I tried to scrape up the remains of my courage. 'We'll look after you, I promise.'

Bit by bit, I brought her back from the edge of panic. I smoothed her hair, murmuring, until finally exhaustion caught up with her and she fell asleep.

I found Daniel at the kitchen table, his head in his hands. There was a map of the area before him, the passes marked out in pencil.

'She's asleep,' I told him.

'Good.' His voice was thick. 'That's good.'

'What're you going to do?' It was the only question that mattered.

He ran his hands through his hair, looked up at me. 'We have to get out. Even if we hid, they'd find us. There are informers.'

He was thinking of Leon, in his smart *milice* blue, of Paul and the boys who patrolled the hills.

'She can't go anywhere,' I whispered. 'Not like this. She has to stay. At least, until — '

'You want to keep her here,' Daniel accused, his face twisted. 'That's what this is. You don't want her to leave.'

'I don't want her to die!'

The suddenness of the words shocked me. I gulped them back, trying not to give in to fear.

'Daniel,' I said, voice shaking, 'she can't go anywhere. Not now.' I wracked my brain. 'We can hide her. We can look after her until she has the baby.' I swallowed hard. 'Perhaps the Germans will have come and gone by then. Or perhaps they won't come at all. Or the Allies, they might have taken Italy, they might cross the border.' I was gabbling, but I had to do *something*. Steeling myself, I reached out and placed my hand on his shoulder. 'I promised I would look after her. I promise you the same.' In that lamplight, Daniel's face looked old. Mine must have too. 'Will you trust me?' I asked.

After a moment, he closed his eyes. Slowly, agonizingly, he nodded.

★　★　★

That night, I didn't sleep at all. I hadn't been able to face the prospect of lying down next to Paul. I knew he'd look at me with that concerned face, and place his hand on my belly and tell me that I had to look after myself now.

Instead, I'd gone to work in the bakery early, listening to Daniel move around the apartment as if trying to walk out the length of the pass on the floorboards. Finally, an hour before dawn, it had fallen silent up there, and I knew he'd given in to sleep.

Papa and I worked in a daze, our hands and bodies following the patterns we'd laid down

365

over the years. Neither of us voiced the obvious question: who would be left to buy the dozens of loaves we made? The day dawned clear, almost offensively bright. A perfect morning by any other standard, the sun warm, with a hint of autumn to come.

We took down the shutters to be greeted by a crowd of faces, wan from sleeplessness. People stood, wrapped in too many clothes, with suitcases and sacks and bundles in hand, waiting to buy bread for their journey.

I couldn't bear to take their money. As one familiar face after another approached the counter, I found myself handing out the loaves, mechanically. It seemed so little. By nightfall, they would be huddled on the bare mountainside and that bread would be gone.

Not long after dawn, the stairs creaked, as I knew they would. Daniel came down first, dressed for walking, in his hat and jacket. A small haversack was slung over his shoulders, his hand in Myriam's. I started forward, about to protest that she shouldn't be moving, but she stopped me with a look.

'Monsieur Corvin,' Daniel said, coming forward, 'thank you for your hospitality.'

My father's face was unreadable as he shook Daniel's hand.

'Good luck, Monsieur Reiss.' He paused. 'I hope we see you again.'

'Me too.'

Papa nodded, took up a *boule* from the cooling tray and handed it over. 'For the journey.'

Together, we watched them walk out of the shop, greeting people in the line as they went, small words, gestures, touches. I had to clench my toes in my boots to keep from following, but when I turned around, Papa was watching me. He jerked his chin.

'Go on,' he muttered. After a moment he picked up my delivery basket, piled it with loaves and placed it in my arms. 'Take these.'

When I got to the square, I didn't move. I just stood, gripping the basket, not knowing what to do. Groups of people were waiting, suitcases and bags beside them, despite what Daniel had said about travelling light. The children were subdued, holding on to siblings or to cases of their own, too big for them to carry. Many were dressed in black, in overcoats and hats. *Like a funeral procession*, I thought bleakly. All around the edges of the square, from windows and doorways, people of the town were watching. People like me.

I saw Wolf standing at the side of a group, a bag on his back and a stout branch in his hand to act as a hiking pole. Wordlessly, I went over and handed him a loaf of bread. He took it, nodded, his face white. I turned away quickly, found other faces among the crowd. When I handed the bread to Andre he thanked me, and put it in his satchel, with his precious *zazou* records. 'The best travelled records in Europe,' he said, but his smile was strained.

I gave a few loaves to one of Myriam's matronly friends, Hannah, who promised to share them with the others. Her three children stood around her, the oldest one, who couldn't have been more than ten, holding the youngest.

'You take care of Madame Reiss,' she said, her eyes bright. 'Send her along to us in Italy as soon as you can.'

I nodded and promised I would, though neither of us knew what waited over the border. Only a dream of safety.

Before long came the signal: the roar of engines, the Italians' jeeps coughing and spluttering into life outside the hotel. I knew they would drive as far out of town as possible, before abandoning the jeeps as the road petered out. Then they too would have to walk. The crowd of people began to move, bunching together, pushing forwards, as if they did not want to be left behind.

At the edge of the square, Daniel and Myriam were saying goodbye. I didn't listen, but I saw the way Daniel looked at her, the way she touched his shoulder, the way he bent to press a kiss to her belly.

He was to go on ahead. He was to guide people across the border, use his contacts in the *Résistance* to try to find safe places for them to stay on the other side. When he'd done that he'd come back to Saint-Antoine for Myriam and, hopefully, for the baby. He met my eyes as he stepped away. In that moment, there was only truth between us. We both loved her; it was as simple and as complicated as that.

With a final nod he turned and joined the stream of people walking out of the square. The trucks rolled forward through the town, soldiers clinging grimly to their roofs. The whole of Saint-Antoine watched as, one foot after another, a thousand people began to walk.

Saint-Antoine

May 1993

'They couldn't have known what would happen, what would be waiting,' Grand-mère says, her voice cracked. 'If I could go back, if I could only go back and tell them.'

Her face is contorted with grief, tears sliding from her eyes, staining her lined cheeks. She is squeezing my hand hard, as if she's worried that I too will walk away and leave her. There's a box of tissues beside the bed. Awkwardly, I reach over and take one out, press it into her free hand.

'Grand-mère,' I say softly, 'if this is too much . . .'

'No!' She struggles to haul herself up on the pillows. 'No, don't stop me. I have to tell this, now I have started.' She looks across at me, her eyes reddened. 'I should have told you and Evelyne a long time ago. You have to . . . to hear this from me. No one else.'

'I know,' I tell her. 'I'm here. And Mum's on her way. We won't leave you.'

She inhales deeply, as if breathing herself into that younger woman's skin, and closes her eyes. When she opens them again, I can tell she isn't seeing me, or the hotel room, but she is back there, in those long, hazy days of early September, when the world balanced on a knife-edge.

Saint-Antoine

September 1943

I barely remember what happened after they left. Those days are like a fog in my mind, pierced with moments of clarity. I think I was half-mad, with the waiting and the fear and the secret I kept from Myriam. Perhaps we all were.

The town felt sagging and desolate, with all of those apartments and rooms emptied of people. The sound of laughter, cigarette smoke and jazz no longer spilled from the hotel; children no longer squealed and splashed in the *gargouille*. Gentle singing no longer drifted from windows. The chairs of the café sat almost empty, no chatter to fill the air.

Not all had taken the path into the mountains. A few had remained with us, those too ill or old or weak to make the journey. *What will the Germans want with me?* I heard one old woman ask, her shawl wrapped protectively about her shoulders. Several children, too, who had come to Saint-Antoine as orphans, had been spirited away to remote farms outside the village, where it was hoped they would be safe.

Everyone was affected by the quiet that fell across the town. It wasn't a peaceful quiet, but an anxious, waiting one; the quiet of a doctor's office, where eyes were lowered and hands pressed together. I found myself willing the minutes away and dreading their passing all at once.

I moved my things to the bakery without discussing it with anyone, and though Paul protested that I should take care of myself, rather than Myriam, and my father frowned when he saw me coming downstairs for the night's work, they knew they couldn't stop me. It was as if the whole town had given itself up to waiting, for the baby, for something that surely must come.

Myriam was distraught. She sank deep into herself, where I couldn't follow her, the way she had when she first arrived in Saint-Antoine. She spent two days after Daniel left sitting by the window in my old room, or lying on the bed, her forehead and belly pressed to the wall, as if she could dissolve into it, become plaster and mortar, free from every human concern.

Twice a day, three times, I had to hurry away from her to vomit as quietly as I could into the toilet downstairs in the bakery. Even I didn't know whether it was anxiety or morning sickness. In the darkness of the tiny closet I would clench my teeth to stop the nausea, squeeze my stomach and try to will away whatever was happening there, praying for my course to come, for it not to be true. I was terrified that Myriam would notice when I came back, pale and sweating, but she never did. She was too far away from me, then.

Most of the time, I tried to forget about myself. I concentrated on Myriam, on coaxing her to the surface when I could. I made her *socca* in the afternoons, and drinks of cool water and lemon balm. I rubbed her wrists with stems of lavender and combed her hair through my fingers, while she lay with her eyes closed and her head in my lap. There were times when I hated the baby inside her. If it didn't exist, then she might have been free, she might have been safe; we could have left this place together.

But then, I would remember that there was no freedom, for either of us. And what of Daniel? What would she have done if she'd been forced to choose between him and me? I didn't know. All I knew was that while she was with me, I would love her, as best I could. And so, I loved the child, because it was part of her, even if I couldn't yet love the idea of my own.

For three unbearable, tremulous days, we waited. On the fourth, the storm broke.

I heard Myriam's cry through the floorboards as we worked down in the bakery, some time past three o'clock in the morning. I stopped, my hands coated in flour and clinging dough, only to hear it again, a harsh moan, as if through gritted teeth. I didn't even wait to wipe my hands before I ran.

She was on her knees in the little bedroom, her face curdled white and red, her eyes huge with fear.

'Celeste,' she gasped when she saw me. 'It's happening.'

My hands left streaks of flour in her hair, on her arms. 'It's all right,' I told her, 'I'm here, I'm here.' But I didn't know what to do, and I couldn't leave her.

'Help!' I yelled, hoping my father would hear. 'Papa, help!'

After that it all happened so quickly; in screams of fear and pain and a soaked cotton nightgown. In salt-sweat and tears, and Myriam's hand gripping mine so hard that her nails drew blood from the skin between my knuckles. Dr Brion came, dishevelled from sleep, and Mama, who was more help than all of us put together, calming Myriam when her panic started to spiral, telling her sternly to breathe, to push, to breathe, to be strong.

And then her screams became a shuddering gasp and another voice filled the room, tiny and new, crying its existence to the world.

Dr Brion cut the bloody cord and placed the new life on to Myriam's breast. She sobbed, staring down at her child. She had a daughter.

⋆　⋆　⋆

I had never seen so fierce a love, amongst such uncertainty and pain. All that first golden morning, with the scent of freshly baked bread filtering through the floor and flour still caught in her hair, Myriam gazed at her child, nursing the tiny being as if in a dream. Sometimes, she would look up at me and laugh, tears on her eyelashes. At other times she would stare into the baby's face, and whisper that she was sorry, that she had never intended to bring her into such a terrible world.

The first time I held the baby, my hands trembled so much I was afraid I might drop her, and I had to sit down on the bed to catch my breath. Her eyes were closed, a tiny pink hand poking from the blanket. I looked into her face and for the first time I felt both wonder that something so beautiful was growing inside me, and a deep guilt, for wishing it away.

Myriam lay watching, propped against the pillows, drunk with exhaustion and happiness.

'My girls,' she said. 'I'll write such stories for you.'

My mother appeared in the afternoon, her old, hesitant self again. She brought with her a neatly folded bundle of baby linen that had once been mine. She looked at me silently, questioningly, and I knew what she was asking: whether I minded if she gave it to a baby that was here, now, rather than wait the months for my own first child. I nodded my agreement, grateful to her.

Carefully, she showed Myriam how to fold thick pads for herself, to catch her bleeding, how to make a napkin for the baby, how to swaddle her in a cotton wrap, how to clean and dress her. But all that softness, all that wonder, could not eclipse the world around us.

'You will have to show Daniel how to do all of this,' my mother said, and glanced at me, before her smile faltered.

'He doesn't even know she exists.' Myriam's face collapsed into grief. 'How can he not know? Where is he?'

We had heard nothing from Daniel or from any of the refugees, though several of the older folk had limped back into town, many hours after they had originally left. They had looked exhausted. Some of them were bruised and bloodied from falls on the mountainside. They could not make it, they told us, their eyes dull.

Some of the farmers and young men had gone up the mountain in their wake and brought back stories of a trail of abandoned possessions: suitcases, silverware, precious items lying out on the scree. People were seen going up the mountain with donkeys, after that, and coming back with laden bags. They'd keep the Jews' belongings safe, they said loudly, until the owners returned.

I didn't want to think about it. I didn't want to think about anything except the fragile bubble of happiness that existed in the small apartment. I clung to it, as the days passed, as if I was holding ever tighter to a rope that had begun to fray. On the fourth day after the birth, after I had finished work at lunchtime, I stood holding the baby, looking out of the window. Her eyes were open, grey-blue and unfocused, and I showed her the sky, the mountains, the swallows that dipped past. It seemed unthinkable — and strangely thrilling — that in a matter of months I would be doing this with my own child. A second later, I saw movement in the alleyway below. A man, staring up at me, his face pale.

I passed the baby back to Myriam, murmured that I had to go out, that I wouldn't be long. She smiled. As I kissed her on the cheek I was enveloped by her scent: soap and skin and a new, soft smell, like powder and milk.

Outside, Paul was waiting. We stood in front of

each other by the back step, the way we had all those months ago, when everything was different. He looked strange. His face was wan, even though his cheeks were reddened, his hair askew, his gendarme's uniform hanging open. The smell of brandy hung about him.

'You — ' His voice cracked. 'You looked beautiful, up there.' He glanced at the window. 'Holding that baby. That's what it could be like, for us.' When he looked down again, his eyes were bright. 'But it won't be, will it? It never will.'

I forced myself to look at him, wanting to take it all away, the pain, the suffering that I'd caused him.

'No,' I whispered. Even a baby would never make us a family. I swallowed hard, made myself go on. 'I'm sorry, Paul. I should never have married you when I knew I felt so differently.'

He made a choked noise and looked away, blinking hard. 'You love *her*, don't you? Even though it's . . . even though it's wrong.'

His words made my jaw clench. *Tell the truth*, I thought bleakly, *even if it's only once*. 'Yes,' I whispered. 'I do.'

He stepped away from me then and laughed, an awful, desperate sound. He was drunk, I realized. My skin prickled with unease. Why should he be so drunk, at noon? It was not like him.

'Paul,' I tried to see his face, 'what's going on?'

He was shaking his head, running his hands through his hair. 'We . . . had a telephone call. From Leon.'

The cobbles of the street, the water in the *gargouille*, all of it seemed to swim.

'Leon?' I heard myself ask. 'Why? What do you mean?'

Paul's voice was thick. 'He called to say he's coming back to Saint-Antoine, with the *milice*.' He looked into my face. 'He called to warn us. He wanted me to get you away, to keep you safe, make sure you weren't involved.'

The Germans, I thought in a daze, *they're coming.*

'How long? How long before . . . ?'

I trailed off, taking in Paul's dishevelled appearance, the reek of alcohol on his breath. 'When did Leon call?' I demanded. 'When, Paul?'

'Just after dawn.' His face was twisted. 'It's too late, they're already on their way.'

Fear struck me like a blow to the gut, and I span towards the door.

'I'm sorry, Ceci!' Paul tried to grab me, but I shoved him away and ran back into the bakery, my heart thundering in my ears.

'Myriam!' I screamed, tripping in my haste. 'Myriam, we have to go.'

She looked up in shock as I tumbled into the apartment. She was nursing the baby, her hair loose and unbrushed, her blouse hanging from one shoulder. I couldn't bear it, that all that gentleness was about to be torn apart.

'They're coming,' I said. 'We have to get out.'

Haste. Hands shaking, spilling, grabbing the wrong thing, and all the while the baby lying red-faced on the bed, crying at the top of her voice.

'We have to go,' I said, grabbing a suitcase. 'We have to find somewhere to hide.'

Somehow, she was calmer than me, pushing aside the suitcase, shoving a satchel into my hands instead. 'Pack for her,' she commanded, wrenching open the dresser drawer in the kitchen, taking out a bundle of papers, an envelope of something that looked like money.

She was prepared, I realized in shock, as I snatched up a handful of the baby linens my mother had brought, and a woollen blanket. She had known this day would come and had planned for it. She had been here before. I felt slow-minded in the face of that stark practicality.

'You had a plan? You and Daniel?' I sounded frantic, and I knew it.

'Yes,' she said, picking up the baby to soothe her. 'If there was a raid I was to try to get out of town. I was to meet him . . . ' She paused. 'At the hut, below the meadow.'

Despite everything, for the briefest second my chest tightened with jealousy.

'Our place?' I asked, slinging the satchel over my body. 'You told him about it?'

'I told him it existed, nothing more. Of all the places I could think of, that was the one that felt safe.'

I nodded, shoving the feeling down. 'How will he know to meet you there?'

'He said he had a way of knowing, of finding out if — ' She stopped, her face hardening. 'When the Germans came. Someone who would contact him.'

I watched as Myriam swaddled the baby

tightly. She seemed to hesitate for a second, before tucking a small, brown envelope into the baby's blanket, so thin it could only have contained a single page.

All I could think, over and over again, was that it was too dangerous. That she wasn't healed yet, that she was still recovering, not strong enough to make the journey over the border, even if Daniel were to come.

But we had no choice. Running was the only thing we could do. Together, we hurried down the stairs. The front door of the bakery was still locked, the square outside quiet in the noon sun. I checked the back door. Paul was gone. *So much the better*, I thought bitterly. A moment later, I remembered something.

'Wait!' I said to Myriam, running into the kitchen.

'Celeste!' she called back. 'Where are you going? We have to hurry!'

From a basket, I grabbed two unsold loaves of *pain bis*. Then I threw a cloth on to the counter, reached for the pot on the shelf and upturned it. Salt came spilling out, like diamonds. I knotted the corners, crammed it into the satchel along with the bread.

In the corridor Myriam was waiting, dressed in her jacket and shawl, the way she had been when I had first seen her. Only now, she held that tiny bundle in her arms. We looked at each other, and the baby gave a squall. It was the only spur we needed.

We hurried through the town, too breathless to talk, taking the back routes. The baby's cries echoed from the archways of cellars, up into courtyards as we made our way through the old streets and out, on to the road that would lead us high above the town, towards the meadow, the apex of the valley.

We were halfway there when we heard the first rumble, like thunder overhead. *Please let it be planes*, I thought, listening to Myriam's laboured breathing behind me. *Let it be the Americans, coming to drop soldiers into Italy.* But the noise didn't grow softer with distance; it grew louder, until I knew what it had to be. I looked over my shoulder, down into the valley.

There was a cavalcade on the winding road. Armoured cars were crossing the bridge, motorcycles, jeeps, a black Citroën, its body glinting like a beetle.

'Celeste, move!' Myriam gasped, shoving me on. 'Don't look back.'

We climbed. The path, which I had usually hiked without thought, now seemed endless. Behind me, I could hear Myriam stifling gasps of pain. No church bells rang, even though the hour must have come and gone. Instead, there were strange, sudden noises: crashes, like doors slamming and voices shouting and a crack that might have been a gunshot. Was Leon down there? He knew about the hut, of course, but whether he would think of it . . . A shudder of nausea overtook me and I had to stop, I had to lean over my knees with flooding eyes before I was sick. Was Leon shoving past our neighbours to haul the few, frail remaining refugees out of buildings, send them staggering towards the trucks? Was he truly capable of that?

Ahead, I saw Myriam stumble, clutching the baby to her. Through her trousers, a dark stain was spreading. Swallowing hard, I got hold of myself and straightened up.

'We have to stop,' I told her, 'you have to rest.'

'We can't.' Her lips were white. 'Not yet.'

When the hut finally came into view, Myriam made a noise, a sob of relief, and sank down in the dirt before it. Cautiously, I peered inside. Everything looked just the same. It was safe, for the moment, at least.

I helped Myriam change the pad she wore, and folded a new one, trying not to show how much it scared me, the sight of that sodden cloth. When that was done, she slumped, all of the hard rationality gone out of her. She simply sat against the wall, her eyes closed, the baby cradled in her lap. Occasionally, sounds would reach us from the town — an engine growling into life, dogs barking frantically — but the path up to the hut remained empty. Finally, though I knew it was superstitious, I couldn't stop myself. I opened the knotted cloth of precious salt, and scattered a pinch of it across the doorstep.

'For protection,' I told her, tying it back up.

'You brought salt,' she said, her eyes heavy. 'Why?'

'Bread for the journey,' I murmured, kneeling to show her the loaves of *pain bis*. 'Salt for the home, for when you arrive in Italy. Then, whenever you taste it, you might . . . you might think of me.'

She didn't say anything, only raised her arm so

that we could hold each other, there on the floor of the hut, the sleeping baby between us.

The waiting was more terrible than the running: half-slipping into a doze only to wake, terrified by the shriek of a marmot, or the rustle of grass, or a sudden scatter of birdsong. Agonizingly, the sun slipped lower and lower in the sky, until it was lost behind the mountain, and the hut grew cold with shadows. I shivered. I had forgotten to bring a jacket. There was nothing to say, and everything, but I didn't have the words. I did what I could and held Myriam's hand. She locked her cold fingers with mine, waiting, like I was, for Daniel to arrive, bringing the future with him.

The moment came, at last, when night had fully fallen. Inside, the hut was almost pitch black, the moon just a thin scraping over the peaks. Out of the darkness, half-dreaming, I thought I heard a bird calling out the time, late as always. *Huit-heure, huit-heure, huit-heure* . . . but I'd never heard that bird sing at night before.

Myriam stiffened beside me, and a moment later we were both sitting up.

'The signal,' she breathed, and I could almost hear her heart thundering as she took a deep breath and whistled softly, low to high, three times.

Then came a rustle of movement, the noise of cloth brushing through grass, and feet were scuffing away my protective scatter of salt. The side of a dark lantern slid open, spilling dim yellow light into the hut. Two men were standing there. I could make out a third in the doorway, his face turned away, on the lookout. One of the men pushed back his cap.

'Daniel — ' Myriam gasped with relief. 'Oh, thank God. Thank God.'

The next minutes were lost to their reunion, to Daniel's wonder at the baby in Myriam's arms. I stood away from them, in the corner of the hut with the other man. For all my relief that Daniel was alive, all my happiness for them, I couldn't watch. I turned my face away, my stomach trembling with nausea.

The man beside me shifted. A hand appeared in my vision, holding a hip flask. I looked up. It was Michel.

'Here,' he muttered.

I took it. Brandy burned my lips. It tasted cold and raw and adult. The sensation was a momentary distraction.

'Daniel,' said Michel, when I handed it back, 'it's time.' He looked at us all. 'You need to decide.'

I watched as Daniel stood, helping Myriam to her feet.

'What's going on?' she asked. 'What do you mean?'

Daniel turned to include me too. He was haggard, I saw now. He hadn't shaved and his skin was taut and grey.

'Italy was a trap,' he said bleakly. 'We got across the border and made for the first town, but by the time we got there — ' He had to stop, swallow hard before he could carry on. 'The Germans were waiting. They must have known the Italians would surrender. They must have been waiting to invade the same day.' He shook his head in the direction of the border. 'It's chaos

384

over there. They're rounding up Italian soldiers, executing deserters and anti-fascists or anyone who doesn't look or sound right. Some of us managed to get away.'

Some.

'What happened to the others?' I asked.

Daniel met my eyes. 'The Germans put up posters in the villages telling us to hand ourselves in, on pain of death. Some did. They were taken. I don't know where.' His voice was dangerously flat. 'Those of us who got away have been hiding in the hills, in barns, in a cave.' He looked at Myriam, defeated. 'I'm sorry,' he said. 'It isn't safe. Nowhere is safe.'

Myriam was shaking with fear, the blanket around the baby trembling. 'Then we stay here,' she said. 'If nowhere is safe, we stay here. Celeste can help us. Perhaps they've already been and gone in the town.'

Michel stepped forward, his hand rasping across his beard. 'No, there are *milice* in town, and the SS, to try to catch anyone risking passage over the mountains.' He looked at me. 'It was bad down there today, Ceci. I'm glad you didn't see it. They took everyone they could find, even the old folk. Some . . . people got hurt.' There was the strangest expression on his hard, coarse face. If I didn't know better, I might have said it was sympathy.

'Who?' I asked, lips numb, already fearing the answer.

'Paul,' he said. 'The idiot tried to stop them from raiding the bakery. He got into a fight with your brother about it, only the German in charge didn't know that they were friends, that they've always fought.' Michel cleared his throat. 'They took a shot at him.'

I couldn't take in what he was telling me. It was as if my brain had frozen over, his words sliding across the top, not sinking in.

'Is he . . . ?' I heard myself saying.

'Still alive, yes. Or he was, three hours ago.' Michel cleared his throat uncomfortably and offered me the hip flask again, but I ignored it, I couldn't remember how to lift my hands. *Paul*, I kept thinking, *Paul, the father of my child*. I saw him again outside the bakery, his eyes bright with pain. He had been prepared to betray Myriam, and yet he hadn't, he'd warned us, even though it had almost been too late. *Paul*.

'We've been here too long,' the man by the door hissed. 'We have to move.'

'Daniel,' Michel said, his voice hard.

In the faint light, Daniel turned to Myriam. 'Michel can get us into Italy. I know some people on the other side now.'

'But you said it's too dangerous over there.' She sounded desperate. 'Perhaps we could get to Nice — '

'We can't.' Daniel took her face in his hands. 'They're blocking everything, the buses, the roads. Italy is still the safest option. If we can travel across country, we can try to make it to the south. The Allies have landed there; they'll be pushing forward any day now.' He forced her to look at him. 'If we can get behind their lines we'll stand a chance.'

'I'll come with you.' I barely knew what I was

saying. 'I have the right papers, I can help . . . ' I trailed off at the look on Daniel's face, as he shook his head.

Myriam didn't see that movement, wrapping the blanket about the baby. 'Daniel, she's four days old, we can't travel across country with her. We — ' She looked up and met his eyes. I had to watch her face shift from confusion to disbelief to a terrible realization.

'They're arresting everyone,' Daniel whispered. '*Everyone.* If we were to be caught, she wouldn't survive, not in the prisons, not in a work camp. We have to do what's best.' His eyes were bright as he looked at me, tears spilling on to his gaunt cheeks. 'It might not be for long,' he told me desperately. 'It might only be for a few months, weeks even, while the Allies advance. This can't go on for ever.'

Myriam choked and held the baby to her chest. I had to stop myself from reaching out to her. 'We can't leave her, Daniel. She doesn't even have a name.'

'Michel!' The lookout hissed, and we all started at the alarm in his voice. 'Torches, on the road. I think it's a patrol!'

'No.' The word broke from me, and I stepped towards them. 'Not yet, please — '

Michel slid the gun from his shoulder. 'We have to move.'

Daniel turned to me then, his eyes wild. 'You'll stay here and care for her.' It was almost a command. 'You promised that.'

'I . . . ' My voice was crushed by what was happening.

387

'Michel, they're coming!'

'This is it.' Michel armed the gun. 'Stay or follow. Your choice.' He turned and half ran from the hut.

The cry that escaped Myriam was like nothing I had ever heard: bone-deep and ragged. She held the baby to her. A moment later, she was in front of me, placing the bundle into my arms.

'Evelyne,' she whispered desperately, 'her name is Evelyne.' She pressed her lips to mine, holding on for one, devastating second and then she was gone, Daniel dragging her away, her cry fading into the sound of footsteps, as they fled into the night.

Saint-Antoine

May 1993

Grand-mère's voice fades into silence. Slowly, the room drifts back; the green shutters open to the warm afternoon, the curtains, billowing gently, her worn hands, resting on the duvet. My body is stiff, as if I haven't moved for a long time. I look up, and only then do I realize that tears are burning my eyes, running down my face. I wipe them away with my sleeve. Of everything my grandmother has said, four words are beating through my mind.

Her name is Evelyne.

Mum.

'Grand-mère,' I start, my voice trembling, 'are you . . . ?'

'No.' She is shaking her head, her eyes closed. 'I'm not your grandmother.' She opens her eyes. 'I'm so sorry, Annie.'

The next moment I'm leaning over, I'm wrapping my arms around the small woman in the bed, so defiant, so vulnerable.

'Don't be sorry,' I whisper, as she clings to me. 'I love you. No matter what.'

She sobs then, and I know she has exhausted herself, has given everything she had to tell me the story, to lay bare the secrets of her heart after fifty long years.

Later, I sit beside her on the bed. All around us, the duvet is littered with photographs, some from her album, some from the pack of old postcards that I bought. Pictures of Saint-Antoine as it was, and of us, as we were. As the afternoon drifts towards evening, she tells me of what came after.

'It was Leon who protected me,' she says, her voice slow and careful now, as if she only has a certain number of words left. 'He knew the baby was Myriam's and he knew they'd arrest me too, if they found out. He didn't report me. But he was never the same after that day.' She shakes her head, closes her eyes. 'After Paul.'

Paul died from the gunshot wound, she told me, a week after the raid. 'After that I couldn't stay in Saint-Antoine,' she murmurs. 'People hated me, they blamed me for what had happened, and there were informers everywhere. The scale of the manhunt was horrifying. People were selling Jews for anything, a hundred francs, a thousand, newborns, the elderly, it didn't matter.'

'And the baby?' I ask her gently. I think I already know the answer. '*Your* baby?'

She looks down at her lap. 'It didn't . . . I miscarried, not long after. My mother said it was the shock of losing Paul.' She turns her face from me, twisted with old guilt. 'But it was my fault. I wished that baby away so many times. In the end, my body listened.'

I wrap my arm around her shoulders. 'It

390

wasn't your fault,' I tell her, but she shakes her head, and I know that this is a burden I will never be able to lift.

She clears her throat. 'Leon . . . ' she says, forcing herself to go on. 'Leon kept the *milice* at bay long enough for me to get to Nice, where I could disappear. I left word in Saint-Antoine with my parents, so that when Myriam and Daniel came back, they could come and find me.

'To anyone else, I was just another young widow, displaced by the war. But it was hard,' her face creases, 'so hard. I found a room with a woman who had recently had a baby herself, and she helped me. She nursed Evelyne in exchange for chores, but there was never any money. After the mountains, living in the city was like a nightmare. The only food that reached us was old, or stale or spoiled; I couldn't simply walk out of the door and gather it for myself. I missed Myriam, desperately, but I couldn't tell anyone what had happened. I had to protect your mother.

'Along with the thought of Myriam, she was the only thing that kept me going. I loved her so much, the way I might have loved my own child. I did everything I could to keep her healthy, to make sure she was growing strong and happy, so that when the war was over and Myriam came back, she would be proud to see how well I'd raised her daughter.' She shakes her head. 'That day never came.'

My head is swimming. *Mum*, I think over and over. *Mum should be the one hearing this, not me. Her parents, her real parents.* I want to tell

Grand-mère to wait for Mum to make it back to France before she says any more. But before I can open my mouth, she's speaking again, and I remember my promise not to stop her. The words are a tide, impossible to keep back.

'Myriam and Daniel were arrested. I don't know where or when. I only know that on the twenty-first of November that year, their names appear on a list of prisoners, transported by train from Italy to Nice. From there, they were sent to the holding camp of Drancy, outside Paris.'

Her eyes are wide, looking straight over my shoulder. 'Of course, I only found that out much later. Nice was eventually liberated and I waited every day to hear from Myriam, thinking she would make her way back from Italy. But the months passed, and I heard nothing. When the war in France was finally over, I went to what was left of the Jewish community in Nice, to see if they had received any word of her. They helped me find out about the arrest. It was they who suggested that I go to Paris. They said that anyone returning from the east would be sent there first.

'And so I did. I took your mother, and moved north, to a city I had never even visited. Every day, I went to the hotel for news. Every day, nothing. Finally, I learned that they had been deported from Drancy in April nineteen forty-four. Their names never appeared on any survivors list.'

Her voice is fading. 'You know the rest. I couldn't go back to Saint-Antoine, even my parents left. It was too painful. And I wanted a good life for your mother, away from all that. So we moved to England, to London, for the simple reason that Myriam had talked about it once.

'We were lucky. I found a bakery with an apartment above it, and I worked hard to bring your mother up well. She was everything to me. How could I tell her what had happened? And so I simply loved her and watched her grow, and whenever she asked about her father or France I would tell her the same thing: that her father had died in the war. That we left France for a better life. There were so many broken families, nobody questioned it.

'Then, before I knew it, she was a young woman, and she was fierce and sharp, just like Myriam, and she was living her own life, studying, travelling . . . Still, I kept silent. By then, I had not spoken of the past for so long, it was almost as if it had happened to someone else.'

She turns to me, and in her eyes I see the young woman she must have been, lonely, grieving, separated from everything she had known.

'I was frightened, Annie. I was so frightened that when Evie found out I had lied for so long, she would hate me for it. She was all I had left.'

'Then why did you let a fight drive you apart?' I burst out. I can feel frustration bubbling up inside me. If only she had *said* something, explained at the time, all those years of silence would never have happened.

She almost laughs, a dry, resigned sound. 'We were having terrible fights then. She wanted to

393

move away with you, take a placement in North Africa, and all those years of fear and guilt, they caught up with me. I was in a bad place. It will sound crazy to you, but when Evie stopped speaking to me, I took it as proof that I had failed as her mother. I kept thinking that if Myriam had been alive . . . ' Her head slumps back against the pillow. 'Like I said, I was not well. Then, when I had the first stroke, years ago, I knew things would only start to go downhill.'

She clenches her hands on her lap. 'It didn't seem fair to ask Evie to care for me when I wasn't her real mother, especially not when she had you to look after and was so busy with her career. Myriam never had a chance to follow her passion. All the stories, all the books she could have written, they died with her. Evie was working in countries I had never even dreamed of visiting. I didn't want to burden her life. I thought . . . I thought Myriam would have wanted her to be free.'

'Well, you don't have a choice about it now,' I tell her, wiping my eyes on my sleeve. 'Mum's on her way. I've told her to fly straight to Nice.' I squeeze her hand. 'She has to hear this from you.'

Grand-mère tries to smile. 'Myriam would be so proud. Daniel as well. I only wish I could go back and tell them about you.'

On the bedside table, the brown envelope sits, with its single, beautifully written page. She reaches for it.

'Myriam left this in your mother's blanket. I think it was the closest she could come to writing

394

to a letter, in case the worst should happen. She never dreamed that we were saying goodbye for ever.' She keeps it close for a moment, before holding it out. 'It's for Evie. And for you.'

I'm about to protest, knowing how much it means to her, but she shakes her head and places it firmly in my hands.

'She may never have had a chance to write our story, but at least now I know she'll never be forgotten.'

Saint-Antoine

May 1993

The summer air buffets my face as the car winds its way down the mountain. Leaning out of the window, I watch the cascade of water in the river far below. It has run through falls and streams, through the *gargouille* of Saint-Antoine, and now it rushes towards its end, in the sparkling Mediterranean. I close my eyes and breathe in the scent of hot road and far-off water, green stone and rock shadow. I open my hand to let the wind rush through my fingers, quick and free.

'Tunnel!' Matteo yells. I pull my arm back in as the mouth of the tunnel looms and glance over at him.

'Thanks.' I smile.

He smiles back, shyly. 'You're welcome, Annie.'

I feel different, somehow lighter than before. I tug at my T-shirt, already hearing my mother's complaints that I don't look smarter. The thought that I'll be seeing her in just a few short hours, that by this evening she and I and Grand-mère will be together at the hotel, is almost too much to comprehend. I shift in my seat, in restlessness, anxiety, and check my watch for the tenth time.

'Are you looking forward to seeing your mother?' Matteo asks, noticing. He's been kind enough to offer to pick her up from the airport, after his weekly meeting at the hospital.

'Yes.' I look out of the window. 'And I'm nervous. I don't know how she'll react to all of this. It's . . . a lot to take in.'

Matteo laughs. 'A lot to take in is an understatement.' He waves at a car, squeezing past in the other direction. 'You haven't told her anything, yet?'

'No. It isn't for me to tell. She should hear it from Grand-mère.'

He nods in understanding. No one in the town has commented on the fact I'm still calling her that, even though they know I'm not truly a Picot, or a Corvin. *She'll always be my grandmother*, I think, remembering childhood birthdays and day trips, afternoons spent baking, grazed knees, evenings curled on the sofa, before she went away. I smile, a little sadly. She may not be well, but there'll be time for new memories, I hope, in the years to come.

As the mountains unravel into foothills, revealing the glittering sea, we talk of this and that; of his work and mine, of my telephone call a few days ago to a furious Iain, about what I'll do now I probably no longer have a job in England. About how long I'll stay in Saint-Antoine.

'If you're still here at the weekend,' he says, as we nudge through the Nice traffic on to the Promenade des Anglais, 'there's a bean festival happening in my grand-father's village, across

397

the border.' I try not to laugh. He glances over, eyebrows raised. 'It's really not as boring as it sounds! There are beans, yes, but there's good wine and food and music. I think you would like it.' He looks over again, cheeks pink. 'If you would like to go, that is.'

'Why not?' I say. 'Thanks.'

He nods. 'I'm sorry I can't have lunch with you today, before we pick up your mother. My meeting will take a few hours.'

'That's all right,' I tell him, looking at the sea and the beach, at the chic hotels and grand streets. After Saint-Antoine, it feels enormous, bustling. 'I'm sure I can find something to amuse myself.'

He drops me near a shopping street off the Promenade des Anglais, and I wave him off, watching his battered car nose its way into the traffic. On the other side of the road, the Mediterranean beckons.

This morning, Grand-mère handed me some money and insisted that I treat myself to lunch in Nice, at one of the expensive beachfront cafés. The sun is so warm, and the food so good, eaten with a view of the sea, that I forget the awkwardness that comes with dining alone.

Afterwards, I wander through Nice's streets, watching people hurry by: tourists with video cameras, mothers chatting as they stroll with pushchairs. It's all so normal, so everyday, that it's hard to imagine this place in the grip of war, fear and tragedy filling the streets. I pause. If I turn left now, I could walk up towards Nice Gare, from where hundreds of people — Myriam

398

and Daniel included — would have been deported. As I hesitate, a group of students walk past, with stacks of books in their arms, chatting loudly in English. It catches my attention, and I peer up the street, trying to see where they came from. A little way along is a building, a sign outside that reads: *ENGLISH AMERICAN LIBRARY OF NICE.*

I check my watch. I still have a little while before I have to meet Matteo, time to look around at least. And who knows, I might be looking for a new job soon. With a smile, I walk towards it and push open the doors.

It's a small place, with modest shelves of books and battered-looking chairs, but it looks well loved. The hush of it, the coolness after the heat outside and the unmistakable smell of old books fills me with comfort. *Home,* I think, walking to the nearest shelf and running my fingers over the hardback spines.

The lady on the desk gives me a smile, her elegant earrings swaying.

'Good afternoon,' she says softly. 'Are you looking for anything?'

'No, thank you.' It feels strange to be speaking English again. 'I just wanted to have a look around.' Two weeks ago, I would have blushed and hurried away to hide in a corner, but now I hear myself say. 'I work in a library in London. Or did, until recently.'

'Do you?' she whispers. 'Well, don't let this place deceive you, dear. We may look humble, but we have quite the heritage. Would you like a leaflet?' She rifles through the papers and flyers on the desk, until she comes up with a folded, photocopied sheet. 'Here you are.'

The library has been lending books from this building for over a hundred years, I read, except for a brief hiatus between 1943 and 1944. My skin prickles as I stare at those dates, at the years that held so much joy and pain for my grandmother. But the library's story is a happy one: although it was forced to close after being used as a meeting place for the *Résistance*, library workers smuggled out as many books as they could, saving them from destruction. After the war, the books began to return, slowly, from where they had been scattered for safety, all across the South of France. The library has been open ever since.

I look around with a sad smile, wondering if Myriam and Daniel ever came here during their short time in Nice, before they arrived in Saint-Antoine. If Myriam had lived, she might have come here after the war. She might she have moved back to Nice to be with my grandmother, and the pair of them might have brought my mother here to look for children's books on rainy days.

Of course, in that world of my imagining, my grandmother would never have moved to England, my mother would never have made the choices she did. I would never have been born, and wouldn't be sitting here now, with nothing of my real grandmother left but a single, handwritten page.

I stand up with a sigh, feeling sadness gnaw at me again. On the other side of the room, there's a card catalogue; old-fashioned wooden drawers that look as though they might have been here during the war, perhaps even since the library started. I kneel down before them and run my fingers over the brassy nameplates, thinking of the work I was doing in Cheshire, using a computer to make these lovely things redundant.

I pull one open. The archivist in me can't help but tut at the messy cataloguing system, organized alphabetically, by author name. Still, the idiosyncratic cards make me smile, some written by hand, some on a typewriter: a glorious collection of all the individuals who have ever worked here.

I find myself opening the 'R' drawer, turning past Raffertys and Ransons and Riches, trying to find the place where Myriam's card might have been. *The book she never had a chance to write.* Rebello, Redman, Rees, Reeves, Rice. No Reiss, of course. I'm about to close the drawer, when something leaps out at me, a single word on a card, flashing past, too quickly to take in. I flick back through them in reverse. Where was it? I stop, my fingertips resting on a yellowed card.

REES, MIRIAM
ROAD OF SALT, THE
NEW YORK, KINGSLEY PRESS, 1952
RECEIVED: 22 AUGUST 1952

I stop, half-crouched in front of the card catalogue, my eyes wide. Slowly, as if at any moment it will turn to dust in my hands, I pull the card from the drawer.

A coincidence, part of my mind is insisting,

just a fluke, thrown out by the universe. I can't stop my hands from trembling as I take the card to the librarian at the desk.

'This — ' I have to clear my throat. 'This book . . . Is it here?'

'Let me see.' The librarian takes the card, peers at it through her glasses. 'Well, yes, it looks like it must be.' She smiles kindly. 'Shall I find it for you, dear?'

Together, we walk to one end of the library, where the fiction section sits haphazardly on shelves.

'Oh,' the lady murmurs, looking at the stacks, 'it's all a bit of a mess, but it should be somewhere . . . Ah! Here we are.'

She pulls out a book. It's a slim volume, cloth-bound, its thin paper jacket tattered by age and use. Calmly, the librarian places it into my hands. The moment I hold it, I know. It just feels *right*. I stare down at the cover, hardly daring to breathe. It's a simple design, deep blue, with a white waving line that could be a mountain peak or the crest of a wave, or a line of salt scattered in the dirt. Beneath it, in bold black letters, the title, that name.

'Is that the one you're after?' the librarian asks, before looking at me. 'Are you all right, dear? You've gone very pale.'

'I'm fine,' I murmur.

I sink down on to the nearest chair, place the book on my lap and slowly, carefully, ease open the cover.

The first thing that meets my eyes is a swirl of green ink.

402

'Most of the books we have here are donations,' the librarian is explaining, leaning over my shoulder. 'Sent in from all over. Not always signed, but I rather like it when they are.' She peers down at the inscription. 'I'm afraid I don't know who the people are, though, perhaps girls who used to work here?'

I can't correct her, can't even shake my head. All I can do is read the words scrawled in that restless, familiar handwriting:

For Celeste and Evelyne,

In the hope that one day, these words will bring you home.

New York, 1952

Epilogue

New York, June 1993

A warm, summer morning in Brooklyn. The rush hour has passed, and the streets are calm. The two women who stand on a corner have already been up for hours, drinking coffee, talking, worrying at their clothes. Now, the older woman stares at the wide, leafy street in front of her, her lined face pale. The younger woman, middle-aged, with dark, close-cropped curls, takes her arm. Mother and daughter, perhaps.

Or perhaps not. The older woman worries at her vivid red lipstick, her brown eyes bright and impatient.

'You look lovely,' the younger woman says.

The older woman smiles a little. 'Thank you, Evie,' she murmurs.

Slowly, arm in arm, they begin to walk. The older woman's steps are slow, halting, but her head is held high, eyes searching every doorway and window. Some of the houses are clean, their windows sparkling. Others are scruffier, straggly plants wrapping iron railings, a dozen different names on the buzzers.

The house they stop at is halfway in between. The steps leading up to the front door are lined with pot plants, a little too wild to be called well-tended. Leggy rosemary and lavender, borage, flowering blue, rocket leaves that seem to have seeded themselves everywhere. Music is drifting from an open window: lively jazz.

'*Zazou*,' the older woman whispers, her eyes fixed on the house.

The younger woman closes her eyes to listen, breathes in the scent of plants. It reminds her of the mountains they left behind a few days ago; the way the breeze spiralled through the windows of the little apartment above the bakery.

A nudge on the arm. The younger woman opens her eyes.

'Have you got the book?' the older woman asks, her voice shaking.

The younger woman reaches into the bag on her shoulder and brings out the slim hardback, with its tattered jacket. Together, they look down at it, at the story they both now know almost by heart.

It's a story of one life-changing summer in the mountains, of love and suffering, of an impossible choice. Of capture and a time near death, of a man, sacrificing his life so that a woman might escape, might live, to find their daughter. Of the time afterwards, spent in hiding and fear and, finally, freedom. Of a return to the place where so much happened, only to find nothing, a trail gone cold. It's a story of searching, of writing, of letters and books sent out into the world in hope, a thousand silent envoys, searching for two readers among millions.

The older woman strokes the cover, then

opens it. Inside, a letter has been placed for safe keeping. The writing is shaky at the edges, less forceful, but still every bit as distinctive as she remembers.

She takes a deep breath and holds out her free hand. The younger woman takes it, and together they climb the steps, brushing past the plants, releasing the scent of mountain herbs into the city air.

Trembling, the younger woman presses the buzzer, with its impossible name plaque: *Dr Miriam Rees*.

Footsteps approach, slow but firm, and the older woman is clutching the younger woman's hand so tightly it hurts, but finally, after decades of silence and sorrow and hope, the door is swinging open.

Grey eyes meet brown eyes for the first time in fifty years, and the older woman feels herself smiling, laughing through the tears.

'My girls,' says the woman at the door.

One day, these words will bring you home.

Author's Note

The Secrets Between Us is a fictional work inspired by true events that took place in the Alpes-Maritimes during the summer of 1943.

From February to September of that year, the town of Saint-Martin-Vésubie, situated around forty miles from Nice, was designated an 'enforced residence' for displaced Jews. Through a combination of sympathy, politics, altruism and the efforts of Jewish Italian banker Angelo Donati, the Italian Fourth Army moved thousands of Jewish refugees into Saint-Martin-Vésubie and the surrounding villages. For one summer, the mountains became something of a safe haven, where the Jews were protected from persecution from German and French forces. It offered respite, relief and a degree of security for the refugees, many of whom had already been fleeing for years.

With the announcement of the Armistice, and Italy's withdrawal from the war, the refugees' safety vanished, and they were left with an impossible choice: stay in villages like Saint-Martin-Vésubie and await the German authorities or take the perilous old salt roads across the mountain passes, to what they believed would be safety in Italy.

Over a thousand refugees made the crossing from Saint-Martin-Vésubie, not knowing that German forces were waiting for them on the other side. Some of those who escaped were aided by *Résistance* members, anti-fascist groups, or French or Italian civilians, who hid the refugees in barns, attics and remote farms, even presenting Jewish children as their own during the round-ups. Many more refugees were captured and interned at Borgo San Dalmazzo, before being sent to Drancy and, ultimately, Auschwitz.

In *The Secrets Between Us*, I decided to set the action in a fictional town named Saint-Antoine, rather than in real-life Saint-Martin-Vésubie. I chose to do this because — while I sincerely hope to bring this underreported area of the Second World War to wider attention — I did not want to conflate my work with the reality of what was experienced by those who were present in Saint-Martin-Vésubie.

For many individuals, that summer in the Alpes-Maritimes was just one chapter in a whole series of heart-breaking, remarkable events. The real-life stories of both the refugees and their French and Italian protectors are ones of bravery and suffering, endurance and survival that need no fictional embellishment.

The Secrets Between Us imagines only a tiny portion of what took place during that period of Italian Occupied France. For those who are interested in learning more about this area and time, I can wholeheartedly recommend the following books and films:

Holocaust Odysseys: The Jews of Saint-Martin-Vésubie and Their Flight through France and Italy, Susan Zuccotti (Yale University Press, 2007)

La Pierre des Juifs, Danielle Baudot Laksine (Editions de Bergier, 2003)

A Pause in the Holocaust (1943: Le Temps d'un Répit), 2009; a documentary directed by André Waksman

Mussolini's Army in the French Riviera: Italy's Occupation of France, Emanuele Sica (University of Illinois Press, 2016)

Wandering Star, J. M. G. Le Clézio (Gallimard, 1992. Translation: C. Dickson, 2009)

Laura Madeleine, Bristol, 2017

Acknowledgements

This has, without a doubt, been the most difficult book to write . . . so far. For helping it into the world, I'd like to thank my family for their support and encouragement, for reading early drafts and for convincing me to keep going.

Thank you to my mother, for coming with me on an adventure to Saint-Martin-Vésubie. Thank you to my dad, for reading literally anything I throw at him, no matter how messy.

Thank you to Lucy, for being there on the days when the bear ate me. To Nick, for help beyond words.

Thanks to Becky and Jude, for cheering me on with wine and cheese toasties and putting up with my pyjamaed slumps. To Kevlin, Chris, Mike, George, Leila, Ian and Viv, for input when I needed it. To Charlie and Tim and Louis, for inspiration.

Thanks to the team at Baked in Bristol, for managing not to look *too* scared when I repeatedly stumbled in to ask questions about *levain*.

To Ed, for always having faith that I can turn vague ideas into viable novels. To Darcy for her editorial trust and patience, and to everyone at Transworld for making this book possible.

Thanks to Pat and, most of all, to my grandmother Iris, for delving back over seventy years to talk about her own — and our family's — wartime experiences.

Thank you all. I couldn't have done it without you.

We do hope that you have enjoyed reading this large print book.

Did you know that all of our titles are available for purchase?

We publish a wide range of high quality large print books including:
Romances, Mysteries, Classics
General Fiction
Non Fiction and Westerns

Special interest titles available in large print are:
The Little Oxford Dictionary
Music Book
Song Book
Hymn Book
Service Book

Also available from us courtesy of Oxford University Press:
Young Readers' Dictionary
(large print edition)
Young Readers' Thesaurus
(large print edition)

For further information or a free brochure, please contact us at:
Ulverscroft Large Print Books Ltd.,
The Green, Bradgate Road, Anstey,
Leicester, LE7 7FU, England.
Tel: (00 44) 0116 236 4325
Fax: (00 44) 0116 234 0205